THE LIVING WILLS

Brendan: *For my mother, Jeri Sullivan. You always told me I could do anything I put my mind to. If they have books in heaven, I hope you enjoy it.*

Rick: *For my father, Eckhard Kaempfer, who died far too young, and inadvertently unleashed a passion for writing in his eldest child.*

PREFACE

The structure of this novel is influenced by the improvisational theater form called the Harold, created by Del Close as a member of the San Francisco theater group the Committee in San Francisco in 1967. On stage, a Harold is a long-form improvisational piece inspired by one audience suggestion and created in the moment by a team of improvisers. In the strictest sense, a Harold contains three separate 'scenes' inspired by the audience suggestion and a theatrical opening. Ideally, as a Harold develops before the audience's eyes over thirty minutes or so, the three scenes begin to connect and reflect one another, coming together in the end to create one coherent performance piece, never to be seen again. Entire books have been written about the essence of the Harold. Our short explanation does not do justice to it. As they say, "You gotta see it for yourself." When it works, it will blow your mind.

This novel is NOT a Harold, only influenced by the form. It wasn't improvised on a stage in thirty minutes, although we did use some improvisation techniques in our process. We do have three interweaving story lines, but this novel was written, edited, rethought, rewritten, and rewritten again. Therefore, the end product of "The Living Wills" doesn't strictly adhere to the Harold form.

Still, we would be remiss if we didn't acknowledge the debt we owe to Del Close.

THE LIVING WILLS

1

THREAT LEVEL RED

As soon as the elevators doors opened on the 17th floor, Reed could smell trouble in the air. This week's front desk receptionist had a look in her eyes that Reed had seen many times, in many receptionists.

"Good morning, Cindy," Reed said, forcing a smile.

She wouldn't make eye contact with him. Reed adjusted his tight collar away from his neck a bit as he made his way through the maze of gray cloth-covered cubicles. Nearly all of them were full already. Not a good sign. Reed didn't like to be one of the last arrivals. It was always better to be somewhere in the middle; unnoticed, unannounced.

Charlie Turner's office door was open. Reed poked his head in.

"Threat level?" he asked.

"Red, with a capital R," Charlie said.

"Great," Reed replied. The pit of his stomach flared.

"He already asked where you were," Charlie warned.

Reed looked at his watch. 8:02. The train was more than a few minutes late this morning. "Oh my God."

"I know," Charlie said.

"That didn't spark the red threat level, did it?" Reed asked.

"What do you think?" Charlie asked.

"Quarterly numbers?" Reed guessed.

Charlie nodded. "Keep your head down. There's a meeting at 8:30 in the conference room."

"Thanks," Reed replied, leaving Charlie to stew in his own quarterly shortcomings.

Reed looked around the office floor at the accountants milling about their cubicles, and they all looked unusually concerned. This had the potential of being a very bad day. When Anderson unloaded on his staff about something trivial like personal phone calls, distractions in the office, dress code violations, or, as Reed had discovered a few times, late arrivals, it was nasty and uncomfortable. But when he unloaded on them about something that was actually important, like quarterly numbers, the scorching heat of his wrath singed navy blue blazers from here to Timbuktu.

When Reed arrived at his office door, he saw a standard piece of 8 ½ by 11 copy paper scotch-taped just above eye level. Not today, of all days. *Is it that time of year already?* The cheap rainbow colored Word-Art font proclaimed the news for all to see.

"*Congratulations Read O'Hern on 27 years with Cap'n Slappy! Best Wishes, HR.*"

"R-E-A-D," he muttered to himself.

Reed calmly removed the scotch tape, and held the piece of paper in his hand as he opened his office door with the other. He flicked on the lights. Reed's office lacked any hint of personality. In fact, his walls were bare other than the corporately mandated Cap'n Slappy poster on the wall behind his desk. He stared at the poster and sighed.

"Christ," he said. "27 years."

Reed coolly crumpled up the piece of paper and tossed it in the wastebasket.

When he took his seat behind the desk, he had only one destination in mind. Reed turned on his computer monitor to double check his quarterly numbers. Yup. Everything was in order. His region of Cap'n Slappy seafood restaurants was due to spend exactly the same as they spent last quarter. Sure, the cost of the small, medium, and laaaaaaaargh soft drink cups went up a bit, but that was offset by savings on the Salty the Parrot plush doll in the Yo-Ho-Ho Kids Meals.

"Thank you, Singapore," he said, as he scrolled down the spread sheet.

Reed printed out another copy of his quarterly report in case it came up in the meeting. He put it in a standard manila folder, wrote "First Quarter 2005" in the tab, and closed the folder. Reed checked his e-mail to make sure there hadn't been any last second directives, and walked out of his office toward the conference room. Sure, it was only 8:15, but the last thing he needed was to be "the meeting straggler." It was bad enough that everyone would be reminded that Reed had once again "pulled an O'Hern" thanks to the ever reliable folks at Metra Rail.

He took his regular seat in the middle of the window side of the table. Charlie arrived moments later and took his seat too, right next to Reed. He was more upset than usual.

"I don't know how I'm going to break this news to Lynée," he said.

"What news?" Reed asked.

"We had a vacation scheduled next week," he explained. He was shaking his head at his own stupidity. "I told her not to buy non-refundable tickets, but she said it was the only way to get the deal. I should have been more forceful."

"Where were you planning on going?"

"One of those all-inclusive places in the Dominican Republic," he said.

Reed nodded sympathetically. He knew that Charlie's new wife had committed the ultimate Cap'n Slappy sin. That's why God made the Wisconsin Dells. It was a rookie mistake, and Charlie's first wife Linda never would have made it.

The conference room began filling up. Cranky Dick Nicholson took his place on Reed's left. He was already grumbling about people "crapping in his pool". By 8:25 every seat was taken except the head seat at the table.

"He's usually here by now," Reed said under his breath to Charlie.

"If I were you," Dick Nicholson interjected, "I wouldn't mention that."

"Point taken," Reed said, his cheeks flushing.

Anderson's personal assistant Annie came into the room, and did a quick head count. She was charged with making sure everyone was in place before His Majesty made his entrance. After a quick check, she left again. Nervous employees cleared their throats one last time. It was too risky to make a noise of any kind once the meeting began.

Conrad Anderson's wiry frame arrived moments later. His thinning gray hair was slicked back above his starched white collar, and his navy and red tie undoubtedly matched the pocket handkerchief in the blazer hanging in Anderson's office closet. He was carrying a mug of coffee in one hand, and a manila folder in the other.

Anderson tried to make eye contact with everyone in the room, but all eyes were firmly glued to the reports on the table in front of them.

"Good morning," he grumbled.

A smattering of meek mutterings returned the greeting. Anderson placed his coffee cup on the glass table, but didn't take his seat. He simply glared through his black-framed Buddy Holly glasses at the fraidy cats that worked for him. Even though nobody saw the glare, he knew they felt it.

"I certainly don't take any pleasure in conducting an unpleasant meeting," he began, taking off the glasses, and rubbing his nose. He placed the glasses back where they belonged and sighed. "But I have the quarterly numbers right here—and the numbers don't lie."

No one said a word.

"Charlie," Anderson spat, not wasting a moment of time with niceties. "Did you take math in high school?"

"Yes," Charlie said.

"Can you tell me what number is bigger—seven or zero?"

"Seven," Charlie said, bracing himself for a body blow.

"So...," Anderson wound up, "A seven percent increase in cost would be *higher* than a zero percent increase."

"Well, I..."

Anderson slammed the manila folder on the glass table.

"Were you, or were you not responsible for the Schooner of Tuna basket order?"

"I was," Charlie admitted.

"And?"

"'Tisket a Tasket' went out of business last year," Charlie reminded him, "and the only other schooner shaped baskets—"

"You checked every single basket company?" Anderson challenged, his voice rising in volume with every sentence. "You're confident that if I researched this personally, I wouldn't be able to find *one single basket company in the entire world* that offered schooner shaped baskets for a price that wouldn't bankrupt us."

"I know these cost a little bit more—"

"Seven percent is not a little more."

"They're still only—"

"Dammit!" Anderson bellowed. "Do you have any idea what corporate is going to do to me when they see these numbers?"

"I'll find a cheaper one," Charlie said.

"When?" Anderson demanded.

"Now," he muttered.

"And when will you stop looking?"

"When I find one," Charlie responded.

"You're excused," Anderson said. He looked through his report for the next egregious violation as Charlie gathered his things.

Charlie pushed his chair back, and tucked all of the paperwork back into his manila folder, but before he could get out of his seat, the room echoed with the sound of a loud crash. When everyone looked up to see what had happened, Anderson had disappeared. All that remained at the head of the table was a knocked-over coffee cup, and an ever growing puddle of the creamette-lightened sugary brown liquid that once resided inside of it. Nobody seemed too concerned that the puddle was expanding toward that dreaded quarterly report.

There was a bigger concern lying beneath the table. Reed rushed past Charlie, and was the first to reach his boss' side. Anderson was face-down on the floor, his smashed glasses by his side. His body lay totally still. Reed tentatively felt for a pulse. Nothing. Everyone gathered around looking for a sign from Reed.

"I think we better call 9-1-1," he finally garbled, although he knew it wouldn't do any good.

Conrad Anderson was dead. As dead as a Salty the Parrot plush doll.

2

What's in a Name?

Waveland Bowl was crackling on a Thursday night. All 40 lanes were packed with the over-40 men's league. The balls rumbled down the well-waxed lanes, crashing into the helpless pins. Beer bottles clinked. Roars of laughter and applause sprang up randomly. There was an energetic hum about the place; grown men, working men, playing a game to relax and forget about their cares for a while. The cacophony was music to Henry's ears as he eagerly walked the long aisle, anxiously searching for his team.

Tonight Henry had news. He had big news. He could hardly contain himself as he spotted his three teammates at lane 23. Henry took the two steps down to where the guys were putting on their bowling shoes. He dropped his duffle bag on the plastic bench, and walked the space like a runway model, twirling and holding his arms out wide.

"Notice anything?" asked Henry.

"The Living Wills?" Ramon was reading the back of the brand new, bright blue letterman's jacket that Henry was sporting. "What the hell is that supposed to mean?"

There were puzzled looks all around.

"I got one for each of us. They're in the bag," beamed Henry. "You gotta admit it's a beautiful jacket, right?"

"Yeah," admitted Oscar, "It's a beautiful jacket. I got no problem with the jacket. But I'm with Ramon. What's the deal with the name?"

"OK, I'll explain." Henry took a deep breath. "I had to act quick. It was a great deal. This guy who parks in the garage, he's a wholesaler. Ramon, you know the guy, silver caddy, always tips five bucks."

"Yeah, yeah," said Ramon. "Dark glasses, heated seats. I know the guy."

"Anyway," said Henry, "he was wearing one of these jackets today when I was parking his car, same real leather sleeves, same stain-resistant, thick cloth construction, same beautiful cobalt blue color, same zip-out winter linings, same fitted cloth at the wrist with the white piping."

"Hey," Ramon interrupted, "I admit, it's a beautiful jacket. It's the most frickin' beautiful bowling team jacket I've ever seen. What's with the name?"

"Ah, that's where my sixty years of fast thinking comes in handy," said Henry. "This wholesaler guy sees me admiring the jacket he's wearing, a jacket just like this except without the name of course. I ask him what it costs and he says he's got a half-dozen that he needs to unload. Somebody over-ordered or bounced a check or something. So I say I'd need four, an XXL, two XLs and one large. He says, 'no problem.' I tell you it's like a dream."

"Henry," Delmar jumped in to get back on point. "What's the deal with the name? I thought we were the Lane Wizards."

"If you'll recall," answered Henry, making his case, "the Lane Wizards sucked. The Lane Wizards were notoriously bad. The Lane Wizards were an embarrassment to the game of bowling."

"Delmar, we talked about this," added Ramon. "We agreed that we should change the name and maybe it would change our luck."

And then Oscar's attention turned back to Henry. "But I don't remember agreeing on a new name."

"That's the joy of this," said Henry. "If you'd just let me finish the story."

"I gotta tell you, Henry, these are some sharp jackets," said Delmar. "They're a whole lot better than these windbreakers we've got now. How did you swing it on our sponsor's notoriously tight budget?"

"That's the beauty of it, if you'd let me finish."

Ramon, Oscar and Delmar sat quietly.

"OK, so I go up to the guy's office on the 23rd floor during my break. He's got quite an operation up there. He's got a machine that sews the lettering on the back, and some other thing that embroiders the team name on the front here," said Henry, holding his hand to his heart. "It's like computerized freakin' magic. He'll do it for free if I take the jackets off his hands today. He's supposed to ship them back to the manufacturer by tomorrow. So I pay him $100 cash for the whole thing, he puts the lettering on with that computer operated machine thing and here we are. Four gorgeous jackets."

"Twenty-five bucks a piece?" asked Oscar. "As the guy who works for our notoriously tight sponsor, I approve. Nice job, Henry."

"Yeah," added Ramon. "And yet the question remains."

"Take a look at the shirts you're wearing, gentlemen," said Henry smugly.

The men stared at one another's baby blue, short sleeve bowling shirts, with their first names sewn over the left breast pocket, an LW for the Lane Wizards in huge white letters on the right side of the shirt, and their sponsor's name, BM&P Toilets, on the back.

"Where are you going with this, Henry?" asked Delmar.

"I saved our notoriously tight sponsor the cost of new shirts!" claimed Henry.

"Huh?" asked Ramon.

"You see," said Henry, pointing to his own shirt. "The Lane Wizards. The Living Wills. Both are LW. New name. No need for a new shirt."

"Once again, as the representative of our notoriously tight sponsor, I approve," said Oscar. "But that's all you could come up with, the Living Wills?"

"Hey, I had to think fast. I didn't have time to send it to a vote. A living will's been on my mind a lot lately, I guess. I've been reading up on it. You know that everyone should have a living will."

"On the back of their bowling jacket?"

"Don't you see? It's a public service," explained Henry. "Nobody thinks about a living will until it's too late. Now when someone asks you, 'Why are you guys called the Living Wills?' you can tell them they should get one so their loved ones can pull the plug when they're in a vegetative state with no hope of recovery."

"That's just great, Henry. If our jackets are public service announcements, couldn't we just be the Brushers and Flossers, or the Prostate Exams?"

"Ah," said Henry, "But those don't start with LW."

"Doesn't anything else start with LW?"

"Actually," said Henry, searching for and finding a crumpled scrap of paper in his pants pocket, "I did think of a few others before going with the Living Wills. Remember, I only had a few minutes to think."

"I'm on the edge of my seat," muttered Oscar.

"The Light Weights, the Limp Wrists, Little Women, Lawrence Welk, the Lemon Wedges, the Lazy Weasels, the Lame Wimps, the Lard Wagons...."

"All right, all right," said Ramon. "Jeez, when you put it like that, the Living Wills sounds almost heroic."

Looks of surrender and exasperation passed back and forth in silence among the four. Oscar held up his beer glass. The others followed. Glasses clinked all around.

"To the Living Wills."

"By the way, Henry, have you got a living will?"

Henry tipped back his beer, pretending he didn't hear the question.

3

It Takes a Village

*W*here can they be? Why isn't she answering her phone? The school called and said it's a nasty scrape, both knees bloody, but no need to worry, she'd be fine. So where are they!?

It sure didn't help that this week marked the Cubs' home opening series against the Brewers. Traffic on Addison was at a standstill. Gina sat in the back row of the eastbound 152 CTA bus, packed to overflow with hopeful Cubs fans crawling slowly toward Mecca. There was buzz around town that 2005 might finally be the year. Gina only wanted to get off this bus and get home.

Gina just happened to live near Wrigley because she'd found a needle in a haystack last fall; a good, cheap apartment in a nice neighborhood that seemed relatively safe for a 25-year-old woman. She'd heard that baseball season turned the area upside down. Now she was getting her first taste, as the mob on the bus spontaneously broke into a raucous rendition of "Take Me Out to the Ballgame." Gina dialed again. The phone rang and rang. No answer, no voicemail.

"Jeez, Libby, get a cell phone," muttered Gina as she slammed the phone shut. "Join the 21st century. Damn."

Gina glanced out the window to read a street sign. Ashland. Her stop was coming up. *Couldn't this bus move any faster?* Gina stood up and began to worm her way through the sardine can of a bus to the side exit. At Southport, Gina squeezed her six-foot frame through the sea of Cubbie blue and finally pried herself and her backpack out the door like a 10-pound newborn from the birth canal. Ah, fresh air.

Most nights Gina would take this opportunity to reach her long fingers into the hip pocket of her barista uniform and light a cigarette for a leisurely walk home. But not tonight. She swept her long, straight, ebony hair from her face and took off running.

Gina barely noticed the crowds of baseball fans as she jogged the two blocks to her gray stone walk-up, praying that everything was OK. She ran up the front walk and opened the gate and the front door of the building without a key. The locks were broken. Gina agreed that these little things were the compromise she made for such a bargain living situation. She didn't bother picking up her mail from the assortment on the entryway floor and raced up the creaky wooden stairs two at a time to the second floor.

Gina pounded on the door of the apartment across the hall from hers, and tried to catch her breath. She heard the television blaring and thought that might be a good sign. She quickly knocked again. The volume on the TV dropped and slow, heavy steps made their way to the door. Two deadbolts and one chain later, the door opened.

"Gina. Please, come on in. Good to see you."

Gina burst into the apartment, still breathing hard. "Libby, where is she? How is she? Where were you? I called. I called a lot."

"Everything's fine, just fine. She's OK. We just walked in the door ourselves," said Libby, her XXL light green sweat suit oddly matching the bright orange she'd washed into her hair. "We went out for new shoes, and for ice cream," Libby whispered.

The eight-year-old girl sitting on the couch turned away from the TV. "Mommy!" she screamed happily, leaping up and racing to Gina, hugging her tightly around the waist.

Emily's knees were wrapped in gauze and bandages, but they didn't appear to impede the little girl's mobility at all. A little dried blood in a few spots, nothing more. Emily was beaming in white shorts, a Hello Kitty t-shirt and brand new pink sneakers.

Gina hugged Emily. "Are you OK, honey? I'm so sorry I had to work. I was so worried about you. I got home as fast as I could."

"I'm alright. We were running around at recess and a big seventh grade boy didn't see me and ran me over and I got big scrapes on both knees and there was lots of blood and they had to carry me to the nurse's office and I had to miss art class and the nurse said the spray wouldn't hurt a bit and she was right," said Emily brightly. "I'm a big girl now."

"Well, I'm just glad you're OK. I was worried."

"Uh huh. And look, I got new shoes. Pink! Libby and I got them. And strawberry ice cream!"

"Libby," said Gina, "You shouldn't have. What do I owe you?"

"Don't be silly," said Libby. "I wanted to do it."

"What would I do without you?" smiled Gina as she stood up, finally feeling a little more relaxed.

"Guess what, Mommy," shouted Emily.

"What?" asked Gina. "You mean there's more?"

"My poem got picked. Mrs. Guercio told us. They're gonna put them in a book for the parents and you can get a copy. And it's gonna be in a big binder and everybody is gonna see it. It's not just like last time when they put them on the wall in the hallway. This is a book. A poem book."

"Emily, tell Mommy the best part," said Libby.

"Oh yeah. They picked my picture. It's gonna be on the cover of the book. It's a picture of the earth from way up in space with stars and stuff."

"Wow. A published author and an illustrator, at age eight. That's just fantastic, sweetheart."

"Would you like some tea, Gina?" asked Libby. "I put on the kettle a while ago."

"No thanks." The last thing Gina needed after a full day of serving coffee was a cup of tea. She closed her eyes for a moment to compose herself, so relieved now that Emily was OK. Emily ran back to the couch and plopped in front of the TV.

Libby smiled a big, cherubic smile. "She's a wonderful girl, Gina. I love having her around and being able to help. Have a seat. You're always rushing around and you never get a chance to relax. Relax."

Gina looked around the room, to the kitchenette strewn with dirty dishes and to the piles of old *TV Guides* and *People* magazines stacked against the far wall, to the overstuffed La-Z-Boy where Libby spent most of her day, an open bag of chips and a Diet Coke on the small adjoining table top, next to the phone. Gina decided the only place to sit was at the dinette table, and pulled out a chrome-piped chair and sat, hopefully for just a short moment. It did feel good to sit, even here.

"I really appreciate you being here for Emily," said Gina. "I just don't know how I'd get by otherwise. You're a life saver."

"You always say that. I love watching Emily. It's the highlight of my day. We were about to have some macaroni and cheese and little hotdogs for dinner, with chocolate milk and a popsicle for dessert, just like always. So tell me about your day." Libby was genuinely interested.

Gina longed to cross the hall and take off her shoes. She'd been standing all day. But this was the small price she paid for a babysitter who didn't charge her a thing. Sure, no homework was ever done, and the TV was rotting Emily's brain, and Emily had consumed enough macaroni and cheese over the last few months to fill a grain silo, but the price was right. In return for an affordable apartment and complimentary daycare, Gina had to talk to her lonely landlady for a short time each evening and be a good tenant. A sweet deal.

"Don't worry about feeding Emily tonight," said Gina as Libby wandered off to the kitchen. "I've got it covered."

"Okey dokey," called Libby from the kitchen.

Gina wasn't quite sure how old Libby was, although by the lines on her face, Gina figured she was in her 60's. But her roundness made her move like she was seventy. And she talked like she was in her eighties.

"There's nothing like a cup of tea after a long day, I always say. And it's good for you too," Libby wheezed as she waddled to the stove. "I heard that it's got those anti-accidents in there to keep away the cancer. I saw that on the Inside Edition program. A big breaking story they had." Libby huffed as she shuffled around the cabinets in search of a clean cup.

Emily was watching an old episode of "The Dick Van Dyke Show". Gina began to nod off sitting on the dinette chair.

"Are you sure you won't join me?" asked Libby, a cup of tea in her hand.

"No, no. Please." Gina stood slowly. "We really should get going. I appreciate the hospitality, and taking care of Emily."

"Don't worry about it. I'll be here tomorrow as always to meet the bus. It gives me something to look forward to. Frankly, I don't know what I'd do without her now. It's kind of quiet around here since mother died, you know."

"Yes," answered Gina, "You've told us. Amazing that she died right on that couch."

"Yes, she died right there on that couch. She couldn't reach her pills. And I was asleep on the La-Z-Boy, the TV on. Mother was hard of hearing, so the volume was up, and I didn't hear her cries, if there were any."

"And you slept right through it."

"Yes. I slept like a baby through the whole thing and when I woke up, she was gone. Well, I mean, she was still lying there, one hand outstretched toward the nitro pills, but she was gone."

"Yes, I'm sorry. It's a sad story."

But Libby sure seemed to enjoy telling it.

"We should get going," Gina said toward Emily on the couch. "Someone I know has some homework to finish, I bet, even if they're injured."

Emily hopped up from the couch, grabbed her backpack, gave Libby a quick hug and walked silently out the door, all without any direction. "Well, good night," said Gina to Libby. "And thank you again."

Gina closed Libby's door. Emily stood in the hallway, and could hear the bolts being secured behind Libby's closed door as Gina opened theirs.

One Thai curry dinner, one chicken fried rice, one glass of wine, one glass of milk, one second grade math worksheet, one spelling quiz review, two Nancy Drew chapters and one hour of 'Survivor' later, Gina announced to Emily that it was time for bed. Emily clunked around the bathroom, reaching up to the faucet on tiptoe, and brushed her teeth. Rinsing was tricky. Emily actually had to leave her feet, hang over the sink on her belly and stick her mouth under the spigot.

"Let's let Dr. Mom take a look at the damage," said Gina.

Emily sat on the edge of the old claw foot bathtub while Gina peeked under the edges of Emily's bandages. The school nurse had overdone it with the wrapping. Gina removed the gauze and slowly exposed the small wounds. She gently washed Emily's knees with a washcloth and soap. She pulled the small first aid kit from the medicine cabinet above the sink, sprayed some Bactine on the scrapes and applied two small band-aids to each knee.

"There," said Gina, "Good as new."

Emily marched to the bedroom, climbed into the queen size bed she shared with her mother and crawled under the covers, sliding to the far side, against the wall. Gina followed Emily into the room to tuck her in. Gina knew that one of these days Emily was going to ask for her own bed or maybe even her own room. Emily was only eight, but she was growing up fast. Just yesterday it seemed she was in a crib. Gina kissed her goodnight, turned out the light and was about to head back to the living room when she heard her favorite word in the world:

"Mom?"

"Yes, honey?"

"How long will we stay in Chicago?"

"I don't know. What do you think?" Gina sat back down on the bed.

"I like it here," said Emily. "It's a short bus ride to school and stuff. There's some nice kids at school. And Libby's really nice. I was just wondering."

Gina reached down and brushed Emily's soft light brown curls from her face. "I think we should just be happy for right now, and not worry. Try to go to sleep, OK?"

"OK," said Emily. Gina made a move to stand. "Mom? One more thing."

"What's that, honey?"

"Is the Ponderosa a real place?"

"What?"

"The Ponderosa. Is it real?"

"What are you talking about, honey?"

"On TV, on 'Bonanza,' they burn that map at the beginning of every episode. So if it's on a map, it's real, right?"

"You watch 'Bonanza'?"

"Sure. With Libby. It's her favorite show and we watch it at four o'clock. With Hoss, and Little Joe and Adam and their dad. Libby says Hop Sing isn't Oriental anymore, he's Asian. And so is that a real map? Can we go there someday?"

"Well, honey. 'Bonanza' is a TV show and it's not real. It was a new TV show before I was born. Even when I was a kid, we only saw reruns. And now you're watching a show that's about 40 years old."

"So we can't go there? But we could have gone there forty years ago?"

"Emily, it's very late. Go to sleep." And Emily snuggled against the wall.

Gina sat on the bed for a moment, thinking about what Emily had said. She didn't want to raise a latch key kid, always moving from city to city without any roots. She didn't want to create a daughter who was raised by strangers, by Libby and the Cartwrights. But for now, what choice did she have? They had each other.

"It won't always be like this," she whispered to Emily, already snoring quietly.

4

OUT OF THE CLOSET

Anyone stepping out of the elevator and into the lobby of MacArthur Harrison Hyde couldn't help but be impressed. The law firm's contemporary lobby with its sleek, clean décor was pristine. The executive conference room, visible from the lobby through beautiful glass doors, looked too nice to actually use. The office of each partner, located at the end of each hallway, was a testament to the firm's power and wealth, from their stainless steel appliances, to their hand carved mahogany desks, to their incredible views of Chicago's skyline.

But if that was the penthouse face of the firm, the young associates like Peter Stankiewicz resided in the outhouse. Not that it bothered Peter. He felt at home in the dingy windowless closet MacArthur Harrison Hyde had assigned him on a lower floor. His desk looked respectable enough; the bourbon cherry finish was lacquered and shiny beneath the piles and piles of paperwork Peter had strewn about. Between the hours of 7AM and 9PM, Peter was sure to be sitting behind that desk in his comfortable ergonomic office chair, in front of five bulging half-open filing cabinets. In fact, every time firm partner Clark Buckingham actually entered Peter's domain, he berated the young lawyer for his disheveled workspace.

"I know exactly where everything is," Peter lied. If Buckingham ever pushed and demanded to have the filing system explained to him, Peter would have collapsed like a house of cards. He simply had too much work, too little space, and too few hours in the day to stay on top of everything.

Of course, Peter was not alone. All the other third year associates also had offices on this floor, and knowing that they were going through the same thing kept Peter sane. One of them, in particular, even helped him out. Her name was Kelly Castle and she had a similarly sized closet down the hall. Kelly was Peter's sounding board, his one-person cheering section, his late night pizza at the office buddy, and for the past six months, much more than that.

She knocked on his open office door.

"Anybody home?"

"Yup," Peter said. "Probably forever. Buckingham's meeting with Albright in the morning and if I don't go through everything we have on the merger..."

"So I guess lunch is out of the question?" Kelly interrupted.

Peter looked up from his paperwork. Kelly was flashing him that toothy smile of hers. Wow, was she blessed with good genes. The graceful high cheekbones of her patrician mother, the dazzling smile her father had used to wow juries for the past thirty years, and of course that Castle name. She may have been a Castle, but she had the heart of a peasant. Peter's.

"Can you bring back something for me?" he asked.

"Sure, what do you want?"

"Where ya goin'?"

"Probably Subway. I've got a mountain of work too."

The phone rang. He held up one finger to let her know he would give her his order as soon as this call was over. She consented with a silent nod, stepped all the way into his office, and shut the door behind her. Peter lifted up the folder that had been covering his phone and picked up the receiver.

"Stankiewicz."

"Hey there, pal. It's me."

Peter knew who it was immediately.

"What is it, Henry? I'm kind of busy here."

Kelly pointed to the phone and mouthed the words: "Your Dad?" Peter nodded to her as he rolled his eyes.

"I thought maybe you could take a few minutes out of your time and have lunch with your old man. I've got something important to talk to you about."

"This is a real bad time. I've got at least eight hours of work ahead of me, maybe more."

"It won't take too long, Pete." Nobody called him Pete. Peter just didn't have time for this today.

"Can't do it," he said. "Maybe another time."

"I'm in the lobby downstairs right now. Maybe I can just come up there and we can talk in your office."

"You're here? Now?"

"Yeah. What floor are you on? I can just hop in the elevator."

"They won't let you up."

"I was just talking to the security guard here and he was sayin' that it wouldn't be a problem if you just called from your desk to let him know I could come in."

Henry had him there. Peter placed the folder he had been holding on top of his computer monitor, as he struggled for a way out.

"Um..."

"He said that he didn't recognize the name Stankiewicz," Henry continued, "So I showed him that 8th grade picture. I said to him, pretend the braces and the zits are gone, and look closely. Now, that's a Stankiewicz. I think he knows who you are now."

"Can you hang on a second?"

Peter put the phone on hold and rubbed his temples.

"Your dad is here?" Kelly asked.

"Yup."

Kelly walked around to Peter's side of the desk, and looked for somewhere to sit. She had been prodding him to get a few extra chairs for the other side of the desk, but Peter was afraid it would encourage Buckingham to visit more often. Kelly sat on the padded handle of Peter's ergonomic chair, and ran her hand along the side of his face.

She was attracted to Peter's boyish features, but she also loved the way that boyish face felt rough to the touch. It wasn't even noon, and already Peter's jaw line was covered with rugged stubble. Her hand lingered, as it often did, on the only smooth spot remaining; the scar just above his chin.

"Why don't you just go to lunch with him?" she asked as she looked into his eyes. "This is the third time he's called you in the last week. There must be something important he needs to talk to you about."

"But this merger," Peter protested.

"You know that's not the real reason you won't see him," she insisted. "Put your issues with your dad aside, just this once. I have a feeling you'll regret it if you don't."

"Regret's a two-way street you know," Peter pointed out.

"He's trying. He's calling isn't he?"

"But this work..."

"You know it's not the work."

"I'm not lying," Peter said. It was fruitless to argue with her, because he knew she was right, but an attorney has an obligation to present the case to the best of his ability. He pointed to the pile of paper in front of him. "I really do have too much work to do."

"You know I would help you," she countered. "We could split up the documents."

"Aha! I thought you said you had a mountain of work too," Peter pointed out. He looked at Kelly with a mischievous grin. "If you keep helping me with my stuff people are going to get a little suspicious, don't you think?"

"There's no rule against helping out your colleagues," Kelly said.

Peter raised his eyebrows. "Yeah, but there *is* a rule against—"

"Just have lunch with your father," she interrupted. She gave him a peck on the cheek and stood up. "If not today, then tomorrow when your research is done. Unless you'd rather have him up here in the office, possibly running into Buckingham, telling stories about that time you were ten years old and threw up on the tilt-a-whirl."

"You can hear everything he says when he calls, can't you?"

Kelly nodded. "He's got a loud voice."

"Just for the record, lots of kids puke on that ride. It's unnatural to spin that fast. I may have had some sort of an inner-ear imbalance."

"I'm not judging."

Peter picked up the phone again.

"Henry, how about an early lunch tomorrow? Want to come back here around 11:00 or so?"

"You mean it?" Henry asked.

"I promise."

"I'll be here with bells on," Henry said.

"No bells," Peter said. "Just Henry."

"Got it."

Henry closed his cell-phone and put it back in his pocket. The security guard was standing by, awaiting a verdict.

"We're doing it tomorrow," Henry beamed. "I'll be back around 11. I'll have Pete smile for you. Just wait until you see that smile. I'm telling you, those braces really worked. Worth every dime his mother paid for them."

5

HOLY SMOKES

Reed was always struck by the incongruities of Holy Name Cathedral. The inscription in the cornerstone read: "AD 1874 — AT THE NAME OF JESUS EVERY KNEE SHOULD BOW — THOSE THAT ARE IN HEAVEN AND THOSE ON EARTH." The inscription looked slightly worn, but not from age. Portions of those words had been riddled with bullets during the 1920s; collateral damage from the murder of gangster Hymie Weiss. A holy cathedral's holy words forever holey.

Holy Name Cathedral also boasted a magnificent 210-foot-tall gothic spire, but the nearby high rises and skyscrapers like the John Hancock Center and the Bloomingdale's Building now dwarfed it, seemingly laughing at the comparatively puny church, daring it to retain its dignity and majesty.

"I didn't even know your boss was Catholic," Lucy whispered to him.

"Even his kids didn't know until they read his will," Reed answered.

They were sitting in the third row pew, awaiting the beginning of Conrad Anderson's funeral mass. Reed tugged at his collar and adjusted his tie. That familiar discomfort was bubbling up inside him. He hoped he could hold it off until the end of the mass, but it wasn't looking good. He looked around, trying to distract himself into peace.

There certainly weren't many mourners on hand. Only a handful of employees from Cap'n Slappy's purchasing department had bothered to show up. Dick Nicholson was there, in the same row, across the aisle. He was attempting to see his watch in the poorly lit cathedral. Reed never understood why Dick had been Anderson's favorite. Dick was only two years away from retirement, but his good attitude had retired many years earlier. If there was a dark cloud in the sky, Nicholson was always able to find it. That dark cloud might have been hovering over his watch at this very moment, preventing him from seeing the hour and minute hands.

The only person who seemed to care at all was Anderson's assistant Annie. It wasn't like she was crying or anything, but at least she had the decency to dress in black. That's something neither of Anderson's ex-wives bothered to do. Those women, who once loved the unpleasant VP/Purchasing for Cap'n Slappy enough to actually marry him, were quietly arguing in the first row. Reed picked up bits and pieces of the conversation, including something about life insurance beneficiaries.

"Where's Charlie?" Lucy whispered.

"In the Dominican Republic," Reed replied. "He had a non-refundable ticket."

Reed looked at his watch again. *What is taking so long for this thing to start?* His anxiety had been building and building and building. It happened in most churches, but this one in particular offered him no chance. The marble-framed bronze Stations of the Cross were speaking to him. The bishop's throne on the altar was speaking to him. The Resurrection Crucifix suspended from the 150 foot high ceiling was speaking to him. They were all telling him the same thing.

Reed gave Lucy a peck on the cheek and stepped out of the pew.

"Where are you going?" she asked.

"I need to get some fresh air," he said.

"The mass is starting any minute," she whispered harshly.

"Don't worry—I'll be right back."

The sheer size of the church's interior made everything echo including Reed's shoes as he walked down the aisle toward the exit, but none of the mourners even bothered to see where he was going. He pulled open those ridiculously heavy doors, walked down the stone steps, and let his feet carry him toward the chiseled cornerstone.

When he stepped into the light, and began to feel the slight chill in the spring air, he calmed down a little bit. He reached into his suit jacket pocket for his pack of smokes. This black suit was his funeral suit, so there were a dozen or so laminated funeral prayer cards in that same inside pocket, but a smoker is never confused by secondary items. The smokes nearly leapt into his hand. The Bic lighter in his pants pocket did the same.

Within seconds the cigarette was lit and a moment later the smoke was filling his lungs. When he blew the smoke out, he was almost back to normal. He reached into his pocket and tentatively pulled out a few of the funeral cards. He stared at them for a moment or two, trying to remember which was which. He started with the fresh one. Conrad Anderson. 1943-2005. That's all it said about his boss. Apparently making your quarterly numbers year after year didn't make the cut. The only thing that mattered was the number of years you lived, and the prayer for your soul.

The next one in the pile was just a few weeks old. Lucy's Aunt Agatha lived to be 87. Nice life. He turned another one over. Old Jack Moran down the street had been almost 90.

Reed didn't dare look at the rest. He knew he was already pushing his luck. One of those cards was bound to chronicle a life that lasted only 18 years. He put them back into his pocket, his anger and anxiety once again bubbling to the surface. Even that man in there, the one they built this magnificent structure to honor, the one who hangs from the 150-ft. high ceiling, the one who took Reed's son away from him forever, even He lived to be 33. That's 15 more years than Will had gotten. And Reed was supposed to sit in that church, and celebrate that?

With his cigarette in one hand, Reed ran his other hand across the chipped stone near the inscription.

"I wonder how old Hymie was," he asked aloud.

Nobody was there to answer him.

Just Reed, a Marlboro, a spring chill, a bullet-ridden cornerstone, and a big black hearse waiting for a very dead boss.

6

THE DAILY GRIND

Delmar Dunwoody was in a hurry. He was always in a hurry. His customers were spread all over town, and Delmar was an old school salesman. As long as he made the effort to meet everyone face to face, instead of relying on the phone or e-mail, Delmar was confident he had a leg up on the younger guys. He always remembered what Oscar Case, his boss and bowling buddy, told him his first day at BM&P Toilets; "You're not selling port-a-potties, Delmar, you're selling yourself."

He pulled into a parking space in front of a fancy frou-frou coffee shop called Al Cappacino's. He could see through the display window that there were at least three people in line waiting for their vanilla mocha three scoop espresso whatevers, and all he wanted was an extra-large cup of coffee. Oh well. He could drive a few blocks to the next coffee shop, Common Grounds, or he could just suck it up and wait in line.

Delmar muttered to himself as he pulled the keys out of the ignition. He was still mad his neighborhood 7-11 had installed that damn security camera. That's where he had gotten his coffee for the past ten years, but ever since that camera was installed, he couldn't avoid looking up at the black and white monitor when he paid. There was only one thing on that monitor as far as Delmar was concerned-- his huuuuuge bald spot. He would never get another cup of coffee from that place. *What full-haired jerk came up with the idea to use that camera angle on the customers anyway? There's a reason God lets most men experience male pattern baldness from back to front. It's not right to rub your face in it.*

Luckily, Al Cappacino's didn't have a camera. That fact alone granted them the first shot at Delmar's business. The line moved pretty quickly too. Another feature in their favor.

"I'll have a large cup of coffee, Gina," he said to the cashier when he got to the front of the line. Delmar always read the name tag and always used the name; another pearl of wisdom courtesy of Oscar Case.

"Should I leave some room for milk?" she asked.

"Nope," he said. "I like my coffee black like my..."

"Women?" Gina finished the sentence for him. She wasn't smiling.

"I was going to say heart," he deadpanned. Not even a flicker of a reaction from Gina. She was busy pouring his coffee.

"That's a joke," Delmar offered.

"I know."

Delmar gave her his warmest sales smile. "Can I ask you a personal question, Gina?"

"Sure."

"Who is the most famous person you've ever served here?"

That was one of his standard conversation starters. Just about everyone loved telling stories about their brushes with greatness. Delmar would drift off during some of the tales (he still couldn't believe his customer in Berwyn considered the weatherman from Channel 2 a "famous" person), but for the most part they were pretty interesting stories.

"Lorne Greene," Gina said.

He didn't say anything at first because he was waiting for Gina to crack a smile. Gina wasn't the smiling type.

"That'll be $2," she said. She slid the cup of coffee across the counter.

"How long have you worked here?"

"Six months," she said.

"And you served Lorne Greene here?" he asked doubtfully. He was giving her his absolute best 'you're messin' with me, right?' smile.

Gina simply nodded.

"When?" he asked.

"Oh, I don't remember exactly," she said.

"How old are you?"

"25".

"Do you even know who Lorne Greene is?" he asked. He had never seen anyone who didn't smile back at his 'you're messin' with me, right?' smile. Was this woman made out of stone?

"Of course, I know," Gina replied. "Gigantic wide face, almost square shaped. Dimpled chin, white hair. Deep, sexy, authoritative voice."

"You're talking about Ben Cartwright?" he asked.

"I know who Lorne Greene is," she said. "Ponderosa Ranch. Adam, Hoss, Little Joe."

Delmar kept waiting for a smile to betray her. Nothing.

"Two bucks for the coffee," she said. "There are people in line behind you."

"I think Lorne Greene has been dead for years," Delmar said, as he handed over the money. "Like maybe longer than you've been alive."

"Well then his ghost likes Grande Lattes," she answered.

Delmar stepped to the side and very slowly walked to the door, shaking his head in disbelief. There was no possible way this girl had served a cup of coffee to Lorne Greene. She was completely full of it. On the other hand, who could keep a straight face while confronting the 'you're messin with me, right?' smile? And if you're going to lie about who you served, what normal 25-year-old would choose Lorne Greene?

He sat in his car, and tried to clear his head of this nonsense. He had about a thirty minute drive to get in the right mindset for his next client, the Taste of Hickory Hills. He checked his little notepad.

It read: "Jim Remak, Hickory Hills Sanitation. 3 kids. Oldest son plays baseball."

He turned the key into the ignition and the engine purred, but Delmar couldn't manage to put the car in reverse. He was staring at the girl behind the counter, clearly visible through two heavy-duty panes of glass, his windshield and her large display window. She was almost a head taller than the other girl working there. A delicious raven haired Amazon.

He turned off the car. Screw it. He had to get a closer look at her. The little bell rang when he re-entered.

"Maybe you were thinking of Shecky Green," Delmar offered from the doorway. "He's originally from Chicago, and I'm pretty sure he's still alive."

She poked her head around the first customer in line. "Nope. It was definitely Lorne Greene."

"He's dead."

The first lady in line nodded in agreement with Delmar. "He's right. He died a long time ago."

"He showed me his driver's license," Gina said, holding her ground. "It said 'Lorne Greene.'"

"What state was the driver's license from?" Delmar asked. He walked back to the front of the line to continue the questioning.

"California."

"A-HA!" he screamed. He pointed at her. "Gotcha! Lorne Greene was a Canadian."

Gina calmly put one finger in the air. "*Was* Canadian. Past tense. He's naturalized."

Still no smile.

Delmar looked at the other people in line. They were all actively involved in the conversation now, eagerly lapping up every word.

"Do any of you have a Blackberry?" Delmar asked. He was looking at the young metro-sexual at the back of the line, with his Mark Shale suit and his hundred dollar shoes. If any of these fancy coffee drinkers had a Blackberry it would be that guy. He shook his head apologetically.

"Sorry, not me."

No one else had one either. It would have only taken a thirty second trip to Google to prove the year Lorne Greene died.

"Do you have any other witnesses?" Delmar asked. Now he was talking to her like she was a suspect, and he was a police detective. The others in line turned to see Gina's reaction.

"Jose was here too," she said. She screamed across the room. "Hey Jose."

Jose was picking up the stray half-filled cups of coffee that people had left behind on the little planks of wood this place called "tables." He looked up to see what she wanted.

"Remember that day Lorne Greene came in here?" she asked.

He nodded and smiled before returning to work.

"See?"

The people in line were not convinced. Delmar spoke on their behalf.

"Hey Jose!"

He looked up again.

"Remember when Queen Elizabeth and her court were in here that one day?"

He nodded and smiled before returning to work.

"That's what I thought," Delmar said. His co-conspirators in line were openly smiling at him now. They had her. "Would you like to take this opportunity to revise your original remarks, Gina? If that's really your name."

"No I wouldn't," she said.

She crossed her arms in front of her. This girl had it all. A young beautiful face and the driest sense of humor he had ever witnessed. This was the ultimate challenge. He couldn't help but smile. A real smile. Just for a second, a brief glimmer of a moment, he thought he saw the corner of her mouth turn upward ever so slightly, before returning to the original stone-faced expression.

"Well," Delmar said, "next time he stops by, make sure you have someone take a picture or something, OK?"

"Jose will do it!" she screamed across the room. Jose looked up, nodded and smiled.

As Delmar pulled out of the parking lot, he recalibrated his brain. Jim Remak in Hickory Hills was probably itching to bitch about the stench in the latest batch of port-a-potties. Delmar had told those guys in the warehouse not to scrimp on the odor-cakes, but times were tough, and Old Man Sullivan was probably making them cut corners. *Time to stop by Enchanted Pastries and pick up some frosted cookies.* Another pearl of wisdom from Oscar Case: a box of frosted cookies has never failed to blunt customer complaints. You just have to make sure you show them the box before they start screaming.

Delmar looked in the rear-view mirror before he turned right on Addison, and got one more glimpse of the coffee shop. If they didn't install one of those bald-cams, or replace the dead-panning barista, they had themselves a new regular customer.

7

CHRYSLERS AND CRISIS

There were once a dozen or so smokers in Cap'n Slappy's purchasing department, and Reed could usually convince someone to join him for a quick smoke break. Outside the parking garage at One North Wacker, below ground, on Lower Wacker Drive, among the damp sewage smell, the occasional rat scurrying by, and the exhaust fumes from the parking garage, they would inhale their cigarette smoke, and exhale a little Anderson animosity.

Then, one by one, the other smokers either kicked the habit, or left the company. That left Reed as the Last of the Marlboro-icans. For the past seven years or so only Henry the parking attendant joined him, and Henry didn't even smoke.

Reed sat on the cement landing near the garage exit and pulled a Marlboro from the pack. Just as he did every day, Henry meandered over to say hello.

"Beautiful day, huh?" Henry said.

"Yeah, spring is here. Gotta love that."

Reed went through the usual charade of offering a smoke to Henry, who always pretended to consider it before declining.

"Did you hear about Anderson?" Reed asked with the cigarette in his mouth. He lit it and inhaled.

"Yup," Henry said calmly. "I saw the paramedics take him from the freight elevator to the alley. He was already dead."

"You ever see a freshly dead man like that before?" Reed asked, exhaling the smoke.

"I'm afraid I have," Henry said.

Reed turned to look at Henry. Henry didn't look back.

"I haven't seen one in eight years," Reed said, before taking another long drag. Reed's tone of voice didn't betray him, but Henry knew what happened eight years ago. They had discussed it many times.

Henry turned back toward the garage and made eye contact with Ramon in the attendant's booth about fifteen feet away. Henry held up all ten fingers and Ramon nodded. Ramon could handle any parking emergency that might arise over the next ten minutes or so. Henry took a seat on the landing next to Reed.

"His funeral was this morning," Reed said.

"I heard."

"I missed some of it," Reed said. He pointed, by way of explanation, to his cigarette. "But I was there for the eulogy. The priest obviously didn't know him. I really hate that. That eulogy couldn't have been more generic. 'Insert-name-here will be missed, but we're all happy that Insert-name-here is in a better place now.'"

"I didn't think you liked Anderson," Henry said.

"Hated his guts," Reed said. The venom in his voice even shocked Reed.

Henry didn't say anything in response. He simply kicked his legs out a bit, and let his work boots thud against the concrete on their way back.

Reed took another deep drag of his Marlboro. He blew the smoke up in the air in a perfect ring.

"Good one," Henry complimented.

"My only talent," Reed said, smiling.

"Yeah, right," Henry replied, grinning mischievously. "I bet Lucy could name a few more."

"You could have asked her yourself," Reed said. "I just sent her back home on the train after the funeral luncheon."

"Why didn't you just go home with her?" Henry asked. "The boss is dead, right? Who is making you come back to the office on the day of his funeral?"

Reed looked right into Henry's twinkling eyes.

"To be honest with you," he chuckled, "I never even thought about it. I'm so used to working all the time, it never crossed my mind."

"That's your problem," Henry said. "Too much working."

"That's for sure."

Henry slapped the concrete between them. "You know what you need?"

"A lottery ticket?" Reed guessed.

"No, a vacation."

Reed laughed. Sitting on a subterranean concrete landing overlooking a rusty green dumpster with overflowing garbage was the perfect environment to suggest a vacation. Reed even thought about it for a second before finding the flaw in the plan.

"Who is going to approve it?" he asked.

"Who is going to say no?" Henry countered.

Reed looked at Henry again. *It couldn't be that easy, could it?*

"I probably should," Reed said.

"Do it!" Henry advised. "Look at you. You're obviously broken up about the boss' death. You need some time to grieve. Grieve somewhere that serves tropical drinks."

That made Reed cackle.

"The sun is not my friend," Reed protested, pointing to his pale Irish complexion. "I'd just get fried and spend the vacation applying salve to my burns."

"Then go north," Henry said. "Go deep into the woods of Wisconsin and throw all of your troubles into one huge hot burning campfire."

"I haven't gone camping in years," Reed said. "I wouldn't even know how to do it."

"Wait right there," Henry replied. He got up from his concrete seat and walked to the parking attendant booth fifteen feet away. He opened the door, leaned in, said something to Ramon and returned with a magazine in his hands. He tossed it onto Reed's lap as he approached.

"Here," Henry said. "Brush up a little."

"Camper's World?"

"That's Ramon's," Henry said. "He said you could borrow it."

Reed flipped through the pages. Ads for tents and lanterns and campgrounds. Articles about backpacking, camping recipes, and family events. It was like a foreign world to modern-day Reed, but a world he lived in many years ago—when he was a young Boy Scout.

"Think about it," Henry implored. "Clear skies. Peace and quiet. A crackling fire. Communing with nature. No stress. No Cap'n Slappy's. No crowds."

"If it only it was that easy," Reed said.

"Remember this," Henry said, patting his friend on the arm. "The only one who's stopping you from doing it now is you."

8

OH YEAH, ONE MORE THING....

Peter punched the button for the lobby, straightened his tie in the mirrored wall of the elevator, took a deep breath and asked himself one more time why he was doing this. The man on the phone was in fact Peter's father, at least biologically that was true. But he hadn't been a "dad" in a very long time. Peter had gotten along just fine without him. *What the hell did he want now?*

The doors opened up onto the cavernous Art Deco lobby of the Flicker Building, with its ornate brass detail and vaulted ceilings, from back when they built office towers that looked like cathedrals. Peter's shoes clicked sharply on the polished stone floors as he crossed the lobby to the security desk.

"Ah, there he is!" announced Henry. "Smile for Marcus here."

Peter nodded shyly to the young black security guard sitting at the desk.

"Yeah, I see what you mean," chuckled Marcus, winking at Henry.

Standing together, Peter and Henry were a study in opposites. They stood about the same height, both a little over six feet. But Henry was a broad shouldered working man in grey work pants and a white dress shirt, with rugged hands, wise old eyes and big voice. Peter was a dapper, thin young man in a navy blue Brooks Brothers suit and polished wingtips, quiet and controlled. Only the long scar along Peter's jaw line seemed out of place.

"Marcus here said that he didn't recognize the name Peter Stankiewicz and I told him that can't be so, since you've been a lawyer here for three years now. So let's clear that up. Marcus, my son Peter. Pete, this is Marcus. Marcus is finishing his undergrad at Roosevelt University, right down the street."

"Nice to meet you, Marcus." And then to Henry, "We better go, and beat the lunch rush. I've gotta get right back."

The Boardroom was a dark, old pub with seating for about 40, not counting the dozen or so seats at the bar. As the name implied, it served the business community. They featured hot, hearty sandwiches and soups at a decent price. There was no fear of tourists or kiddies on field trips finding this joint. At 11:15, Peter and Henry were still early enough to grab a table, although the bar was already standing room only. The place opened at 10am and some of the patrons, no doubt, had been here since then. And they would be here all day. Peter usually didn't have the luxury of a true lunch hour. He hoped no one recognized him.

"So, Henry, what's up?" asked Peter as they sat down.

Henry wasn't ready to dive right in just yet. He started slow.

"Well, Pete. How's the love life? Your mother says you're getting married. I think that's great. If you are ever looking for marriage advice, let me know."

"You're kidding, right?"

"Why not, son? I've been married several times. Don't you think there's some wisdom I might have to share?"

"Well, Henry, I guess you might have some 'wedding' advice, seeing as you've been through the ceremony so often. But your post-wedding day track record is kind of weak, don't you think?"

"I'm proud of that record. I like to call it 'three marriages, no convictions'."

"Anyway, I'm not engaged. Mom just likes to think that. I think she wants to have a grandchild. And you know Mom. Well, maybe you don't. But she's got a perfect vision of how she thinks things are supposed to be, and apparently it's time for me to get married. All part of the plan."

"Your mother's a good person. But she always needed a plan," Henry smiled.

"Do you know what you're gonna have?" asked Peter looking at the menu one more time and nodding for the waiter to come to the table.

"Yes, sir," muttered the elderly waiter as he appeared tableside. "Are you ready to order?"

"I'm ready," said Peter, "Henry here has a little harder time settling on an option. I'll have the soup and the grilled chicken sandwich, hold the mayo."

"Hold the mayo? What's the point of that?" mumbled Henry. "My son, the dietician. I'll have the beef au jus sandwich and fries. And have you got one of those near beers? An O'Doul's or something?"

"Yes, sir," said the waiter. "Anything for the boy?"

Hey, the boy is a 28-year-old attorney. He can order for himself.

"I'll have a club soda. And a lime. Thanks."

The waiter nodded and left.

"So, non-alcoholic beer," said Peter. "What's the occasion?"

"Well," smiled Henry, pointing to his crisp white shirt which clearly indicated that he worked for Ace Parking Lot Services, "I'm going back to work from here. And they kind of frown on the whole drinking and driving thing."

"Are you sure you can get away like this?" asked Peter.

"Oh yeah, this is dead time. Busy in the morning rush, with all those people dying to get to their offices. They must be giving stuff away up there. And then busy again late in the afternoon. All those same people running to their cars like the building was on fire, and looking forward to sitting on the highway again for an hour or two. But around now, nothing happens. No one enters. No one leaves. It's like the building is on 'lock down.' And Ramon's got me covered. All is well. It's a simple gig. I've got it pretty darn good."

"As long as you're happy."

"I'm happy. Trust me, I know. I've been unhappy often enough to know when I'm happy. I go to work, I come home. I watch a ball game with my feet up, and a hot meal in my belly. A good woman sitting in the next room doing, I don't know, whatever she does in there. And the bills are paid. What more could I ask for?"

"Great. I think that's just great."

The place was filling up with a lunchtime crowd. It was getting louder.

"Oh, yeah," said Henry. "I wanted to learn more about this girl in your life. It is a girl, right? You're not gonna go to the dark side on me, are you? Cuz I'm not sure how to deal with that, although I got nothing against the whole mano a mano thing. I just think it's a shame when there's so many beautiful women out there."

"No, Henry. It's a girl. I mean, she's a girl, a woman. Yes." Peter rolled his eyes. *Do I really share genes with this caveman?*

"OK, then. So what's she like? I don't even know this girl and she's on her way to being family."

"Family?" asked Peter quietly, his hand shaking as he grabbed his drink.

Henry caught the verbal jab and nodded. *Is it getting warm in here?*

"So," said Henry, suddenly awkward, "Tell me about this girl."

Peter took a deep breath.

"Well, Kelly's a lawyer too. We met while we were interning at MacArthur Harrison during law school. Kelly went to Notre Dame. So now we both work at the same firm, and no one is supposed to know about us because it's kind of frowned upon. But these lawyers, it's a very close group, I spend my entire life there, and these are smart people, and I kind of think that they suspect."

"Kelly, that's a nice name. Of course it could be a boy name too. Are you sure you're not..."

"No, Henry. Trust me, she's a girl. I've checked."

"Good. So when do I get to meet this alleged Kelly?"

"Wow, Henry. I don't know. I didn't think that would interest you."

"Why wouldn't I want to meet my son's sweetheart?"

Peter wanted to launch into him. But instead, Peter took a long, slow drink of his club soda and resisted the urge.

Henry broke the silence. "I'm not very good at this. I know I haven't been a great father. I'd like to take another shot if it's not too late."

"Gee, Henry. Nice timing. I'd say you're about fifteen years late."

Henry cleared his throat. "I realize that I haven't been around. And I know I can't take any of the credit for your success, but I am proud of you."

"Really?" asked Peter, trying to remain calm. "What do you even know about me?"

Henry looked around the room, conscious that they were in a public place.

"First of all," said Henry, lowering his voice, "I know some stuff about you. I know you're smart, although I'm sure you didn't get that from me. I know you're a good man, and you take care of your mother. I know that you don't like mayonnaise on your grilled chicken sandwich. I know that you're incredibly busy being an associate working his way up this law firm with very little time for anything else. And I know that every once in a while, you do have time for lunch." Henry paused, and took a breath. "Thanks for coming down."

The drinks, soup and sandwiches all arrived at once. "Enjoy," muttered the waiter.

The two men arranged their plates and began to eat.

"So," said Peter, searching for something. "How's the latest Mrs. Henry Stankiewicz? Katherine, right? How's she doing?"

"Well, I'll tell you one thing. I'm pretty sure she'll be the last Mrs. Henry Stankiewicz," Henry smiled a half smile and took a big bite of his sandwich.

"That's good to hear, Henry. You really think she's the one, finally?"

"Maybe," Henry answered, swallowing the bite. "But more likely it's just that I won't make it to wife number four. The doctor tells me I've got cancer, and it's pretty serious."

Henry took another large bite of his sandwich. For a moment, Peter thought he must have misunderstood what Henry had said. Peter sat back and tried to collect his thoughts. Then he leaned forward again and looked Henry in the eye.

"What? Cancer? What kind of cancer?"

"Whaddya mean, 'what kind of cancer'? The bad kind."

"Henry, they can take care of that now. They've got chemo and radiation and things." Peter couldn't think about his meal, although Henry continued to devour the au jus.

"No, son," Henry managed between gulps. "They say they could try that stuff but it's complicated and they really don't think it would do anything positive, and it would just postpone the inevitable. Here, I wrote it down. I figured you'd ask something like that." Henry set down his sandwich for a moment and handed Peter the crumpled napkin from his shirt pocket. "It's terminal. Eat your soup."

Peter tried to decipher Henry's handwriting, reading aloud. "Diffuse large B cell non-Hodgkin's lymphoma. Is that it?"

"I think so. Doctors talk kinda fast. It's something like that."

"You seem awfully calm about all this."

"What do you want me to do? Sure I'm scared, but these are the cards I've been dealt. I've gotta play them. One of the reasons I wanted to have lunch is to see if you could write a living will for me. They tell me it's an important thing to have, so they can flip off the machines if I become a vegetable. You being a lawyer and all, I figured you'd be the man for the job. I'd pay you of course, and I'm sure you do these things all the time."

"Alright, I just need a second to…" Peter stopped talking and chugged his club soda. "OK. Look, Henry, first of all, I have never written a living will. I'm sure it's pretty simple and I'll figure it out and I'll do it. Second, don't even think about paying for it. And third, well, do you have any idea how much time you have?"

"No. They say it's a tricky thing. No way of knowing, but I thought I should put my ducks in a row. And one more favor, please keep this just between us, OK?"

"OK."

Peter looked up from the table, realizing that the restaurant was now absolutely jammed with loud, and hungry businesspeople. *When did this happen?*

"Look, Henry," said Peter tentatively. "I'm sorry."

"I know," said Henry. "Now when am I gonna meet this Kelly?"

9

A HOUSE DIVIDED

Reed had never quite gotten over the name etched into the glass doors of the corporate offices on the 17th floor, even after all this time.

The company lore begins in the early 1960's. There was a local Cleveland children's show, "The Cartoon Fun Parade," featuring Captain Happy, a goofy pirate who introduced cartoons and talked to puppets. Benny Carson, the actor who portrayed Captain Happy, was always looking for an angle. He knew he couldn't be a TV pirate forever and wanted to capitalize on his local fame.

Benny became convinced that what the world needed was another seafood fast food outlet, and seeing that he was a pirate, Benny should open Captain Happy's Seafood Restaurant, serving deep fried fish products to children without palates and their undiscriminating parents. Benny opened three outlets in Cleveland and they were doing surprisingly well. Benny was on top of the world.

He drank, got divorced, and lost the TV gig. His former employers insisted that they owned the Captain Happy name. And so Benny, in a drunken blur one evening, changed the restaurant's name slightly, changed the color of the good captain's uniform and switched the eye patch from the right eye to the left.

Hence, Cap'n Slappy's was born. Over the years, Benny expanded the chain throughout the Midwest, bringing frozen seafood to people who'd never seen an ocean. In the 1980's, Benny sold out to an investment group, took his money and moved to the Florida Keys and became a real pirate.

Since then, Cap'n Slappy's had been a consistently profitable contributor to the HKY Restaurant Group, which also included Tricky Chicky, Custer's Last Burger and the Donner Party Pavilion; never spectacular, not really growing, but a reliable, steady revenue stream with 250 locations throughout the Midwest and parts of the Northeast. In 1978, the headquarters were moved to Chicago. Reed was hired in the purchasing department that very year. He never expected that he'd still be there 27 years later.

That evening, Reed climbed onto the 5:25 pm Rock Island train home just like he'd done every weeknight for as long as he could remember. He walked to his seat. He actually considered it 'his' seat and was offended when some rookie unknowingly sat there. On those days, Reed couldn't think straight for a moment and had to remember which other seats were not taken by regulars. He couldn't ask the offender to move. They didn't know better, and that would also break the code of strangers. But he couldn't sit across the aisle. Bald, bushy eyebrows guy always sat there, one row back was bubble butt woman's seat, and against the window was always cardigan sweater guy's spot. He'd have to select from the seats that a regular didn't claim. Otherwise he'd cause a ripple effect of people ousted in silence, always in silence, from their regular seats. Fruit basket upset.

Thankfully for Reed, today his seat was waiting for him like an old friend, something to be counted upon. Reed sat down and relaxed. For the third straight evening, he pulled out the *Camper's World* magazine that Henry had given him. This time he lost himself in an article on the new line of Coleman lanterns.

The rhythm of the train rocked Reed into a comfortable lull. Twenty-six minutes later, he stood up and exited the train at his stop, 95th Street at Longwood Drive, without looking up and without having to hear the conductor's announcement, like an old man who didn't need an alarm clock, whose body just knew it was time to wake up. He walked off the train to the familiar station and joined the thirty or so other exiting passengers who silently assimilated into the community, some into waiting cars, others like Reed just walking the few blocks home.

Reed still had analyses to review. He still had reports to complete, even though they had been just piling up in the inbox of a dead man in the corner office for a week now. The new guy will probably change procedures; that's what the bastards usually do. They'll decide they're going to make their mark by changing the weekly reports to bi-weekly and the monthly reports to weekly, including a new teleconference on Mondays and a new quarterly performance review to replace the old semi-annual review. That will show them who is in charge. Until that change came, Reed would keep sending reports to the dead man's desk. Reed's paycheck kept coming by direct deposit and he wasn't going to rock that boat.

Reed marched through the evening mist until his feet led him like a sleepwalker to the front steps of his modest red brick Colonial home. The front door was unlocked. Reed stepped into the entryway, hanging his JC Penney overcoat in its place. For a moment, Reed remembered days gone by when he'd stumble over baseball gloves and hockey equipment, when his son's youthful energy easily filled the entire house. Pictures of Will filled the walls, but the little boy Reed remembered was long gone. Now it was Reed and Lucy, alone.

"Hi, honey. How was your day?" It was Lucy. Of course it was Lucy, who else would it be? Every night the same greeting, in the same lilt. And the same response.

"Fine. Fine."

The only adjustment over the years had been the drink she offered him as he entered the kitchen. It had been soda when Will was young, followed by a glass of milk with dinner. This era was followed by the Budweiser years, and then the days of gin and tonics. For the last eight years, it was club soda and a lime. No calories, no ill effects, no bad aftertaste.

Kind of like Lucy.

Reed knew he loved Lucy, but sometimes he had to remind himself. She'd been through a terrible ordeal, he knew. And so he gave her the space she needed. But something had to give. The inertia was stifling. Of course, he wasn't sure if Lucy agreed. They hadn't had a real conversation in years.

"What's for dinner?" asked Reed, out of habit.

"Well, it's Tuesday. That's meatloaf night. It should be ready in about ten minutes."

Reed plodded upstairs to the bedroom, hung up his jacket and tie, went down the hall to the bathroom and splashed some water in his face, staring into the mirror at the gray around his temples, the cavernous wrinkles around his eyes and indentations on either side of his nose, left by his ill-fitting reading glasses. He stepped back and observed the slight gut that was pressing against the lower buttons of his short-sleeve white polycotton dress shirt. Reed leaned forward again and stared into his own green eyes, hoping for an answer. *Who is this old man in the mirror? When did this happen?* He plodded back down to the kitchen. Dinner was waiting.

"I want to go camping."

There, he said it. Sitting at the kitchen island, between bites of meatloaf. Lucy looked up from her plate, sipped a bit of water and said, "What?"

"I want to go camping." The ice had been broken and Reed was glad he'd said it.

"What are you talking about? Camping? Where did this come from?"

"I've been thinking about it for awhile now. I just want to try something new. I want to sleep under the stars, enjoy the great outdoors, commune with Mother Nature."

"It just seems awfully sudden, don't you think?"

"I thought it might be good for me. To escape for a day or two."

"Escape? From what?"

"Just the pressures of work and life and all that. Everyone needs a break."

"I've been working at the library for fifteen years. I don't need a break," said Lucy. "You're planning to do this alone?"

"Well, no. I was hoping you'd like to go, of course." What were the odds of that? Lucy didn't even like picnics. She thought they were pointless. Why would someone sitting in a perfectly good house with a stove and refrigerator, with a roof over her head, climate controlled air and no bugs want to leave all that to sit in the hot sun, sweating, and swatting flies, only to have to pack it all up and head back into that nice, comfortable home where she had wanted to be in the first place?

"How did this whole train of thought get started?" Lucy asked.

"I don't know," shrugged Reed. "Lots of things, I guess. Work, and now the whole Anderson dying thing. It just got me to thinking about the future and mortality and 'what's it all about' and, I don't know, I need to get away and clear my head."

Lucy looked across the table at Reed. "It's like I don't even know you."

"What do you mean? Nothing's changed. I just feel like I'm in a rut. I thought the fresh air and the great outdoors might give me some new perspective."

"That sure sounds like you want to be alone."

"If you'd like to come along, I think that would be great. If you don't, I totally understand."

"Wow, that's a hearty invitation. You want time to get away. What am I supposed to think? You never tell me anything. You never mentioned a word before about 'clearing your head' and 'new perspectives'. Now, bam, out of the blue, this! You want to go camping?"

These were the moments that made Reed uncomfortable. When they didn't talk, it made him anxious. And when they talked, it made him anxious.

Reed did love Lucy. But if Lucy didn't want to go camping, Reed was OK with that too.

10

MOTHER KNOWS BEST

One good thing about working late in Chicago is avoiding rush hour. Peter was sailing north on the Kennedy with the windows down, his '98 Accord purring smoothly and his girl at his side. Seven years of college did not go down the drain. Yeah, they worked him to the bone, but the benefits to his personal life had proven substantial.

"So, I just want to prepare you for a few things before we get there," said Peter, his tie loosened, his jacket hanging in the backseat, but otherwise still in his lawyer garb.

"What's the big deal? I've met your mother before," smiled Kelly, still looking fresh after twelve hours of legal grunt work. *How does she do it?*

"Yes, but only on neutral territory, with other people around. And back then you were just a girl I was dating. Now she thinks it's serious."

"Isn't it?"

"I'm bringing you to her home, aren't I? I just know my mother. She's a wonderful woman, but she has a plan. She has high expectations for her boy. I would consider this a test. And the apartment gets very few visitors. It's a big deal."

"You've never brought a girl home before?"

"Not even Prom. I've avoided it as long as possible. But sooner or later, I knew this day would come. And now you'll have to run the gauntlet." Peter took the Lawrence Avenue exit and headed west.

Kelly was cool under pressure. "Is this the way you brief all of your witnesses, counselor? You give them a three-minute warning and scare them to death before they take the stand?"

Peter was now cruising into Jefferson Park, his old neighborhood on the northwest side of the city.

"Oh, yeah. I almost forgot. I would also avoid any discussion of religion, politics or sex."

"Bummer," said Kelly, "I had a whole lot of sex questions all lined up for her."

"Also no talk about NASA, sharks, Muhammad Ali or sushi."

"Wow. What's left to talk about? I think I'll just nod my head and smile a lot."

"Perfect," said Peter, turning onto his old block, finding a parking spot beneath a giant oak that towered over the narrow street.

Every time he came back to this block, his memory flashed to hot summer evenings playing hide and seek, or capture the flag, running down gangways through the alley and over the chain link fences between backyards. Peter's block had been home to at least a dozen kids around his age. Some of their parents still lived here, but it had been years since Peter had seen any of them.

Peter and Kelly walked to the brick two-flat and rang the bell. The buzzer buzzed and they let themselves in, trekking up the narrow stairway to the second floor apartment. At the top of the stairs, Peter's mother stood in the doorway, wearing a comfortable silk blouse, khakis and sandals. Her graying coif was held together with enough hair spray to raise ozone threat levels.

"Come in, come in." Evelyn ushered her guests.

"Hello, Mrs. Stankiewicz, nice to see you again," said Kelly.

"Please. Call me Evelyn. Can I get you something to drink? Peter, why don't you get us both something to drink? Kelly, what would you like to drink?"

"Oh," Kelly hesitated, "Surprise me, Peter."

"No surprises for me, Peter. I'll have a Jack and Coke," said Evelyn, leading Kelly into the living room. "Well, I was working late too as it turns out. I'm on the alderman's committee for crime prevention and the meeting ran a little long. Luckily I had a pot roast in the crock pot all day. It's Peter's favorite, you know. And it's so simple, you just drop the roast in the crock pot in the morning, come home, boil some egg noodles, chop up the roast, heat some cream of mushroom soup and gravy, mix it together, and that's it. Of course it is a huge meal for just me, but it's nice to have company."

"Here we are," announced Peter, "One Jack and Coke and two chardonnays. Mom, dinner smells great."

"Good. Now let me check on it." Evelyn excused herself. Peter sat down on an armchair, across from Kelly.

"So, how's it going?" whispered Peter.

"Fine. I haven't said a word and already I have the recipe for your favorite meal."

"I guess she's lulling you into a false sense of security."

"Whoa!" interrupted Kelly, "What the heck is that?"

Kelly stood and looked at an 8X10 color photo of Peter at age twelve hanging above the couch, braces gleaming, and a shock of long, thick brown hair taking up most of the frame. Kelly turned and took another look around the room. She hadn't noticed them when she first sat down.

"It's some sort of a shrine," she said in amazement.

There were at least fifteen pictures of Peter at various ages everywhere she turned. In a graduation gown, a Prom tux, a Little League uniform, at a Bears game. Some of the photos were large, some small. The one over the couch even had its own light source, a fluorescent lamp attached to the frame and shining upward.

"I should have warned you. My mom thinks a lot of me."

"Well, I think it's cute." Kelly snuck Peter a quick peck on the cheek.

"Dinner is served," said Evelyn, walking into the room. Peter wondered if Evelyn had caught the display of affection. Kelly kissed Peter again to make sure she had. Evelyn smiled.

As she left the room, Kelly noticed another display. Smaller. On an end table. Several photos of a very pretty young girl, with soft, light brown hair, sparkling green eyes and a very fair complexion.

"Is this Sarah?" asked Kelly.

Peter paused. "Yes, that's her." He looked at the photos for a long, quiet moment.

The meal went off without a hitch, thought Peter. No dangerous topics, just small talk and lots of pot roast and noodles.

Dinner ended and it was nearly 11pm, according to the cuckoo clock on the wall. Peter knew he'd have to tell his mother. He had put it off long enough. Kelly carried dishes to the kitchen where Evelyn was making coffee.

"Decaf only, mom," called Peter from the dining room, sitting alone. "It's way too late, and we all have early days tomorrow."

"Of course, honey." Evelyn brought in a tray of cookies with the coffee, and Peter stood and poured them each a cup.

"Mom, I need to tell you something." Peter's tone was serious, and Evelyn's ears perked up. It was not the typical lead-in to an engagement announcement that Evelyn might have expected. Peter sat back down. "It's about Henry."

Evelyn looked confused. Kelly focused her attention on her coffee, considering whether she should actually be sitting there for this.

"Well, what is it?" asked Evelyn, now concerned.

"Look, it's probably not my place. And he's not your concern, I know."

"Well, he is your father. And that was a long time ago. And things change." Evelyn had clearly taken a lot of steps that took years for her to get to this point of peace and resignation. Peter wasn't sure he was quite there yet. No, he was definitely not there yet. But he plodded on, thinking his mother deserved to know.

"Henry's dying. Now I don't expect you to do anything about it. In fact, there really isn't much you could do if you wanted to. I had lunch with him today, and he told me. He told me so that I could write up a living will for him. If I wasn't a lawyer, he may never have told me. It's some kind of rare cancer. I looked it up today. It's pretty nasty stuff. He's not sure how long he's got. I thought you should at least know. Frankly, I'm a little pissed. I mean, he just throws this in my lap. I don't know how to handle this."

Kelly sat uncomfortably. Evelyn seemed to deflate as she leaned back in her chair.

"Tact was never your father's strong suit. But I imagine he's a little scared, even if he'd never admit it. He's had a pretty scattered life, you know. He doesn't have many people he can turn to, I'd imagine."

"So I'm the lucky one, huh?" said Peter. "Honestly, I can't see what you ever saw in him."

Evelyn took a long sip of her coffee and began quietly.

"Your father was a charming young man." Evelyn closed her eyes for a moment, remembering. "He swept me off my feet with his jokes and stories. He was quite the catch. We were together when he was drafted, and I vowed that I would wait for him. And so I did. He came back two long years later, scarred, physically and emotionally. He asked me to marry him. Of course I said yes. I thought that I could heal him, and that whatever issues he had would be temporary. We got married. A few years later, you came along. And then Sarah. We had some wonderful times. It wasn't all bad. And I thought things might change for good. But he continued to struggle, on and off, over the years. Finally, he left, and I knew that it was for the best."

The best for whom? thought Peter.

"And he still sent a check every month to help support you and Sarah."

Peter wanted to shake his mother by the shoulders. Instead he tried to be as calm as possible, remaining seated. "Mom, he left us. He left me. I didn't need his money. I needed a father. And so did Sarah. Time doesn't heal those kinds of wounds."

Kelly had never heard this from Peter before. She walked over behind Peter's chair and put her hands on his shoulders.

Evelyn nodded in sympathy. Finally she said, "I'd like you to do something. For me. Don't do it for Henry, do it for me. Please."

Peter considered it for a moment and saw the pain in his mother's eyes. "All right, Mom," Peter said with resignation, "What is it?"

"I'd like you to tell his old army buddies."

"Henry didn't want me to tell anyone."

"Your father always had a special place for the men he fought with. Those men went through hell together and I know they would want to know. I still get Christmas cards from a few of them. I first met them when they all flew in to Chicago for the wedding. That was some party. You should have seen Henry light up when he was around them. It's been a long time, and a few may be gone by now, but see if you can find them. They should know."

"How am I supposed to do that?"

"Hang on." Evelyn excused herself from the table for a moment.

Kelly sat down in the empty chair next to Peter and held his hand tightly. If she hadn't, Peter might have taken the opportunity to break for the door.

Evelyn returned with a cardboard box filled with cards. Shuffling through the contents, she found what she needed.

"Here it is. I knew one of them was local. I don't have a phone number but there's a return address in Wilmette. Maybe he would know how you could contact the others."

Peter was about to protest, and got a kick in the shin under the table from Kelly.

"OK, Mom. Whatever you want."

11

THE GREAT OUTDOORS

Reed had been practicing setting up the tent all week. Every night when he got home from work, he ate dinner with Lucy, then went out to the yard and timed himself. By Thursday, he had it down to a science. It took Reed exactly eight minutes to set it up; every single pole, stake, and flap. These new tents were so much easier than they were when he was a kid.

Reed had done some online research about area campgrounds and finally selected the Bong Recreational District just over the Wisconsin border. He and his college roommates had always laughed when they saw that sign at exit 340. They didn't know the campground was named after a World War II flying ace; their simple college minds had instead imagined vast woodlands filled with marijuana plants. The wiser, older Reed just knew it was far enough from Chicago to feel like he was "away".

Halfway there, Reed began to question his choice. His research hadn't told him that the interstate was down to one stinkin' lane for a good twenty miles just north of Chicago, although he probably should have known. After spring has sprung, any interstate near Chicago was sure to be under construction. It was as inevitable as death, taxes, and Illinois governors going to prison. Reed tried to stay positive. This weekend was going to be about relaxing, breathing in nature, and replenishing his soul.

But, dammit, he should have taken off the whole day like Henry suggested, instead of just the afternoon. Now instead of arriving at a decent hour, Reed was arriving just as it was getting dark. That was going to make tent set up a little more difficult. Thank God he splurged on that Coleman lantern. That baby was going to save him.

Reed rolled down the windows as he entered the Bong campground looking for site number 57. He turned off the paved road and could hear that comforting sound of the tire rubber interacting with the gravel path. That sound was enough to make him feel like he was getting away from it all.

He pulled into his stall, climbed out of his Camry, stretched his legs, took a deep breath and began to unload. The crickets were chirping. He could hear bullfrogs in the distance. Reed looked up at the sky and marveled at the stars. There were a few black clouds rolling in from the west, but there were more stars than he had ever seen in the east. It was almost light enough to see what he was doing.

"Didn't I tell you, son?" he said looking up at the sky. "We're finally doing it."

He lit the Coleman lantern and flooded his tiny little site with enough light to set up the tent. Reed got to work. He laid out the tarp, and unrolled his tent into position over the tarp. The two black poles went on the outside, the two orange polls went on the inside, and the rain flap went...

Uh oh.

Reed saw it in his mind. The rain flap was still on his deck at home. He looked up at the sky again. Those black clouds were definitely headed this way, but that didn't mean it was going to rain. It was probably going to be fine. Heck, without the rain flap, it would even take a minute off his tent set up time. Think positive.

Sure enough, in seven minutes flat, it was all staked and ready to rock. He went inside to get it all comfy. He unrolled his padded mat and sleeping bag. He set up his pillow just so. Then he gave it the ultimate test; he lay down on the sleeping bag and looked up at the sky through the mesh roof.

"This is going to be an awesome view," he said to himself. "Absolutely perfect."

With the inside of the tent perfectly prepared, it was time to get the campfire going. Site #57 had a nice little fire pit, and all it needed was firewood. This campground didn't allow you to bring your own wood because of the Asian tree beetle scare, so Reed walked the hundred yards or so back to the shack near the campground entrance. He remembered seeing a sign saying they sold bundles of wood there. $5 seemed like a reasonable price.

When Reed returned, he arranged a few of the logs into the shape of a tee-pee, put some newspaper beneath it for kindling, and then lit the fire. Twenty minutes later the fire was beginning to take shape. The crackling of the burning wood was such a soothing sound. This was as close to heaven as he could get.

Reed took a look around the grounds. "I wonder why this place is so empty on a Friday night," he asked himself. There was only one other camper in this entire row; on the other side of the well, the site closest to the latrine cabin. That guy had obviously paid a little extra for an electric hookup. He needed it for his RV.

"That's not even camping," Reed said.

Reed sat down on a rock next to the fire and reached into his pocket for his cigarette lighter. He noticed a few black dots around his knee. He pulled the lantern over to get a closer look. They were bugs of some kind.

"Oh no."

Three little ticks had burrowed their little black heads into his skin around his knee. Reed remembered from his Boy Scout days that ticks had to be pulled out carefully. Otherwise they would leave their heads behind under the skin, and that could cause all sorts of problems. He pulled out all three ticks without too much effort.

"There, that wasn't so bad."

He turned his knee around to see the back side of it, and there were a few more. That's when he noticed his other knee was covered too. He must have gotten them when he walked through that long grass on the way to the shack.

Reed patiently plucked the ticks off one by one, flicking them into the fire. *Die, you blood suckers, die.* While he was killing them, he had another awful thought. *What if these things found a home in more unmentionable areas?* He had to check, even if it meant shining a lantern on an area that wasn't normally illuminated quite so directly.

Suddenly, the sky lit up with lightning. A thunderclap followed. Reed was counting the seconds. He had read that each second meant about a 1/5 mile of distance.

"Still a mile away," he said. He put his finger in the air. "Feels like it's blowing slightly north. It'll probably blow past."

He tried to find a secluded spot to check out his unmentionables, and settled on a spot right next to his car door, out of sight from the other camper in the RV. The lantern light bounced off the metal to give a little additional light.

"Thank God," he said as he pored through the nether forest. "Clean as a whistle."

The sky lit up again. This time the thunderclap followed only two seconds afterward.

"Oh no."

Reed looked at his mesh tent roof and cursed himself for leaving the rain flap on the deck. How could he be so damned stupid?

"Wait a second," he said to himself. "I think I have a blanket in the trunk."

Reed rummaged around his trunk trying to find a rain flap substitute. The blanket was gone. He must have taken it out when he packed. Maybe he could yank the tarp out from under the tent and throw it over the mesh roof, but then the bottom of the tent would get soaked. *Come on, nature boy, think of something.*

Lightning, followed almost immediately by thunder, rang through the air once again. Reed didn't have long now. A gust of wind came through and the air temperature immediately dropped ten degrees. That tent had to be taken apart fast. First he grabbed his pad, sleeping bag, pillow and backpack and threw them in the back seat of the car. There was no time to put everything away nicely and neatly like he wanted. He pulled out the stakes and began throwing them in a pile. The last stake missed the pile and knocked out the Coleman lantern.

Only the campfire illuminated the campsite now, and it looked like Mother Nature was going to take care of that little detail very soon.

Reed pulled out the black and orange poles, collapsed them into smaller piles, and started rolling up the tent. That's when it began. The raindrops were huge; the kind of drops that felt like you were getting hit by water balloons. Reed's tent now lay on the ground and was quickly soaked, but he was a man on a mission. He rolled it up, and without putting it back into its bag, threw it into the trunk. He threw the stakes and poles on top of the wet tent, and slammed the trunk shut. Reed's only remaining piece of equipment was the lantern. It was still hot, but a few seconds of that pouring rain was probably enough to cool it sufficiently to put it in his car.

As he ran past the campfire to retrieve it, the struggling orange light of the dampening fire illuminated the remaining ticks on Reed's legs. The rain was washing a few of them off, but those suckers were hanging on for dear life. He grabbed the lantern and made one last mad dash to the car. The rain was pounding him the whole way there. His polo shirt and khaki shorts were now pasted to his body. He was completely drenched; sweat mixed with the rain began to cascade over Reed's eyes. He felt ten pounds heavier thanks to the absorbency of his clothes.

It wasn't until Reed was inside his car, sitting behind the steering wheel, creating a huge puddle on his vinyl seats, that he finally exhaled. There were times when that sound of falling rain was soothing. This was not one of those times. The raindrops were so heavy and were coming down with such force, it sounded like they were denting the car with each violent clunk.

Reed leaned the driver's seat back as far as it could go and watched the rain smack down on the moon roof. Just like the pioneers would have done. He couldn't help but chuckle.

"So much for the great outdoors," he said in the general direction of the pounding roof. "Or is that you up there pulling strings to make sure I don't appreciate it without you?"

Reed put the seat back in the upright position, inserted the key into the ignition, and started the car. He couldn't see much through the pouring rain. There were no lights at all now; even the campfire had been extinguished. Reed turned on his brights. He needed to get the hell out of this place. He remembered seeing a sign for a fairly nice hotel a few miles back, just off the highway.

It only took a few minutes to get there.

Reed pulled into the parking lot and under the canopy of the Shady Vista Inn. He grabbed his backpack, climbed out of the car and got soaked again, even under the canopy because the rain was blowing sideways in the gusty wind. He entered through the huge oak doors. Reed dripped all over the nicely carpeted hotel lobby floor as he waited behind the only other patron at the front desk. Reed looked around the charming old inn. Someone had really taken care of this place, filled with antiques and paintings of the Wisconsin countryside. Reed's shirt clung to his chest, and he felt cold and tired. The man in front of him was being helped, but he sounded more than a little agitated. Apparently Reed wasn't the only one having a bad day.

The man was screaming at the clerk; his face contorted with rage, his tone of voice incredibly snotty. "How can there not be a single room in this hotel?"

"Well sir, I'm sorry, but you don't have a reservation."

"Are you checking the entire hotel?" the man bellowed at the clerk. "Take another look at your computer there. There has to be a room in this fucking hotel somewhere."

The clerk clicked on the keyboard a few times.

"I'm sorry, sir. There's nothing I can do. There's a motel about twenty miles north of here."

"I'm not driving in that storm for twenty miles!"

"I'm sorry, sir, that's all I can do."

The man turned around and looked at the soaking-wet Reed standing behind him. "Can you believe this guy?" he said to Reed. "This is Wisconsin, in the middle of nowhere. There's no way the entire hotel is booked."

"We have a family reunion here this weekend," the clerk explained.

"Well then call them up and tell them to share a fucking room," the man snapped.

"You know I can't do that," the clerk said. The clerk was visibly upset but maintained his composure.

"Well thanks for nothing," the man spat, and stormed toward the door.

Reed and the clerk watched the angry customer until he was out of view. When he was gone, Reed met eyes with the clerk, and then noticed his name tag on his green cardigan sweater. Kenny couldn't have been more than 25 years old. He was struggling to keep it together after that ugly confrontation.

"Sorry about that, Kenny," Reed said.

Kenny waved him off. "Not your fault."

"And sorry about dripping all over your carpet."

"Don't worry, sir," Kenny said, a reluctant smile emerging. "I'm sure you won't be the only wet one tonight."

"You know, I just have to say," Reed said, "I thought the way you handled that guy was very impressive. He was being a complete jerk, and you never lost your cool. Nice job."

The lights in the lobby flickered for a moment as another thunderclap sounded nearby, but Reed noticed the clerk was suddenly standing taller than he was a moment ago.

"So," Reed continued. "Where is that motel you were talking about?"

Kenny clicked a few keys on the keyboard. "Your reservation is right here, sir."

"No, I don't have one," Reed said. "I was camping and..."

"Well, we didn't think you were going to make it so we actually gave your room to someone else. Sorry about that."

Now Reed was really confused.

"The only thing I can do is give you the Brentwood Suite," Kenny continued. "It's actually the only room we have left. I'd have to give it to you for the lower basic room rate. Would you like to put that on your credit card?"

"Really?" Reed asked.

"Yes, sir," he said. "And once you're settled, we can run those wet clothes through the dryer for you. Just leave them outside your door. Room service is available until 11pm. Here's a coupon for a drink at the lobby bar, and for breakfast in the morning. Enjoy your stay."

"Thank you so much, Kenny."

Kenny smiled. "Thank you too, sir."

12

You Could Hear a Pin Drop

Living Wills varsity letter jackets were hanging on hooks behind lanes 11 and 12, and the team members were all wearing their "LW" bowling shirts. Despite their snappy bowling attire, bowling, as always, was taking a back seat to good old fashioned male bonding for team members Henry Stankiewicz, Oscar Case, Delmar Dunwoody, and Ramon Munoz.

Henry was wiping the tears away from his eyes in mid-story. Delmar was sitting next to him, his attention rapt. Oscar Case was rolling his eyes.

"So, I got home that night and had the ring in my pocket," Henry continued, suppressing a laugh. "I looked around the house for a place to put it away for safe keeping, but I couldn't find one."

"We had both agreed to wait until Valentine's Day," Oscar interrupted. "Don't forget that point."

"Well, yeah, but it was mid-January, and that was a whole month away," Henry said. "I knew I was seeing Evelyn that night, so I thought what the heck..."

"But it was a Tuesday night!" Oscar said. "Who proposes to his wife on a non-descript Tuesday night?"

The story was interrupted by the sweet sound of Ramon's silver ball hitting the pocket perfectly.

"STRIKE!" Oscar said. "Way to go Ramon!"

Ramon returned to high fives all around. They all called him "The Ringer" because he was by far the best bowler on the Living Wills team. Ramon's 175 average was the only reason they weren't dead last in the Thursday Night Over-40 League standings.

Delmar didn't technically meet the league's age requirement. He wasn't 40 yet; he just looked it. As for his bowling prowess, suffice it to say that if they called Delmar "The Ringer," it would have been sarcastic.

"Then what happened?" Delmar asked.

"You're up Henry," Ramon reminded him.

"Finish the story," Delmar said.

"Oscar can tell you the rest," Henry said. He walked up to the ball return and held his hand over the air to dry off his sweaty palms. He leaned back to hear Oscar tell his story, to make sure the old goat got the details right.

"So, Henry proposed to Evelyn that very night. We were supposed to do it on the same night... a month later. We had it all planned out, both of us were going to pull the rings out at the same table, at Chez Paul's, at the same time. It would have been one for the ages," Oscar yelled toward Henry, mock anger in his voice. "We had an agreement!"

"Tell him about the phone call," Henry said. Etiquette required him to wait for the man in the next lane to bowl first, but Henry would have let him go anyway. He wanted to hear the story again.

"So Henry called me up when he got home that night," Oscar said. "He said, 'Hey, I've got some big news for you. Evelyn and I are engaged.' I thought he was kidding, so he said, 'No, really, I asked her tonight at the Chinese restaurant. She said yes.'"

"Tell him what you said to me," Henry said. He couldn't contain a huge smile.

"I said, 'Fuck you,' and hung up the phone."

"You didn't," Delmar said. He loved hearing his boss tell stories like this. The other guys at BM&P Toilets had no idea that Oscar Case had this side to him.

"I did."

"Evelyn thought you were the biggest dick alive when you did that," Henry said.

"*You* were the dick," Oscar said. "We had an agreement."

Henry hit his mark, but he pulled his ball a fraction too far. It was heading right for the head pin. Split. He was unfazed by his typical lousy bowling, and came back to the scorer's table with a grin on his face.

"Tell Delmar how long it took you to ask Margaret to marry you after that," Henry said, as he waited for his ball to come back.

"I'm heading over to the bar," Ramon interrupted. "Three Old Styles and an O'Doul's?"

They all nodded. Ramon went for the refreshments.

"Tell him," Henry insisted.

"I was pissed at you," Oscar said.

"So, of course, he took it out on Margaret," Henry said.

"I didn't take it out on her," Oscar explained. "What do I always tell you, Delmar? Save your best material for when it's time to close the deal. Henry took away my best material. He's been stealing from me since high school. So I had to come up with a new plan."

Henry knew he couldn't pick up both sides of the split, so he went for the ten pin and knocked it over for a nine.

"Oscar, you're up," Delmar said.

"Anyway, that was 30 years ago," Oscar said, heading to the ball return. "At least I'm still married to the same woman."

"Yeah," Henry said to him, nudging Oscar as they walked by each other. "But I've gotten to propose more often than you did."

"Speaking of failed marriages," Oscar said. "Delmar's got a new girlfriend."

"I do not," Delmar said. He gave Oscar the evil eye. "All I said was that there's a cute girl at Al Cappacino's coffee shop near my place."

Oscar grabbed his ball, and prepared himself to bowl. Unlike his high school buddy Henry, Oscar Case took his bowling seriously. His 150 average was second best on the team, and he was dedicated to never taking a single frame for granted. He was concentrating as

Ramon returned with the beers, and Henry probed Delmar about this new woman.

"Are you sure this one isn't going to turn into a lesbian too?" Henry joked. "You should show her a picture of Brad Pitt and one of Angelina Jolie and ask her which one is better looking."

"My ex-wife wasn't a lesbian," Delmar protested. "She just moved to Vermont."

"Same thing," said Henry.

Ramon guffawed.

"Very funny," Delmar said. "Besides, I haven't even asked her out yet."

"Why not?" Henry asked.

"Like Oscar says, I need to use my best material to close the deal. I'm still working on a plan."

"You don't need a plan to ask out a woman," Henry said. "Just ask Ramon. He met Carmen when he was parking her car."

Ramon was in mid-swig of his beer, but he still managed a smile at the memory.

"I'm not sure what it is about her," Delmar explained, "But I think we'd really hit it off. She's got this evil sense of humor. When I asked her the question about the most famous person she ever served..."

"You asked *her* too?" Henry interrupted.

"I ask everyone," Delmar explained. "It's a conversation starter."

"Was it better than the one the cabbie told you?"

"Yup," he said. "Better than Yo Yo Ma."

"Who did she say?"

"Lorne Greene."

"Isn't he dead?"

Oscar returned to the conversation after he got a 9 on his first roll. He left the darn five pin standing. He couldn't help but add his two cents when he heard what they were still talking about.

"Tell Henry how old she is."

"She's 25," Delmar said.

"If she's 25, then Lorne Greene is impossible," Henry said.

"I know!" Delmar gushed. "That's what I loved about her. She's got that little evil streak."

"But she's 20 years younger than Delmar is," Oscar pointed out.

"She IS not," Delmar protested. He began to whisper so the guys on the other team couldn't hear him. "It's only 13 years."

"So what?" Henry said. "If it's meant to be, it's meant to be."

"I told you Henry would be on my side!" Delmar said. He held his hand out for a high five. Henry slapped it enthusiastically.

"Henry's a three-time loser," Oscar reminded him.

"Hey!" Henry replied, feigning hurt. "This third one hasn't failed yet. Let's be fair now."

"I was thinking of researching today's music a little before I asked her out," Delmar said. "What if she likes rap or something?"

"So what?" Henry said.

"I'm already a little too old for her," Delmar said. "I don't want it to be *that* obvious."

"Tell her you love the disco they play here at the bowling alley," Henry replied.

"Do you want this man to ever get laid again?" Oscar asked. He was holding his ball in his hand. "I think researching isn't a bad plan. Why don't you call my ten year old grandson? He could probably get you up to speed on rap. I won't let him play it in the house, but he's got a ton of it on his iPod. I always say to him, 'Hey Tommy, do you know how to spell rap? It's spelled C-R-A-P. The 'C' is just silent."

Delmar smiled. Oscar was a very wise man.

"Pick up your damn spare," Ramon urged him. It was like these guys didn't know they were bowling.

"Right," Oscar said. He lined up his mark.

"Look, you can do that if you want," Henry said, "But if you ask me, I think you should just ask her out. What's the worst that can happen? So she says no. You'll be in the same boat you're in now."

"But I don't want her to say no," Delmar said. "That's why I need a plan."

Oscar picked up the spare.

"Nice ball, Oscar," Ramon said. High fives all around as he returned to his seat. "Delmar, you're up."

Yes he was. The question was, was he ready to take his shot?

13

PURPLE HAZE

Peter was a little nervous about having Sunday brunch in Wilmette. He had met Kelly's parents a few times, and they seemed like very nice people, but they were from a totally different world. They were from the ritzy North Shore. He was from blue-collar Jefferson Park. It didn't matter that it was only 11.13 miles away. It might as well have been a different planet.

Peter had a slight pang of guilt that he hadn't driven out there early with Kelly, but he hadn't *technically* lied when he said he had work to do at the office this morning. He always had work to do at the office. He just didn't actually do it. Instead, he waited at home until the last possible moment, and then hopped in the car to arrive precisely when the brunch was scheduled to begin. The later he arrived, Peter figured, the less time he had to choose the wrong fork, or misidentify a smoked fish.

Wouldn't you know it? He arrived in Wilmette early anyway, because there was absolutely no traffic on Sunday. Now Peter had time to kill, so he was just driving around. He was hoping that nobody would call the cops on the guy in the Honda Accord driving five miles an hour, oohing and aahing over the gorgeous Tudors and Colonials.

He had driven around the neighborhood a few times already and each time he did, one of the nearby streets, Greenbriar Lane, rang a bell in his head. He tried to visually recall his company Christmas card list, thinking it must have been one of the partners from his firm that lived on this street, but then it hit him.

He reached into his glove compartment and looked for the card his mother had given him. Sure enough. His father's Vietnam buddy Hendrix lived on Greenbriar Lane in Wilmette. Should he do it now? His mom had already called him a few times to remind him, and he had just been putting it off.

Maybe this is a sign.

When he pulled up in front of the house on Greenbriar, Peter was impressed. This was easily a multi-million dollar Tudor. It was only a two-story home on a quarter acre lot, but it was large and solid and classy. The big beautiful bay windows probably cost more than Peter's dinky River North condo. Apparently not all of Henry's Vietnam buddies followed in Henry's ne'er-do-well footsteps.

When Peter walked up the driveway, he started getting a queasy feeling about this task. How in the world was he even going to bring this up? "Hello, we've never met, my father is dying." He went through a half dozen possible opening lines in his head before he arrived at the front door. He still hadn't decided on one, but there was no turning back now. He raised his hand to knock, but then noticed the mailbox next to the door said "Bradley."

Wait a minute. Something wasn't right here. The card his mom had given him said "Hendrix." *What if Mom had an old address?* As he pondered his next move, the front door opened, scaring Peter out of his skin. It jolted him back to reality.

A lovely African-American woman wearing a casual floral dress was staring at him.

"Can I help you?" she asked.

"Yes," Peter said. "Listen, I hate to bug you, but do the Bradleys live in this house?"

"Yes," she said.

"That's weird," Peter said, looking back at the address on the card in his hand. "Oh well, never mind. I guess they moved. Never mind. Sorry to bother you."

Peter started walking back toward his car.

"Who are you looking for?" the woman asked.

Peter turned around, and continued walking backwards.

"I'm looking for a man named Hendrix," Peter said. "I guess he doesn't live here anymore."

"Wait," she said.

Peter stopped in his tracks. The woman smiled.

"That's my husband," she said. "But only his buddies from Vietnam call him that."

"Is Henry Stankiewicz one of them?" Peter asked.

She smiled again. "Do you know him?"

"I'm Peter Stankiewicz," he explained.

"Henry's son?"

Peter nodded.

"I'm Susan Bradley," she said. She motioned for Peter to come back. "Come on in. James is at the store, but he'll be so excited to meet you. He should be home any minute."

Peter followed her through the foyer and into the spotless living room.

"Have a seat," she said, pointing to the huge plush fawn couch. "Can I get you lemonade or something?"

"No thank you," Peter said. He took a seat, sinking a few inches into the soft fabric. *Wow, this couch is unbelievably comfortable.*

Susan took a seat in the wingback chair, just to the right of the round hardwood timber coffee table.

"This table is beautiful," Peter said. "Is it an antique?"

"No," Susan said. "Konteaki Furniture Store."

Peter nodded as if he knew what she meant. This was more evidence that he made the right call by not showing up early for brunch. He could small talk, but not with rich people.

"So you're the famous Stankiewicz boy," she said.

Peter didn't know how to respond. "I suppose that's me."

Susan looked Peter in the eyes. "You know, you really don't look much like your father, but I still should have recognized you. You haven't changed much."

"Did we already meet?" Peter asked.

"No, but I've seen the home movie. Your dad brought it over and we watched it together. It was a long time ago, though. I don't think he had even moved back to Chicago yet."

"Home movie?"

"Yes," she said. "You know the one I mean."

Peter was confused.

"The one that the guys always joke about."

Peter shook his head.

"Oh c'mon," Susan said. "The one he showed to everyone. The Christmas video. James said that Henry made them watch it at all the reunions. You and your sister, and..."

"I've never seen it," Peter interrupted as politely as he could muster. "I haven't seen too much of Henry over the past 15 years or so."

"Of course," Susan said. She suddenly looked a little uncomfortable. "So what brings you out to our neck of the woods?" she asked.

It was the moment of truth, and none of his semi-rehearsed lines seemed appropriate. Peter just decided to wing it.

"Actually, I've got a brunch date not too far from here. I just recognized your street address as I was driving by. I need to talk to your husband about something, and I've been putting it off for awhile. When I saw your street, I figured it was a sign that maybe I shouldn't put it off any longer."

"That doesn't sound good," she said.

"I'm afraid it's not."

Now it was Peter's turn to feel uncomfortable. He fidgeted with his hands, not really sure how to continue.

"Is Henry OK?" she asked.

Peter shook his head. "No, Henry has cancer."

"Oh no."

"The doctors told him it was terminal."

"Damn," Susan said. "Is he in the hospital?"

"Not yet, but it's just a matter of time."

"How is he handling this?" Susan asked. "After all he's been through..."

"You know how he is—he doesn't want anyone fussing over him. He doesn't even know I'm here. My mom is the one who asked me to tell his army buddies. I hope I'm doing the right thing."

Susan came over to the couch, sat next to Peter, and put her hand on his.

"You're doing the right thing," she said, comforting him. "All of these guys are as stubborn as Henry, including my James. They suffer in silence. Henry may say he doesn't want anyone to know—and he probably thinks he means it too—but he would be hurt if James or Sonny or Hick didn't tell him if they were in the same boat. You're doing the right thing."

She patted his hand again.

The front door opened, and in walked a 60-something year old man carrying a bag of fertilizer. He held it up in the air toward Susan.

"Honey? Is this the kind you needed?"

"Yes," Susan said. "But put it around the back by the garden."

"Can do," James said. He was looking at Peter as he said it.

"James," Susan said. "We've got company. This is Peter Stankiewicz. Henry's boy."

James didn't smile. He simply put the bag down, and came over to shake Peter's hand.

"James Bradley," he said.

"He was looking for a man named Hendrix," Susan said, laughing at the suggestion. That finally brought a smile to James' face.

"Your dad's the one that gave me that nickname," he explained.

"Where did it come from?" Peter asked.

"My first name is James—so he started calling me Jimi. And he said I looked like Jimi Hendrix, so that's what everyone started calling me."

Peter looked at the freckled heavy-set balding 60-something black man standing in front of him and tried to picture him with long sideburns, a wild afro, and psychedelic clothes. Nope, that vision just wasn't coming to him.

"Did you ever look like Jimi Hendrix?" Peter asked.

"No, but your dad said we all look alike."

Peter cringed.

"That was just Henry being Henry," James said, waving it off. "So you're little Stankiewicz, huh?"

Peter nodded.

"My son, the hot shot lawyer," James said, channeling Henry.

Peter recognized the impersonation, and managed a polite grin.

"Well it's great to finally meet you," James said. "You want a beer or something? It's gotta be happy hour somewhere in the world right now."

"I can't stay," Peter said. "I have to be at a brunch in a little while and it's not far from here. There's just something I need to talk to you about if you've got a second."

James stared at his houseguest for a moment, and then looked over at his wife. She couldn't hide her concern.

"OK, come back to the garden with me," James said. "We can talk back there. You mind helping me carry some of these bags?"

"Sure, no problem."

"James!" Susan said. "He's all dressed up for brunch."

"Oh, right, sorry," James said.

"It's OK," Peter said.

"It absolutely is *not* OK," Susan scolded.

Peter and James exchanged smiles, and he motioned with his head for Peter to follow. James picked up the bag on the way out.

"Don't you dare let him carry one of those bags," she called after them on the walkway out to the car.

"Yes, dear," James replied. He turned to Peter. "I probably say those two words more than any other words in the English language."

James grabbed another big bag out of the back of his Chevy Blazer, added it to the other, and motioned with his head for Peter to shut the trunk and follow.

"I figured everyone in this neighborhood had a lawn service," Peter said.

"Nah," James replied. "I sit in the office all day. I need a little outdoor work to keep me sane."

He led Peter around the side of the house to a private backyard garden, complete with a waterfall and a pond. He threw the bags of fertilizer in a pile near the rosebushes, and James motioned for Peter to take a seat in one of the cushioned chairs overlooking the pond. Peter could see orange and white fish swimming beneath the surface as he took a seat.

"Are those Koi?"

"Yeah," James replied. "Susan gives me a hard time because I spend way too much money on those things. I don't know what it is about them. They relax me."

"Do you have a stressful job?" Peter asked.

"I own Bradley Carpet," he said.

"I've seen the commercials," Peter said.

"Promise me you won't sing the jingle," James replied with a smile. "I hear it about fifty times a day."

James reached into a bag of fish food laying at the edge of the pond, grabbed a handful and tossed it in. As the waterfall gurgled and splashed, and the breeze blew through the trees in the garden, James adjusted one of the beautiful stones surrounding the pond. When he completed his tidying, he looked at his guest.

"Well little Stankiewicz," he began, "I have a funny idea you aren't here to tell me good news. Am I right?"

Peter couldn't look James in the eye. "No, I'm afraid not. Henry is pretty sick."

"What's he got?"

"Inoperable cancer. Although you'd never know it if you saw him," Peter said. He forced himself to smile. "He still looks and acts exactly the same."

That made James smile. "Same son of a bitch, huh?"

"Yup," Peter said. "Listen, I hope I'm not out of line for just showing up like this."

"No, of course not."

The two men stared at the Koi pond. Peter felt uncomfortable in the silence, but he didn't want to interrupt the train of thought going on inside James's head.

"I should call him," James finally said.

"If you do, don't mention I talked to you," Peter pleaded. "You know how Henry is. He would probably be mad at me for telling you."

James nodded.

"Do you have the numbers for some of the other guys?" Peter asked. "I promised my mom I'd let them all know."

"Yeah, sure. Come on in."

James motioned with his hand for Peter to follow, and kept talking as they walked across the stone patio toward the sliding glass doors.

"You know, I've asked that bastard to come up here and have dinner with Susan and me a thousand times since he came back to Chicago, but I don't think he's been over to the house more than a couple of times."

The glass doors opened to a luxurious rec-room.

"Wow," Peter said, admiring the décor. "I bet he liked this room."

"Yeah," James laughed. "This is my room. The rest of the house is Susan's."

A billiards table, with a maple core and topped with beautiful green felt, took center stage in the middle of the room. One corner of the room had a stunning oak bar with three bar stools. The other corner of the room was set up as a home theatre with luxurious black leather chairs and one of the largest widescreen televisions Peter had ever seen. It must have been a 64 incher.

"Have a seat," James said. "Let me see what phone numbers I have in my Rolodex upstairs."

When his host departed, Peter wandered. This room was every man's dream, and one of Henry's buddies was living it. Peter took a seat at one of the barstools and spun around a few times. When the chair came to a rest, he noticed the large framed photo hanging on the wall behind the bar; twelve military men posing with their rifles. Peter hopped out of the barstool to investigate.

He definitely recognized that face in the middle of the top row. Henry looked so young and strong in the picture. All of them did. There was James in the bottom row, kneeling with his rifle. He bore no resemblance to Jimi Hendrix at all. Although, the guy kneeling beside him sort of did.

"That's our squad," James said, jarring Peter, who hadn't heard him approaching.

Peter pointed to the picture. "This guy next to you actually looks a little like Jimi Hendrix."

"Yeah, I guess so," James said, chuckling. "That's Hot Rod. He did have a little Jimi Hendrix in him, now that you mention it."

"Does he still look like that?" Peter asked.

"We lost Hot Rod years ago."

"I'm sorry," Peter said.

Hendrix started identifying the other guys in the picture. "This young guy here is Lieutenant Medina — he was the leader of our entire platoon. Didn't really get to know him that well. He died about six weeks after this picture was taken." He pointed to the slightly older man in the bottom row next. "This here's Sergeant Retter."

Peter couldn't put his finger on exactly why Sgt. Retter looked like the most stereotypically military of this motley bunch. It might have been his firm upright posture, or his very short hair, or it might have just been that he was the only grown up in the picture.

"He was the leader of our squad," James explained. "We lost him too. The rest of us made it back though. We still get together for a reunion every other year or so."

"So these are the guys I should contact?" Peter asked.

"This is the guy right here," Hendrix said, pointing to the baby-faced guy at the end of the bottom row. "That's Sonny. He's the guy that puts the reunions together. He would definitely be able to help you get in touch with the other guys." He handed Peter the Rolodex card with Sonny's name and phone number. "You can keep it. I've got it in the computer too."

"Thanks."

Peter didn't know what else to say. "Look, I'm really sorry."

James put his hand on Peter's shoulder. It looked like he wanted to say something in response, but the words never came.

14

ANOTHER CUP O' JOE, LITTLE JOE?

Delmar sat in the parking lot of the strip mall off of Addison. He had watched her open the shop at 5:30am. Now it was 6:15 and he was still trying to figure out what he was going to say.

He needed a cup of coffee badly. Her coffee.

The days away hadn't dimmed his desire. Every time he'd closed his eyes last night he'd seen that raven hair. At first he'd thought it was just the blackout he experienced when the blood rushed to his head. He had read somewhere that blood flow to the head reversed male pattern baldness, so he'd once stood on his head every night for a month. No new hair, just black spots in his eyes when he stood up. Delmar wondered if he might have even accelerated the baldness by spending all that time upside down, rubbing his barren pate into the shag carpet.

Last night it was a different vision. He hadn't seen spots. He'd seen a silky ebony mane. The dizziness had been about the same.

Why was this so difficult? Delmar considered himself a smooth talker, a salesman who could handle the toughest customer. And now one beautiful barista was turning him into a blithering bowl of Jell-O. What was happening? He'd thought the whole thing absolutely to death. She was young enough to be his, well, much younger sister. And here he was watching her from his car. *Am I a stalker? Is this how it starts? 'I didn't mean to frighten her, officer, but I just had to be near her.'*

Delmar looked up again. Two men wearing orange overalls and huge tool belts left the store with giant lattes. Now there were no customers in the shop. A break for Delmar. He took a deep breath, grabbed the folder he'd brought along, climbed out of the car, shook off the cobwebs and entered the store.

"Good morning, Gina."

"Well, good morning. Will you be having the usual?"

Wow. The usual. She'd only served him once before and she remembered his order. Did she do this for everyone or had he been on her mind too? Delmar laughed at the ridiculousness of the notion. "Yes, Gina. The usual."

Gina poured a large, black coffee. "Black, like your heart, right?"

Delmar was speechless. The dizziness was beginning to return. But it was Delmar's move now. He paid for the coffee and took a big swig. Gina stood quietly at the register. Delmar watched her long, strong fingers as she rang up the sale and handed Delmar his change. Their hands touched briefly. With his eyes locked on hers, and his brain disengaged, he casually dropped the handful of money into the tip cup, meaning he'd just paid ten bucks for a two dollar cup of coffee.

"Thanks very much," said Gina.

Delmar's brain snapped back to reality and raced through all the sales tricks in his bag. *This is it. I have the customer's attention. The customer's body language is positive. She's left me an opening, and there is no one else in the shop. What am I waiting for?* There was an awkward silence while the energy in the room faded.

Delmar finally mumbled, "1985," and shifted his feet, looking at the ground.

"Excuse me?" said Gina.

"I, uh, 1985," muttered Delmar, clearing his throat.

Gina's dark brown eyes scrunched for a moment. "I don't understand."

"Lorne Greene. He died in 1985."

Gina waited in silence. Delmar's heart was pounding. He knew now that this was a stupid tactic. He hadn't thought it through. *The customer is always right, and now I'm challenging her. Just walk away now.* But he couldn't walk away now. What would that say?

"You see, I Googled Lorne Greene the other night," Delmar added quietly, occasionally daring to make eye contact, "and every reference indicated that he died in 1985 at age 72 and he's buried in his native Canada." Delmar held up the folder without opening it. "So, you see, that would mean that he couldn't have been in here anytime in the past six months for coffee."

"I see," said Gina. And she could barely contain herself any longer and a smile started to crack along the edges of her mouth and she turned away from Delmar, pretending to clean a coffee cup in the sink, before he could see her entire, huge grin. She collected herself and forced a stern look onto her face, looked Delmar straight in his puppy dog eyes and said, "So you're calling me a liar."

Oh, crap, what was Delmar getting himself into? He had to think fast.

"No, no, no. Of course not. I'm not saying you're a liar. I'm, well, I'm just saying, you see, well, that you were mistaken. I'm saying that the man probably said he was Lorne Greene, but he was actually a Lorne Greene look alike, maybe a Lorne Greene impersonator."

"Are there a lot of those?"

"I imagine if you looked and sounded enough like Lorne Greene, you might be able to make a buck or two."

"Is that why you came in here today?" she asked, looking Delmar straight in the eye, "To tell me that Lorne Greene was dead?"

"No. I just wanted a cup of coffee, so I thought I'd make some conversation. I don't know what I was thinking. I didn't mean to argue with you. Really. I just, I don't know, I just, well, I'm usually much better at this. I'm in portable toilets. I mean I'm in the portable toilet business. I'm an account executive, a salesman, and I talk to people all day and I usually have a real gift of gab, and you, you just, I mean the other day, when I was in here, and…"

Delmar was flailing now.

"I better just go. Thanks for the coffee. Sorry about the whole Lorne Greene thing."

Delmar turned and headed for the door. What an idiot he'd been. Glancing outside, he saw a young couple getting out of their car and heading for the coffee shop. He had one last moment before he and Gina would be interrupted. Delmar turned around and walked quickly back to the counter. Gina was still standing there, arms crossed, watching his every move.

Delmar looked deep into Gina's brown eyes.

"I find you intriguing," he said.

And he started back for the door. And he kept walking, his head swimming. *Did I just say what I think I just said? Can I take it back? No. I don't want to take it back.* Delmar reached the door. Gina hadn't said anything in response, but Delmar could feel her eyes staring into the back of his bald, now sweaty head. He held the door open for the incoming customers, and walked to his car without turning around.

"Now what?" he muttered, closing the car door behind him. His heart was racing. He started the engine and headed to his first appointment of the day. He would go over those words a hundred times today. "I find you intriguing." God, had it sounded as hokey then as it did now, on continuous replay in his brain? Why didn't he look back and catch her reaction? Was she smiling, laughing, rolling her eyes? *Oh, God. What now?*

15

HOME SWEET HENRY

Peter and Kelly pulled up slowly to the unassuming home in Roscoe Village, a neighborhood of single family homes and two-flats, on tree lined streets on the north side of the city. The area had seen its share of gentrification in recent years, with developers eagerly buying up the most dilapidated homes, tearing them down and replacing them with sleek, red brick monstrosities, the urban versions of McMansions. But Henry's beautiful, old home appeared to remain preserved happily in the 1920s, a charming, brown brick wonder of residential architecture called the bungalow.

Of course, it wasn't really Henry's. It had come along with wife number three.

Peter took a deep breath and stared at the house.

"Shall we get out of the car this time?" asked Kelly. "Or do you want to take another tour of the area?"

This was actually their third time pulling up to the front of the house. Peter had also cruised through the alley behind the house once.

"Someone's gonna think we're casing the joint."

"We are," said Peter. "I really can't believe my father has a home with a yard and a garage and a wife and a front porch. I've always pictured him as a vagabond, suitcase in hand, wandering and unsettled. It's a lot to grasp."

"I can't say that I know how you feel. But are you sure there's not more to it? I've never seen you like this."

"The man is dying. And I barely know the guy. He's acting like everything is fine. I don't even know how to have a conversation with Henry. We've never talked about anything. How do sons and fathers talk?"

Peter looked toward the house to see if anyone was watching them from inside.

"Henry was MIA for over a decade," Peter continued. "Since he's come back, he pops in every few months. Usually we talk like strangers, distant and vaguely polite. Then the very first 'real' conversation I have with him, I'm twenty-eight years old. I'm finally about to tell him what an asshole he's been. And he blurts out that he's dying."

Kelly knew better than to interrupt Peter now.

"I missed out on the 'birds and the bees' talk, and the 'today you're a man' talk and the 'son, have I told you I'm proud of you' talk, and we jumped right to the 'son, I'm dying' talk. Bam. How am I supposed to respond? You know, we sat at lunch the other day after he dropped the bombshell and he just had a great time, eating every scrap of his meal, finishing his beer with a look of satisfaction, and then right back to work. I was a wreck. He was unfazed. I don't get it."

"It's a nice house. Should we check out the inside?" Kelly smiled.

"You're probably right," Peter sighed. "It's his life. If he doesn't want to be miserable, then screw it. Why should I take on the burden? To hell with him."

"That's the spirit. Now let's go enjoy ourselves. I'd like to meet your father."

They climbed out of Peter's car. Kelly carried the bottle of mid-priced Merlot and Peter handled the six-pack of Guinness bottles. They walked along the sidewalk, up the old concrete steps, and rang the bell.

The heavy wooden door opened and an angelic looking woman in her late 50s greeted them, an apron over her dress, and a spatula in her hand.

"Hello. Please come in. I'm Katherine. I'm just finishing up in the kitchen. Welcome, welcome. It's so nice to meet you."

Something smelled great, wafting from the oven.

"You must be Peter of course. You have your father's eyes. And you're Kelly. Please come in. You can just hang your coats on the hooks behind you. Oh, and you brought wine. Thank you. And beer. If you could just bring it into the kitchen. Your father ran out..." A twitch went through Peter's mind. Of course, he ran out. "...for some ice cream, for dessert. He should be back in a moment."

Wow. Henry had landed right in it. Peter looked around. Norman Rockwell must have had this house in mind. The floors were a beautiful, dark oak matching the woodwork. The dining room table was set with a fine linen tablecloth, and had a vintage chandelier hanging above it. There were fresh flowers neatly arranged in vases throughout the rooms, and even a rocking chair in the living room, where someone (surely not Henry) had left a half-finished sweater and needles hanging out of a basket.

Peter felt like he was in the twilight zone. Had they walked into the wrong house? He'd been expecting Katherine to be a tough old broad with a rasp in her nicotine-stained voice, a beer-buzzed, world weary bag of bones living in a cluttered, whiskey-blotched mess. But instead he got some weird amalgam of Aunt Bee and June Cleaver. How did Henry end up with such a proper, sweet woman?

"Why don't the two of you make yourselves at home? The glasses are in the china cabinet, in the dining room. You can put the beer in the refrigerator, and please open the wine if you don't mind. I just have to tend to a few loose ends here. And please relax in the living room."

How could anyone NOT feel at home here? Peter and Kelly happily did as they were told, adjourning to the overstuffed paisley sofa in the living room, placing their wine glasses on coasters on the well-polished oak coffee table. They admired the framed photos on the walls. Katherine was obviously a widow, the mother of two boys and a girl, and a grandmother of at least four or five. Lucky kids. Peter wondered what they thought of Henry.

A door opened somewhere at the back of the house and whooshed shut. Heavy steps up a few stairs to the kitchen, a few muttered pleasantries, and then he burst into the living room.

"Well, you made it," Henry bellowed. Peter stood up. Henry considered hugging Peter and settled for shaking Peter's outstretched hand. "Great to see you."

"Henry," said Peter as his father released his grip. "Henry, this is Kelly."

Henry pushed his son aside like a child who was just shown a shiny, new bicycle, and doesn't need his old toy anymore.

"Kelly." Henry stepped toward the girl and there was nothing else in his world. "Has anyone ever told you that you look like Grace Kelly? It's a remarkable likeness really."

Kelly blushed.

"Henry, you're embarrassing her."

Henry looked at his son. "Who are you again?"

"Henry, really. You're making Kelly uncomfortable."

"OK, OK." Henry stepped back. "Peter was right. You're definitely a girl."

Kelly gave a puzzled look to Peter.

"Henry thought you might be a man. He was apparently concerned that not having a male role model as a boy might have led me to homosexuality. Right, Henry?"

"Something like that." Henry was still focused on Kelly. "But this is definitely a girl. I can spot them. In fact I'd like to think of myself as a bit of an expert on the subject, and this is a fine example of the female of the species. No question. Well, who needs a drink?"

The wine glasses on the coffee table were still full.

"OK, I guess I do. Excuse me." Henry left them alone for a moment.

"He's charming."

"What?!! Why is it charming when an old man acts like that, and it would be disgusting if I said that stuff?""

"Because he's harmless. Because he's an older man." Kelly paused and looked Peter in the eye. "Because he's dying."

"I'm beginning to wonder. He sure doesn't act like he's dying. I don't know him well, but he seems in fine spirits," said Peter. "I haven't heard him cough or wheeze or anything."

"Well, Dr. Stankiewicz, remind me to get a second opinion if I ever get sick."

Katherine's lilting voice called from the dining room.

"Dinner is served."

"I'll go see if Katherine needs help in the kitchen," said Kelly. Peter sought out Henry into the dining room.

"I almost forgot," said Peter to Henry, pulling a thick envelope from the inside pocket of his sport coat, "Here's the document you needed." Peter handed the packet to Henry.

"Thanks," Henry whispered, and he quickly put the envelope into a drawer in the buffet without looking at it. It was clear he didn't want Katherine to see it.

Peter was puzzled. "Doesn't she know?"

"She knows," said Henry, "She's known right from the start that I was damaged goods. But I'm trying to take care of this myself."

The women entered with a plate of carved flank steak, and a bowl of garlic mashed potatoes. Salad and bread and steamed asparagus were already on the table. This was to be a feast. Peter noticed that Henry hadn't taken a Guinness and instead was drinking a much, much paler ale from a pint glass. No telling what brand. Peter had figured Henry for a man who enjoyed a heartier brew.

Henry raised his glass as the women sat down. "A toast. To families. New ones and old ones." Peter hesitantly raised his glass. Kelly looked at him from across the table as if to say that now was not the time to make a scene. Let it pass.

* * *

Peter helped Katherine clear the table while Henry invited Kelly to the living room where coffee would be served.

"That was a magnificent meal," said Peter, carrying a stack of dinner plates and following Katherine into the kitchen.

"You know your father is very proud of you," Katherine smiled, certain they were alone. "You should have seen him when you agreed to come to dinner. He was like a school boy making sure that everything would be just so. He ran out just before you got here and bought seven different pints of ice cream because he didn't know what you liked."

Distant laughter echoed from the living room.

"I don't like ice cream," Peter smiled. "But it was a nice try."

Katherine began to rinse the dishes before placing them in the dishwasher.

"You have a very nice home. It's very, uh, homey."

"Thank you, Peter. Frank and I bought this place about 30 years ago, when the kids were still small. We got a lot of use out of it."

"I saw the pictures in the living room."

"Yes, we were blessed with three healthy, happy children. Michael is an architect, he lives in Phoenix. Amy is a teacher right here in Chicago. And Kevin is an electrical contractor in the south suburbs. They're all doing very well. They're good kids."

Peter grabbed a dishtowel off of the counter and began drying the large pots that Katherine had washed in the sink.

They worked in silence for a while.

"So," ventured Peter awkwardly, "How did you and Henry, I mean, you know. I mean I know it's none of my business, but…"

"I think I understand," smiled Katherine. "Let me try to explain. Frank passed away about six years ago. He was always very healthy and then one morning he just didn't wake up. He died in his sleep. It was pretty lonely around here until your father showed up."

"How did that happen?"

"Well, Frank had always been handy, he could fix anything. But now he was gone, and little things continued to need repair. It's an old house," said Katherine. "The backyard fence needed fixing. My neighbor knew Henry from the bowling alley. He knew that Henry was handy. Henry fixed the fence, and we got to know each other."

"It's just that, well, don't take this the wrong way but..."

"I don't seem like Henry's type?" offered Katherine.

"Well, I mean it's that he's so rough around the edges and you're so..."

Katherine smiled. "Maybe it's true that opposites do attract."

"Yeah, but this is like *Beauty and the Beast*."

"I'll take that as a compliment. But people in their 50's and 60's get together for different reasons than people in their 20's and 30's. It's about being comfortable with someone, being a companion. And Henry and I are very comfortable together."

"Of course," said Peter, ashamed that he'd pried.

"Please don't be shy," said Katherine. "I enjoy your questions. No need hiding anything. What's the point? Right?"

"Right," said Peter, feeling more at ease, "Well, how do your kids feel about Henry?"

"It was very hard at first, especially seeing him living here, where they all grew up. We got married mainly for their sake I think. And Henry insisted on a prenuptial agreement."

"Uh oh." Peter now had an idea of Henry's game. "What's in the agreement? I'm an attorney, you know."

"So I've been told," winked Katherine. "The agreement states that Henry has no claim on this house or anything I own, including life insurance or anything else. I thought he was being a bit extreme, but he wouldn't marry me without it. He wanted my children to know that he had no desire to replace their father and that his intentions were honorable."

"How's that working out?"

"It's been good. I think they appreciate the fact that I'm not alone. Henry and the kids get along well, but then your father is a charmer. The grandkids call him Pappy Henry. It's different than grandpa, which didn't feel right."

Peter felt something new. A tinge of jealousy.

"Well, I'm glad it seems to be working out."

"Yes. Of course none of us planned for this cancer," said Katherine.

"Do your children know?"

"No. Henry insisted. He said it's not their problem. And what could they do?" Then her voice cracked and the veneer lifted. "What can any of us do?" she cried softly.

"I'm sorry," said Peter, not knowing what to do or say.

"He's such a good man," said Katherine, wiping her tears with a dish cloth. "He's still so young. And then the cancer started eating away at him. He's in such pain but he won't let anyone see it. He doesn't want any pity. I feel so helpless."

"I'm afraid I'm not very good at this," said Peter, not sure where to look and then finding Katherine's eyes. "Is there anything I can do for you?"

"For me, you've done enough already. It's good to talk to someone. I appreciate that you let me talk." Katherine took a deep breath and composed herself. "And for your father, nothing could be better medicine than you being here. I can tell a difference even tonight, when you're around."

Peter had dried all of the pots and put them on the counter. He looked around the kitchen to see if there was anything left to wash or dry.

"Your father talks about you a lot, about you and your sister," said Katherine. "My children are about the same age as you. We compare notes. We talk about when you were small. It usually leads to a tear in Henry's eye. He's really an old softie."

"That reminds me," said Peter. "I do have one more question. Has Henry ever shown you any pictures or anything from when my sister and I were kids?"

"No, although he has mentioned an old film or something that he used to have. I guess it's gone now. We were watching some old home videos at my son's house one night and Henry told me."

"Does he have any idea where that old tape might be?"

"If he does, he didn't tell me. And I didn't want to push the subject."

Katherine closed the dishwasher door and turned it on.

"Now if you'll take in the coffee tray, it's a bit heavy for me. I'll follow with the pie."

Peter turned to Katherine before they left the kitchen. "Katherine, can you do me a favor? Don't mention to Henry that I was asking about the tape."

"Your secret's safe with me," said Katherine.

16

GIRL POWER

Gina and Emily ate breakfast and dinner together in their dining room whenever they could, although calling it a dining room was a bit of a stretch. It was really just a semi-partitioned section of a rather inadequate living room.

Gina had done her best to make this apartment a home. She was thankful that Libby had given her an insane break on the rent to get tenants she trusted, and the location was really fantastic, but the physical space was a little cramped. The entire apartment was less than 700 square feet. Gina knew that one day this place wouldn't be big enough for both of them, but for now they were making do, doing their best to concentrate on the positive by covering up the negative.

The cracks in the plaster walls were everywhere, but the worst of it was disguised nicely by the framed Paris Match poster she bought for $8. The fake fireplace built into the wall may have had a chipped stone mantle, but no one could see it beneath the cloth runner that covered it. On top of this she placed a handful of framed photographs of mother and daughter, giving the living room a homey feel. And though the hardwood floors were a little scuffed—a throw rug here, and a little nightstand there, and voila! It was almost passable.

And recently, thanks to two months' worth of tips, they now had a very comfortable maroon couch that would probably have to be replaced by a sleeper-bed someday, and a gently used, but fairly sturdy dining room table Gina bought off the lady down the street. It might not reside in a real dining room, but it was definitely a real dining table.

Emily picked at the ham steak and black beans on her plate with her fork. Across the table her mother did the same.

"Mom?"

"Yeah," Gina said, without looking up.

"This dinner isn't very good," Emily said.

"I know."

"The ham is a little chewy."

"Just eat it."

Emily picked at it some more. She plunged the fork into a small square piece of ham, and gingerly placed it into her mouth. She chewed and chewed and chewed. After ten more seconds of chewing, Gina looked up at her daughter. When they met eyes, Emily smiled, cheeks still full of incredibly well-chewed ham steak.

"It's good exercise for my mouth," she garbled.

Gina smiled back. "You can take your plate to the kitchen, but no snacks later tonight if you get hungry."

"Thanks, Mom. Do you want the rest of my ham?"

"Ugh," Gina said. "Just throw it out."

Emily went into the little galley kitchen, opened the cabinet door under the sink and tossed the ham into the garbage can. She rinsed off her plate, and put it into the left sink basin, before returning to the dining room table. Her mom was still picking at the same chewy ham and mushy black beans. Emily noticed that she hadn't actually eaten any of it. She stood right next to her mother.

"Everything OK, Mom?"

"Yeah, just great," Gina said.

"Did you have a bad day at work?"

"No, it was fine."

Emily gave her mother a hug from the side, before climbing into her lap and giving her a proper one. Gina pushed the wretched dinner toward the middle of the table so that Emily wouldn't get mushy black bean stains on the back of her shirt.

"Can I ask you a question?" Emily asked.

"Sure."

"Why are boys so stupid?"

Gina laughed out loud. "Honey, I'm afraid no one is smart enough to answer that question. Why?"

"Remember David?"

"Your 4-square pal?"

"Yes."

"Is he stupid now?" Gina asked.

"Yes."

"What did he do?"

"He won't talk to me anymore."

"Why not?" Gina asked.

"I was on a swing last week and he asked if I wanted a push," Emily explained, "and then Billy and Stu saw him and screamed 'David loves Emily!' and did these kissy-faces."

Gina tried to keep a serious look on her face. "And now he won't talk to you, huh?"

"Yeah."

"You want to know what I think?"

Emily nodded vigorously.

"I think Billy and Stu were right," her mother said. She tapped Emily on the nose. Emily furrowed her brow, totally lost. "That's why he isn't talking to you," Gina continued, "because now he thinks that you know, so now it's too embarrassing to talk to you."

"That doesn't make any sense," Emily said.

"Sometimes boys just don't know how to show girls that they like them."

Gina got up from her chair, lifting Emily as she did. She placed Emily on the ground next to her. She gave her a kiss on the cheek.

"C'mon, help me clean up the kitchen."

The mother-daughter clean up crew brought everything into the kitchen; the sticky brown pot of beans, Gina's plate and silverware, and her empty wine glass. Gina dumped the leftover beans into the garbage can beneath the sink while Emily washed off her mother's plate and silverware and placed them in the sink.

When all the dishes were in the left basin, Gina turned on the hot water, squeezing out a little liquid dish soap as the water filled the basin. Emily knew her role. She grabbed the dishtowel from the little hook on the door beneath the sink and held it her hands; ready for duty.

"Mom, do you really like 'Bonanza'?" Emily asked, as the soap bubbles started forming in the sink.

Gina looked at her little girl's facial expression. It was earnest. It was serious. It was honestly wondering about a 40-year-old television show... again.

"Not really," Gina said, bracing herself. "Why do you ask?"

"I found that folder in the bedroom," Emily said. "It has all sorts of information about Lorne Greene. Was Ben your favorite?"

Her mother suppressed a chuckle. "An eight year old in the 21st century shouldn't know this much about 'Bonanza'. Remind me to talk to Libby about that."

"She doesn't have cable, Mom," Emily protested.

"Neither do we," Gina reminded her.

Some of the beans were stubbornly refusing to leave the side of the pot, and Gina scrubbed at them. Emily was waiting patiently, dish towel in hand.

"Did you see that Lorne Greene was in "Battlestar Galactica' too?" she said to her mother, over the sound of scrubbing. "I've heard David talk about that show."

"I think that's a different version of the show," Gina explained. She finished up the pot and handed it to Emily. "They remade it recently. Lorne Greene was in the original one thirty years ago."

"Which one is better?" Emily asked.

"I've never seen either one," Gina admitted.

Emily dried the pot, and then placed it into the bottom cabinet, inside of the frying pan. She had gotten pretty adept at rearranging the dishes. They only had four full-sized cabinets in the tiny kitchen, and one of them doubled as a pantry.

"So if you don't like 'Bonanza' or "Battlestar Galactica'," Emily asked as she waited for the next dish, "why do you have that folder?"

Gina smiled. "It's a long story, but a man at the coffee shop gave me that."

Emily's eyes lit up. "A man?"

Gina handed her daughter another clean dish, doing her best to downplay this development. "Yes, a man," she said. "But a really dorky, slightly older one. Although, there is something cute about him."

Emily was drying the dish, but she wasn't giving the job her usual amount of attention. "Is he going to be your boyfriend?" she asked.

"He hasn't asked me out," her mother said, "but I know he likes me."

"How do you know?" Emily asked. She wasn't tall enough to put the clean dishes into the cabinet above the sink, so she rested the dry dish gently in the right sink basin drainer for Gina to put away later. "Did he stop talking to you like David did to me?"

Gina raised her eyebrow conspiratorially. "He said 'I find you intriguing.'"

Emily let that sink in as she waited for the next drying job.

"What's he like?" she finally asked.

"He's a little odd," Gina admitted. "I don't know what it is about him. I was talking to Kathy about him at the shop and she thinks I'm crazy. He's too old, he's too smarmy, and he doesn't dress like he belongs in this decade, but I kind of like him. I don't think he'll ever ask me out though. He's like David. He doesn't know what to do."

"Does he know about me?" Emily asked.

"It hasn't come up," Gina said.

Emily grabbed her mother's wet arm. "Don't tell him, Mom," she said emphatically. "Remember what happened with Sean?"

Gina looked her daughter in the eyes. "How many times do I have to tell you? That wasn't your fault. He was a creep."

"But I heard him tell you that he couldn't deal with—"

"Like I said," Gina said. "Creep."

"But you liked him."

"But I *love* you."

Gina hugged Emily.

"I still think you shouldn't tell him," Emily said into her mother's hip, mid-hug. "You know how stupid boys can be."

17

The Parking Garage at Delphi

Reed sat on the cement landing near the garage exit and pulled a Marlboro from the pack.

"Good to see you, Reed. How are things up above?"

"Don't ask," mumbled Reed. "Life just got complicated."

Henry took up his regular spot on the opposite wall. "You mean it was simple up until now?"

Reed shook his head and smiled.

"How was the camping trip?" Henry's large feet dangled from his seat on the wall.

"Well, it didn't turn out to be much of a camping trip," continued Reed. "Maybe Noah would have enjoyed it. The rain was torrential. I almost needed an ark to save me and all the little woodland creatures from the flood. I ended up in a swanky hotel suite eating Swiss chocolate, ordering room service and watching Sports Center."

"Sounds awful," said Henry.

"I gotta tell you it was absolutely surreal. Out there in the middle of nowhere, in a driving rainstorm, soaked to the skin, my dreams of a quiet weekend communing with nature flushed down the creek, with ticks gnawing at my kneecaps, I show up at a hotel with no vacancies and I end up warm, dry, rested and pampered in a suite fit for a king."

"And how do you suppose that all happened?"

Reed stood and faced Henry. "I've been thinking a lot about that. It's gonna sound crazy but I can only think of one thing. The hotel desk clerk, this kid named Kenny, told the very obnoxious customer ahead of me that the hotel was completely occupied. The customer went nuts, said some nasty things and Kenny handled it very professionally. I stepped up to the desk next and expected to be told the same thing, no room at the inn. But I made a point of telling Kenny that I was impressed with how well he'd responded to the nasty customer. Instead of being sent back out into the storm, this clerk gives me the best suite in the house, for the price of a regular room."

"Yeah, well it's a shame you didn't get what you needed from the weekend."

"It wasn't bad," answered Reed. "It just wasn't what I was looking for."

"What were you looking for?" asked Henry.

"The answers, you know, to the big questions," said Reed nonchalantly. "Why are we here? What should I be doing with my life? Simple stuff like that."

Henry shook his head.

"Those are some pretty high expectations. To be fair, I never promised that you'd find all the answers by sitting in the woods for a night. I just said that you needed a vacation."

"Good point," mumbled Reed.

"I've told you before, my friend. Everything happens for a reason. Even the rain. Don't try to overthink it. Life isn't as random as it seems."

"Sounds simple."

"I try to keep things uncomplicated," said Henry.

Reed watched a homeless man pushing his shopping cart down the murky alley. For just a second, Reed actually envied the homeless man's freedom.

"So how's your son? Weren't you supposed to have dinner the other night?" asked Reed.

"It was great. He even brought along his girlfriend. It was very nice."

"Hang onto that, Henry," said Reed very seriously. "Don't let him slip away."

Reed pulled another cigarette from the pack, examining it before lighting it.

"Absolutely," said Henry solemnly. And then to change the subject, "So, anyway, when you first entered my office here you said something about 'life just got complicated'. What's that about?"

"As we speak there's a memo going around our offices. An announcement from management. They've chosen a replacement for Anderson."

"Is it Nicholson? Oh, man, I'm sorry. You know that I've parked that bastard's car every day for over seven years now without a single tip?"

"Not Nicholson," said Reed quietly, and he turned and looked directly at Henry.

"Holy crap," exclaimed Henry.

"Yes," muttered Reed. "You're looking at the new Anderson."

"Congratulations. You look thrilled."

"I almost turned it down, you know. I just don't have enough 'screw you' money in the bank to walk away. An accountant nearing 50 with one job on his resume isn't going to open many doors. So if I said 'no', I'd be engraving my tombstone. I'd be running in place, a gerbil on a wheel from here on out. Worst of all," Reed paused, "If I didn't take it, they'd give it to Nicholson."

"Yeah. Well, you got one thing wrong," said Henry. "You're not 'the new Anderson'."

Reed looked at Henry quizzically.

Henry shrugged his shoulders. "All I'm sayin' is you don't have to be the new Anderson. Play it your way."

"OK. How's that?"

"Listen. Anderson, if he'd been a smoker and come down here to light up, he would never have talked to me. I parked Anderson's car once in a while and it was like I was invisible. I know the type.

They got their name on the door, I got mine stitched on my shirt, so they're above me, they think I got nothing to offer, I just park cars. And Nicholson, don't even get me started. But you're not like that. You couldn't be. So you're not the new Anderson. Just treat everybody the way you treated that hotel clerk, with respect. Appreciate them for what they do, and tell them. Acknowledge it, celebrate it. You know, Reed, you're a good man, and you'll be a good leader. Go up there and tell those people that there's a new sheriff in town, and things can be different."

"I just don't think it's gonna be that easy, Henry."

"Look, I've been listening to your stories for years now. I've got a pretty good idea of how things were up there. This is your chance to change things for the better. Anderson enjoyed making people miserable. Life is short. Be happy, for cryin' out loud. And let the people around you be happy. What's the worst that could happen?"

Reed shook his head. "Now don't take this the wrong way, but why are you down here parking cars?"

"Everything happens for a reason," Henry winked. "Now I gotta get back to work. How about you?"

18

EYE OF THE TIGER

Delmar had planned it all out in his head. Today was the day to make a move. Thursday or Friday would be too presumptuous. It was too obviously "date-like." But Tuesday was perfect; non-threatening as can be. Nobody already has plans on a Tuesday night.

Delmar's plan was simple. Show up just when she gets off work. Make it all very casual as if this was just something off the top of his head, jokingly telling her where he was going for dinner, and asking her if she wanted to come along. If she said no, he could pretend it was a joke.

But if she said yes...

Well, it had sounded so good when he was out on his calls today. But now that he was sitting here in the parking lot, it suddenly seemed like a terrifying proposition.

Do it, Delmar. Eye of the tiger.

He took a deep breath, and opened his car door. By the time he was on the sidewalk outside the coffee shop, Gina's eyes met his through the pane glass window. He looked directly down to the ground, and opened the door. The bell rang as he entered. There were three people in line ahead of him.

Casual, Delmar, casual.

Gina was staring at him when he looked up, in the process of taking off her apron. He pretended like he was seeing her for the first time.

"Oh, hi," he said. "You're still here?"

"A little late for a cup of coffee, isn't it?" she asked.

That little comment completely threw Delmar off his game. *Dammit! Of course.* She had only seen him in the morning. He had never been here in the evening before. She was probably on to him. Knowing her wicked sense of humor she was about to bust his chops. The rejection was already creeping into his heart, and it paralyzed his ordinarily gifted tongue once again.

"Well, I..."

"Are you done working?" Gina asked.

"Uh huh."

"Good day in the toilet business?"

"I've done my duty," he answered. "That's D-U-T-Y." It was his standard witty retort to the question he got fifty times a day.

Gina betrayed herself with a smile.

"Is that a smile?" he asked.

She wiped it off her face. "I don't know what you're talking about."

They stood a few feet apart, looking at each other. Despite Delmar's well designed plan, he suddenly couldn't execute. He was blowing the sale. Time to punt, and return with a better plan another day.

"Listen, about what I said the other day..."

"Got any plans?" Gina asked.

"You mean right now?"

"Yeah."

"I... uh... well... no... no plans."

"Want to grab some dinner?" she asked. "My shift is over." She pointed to the selection of food in the tiny refrigerator section; a few boxed salads and $7 sandwiches, and this morning's leftover muffins, donuts, and scones. "I'm starving and *that* is not going to do it for me. There are a bunch of restaurants around here. We could grab a bite to eat if you're up for it."

When Delmar realized what was happening, his confidence returned. It was a rare day indeed when the sale came to him instead of the other way around, but he did have some experience with this. This was like the day he bumped into that guy from the 16-inch softball tournament out in Mt. Prospect the same day their Port-A-Potty company stiffed them. Could Delmar deliver twenty of the Gladder Bladder models by Sunday? You better believe it. Always say yes, and then figure out how to pull it off.

This was even better, because this time he already had a plan.

"Actually," Delmar said. "If you don't mind driving a few miles, I know a place that you would absolutely love. Did you drive to work?"

"I took the bus," Gina said.

"I'd be happy to give you a ride," Delmar replied.

"Sure, what the heck," Gina said. "I just need to call my girlfriend. She was going to meet me at the bus stop, and I don't want her to wait for me."

"Oh, sorry. I don't want to intrude on..."

"It's OK. Just give me a second."

Gina pulled out her cell phone and walked a few paces away from Delmar. Libby answered the phone on the second ring.

"Hello?"

"Libby?"

"Gina? Is something wrong?"

"Um, no, could I talk to Emily for a second?"

"Sure."

Delmar walked up to see if Gina was OK, just as Emily picked up the phone.

"Mom?"

"Hang on a second."

Gina put her hand over the phone, and talked to Delmar. "You can go out in the car if you want. I'll just be a second."

Delmar nodded and did as he was told. Gina didn't dare continue until Delmar was out of listening range. When he was gone, she resumed the conversation.

"If it's OK with you and Libby, I'm going to be late tonight, honey," she said.

"Why?"

"I'm going out to dinner with someone."

"DID HE ASK YOU OUT?" Emily shrieked.

Gina was happy she had shooed Delmar out of the shop. He would have definitely heard Emily's piercing voice.

"Actually, I asked *him* out," she said. "I don't think I've ever done that before."

"Way to go, Mom!"

"Are you sure it's OK?"

"Uh huh."

"Thanks honey," Gina said. "You can stay up until I get home." She knew Emily wouldn't be able to sleep until she heard all the details anyway.

"Libby doesn't have any plans for tonight, does she?"

"Are you kidding?" Emily said. "We've been playing canasta."

"Great," Gina said. "Can you put Libby back on?"

Delmar was watching Gina on the phone from outside the pane glass window and saw the giddiness in her eyes. And she was smiling. Smiling! Was it even remotely possible that *he* had something to do with that? It didn't seem likely.

Maybe her girlfriend is telling her a funny story. Yeah, that's probably it.

Gina shut the phone and came out to Delmar's car. She got in the passenger seat, and closed the door behind her.

"Everything OK?" Delmar asked.

"Yup," Gina replied. "I was just giving my girlfriend your license plate number and a general description of you and your car in case something happens to me."

Delmar stared at her face. She wasn't smiling... until she saw his worried expression. Then a flicker of a smile betrayed her again. That was a smile Delmar knew well. That was the mirror image of his patented "I'm just messin' with you" smile. He smiled back.

"Well, there's goes that plan," he said. "I even had a shovel in the trunk."

"Maybe next time," Gina said.

They drove in mostly silence, but arrived at their destination only a few minutes later. Gina laughed out loud when they pulled into the parking lot.

"Ponderosa Steakhouse!" she said. "I didn't even know these restaurants were still around."

"It's the last one in Chicago," Delmar said. "I checked their website."

Delmar put the car in park, and turned off the engine. He had a very serious expression on his face. "There's something I have to know before we get out of this car."

Gina looked concerned.

"What?" she asked.

"Which one of the Cartwrights is your favorite and why?" he asked.

"Why does it matter?" Gina asked back. She was eyeing Delmar suspiciously.

"It matters because you can tell a lot about a person based on the Cartwright they choose."

"Like what?"

"I can't tell you that," he said. "It will cloud your decision."

"Hmmm," she said. "The depressing thing is that I actually have an answer to this question. My dad loved that show when I was kid, and just over the past week or so I've seen a few reruns."

"So, which one is it? Ben, Adam, Hoss, or Little Joe?"

"I can't deny it," Gina said, all too aware of her un-hipness. "I'm a Ben fan."

"Not Little Joe?"

"Joe was too much of a pretty boy. I've been there, done that. Plus, Little Joe always had to be rescued by Ben or Hoss."

Delmar smiled. That was the right answer.

"What does that mean?" she demanded.

"It means you can appreciate a balding man," Delmar said. "Not many women are as evolved as you are."

"Ben wasn't balding," Gina replied, chuckling at Delmar's approach. This guy was getting cuter all the time. What a strange duck.

"Yes he was," Delmar informed her. "It was a piece."

"No!"

"Yes, and a damn fine one," Delmar said. "I tried to do some research into where he got that 'Bonanza' piece, because it was so much better than the one he wore in "Battlestar Galactica'."

They got out of the car and headed across the parking lot. As they walked side by side he couldn't help but notice that she was an inch or two taller than he was. Gina was all-woman.

"Don't you dare get a hairpiece," she implored. "That is so creepy."

"But you liked Ben."

"I liked his firm hand," she said. "The way he was such a caring father. The way he was a voice of reason in a town full of half-baked trigger-happy idiots. It had nothing to do with his hair or lack thereof."

Delmar hadn't actually been inside a Ponderosa Steakhouse for at least a decade. He forgot that you order at the counter, and then they bring it back to your table. He quickly made up his mind. That 10 oz. sirloin was calling his name. While Gina was looking over the menu posted high above the counter, Delmar was looking over the beautiful woman about to share a dinner with him.

"So, your dad turned you on to 'Bonanza'?" he asked.

"Sort of," Gina said. "Believe it or not, there's a little girl in my building that's an even bigger fan. She won't stop talking about the show. She's the one that made me watch several episodes this week."

"A little girl?"

Gina averted her eyes as she explained it. "My landlady's daughter. She's eight. They don't have cable, so they watch 'Bonanza' reruns every afternoon."

"Sounds like my kind of girl," Delmar said.

Gina smiled.

19

FOLLOW THE CLUES

The door to Peter's office served no purpose. A closed door was supposed to indicate, Peter believed, that the occupant was busy, focused, and did not want to be disturbed. Perhaps this diligent person was doing some work which required quiet, and a lack of interruption. But Peter's door was just a big piece of wood with a knob on it that people moved whenever they felt like it. Coworkers, when they did bother to knock, did it as they were opening the door. So what was the point? Buckingham didn't even bother knocking. He just burst in anytime, always with some urgent assignment that he needed "pronto".

Luckily for Peter, one great thing about MacArthur Harrison Hyde was that they had lots of conference space, lots of rooms of all sizes for meeting with clients, quiet well-appointed sanctuaries, and most of the time these rooms were empty. So if you needed some privacy, you could find it. Peter still took some precautions by coming in here at lunchtime, and bringing along his cell phone. Every work related expense was connected to a client. It was all about billable hours. So make your personal calls, but try not to let them show up on the company records. Peter thought that this was a reasonable expectation.

Peter heard the phone ring in Charleston, South Carolina. The reception in this conference room was surprisingly clear. "Hopkins

Realty," answered the man with a slight southern drawl. "Sonny Hopkins at your service."

"Mr. Hopkins?" began Peter, tapping a pencil nervously on the table. "You don't know me, but I think you know my father. His name is Henry Stankiewicz."

"Why of course I know Henry." And then he added carefully, "How is Henry?"

"Well, that's kind of what I wanted to talk to you about. He's not doing well."

"Damn it," whispered Sonny. "Let me sit down. Damn it all."

"I talked to James Bradley, Hendrix I mean. And he suggested that I call you. He thought that you could spread the word. My mother believes that the guys in Henry's squad should know."

"Whoa. Now I pride myself on my memory. Let's go back a little there. Now you must be Peter, right?"

"Yeah, that's right."

"OK, so you've gotta be about 30, is that right? And your mother is Evelyn?"

"I'm actually 28, but very close. You're good."

"Does your father know that you're calling me?"

"No. I'm doing this for my mother."

"OK, so let's do what our mothers ask us to do. What's the prognosis?"

"Well," sighed Peter, "It's cancer. It's apparently inoperable. He's still up and about, he's still going to work every day here in Chicago. You wouldn't know that he's sick to look at him."

"That's Henry," said Sonny. "If he's in pain, he's not gonna let anyone know. It's just not his style."

"Yeah, well, I guess I don't know him that well," muttered Peter.

Sonny caught the sarcasm in Peter's voice but let it slide.

"How long do they think he's got?" asked Sonny.

"He didn't say. He wanted me to draw up some papers, a living will and such. I'm a lawyer. It seems like he's getting his things in order. But I don't know how long he's got. My mother said he was pretty close to you guys, certainly closer than he's been to us."

Part of Peter was surprised that those words came out that way.

"We've met, you know," said Sonny. "You probably don't remember. I think you were about two. I was visiting Chicago with the National Realtors Association. Anyway, your father couldn't stop bragging about you, how you'd walked before the other kids, and how you could throw a ball, a sure sign you were an athlete. I stopped by the house and you were glued to your daddy's side the entire time. And your dad loved it. It made me smile to see him so happy, given what we'd all been through."

"That must have been the house on Laramie," said Peter.

"My memory's good, but it's not that good. I do remember that it was a small brick house with a fenced-in backyard and a white garage. Does that help?"

"Yeah, it does," smiled Peter. "That was a great little house."

"Look, Peter, I know you don't know me, and I may be way out of line here. But maybe you're being a little rough on the old man. I know he wasn't always there. It must have been tough to grow up without a father. You've got a right to be pissed." Sonny paused for a moment and listened. "You can stop me anytime."

"Go on," said Peter.

"Well, if you don't mind me getting too personal, Peter, I'd like to tell you a few things about Henry that he'd never tell you. Henry had a rough time after the war. He tried hard to deal with it and did a lot better than some other guys I know."

"I'm not sure I know what you're talking about," said Peter.

Sonny cleared his throat on the other end of the line, and continued.

"The doctors have fancy names for it, but the bottom line is that your dad got hit hard. You can't just pretend that seeing your friends killed in front of your eyes on a battlefield isn't gonna have some effect. When Henry came home he was in a lot of pain, he had some bad episodes, including some fits of rage that he couldn't control. Of course he never saw anyone professionally about it. He'd see that as a sign of weakness. The guys might talk about it among themselves, but he wouldn't have burdened you with it."

Peter closed his eyes. The line was silent for several moments.

"Thanks," said Peter finally. "My mom has alluded to that, but Henry's never said a word."

"Yeah, well, you didn't hear it from me," said Sonny. He quickly changed the subject. "Hey, I was at your parents' wedding. That was quite a party. I remember dancing on tabletops and just having a ball. When you talk to your mother, please give her my best."

Peter smiled at the thought of what that happier time must have been like. Then he came back around.

"Sonny, I almost forgot. Did Henry ever talk about any home movies he had?"

"Oh man," Sonny chuckled. "He carried that videotape with him like it was gold. Whenever we'd meet for a reunion he'd have it with him, and he'd show it to anyone who was interested, and some of us who weren't."

Sonny chuckled again.

"One night we were hanging out in the lobby bar of the hotel we were at in Indianapolis. The concierge had found him a VCR and Henry had set it up in the business center. We sat around drinking beer and your dad gave the play-by-play. I still remember some of it. Let me see, there was you opening presents, throwing a baseball to your sister, and you both riding on Henry's back in the living room and giggling so hard that you fell off. Your mom must have been holding the camera for that. There were lots of great images on there. That much I remember. You made a beautiful family. Watching the tape became a late night tradition over the years with a few of us, me, Hendrix, Hick, your dad and a few of the others. Henry wouldn't let us end the night without seeing it again. Seventeen minutes captured forever."

Sonny's voice became more contemplative. "The last couple times we met, he didn't have it with him, and I figured he must have forgotten, or the tape just wore out. He didn't say and I didn't ask."

"So you wouldn't know where it is?" asked Peter.

"Have you asked the reigning Mrs. Stankiewicz?"

"Yes. I asked her the other night. She said she's never seen it, but she'd heard Henry talk about it once in passing and that she's sure Henry doesn't have it."

"OK, let's see. Now the last time I saw that thing was in Indianapolis. That was about ten years ago, so that would mean Henry was married to Nancy. They lived down in Oklahoma, a small town by the name of Judd, which I always remember because of the musical. But that was ten years ago. She may not be there anymore, and I don't have an address or a phone number for her. But if that tape still exists, she might have it."

"I'll check it out."

"Good news for you though. Nancy took Henry's last name. I remember joking that they were probably the only two Stankiewiczes in the state of Oklahoma. If she's still down there, she should be easy enough to find."

"Thanks," said Peter. "Can you get the word to the rest of the squad?"

"I should be able to do that. I stay pretty current with the contact information on these guys. Of course, I don't know what happened to Hick."

"Hick?"

"Gary Hickman. Yeah, Gary definitely would want to know about Henry--that is if anybody knew how to reach him. I don't know where he is. The last note I have here in my file for him says, 'See Henry'."

"Well, if you can tell the others, my mother would appreciate it. Thanks for your time."

"It was a pleasure to talk to you, Peter. I only remember you as a two-year-old hanging onto your father's leg, and of course on that video. I'm sure you're a fine young man," Sonny said.

"I wouldn't go that far," Peter replied.

"Anyway, please take care of your father. I know he doesn't want any fuss, but he'll be in our prayers, and please keep us informed. I'll spread the news. The guys will want to know. But I won't let them know my source. Hang in there."

"Thanks, Sonny."

Peter hung up and sat back for a moment, letting this new information sink in. So maybe his mother hadn't just been covering for Henry all these years.

20

YEAH, WE'RE MOVIN' ON UP

Reed had gotten home late that night, which was unusual. He had called ahead to tell Lucy to eat without him, he would warm up dinner for himself when he got home. Now, at 8:45pm, Reed sat at the kitchen table enjoying a hot plateful of chicken casserole and a side salad. Lucy remained standing, leaning her back against the countertop, her hands folded in front of her. The silence was broken only by an occasional fork clinking against a plate, or a water glass being set down. Neither said a word for nearly five minutes. The entire house appeared to be still.

The small kitchen table had three chairs. Reed always sat on the side nearest the pantry door. Lucy always sat opposite him, close to the stove and refrigerator if anything was needed. The chair between them was empty. For a long time now.

Reed munched on his salad, cleared his throat and nonchalantly mentioned, "They've brought someone in to replace Anderson."

"Who is it? Somebody from the department? Is that why you were late tonight?"

"Yes. That had something to do with it."

Lucy nodded. "Is it that Dick Nicholson? Please tell me it's not."

"No, it's not Dick. But it's someone who's been there a while and knows the operation pretty well."

"Well, that's good, I guess. You won't have to show them the ropes. You think they'll be a good boss?"

"I don't know. This guy's never actually had this kind of personnel responsibility before. He's really a numbers guy."

"From what little I've heard from you over the years, I can't imagine he could be worse than Anderson. Who is it?"

Reed looked up from the table in silence, looked Lucy in the eye and lifted his eyebrows a few times.

"What?" asked Lucy.

"Me," Reed said casually, and returned to his salad.

"You? Really?"

"You seem surprised," smiled Reed.

"Don't take this the wrong way," said Lucy. "But I didn't even know you were in the running. How does that work? Did you apply for it? What does it mean? More work? More responsibility? More pay?"

"Yes, it means all of those things."

"When did all this happen?"

"Today. Karen Barnett from corporate called me up to her office. She said the job was mine if I wanted it."

"Did she tell you why?"

"Why what?"

"Why you? I mean, you're an accountant. This is a management job."

"I'll be managing a bunch of accountants."

"Right," said Lucy. She sat down at the table and tried to organize the many thoughts and questions running through her mind. "Did you have a choice?"

"Yes. I could have said 'no'. And believe me, I was as surprised as you are now. My first instinct was to turn it down."

"Do they give you any training?"

"Yes. They signed me up for some intensive leadership development training over the next three days."

"Think it'll help?"

"I don't know. I've been reading the manual. It's got some good ideas. A lot of it seems like common sense. But that doesn't mean it's easy," said Reed, taking another drink of water.

"Your first day as boss and already you had to work late," Lucy said. "Is this part of the job?"

"After I accepted the promotion, I didn't want to go right back to the office. There was an email memo sent around announcing the change. And I needed to not be there. I needed to figure out how I was going to handle it. It's a little overwhelming. And so I waited until after five o'clock and went back into the office with a maintenance guy and moved my stuff into Anderson's office after everyone had left."

"You said you thought it was the job that killed him. And now you've got that job. Have you thought about that?"

"Sitting in his old office is going to be a constant reminder. I want it to be a good reminder, to keep some perspective and never get so caught up in the minutiae that I forget what's important. It wasn't the stress of the job that killed Anderson, it was his inability to handle that stress."

"What's the difference?"

"Remember my camping trip? The guy ahead of me in line at the hotel went ballistic, and reacted way out of perspective with the situation. His reward was that he was thrown out into the storm. On the other hand, I ended up in the first class suite. Henry helped me see what it meant."

"Henry? Who's Henry?"

"He works in the parking garage of our building. He's the one that actually recommended that I go camping in the first place."

"And this parking attendant is now your life coach or something?"

"That's where I went this afternoon. The president has Camp David. I've got the parking garage. I do a lot of my best thinking there."

"With this Henry?"

"Everything happens for a reason, Lucy. Even if we don't realize it at the time. For example, I went camping and I came away with a leadership skill. All I did was treat the hotel clerk with the respect he deserved, and my weekend was made a lot easier. I can do the same thing at the office. Henry helped me to see that. How many times have I seen someone doing something well and not said anything?"

Lucy brushed some bread crumbs off of the table and into her hand. "It's that easy, huh?"

"Well, I realize there's more to it. But that's a good start."

"I'm sure there's more to it. You'll have to go camping again."

"I haven't even mentioned the biggest part of it, because I'm afraid of what you'll think," said Reed. "But I guess now's the time."

Lucy had Reed's full attention. Reed hadn't been this open in a long time.

"I think Will had something to do with it. I could feel his presence all that weekend."

Lucy got up to do some dishes at the sink. Reed stood up and followed her.

"Really, Lucy. The spooky way that the storm blew in, the appearance of that hotel in the middle of nowhere, the confrontation in the lobby, the great room. I could feel him there. And now I think he was telling me something."

"Stop it," begged Lucy, not turning to face him. "I don't want to hear it."

But Reed persisted.

"Will's gone and we can't bring him back. What's so wrong in thinking that he might be looking out for us? I get comfort from that."

"I just don't want to talk about it," said Lucy looking down into the sink.

"Maybe Will was trying to tell me something. Something about how I spend most of my time on this planet, in that office. I can make an inane job more rewarding. I don't have to die like Anderson. I'm better than that. And those people I work with, my friends and colleagues, they are good people too. They need me. They need a boss they can trust, and who gives them the respect they deserve. It's not brain surgery. I can do this. This is what I'm supposed to be doing right now."

Lucy turned and faced Reed. "Because you're getting messages from our son?"

"If I didn't take this job, it would have gone to Nicholson. And those good people who have spent most of their waking hours for years in that miserable sweat shop just to support their loved ones, they would have had to deal with more of Anderson's shit." Reed's voice began to crack. "I'd like to think Will had something to do with what's been happening. If I'm wrong, so what? And I know it's not like I'm curing cancer or eradicating poverty, but it's something tangible I can do. I'm a small man in a small job. But maybe it will lead to something else. Right now, I'm just following the signs. This is an opportunity that I need to take."

Lucy walked out of the room. Reed continued, calling up to her as she climbed the stairs.

"I've been grasping at straws for eight years now, trying to figure out what the point of it all is," said Reed. "I feel like I'm finally starting to move forward again."

Reed heard the bedroom door close and stood at the base of the stairs alone.

21

RENEGADE

Peter knocked on the door because there might have been someone in the office with her, and it just wasn't right to barge into the middle of a meeting. Peter and Kelly seemed to be the last two on the floor that treated each other with professional courtesy.

"Yes?" she answered from the other side of the door.

"Miss Castle?" Peter said. He used a very respectful tone of voice.

The door flew open a moment later, coyly held by a gorgeous lawyer with a toothy smile. "Mr. Stankiewicz?"

"Do you have a moment?"

She looked up and down the hall before responding. She was feeling a little playful, but not playful enough to take any chances in the office. "Why yes, I do, Mr. Stankiewicz. Which case is this regarding?"

"The living will."

Kelly's smile faded. "Come on in."

Her office was exactly the same size and shape as Peter's, but it didn't resemble it in the slightest. For one thing, her walls were not blank white slates. She had hung a few very tasteful photographs, including a beautiful black and white shot of the Chicago skyline circa 1959. There was something about that photograph of the

Prudential Building towering over Michigan Avenue that lent respectability to her office.

Her desk also couldn't have contrasted more with Peter's. Kelly's was tidy and organized. Only three items were deemed important enough to grace the surface; a laptop, a jam-packed in-box, and a framed photograph of her parents taken at a charity ball a few years ago. Kelly thought her father looked dashing in that tuxedo.

She closed the door behind them and motioned toward the chairs across from her desk. Peter sat on the nearest one, and Kelly took her place next to him, in the other cushioned guest chair. Peter reached into his suit jacket pocket, and held up a piece of paper.

"I can't believe I'm doing this," he said.

"United Airlines?" Kelly asked, grabbing it out of his hands. "Is this an e-ticket?"

"Yup."

"To Oklahoma City?"

"Yup."

She pointed to the center of the e-ticket. "This leaves in the morning."

"I know," Peter said.

"May I ask why?"

"Remember that home movie I talked to you about."

Kelly nodded.

"I'm pretty sure I know where it is," Peter said.

She pointed to the e-ticket again. "Oklahoma City?"

Peter nodded.

"Peter," Kelly said. She tried to make her tone of voice as soothing and understanding as possible, while still conveying the seriousness of the situation. She handed him his e-ticket back, and clasped his hand when he grabbed it. "You can't just get on a plane and fly down to Oklahoma City. You don't even know if that tape still exists."

"It has to," Peter said. "The way everyone talks about that video, there's no way Henry would have allowed it to be destroyed or ruined. So, I've done some investigating, and the trail most definitely leads to Oklahoma City. Henry's ex-wife Nancy is a long-haul trucker, and lives near there in a town called Judd."

"Why don't you call her first to make sure she's got it?"

"I did," Peter explained. "Her voicemail message says she'll be back in town the day after tomorrow. I left a message saying I'll be there when she returns."

"Why don't you just wait until she gets back, and then call her, and ask her to send it to you?" Kelly asked.

"It's too risky."

"Risky how?" she asked.

"Look, I don't know her. She might not even return my call. For all I know, she hates Henry. I have a much better chance of convincing her in person..."

"But if she hates him..."

"Maybe she doesn't hate him," Peter countered, anticipating Kelly's argument, "but I still wouldn't trust her to send the tape in the mail. What if it got damaged en route? I'd want to go down there to pick it up anyway. I hate to say it, but time is ticking. I can feel it in my gut. I just know I have to do this now. I'm getting on that plane tomorrow morning."

"Whoa," she said. "You really are going crazy, aren't you?"

Peter acted offended. "Don't look so shocked. I've done some crazy things in my day."

Kelly laughed out loud; a guttural guffaw. "Yeah right. The craziest thing I've ever seen you do was refuse to take a new plate for your second helping at the salad bar."

"Most men wouldn't have *dared* to blatantly disregard that sign," Peter pointed out. He smiled at her.

"Peter..."

"I know what you're going to say."

She said it anyway. "Buckingham will kill you."

Peter gave her an exaggerated coughing display. "I feel the flu coming on," he said.

"You don't cough with the flu," Kelly advised. "You're terrible at this. Have you ever called in sick before?"

Peter shook his head.

"Have you really thought this through?" she asked. She looked into his eyes for additional clues. She didn't see anything but turmoil. "What is this really about?"

Peter pointed to the picture on Kelly's desk. "You don't understand because you have the perfect family. Your childhood was perfect."

"I wouldn't say that," she began, but Peter cut her off.

"This video has something that I have to see," he explained. "A happy childhood. *My* happy childhood. I vaguely remember it, but so much has happened since then, it's like it never existed. If I could actually see it..."

Kelly looked sympathetic, but slightly confused.

"I know that doesn't explain it very well," Peter said.

Kelly squeezed Peter's hand. "What can I do to help?"

"If someone asks about me just say that you've never seen anyone look that sick before," Peter said. "Play it up big. I'm hoping this won't take more than a day or two. I work seventy damn hours a week here. I'm entitled to one or two lousy sick days, don't you think?"

Kelly nodded.

"You think I'm crazy don't you?" Peter asked.

Kelly nodded again. "Crazy, but cute."

22

THE BOOK OF LOVE

The Living Wills were having a very bad bowling night, but Ramon and Henry were laughing so hard they could be heard five lanes away. Ramon's laughing, unfortunately for the team, had led to a 6-10 split, killing their chances of winning the last game. Henry's laughing had nearly shorted out the electronics on the scoring table because it was preceded by a Danny Thomas-worthy spit take of O'Doul's.

Only Oscar Case wasn't laughing. He couldn't believe his ears. "You took her to Ponderosa Steakhouse?!" he screamed.

"Yes, Ponderosa Steakhouse," Delmar sheepishly admitted. "I'm telling you, she loved the gesture. She got the Lorne Greene joke right away. I think we're making a connection."

"Did she give you a good night kiss?" Henry asked as he wiped the beer off the table with his shirt.

"She kissed me on the cheek when I dropped her off," Delmar replied.

"Oooooh," all three of his teammates replied at the same time. The tone of the ooh left little doubt about their interpretation.

"Not good," Ramon said.

"That might be a kiss off," Oscar said.

"Yeah, I don't know, Delmar," Henry said. "In my day that wouldn't have been a bad sign, but these young girls today..."

"Do you want to save this thing or not?" Oscar asked.

"I really don't think it's in danger," Delmar said. "I could just tell."

"No offense, buddy," Henry said, "But let's just say that your track record of 'just being able to tell' with women isn't so hot. Do I need a blow in a call to Vermont?"

"Look who's talking!" Delmar responded.

The Delmar bashing was interrupted by Max Hack, the captain of the opposing team—the Minds are in the Gutters. He extended his hand to Ramon while the rest of the Gutters were putting on their street shoes.

"Good game, guys," he said.

"Good game?" Ramon responded. "We lost by 40 pins."

Hack smiled. "Yeah, good game for us. See you guys next week."

The rest of the Living Wills gave him a wave except Oscar. He was still staring at his young protégé, incredulous at his ineptitude. He repeated his earlier question.

"Do you want to save this thing or not?"

"Of course," Delmar answered.

"Well then you've got to take this thing to Defcon 5," Oscar advised. "This next date has got to be the other end of the spectrum. She's got to be dazzled and impressed. There is only one way to truly impress a woman."

"Jewelry?" Ramon guessed.

"No," Oscar said, trying to shush him with his hand. "That comes later. You've got to snare her first."

"Make her laugh," Henry advised.

"NO!" Oscar said, shushing him too. "Don't listen to him. He's a three time loser."

"Two!" Henry protested.

"What is it?" Delmar asked. Even he was curious now.

"Dancing," Oscar said. He crossed his arms in front of his body, supremely confident in his wisdom. "Every woman in the world LOVES to dance, and every guy in the world avoids it at all costs. When they find one that loves to dance too, or at least pretends to love it during the mating process, they will never, ever let him get away. It's a proven fact."

The entire Living Wills team sat in silence for several seconds mulling the suggestion. Only the sound of pins being knocked over a few lanes away could be heard; the Ten-Pin Tattlers versus the Twisted Turkeys. Judging by the self-satisfied grin on the Turkey captain's puss, the Tattlers may just have tumbled out of first place.

"That's the stupidest thing I've ever heard," Henry finally said. "Delmar couldn't dance to save his life."

"Wait a minute," Delmar protested, "I'm not that bad."

"But what do you dance to?" Henry asked to illustrate his point. "This is a young girl. She's not going to want to dance to that disco crap you like."

"Whoa, whoa, whoa," Delmar said, holding his hand out. "The O'Jays are not crap!"

"Henry's right," Oscar said. "To a 25 year old, the O'Jays might as well be the Ben Gays. It sounds old."

"I'm not that old," Delmar pointed out. "I'm only..." he looked over at the last Gutter team member zipping up his bowling bag. He didn't appear to be paying attention, but Delmar whispered anyway to avoid giving away his flagrant Over-40 League rule-breaking. "I'm only 38."

"You know where you should go? That club over on Diversey," Oscar said. "What's that place called again, Henry? It used to be that Go-Go place when we were in high school."

"Oh," Henry said. He snapped his fingers a few times. "The... the... Vinyl Boot!"

"Yeah, the Vinyl Boot," Oscar said. "What's it called now?"

"Iron Crystal," Ramon informed them.

"That's it!"

"I really don't think she's an Iron Crystal kind of girl," Delmar said. "Plus, I would hate that place."

"This isn't about you," Oscar pointed out. "This is about her. Remember the first rule of sales."

"Know your customer," Delmar replied.

"Exactly! She's 25. Twenty-five year olds go to places like Iron Crystal. They eat that shit up. How bad can it be? Wear black clothes, go in and sway a little to the ridiculously loud thumping, then lean in close to talk to her on the dance floor because you have to--it's too loud. And then, when you're both screamed out, and getting a little sweaty, ask her to go outside and get some fresh air. By then you'll both be comfortable touching each other a little and she'll be so damn impressed that an old guy like you is as hip as you are, and before you know it..."

Oscar smiled. He didn't need to say the rest.

"I don't know," Delmar said.

"I don't know either," Henry said. "I've only seen that dancing thing work one time in my entire life. My buddy Gary picked up this nurse in Nam after they spent the whole night dancing to Country Joe & the Fish."

"I like those guys!" Delmar said.

"Oh dear God," Oscar interrupted. "You've got to be kidding me. Do you know what the name Country Joe and the Fish sounds like to a 25-year-old? 'Old Country Buffet and the All-You-Can-Eat-Fish-Fry'."

Henry cackled. It may have been one cackle too many in a night full of them. He held his side and winced in pain. Only Ramon noticed it.

"You OK, Henry?"

Henry waved him off.

"Have I ever steered you wrong?" Oscar asked Delmar. "When Century Builders was getting ready to break ground on that high rise, who told you to bring them frosted cookies?"

"You did."

"And did you make the sale?"

Delmar nodded.

"Who gave you that tip about Addison Fest a week before they announced they were going to bring in Joan Jett and the Blackhearts?"

"You did," Delmar admitted, smiling at the memory. His boss was indeed a very wise man. "I'll never forget the look on that Kwikker Krapper salesman's face when he showed up on the day of the announcement and Addison Fest told him they already had a port-a-potty company."

"I'm telling you, kid," Oscar finished, "I know what I'm talking about here. Wooing a woman is just another form of sales. Go in with a plan and execute it. Here's your plan: Wear black. Take her dancing. And pretend to enjoy the loud thumping music."

"Maybe you're right."

"Of course I'm right. And whatever you do, don't even think about letting her know what kind of music you listen to. Hell, I'm more than twenty years older than you are, and I don't even listen to that stuff anymore. You know what the name Sly and the Family Stone sounds like to a 25-year old?"

Henry was still holding his side and smiling through the pain as Oscar looked around at his Living Wills teammates. He didn't venture a guess at Oscar's query and neither did Ramon or Delmar.

"C'mon," Oscar prodded.

"Sly and the Kidney Stone?" Delmar finally guessed.

"I was going to say Sly and the Gall Stone," Oscar said with a smile, "but that's not bad. What did I tell you about this guy, Henry? He may not look like much, but Delmar here is the best pupil I've ever had. Do us proud, kid. The reputation of the entire Living Wills team is at stake."

23

DEFROSTING

Cold was the safest, Reed figured. And so Reed gathered a load of dark clothes, jeans, shirts and blouses, and tossed them in. *Are you supposed to add the soap first? Too late now.* Reed set the dials for a large load in the regular cycle, poured in some detergent and pushed the dial in. The machine began to purr.

Reed looked around the musty laundry room, at the washer and dryer, the furnace, the water meter, the electrical breaker box, the water heater and the utility sink. Reed was standing in the power center of his home, a room he spent as little time in as possible over the years. Standing there in his short sleeve, light blue dress shirt and matching blue, polyester tie, Reed realized that if any of these things ever broke down, he wouldn't have the slightest idea what to do except dial the phone, write a check and balance the bank account.

Reed looked at his watch. Lucy would be home soon. He climbed the stairs from the basement, crouching at a spot where the ceiling forced a six foot tall man to duck a bit. The stairs creaked. He turned off the lights at the top of the stairs, which led into the kitchen. From the kitchen counter, he grabbed the wrapped fresh flowers he'd bought near the train station and went in search of a vase. *Where does she keep things like that?*

Reed searched the pantry, looking on the highest shelves among the items that weren't used very often, the bread maker and the crock pot and the good silver. He looked in the hall closet, and finally found a tall, thin vase with an arts and crafts class quality paper-mache design at the top of the linen closet. Reed brought it to the kitchen, cleared the thin layer of dust from the vase, shoved the half-dozen red roses into the vase and brought it to the dining room, placing them on the buffet.

Reed had seen a white table cloth in the linen closet and returned with it quickly. There were deep creases in the folds, which he tried to smooth out as he spread it on the heavily polished, dark wooden table. There were chairs for six. Which two places should he set for him and Lucy? As far as he could remember, they'd never eaten in the dining room by themselves. For symmetry's sake, he chose the two end spots. He placed the flowers in the vase at the center of the table and went off in search of china.

After looking in the kitchen and the linen closet, Reed returned to the dining room and found the china in, of all places, the china cabinet above the buffet. These had been wedding gifts nearly 30 years ago, but they had seen little use in the last decade. Reed set the table and as a bonus found two candlesticks and candles in a drawer of the buffet. *What else? What else?* Lucy would be home soon. Reed couldn't remember the last time that he was alone in the house on a weekday afternoon before 5:30. When he had left the office early today, he'd felt like he was playing hooky.

Lucy had only worked the morning shift at the library today. She would be home soon from her regular Wednesday visit to her parents, in their eighties, still on their own and going strong. They lived just two miles north, in the house that Lucy had grown up in. Lucy spent Wednesday afternoons at their house and Sunday mornings with them at St. Barnabas Church, followed by brunch at the Beverly Inn. Her brother had moved to St. Louis a few years ago. Lucy knew that one of these days, she would become a full-time care giver again.

Lucy would be home in 20 minutes. Reed made the call to China Garden, and ordered General Tso's Chicken, extra spicy, the Kung Pao Beef, two hot and sour soups, and an order of pot stickers. They said they'd arrive in a half hour, which would be just about right.

Reed put out wine glasses. Reed's glass would hold seltzer water, but Lucy still enjoyed a nice glass of chardonnay with dinner. A bottle was chilling.

Reed heard the garage door opening. Lucy was home. *What else? What else? Ah, music.* Reed turned on the CD player and crossed his fingers that the selections were appropriate. Sinatra. Things were going well. "The Lady is a Tramp." Well, if you listen to the lyrics, it's about a classy broad. Good enough.

Lucy's keys played with the lock to the back door. Reed stood back in silence and waited. Lucy entered and closed the door behind her. She turned quickly and was startled to see Reed, began to scream and caught herself. "Oh my God, don't do that. You nearly scared me to death. What are you doing here? I know I'm not late. Why are you home so early?"

"I don't know. I just felt like it I guess."

"Just felt like it," Lucy echoed as she took off her coat. "Is this promotion going to your head? Do you make your own hours now?"

"I just wanted to be here, with you. What's wrong with that?" And he gave her a kiss on the cheek, walking past her, through the kitchen *...she gets too hungry for dinner at eight...* and into the dining room. Lucy, in her khaki pants and kick-around, light blue polo shirt, followed him curiously.

The washing machine began the rinse cycle, and Lucy heard it through the floorboards. "You're doing laundry?"

"Yeah, I actually located the washing machine and thought I'd give it a shot."

"Did you spill something? Did you have a shirt you needed?"

"Nope. Just thought I'd do a load of laundry. What the heck."

"What's all this about?" Then she spotted the roses and the china. Lucy stood in the dining room with her hands on her hips. Reed moved to the kitchen, got the wine from the refrigerator and returned with the opened bottle.

"Care to sample the wine, madam?" Reed poured Lucy a glass and handed it to her.

"Did you get fired?" she asked.

"No."

"We were going to have chicken tonight. It's Wednesday. It's defrosting on the kitchen counter. Is that still in the plans or have you taken that over too?"

"Taken it over?"

"Well, you're doing the laundry. You're setting the table in the dining room."

"And I ordered from China Garden. Remember how you liked their General Tso's Chicken? So I guess we are still having chicken. Or at least you are. I'll be having the Kung Pao Beef. It'll be here in a few minutes. Why don't you just sit and relax? I'm sure you've had a long day with your parents."

"What is that supposed to mean? I love my parents."

Reed was trying to keep up the positive. "Of course you do. That came out wrong. Look, why don't you just relax and sit down and enjoy your wine?"

"What are you going to do? Another load of laundry? Why don't you empty the dishwasher while you're at it? I probably don't put the silverware back in the drawers the way you like it. Why do you have to surprise me like this?" And Lucy stormed into the kitchen after Reed.

Reed was ready and moved in, swooping her into his arms. "I love you."

Lucy tried to get away. "Just let me go, please."

"Listen to yourself. I was only trying to do something nice for you. OK?"

"OK. Now will you let me go? I have to put the chicken back in the refrigerator or it will spoil. We'll have it tomorrow. Now please let me go."

Frank had moved on to another song. ...and then I go and spoil it all by saying something stupid like I love you...

Reed let go of Lucy. "He's not coming back," Reed said quietly.

"Who? What are you talking about?"

"He wouldn't want us to still be wallowing in this. It's been eight years now. We never talk about it. We have to move on."

"Move on? Move on to what? I can't move on. You seem to believe that some roses and a take-out order can make things all better. Well they can't."

"Hey," Reed yelled, surprised by his anger, "You're not the only one who lost a son, OK? Not a day goes by that the pain doesn't eat me up. I see Will everywhere and I think of him constantly, probably more than I would if he were still alive. He was my son too. And we did a damn good job raising him and it's not our fault that he's gone. I never would trivialize your pain, our pain. But I've been thinking a lot lately, about why I'm here, and what I should be doing with my life. And as hard as it sounds, I know I should not be living in the past. Dammit, I just thought I'd do something nice for you today. For no other reason than that I love you, and I, well, I miss you. We live in this house together but separately. Every time I mention him, you shut down, you turn away. I know it hurts. I thought it would get better over time, but it hasn't. It still hurts. And it hurts even more when I can't talk to you about it."

The doorbell rang.

Lucy stood there with tears in her eyes. "I don't know if I can. I just don't know."

Reed was shaking. He hadn't planned such an outburst.

The doorbell rang again.

"I tell you what," Lucy said softly. "Why don't you answer the door? I hope you remembered the sweet and sour soup."

24

ONE BIG HAPPY FAMILY

"Hello, hello," said the woman who answered the door. "You must be here to pick up Emily. Please come in. We were just serving cake and opening presents."

"Thank you," said Gina, stepping into the foyer.

The big house was buzzing with the screams and giggles of unseen eight-year-old girls, fueled by soda and pizza. The woman walked Gina past the formal dining room which was strewn with a pleasant disarray of wrapping paper and half-eaten cake slices and plastic cups and forks. She talked as she walked.

"I'm sorry, we haven't actually met. I'm Rosie's mother, Janet. Thank you so much for bringing Emily. We were so happy she could make it. Would you like some coffee?"

"No thanks," said Gina. Like the drug dealer who saw what the junk did to his clients on the street, Gina never touched the stuff.

"Well, we've also got plenty of cake and ice cream, as you can see. Please feel free to grab a plate."

The whirling dervish of a woman stopped for a moment, took a breath and focused on Gina. "So are you Emily's nanny? Or her sitter?"

"No," grinned Gina, "I'm her mother."

"Oh, I am so sorry," said Janet, "Please don't take this the wrong way. But you just look very young. How do you do it?"

"It's easy," said Gina. "I *am* very young."

"Oh… I see."

They entered the kitchen, and Janet announced to the other second grade parents in the room, "Excuse me, everyone. This is Gina, she's Emily's mom. Now I have to run back in there and manage the insanity."

The other parents politely introduced themselves and attempted to include Gina in the conversation.

"So, Gina," said one of the dads, hoping to bring her into the conversation, "What happened to your property taxes this last go-around?"

"I rent," said Gina.

"Could be a smart, short-term move," added one of the mothers. "New to the area. Get a good feel for the market before you invest."

"Yes," said Gina. "Something like that."

"Well, I'm Monica Ryan, Nicole's mom," the woman said, handing Gina her business card. "When you're ready, I'd be happy to help you."

"Thanks," said Gina, looking around. "Will you excuse me for a minute?" She really needed a cigarette.

Gina noticed that the kitchen looked onto the backyard. She drifted toward the door and wandered outside to a small deck. Gina descended a few wooden stairs to the yard level and found herself smack dab in the middle of another party.

There were lots of children of different ages, some in diapers, most in play clothes and a few in teenage 'attitude wear'. About a dozen adults, including a couple in their eighties, were sitting in lawn chairs, drinking beer, sharing stories and dodging the various projectiles the kids were throwing around.

A large, jovial man of about 45 got up from his chair when he spotted Gina.

"Hello," he said. "I'm Rob, I'm Rosie's dad. You must be a Bell parent."

"I'm Gina. Yes, my daughter's at the other party, inside. I didn't realize there were two parties. I'll just go back inside."

"Actually," said Rob, "It's the same party. These are the relatives, Rose's cousins, aunts, uncles and grandparents. Inside are Rose's school friends. Rosie wanted two parties. This was our deal. One day for everyone. The friends' party is wrapping up. The relatives will be here all night."

"Big family," said Gina.

"Too big, maybe," Rob laughed. "But what's better than family, right?"

"Right," nodded Gina. "Well, I better get back inside. Nice to meet you, Rob."

"Nice to meet you, Gina."

When Gina got back to the kitchen, things were breaking up. Parents and classmates were saying their goodbyes to Rose and her mother. Each girl got a goody bag on the way out. Gina thanked Janet for having Emily. Emily gave Rose a birthday hug.

Gina and Emily walked out into a gorgeous spring evening in Chicago. On another day, they might take the bus, but today was a great day to walk the twelve blocks east to their apartment.

"So, did you have a good time?"

"Yeah."

"What did you do?"

"We played dress up. Rosie's got lots of fun costumes. And her basement has a million toys. They had a piñata in the yard."

"Did you have fun?"

"Yeah. The girls in the class are nice to me, even though they've been together since they were way back in kindergarten and I'm new."

Gina smiled. Kindergarten was two long years ago.

"I think Lisa is my best friend though. She doesn't have a dad either. She has two moms."

"Well," said Gina, "You're going to have to settle for one."

"I know," smiled Emily. "I only have one mom, but she's the best one ever."

They were taking side streets whenever they could, to avoid the traffic and noise. Emily took Gina's hand when they crossed a street. Gina knew that one day soon Emily would stop needing to hold her hand.

"It sure was crazy, Mom."

"What was crazy?"

"All the people at the party. The doorbell just kept ringing and all these people just kept coming in. Not just kids from school. There were tons of other people. I think they were Rosie's aunts and uncles and stuff. Every time we were in the middle of playing something, Rosie had to go say 'hi' to cousin Bill or give Grandma and Grandpa a kiss or something."

"Uh huh."

"Yeah. And when we sang 'Happy Birthday' we had to do it in the backyard so we could fit everybody. There was like a hundred people standing around the cake and all singing."

Gina and Emily walked past the Baskin-Robbins at Lincoln Avenue. Under other circumstances they might have dropped in for a treat, but Emily had been dosed with enough sugar today. She didn't even ask Gina if they could stop.

The rest of the walk home was very quiet. Both mother and daughter appeared to be lost in their own thoughts. Climbing the hallway stairs to their apartment, the fresh spring air turned musty. The peeling paint on the walls revealed a little more plaster than it had the day before.

Gina unlocked the apartment door, entered with Emily and locked the door again behind them. Emily turned on the fan in the window to cool the room. Gina sat on the couch and kicked off her shoes. Emily stood facing her mother.

"Mom?" said Emily.

"What is it, honey?" asked Gina, closing her eyes and rubbing her temples.

"Can we live in a big house like Rose?"

"It's not about how much stuff you have. Remember?"

"I know," said Emily, slumping on the couch beside Gina. "It's just that there was so much going on, there were so many people there too."

Gina sat up, tensing a bit. "What's the matter with what we have?" Her voice rose. "I'm doing the best I can!"

"I know," said Emily, a little scared that she'd upset her mother. "I didn't mean…"

Gina stood and looked down at Emily. "Look, we may not have the fancy things your friends have, or a big house, or all that family, and all that. Biff and Muffy were in the kitchen trying to sell me a house! How am I supposed to do that?!" Now she was yelling. "Be thankful for what you have. You think I like making double lattes all day? You think that's my dream? I work my butt off just to barely make ends meet! Wanna go back to Kansas City? Or Denver? Remember that?"

"I'm sorry, Mommy," sobbed Emily. "I'm so sorry."

Gina picked up Emily and held her very tightly for a long, quiet moment.

"No, baby," said Gina softly, "I'm the one who's sorry. I didn't mean to yell. I'm not mad at you. I love you so much."

Gina stood Emily back on the ground and knelt in front of her. Gina was now looking Emily straight in the eye. "I love you more than anything in the whole world. I just want you to be safe and healthy and happy."

"I know," said Emily, hugging her mom. "I love you too."

25

OKLAHOMA TRANSPLANT

Peter pulled into the long gravel driveway and followed the path back toward the house; a long ranch-style home with an unattached garage almost as big as the house itself.

Over the past twenty-four hours it seemed like he would never reach his destination. The flight to Oklahoma City begat the long drive to Judd, which begat the night at the truly nasty Round Barn Motel, which begat the wake up door knock from a clerk named Earl, which begat the many misadventures caused by Earl's impossible-to-follow directions to Nancy's house. But finally, finally, he was here.

Peter was a little concerned by what he saw when he turned off the car engine.

"Dammit," he muttered to himself.

He couldn't see Nancy's rig anywhere. Was she even here? He slammed the car door as he got out, hoping that would serve as an alarm just in case she was inside the completely silent home. As he approached the front walk, he tried to peek inside the windows. The blinds were all drawn. The house looked dark and empty. She probably wasn't home yet, but what the heck.

Peter held his fist out and was about to knock on the front door, but was suddenly overcome by anxiety in the pit of his gut. He took a deep breath and knocked on the door. Three firm loud knocks. Peter was surprised to hear some rustling on the other side of the door. Somebody was home after all.

The door opened moments later and a short but voluptuous 40-something blonde was standing there. She was wearing a baby blue nightgown, a sleeping mask pulled up above her eyes, and an agitated expression on her face.

"Whatever you're sellin', I ain't buyin'," she said. She moved her hand to her hip. This woman was ticked off.

"I'm not selling anything," Peter said. "I'm sorry, did I wake you up?"

She pulled off her sleeping mask. "What do *you* think?"

"I'm sorry," he said.

"I just got home from a 16-hour drive three hours ago," she said. "You better be with Publisher's Clearinghouse, and you better be offerin' me a gigantic million dollar check, or we're gonna have some problems."

"I'm Peter Stankiewicz."

Nancy stared at him for a few seconds. Peter was unnerved.

"I left you a voicemail saying I would be stopping by today," he clarified.

"Oh," she said. "I didn't even check the messages when I got home."

Peter tried to smile to put her at ease. It didn't seem to be working. The more she didn't smile back, the more nervous he became.

"I can come back later if you prefer."

"You're Henry's son?" she asked.

"Yes."

"Don't you live in Chicago?" she asked.

Peter nodded.

"And you came all the way down here to see me?" she asked.

Peter nodded again.

She opened the door all the way and motioned for Peter to come in. Peter tentatively entered the house. Nancy followed him in, and then darted around the living room picking things up and throwing them all in a pile on the big chair.

"Sorry about the mess. I just got back from the road. I kind of just threw my shit everywhere."

"Don't worry about it," Peter said. "You should see my condo and my office."

"Just like your dad, huh?" she said. Her first smile was beginning to emerge. Peter didn't have the heart to make it go away.

"Yeah, guess so," he said.

"Well, then, if you're just like Henry I better go put on a robe," she said with a wink. "You want some coffee or somethin'?"

"That would be great."

"Hope you drink it black," she said from the kitchen. "I haven't been home for a few days and don't have any fresh milk."

"That's fine," Peter announced. He wandered around the living room looking at the framed pictures on the wall. There was a cute picture of Nancy as a little girl—it looked like it was taken in the 60s because the color was slightly faded. Another picture featured Nancy standing in front of her bright green rig. And then there was the big one in the middle of the wall; Nancy and Henry's wedding picture. It looked like it was taken in a chapel in Vegas. The minister was dressed as Elvis Presley.

When Nancy returned she was wearing a fuzzy white robe with the Hilton insignia on the pocket.

"It'll take a few minutes to brew," she said. "Have a seat."

Peter took a seat on one end of the couch and Nancy sat on the other end of the couch.

"So what is this bad news?" she asked.

"It's about Henry," he said.

"I figured," she said. "Is he gone?"

"Not yet," Peter said. "But his doctors have told him that he doesn't have long."

She broke into a great big smile. "He really hung in there, didn't he?" She reached across the couch and playfully slapped Peter in the arm. "That tough old goat! I miss him, I really do, but I'm glad he moved up to Chicago. Before he got his transplant, we researched the best places for aftercare, and you should have seen the smile on his face when we found out Chicago was one of the best. Ya'll got some good specialists up there."

Peter's head was spinning. "Transplant?!"

"Well, not the transplant itself," she said. "We had that done at the VA in Oklahoma City. He was in the hospital already—it looked like he wasn't gonna make it—and the doctor came in and said 'Henry, we got a liver!' If he didn't get it that day, he wouldn'ta lasted more than another day or two."

"I had no idea," Peter said. "He never told me he had a transplant."

Nancy laughed. "That doesn't surprise me. Always the tough guy. I tell you what, Peter, I never had more fun in my life than I did with your father, but he sure drove me crazy. You know how long he was hurtin' before he even went in to see what was wrong? And then once he finally found out he had a bad liver, he tried to manage it on his own. He watched what he ate and drank. He didn't take the pills they gave him. But it was a losin' battle, he was gettin' weaker and lookin' real jaundiced. His eyes were turnin' yellowish. If his buddy Hick wasn't down here visitin' when he collapsed in the driveway one day, Henry would never have gone back to that doctor. Hick took him to the VA kickin' and screamin'. He saved Henry's life."

"Wow," Peter said.

Nancy reached out and patted Peter's shoulder. "I'm so happy for you and Henry that y'all got to spend these last few years together. I'm sure you know how much you've always meant to him."

Peter held his tongue.

"He had a videotape of you guys that we musta watched a thousand times. His whole face would light up when we watched that thing. I'll be honest with you, sugar, I put that video in the VCR a few times myself just to cheer him up when he was down, or when he was goin' through one of those spells he brought home from the war—you probably remember those. Poor guy. That video was like a happy pill."

Peter shook his head. "I've never seen it."

"Really?" she was genuinely shocked. "That makes you about the only person in this whole country that hasn't seen it. He showed it to everyone."

"That's what I hear," Peter said. "One of the reasons I came down here was to find it for him. Do you still have it?"

"Doesn't Henry?"

"He doesn't know that I'm looking for it," Peter said. "But I asked his current wife..." Peter stopped himself, realizing that he might have said too much. Nancy touched his arm again.

"Oh don't worry about it," she said. "I knew he was gonna remarry if he lasted more than a year or two with that new liver. That horny old goat wouldn't be able to last a week without a little somethin'."

Peter wouldn't be able to look Katherine in the eye the next time he saw her.

"The divorce was my idea," Nancy continued. "Chicago was the place for him. That's his hometown—he was a Chicago boy through and through. Plus, you were there, and Sarah was there, and some of the best treatment in the world was there. He wouldn't have wanted to live his last breath in this little town..."

"And you didn't want to go to Chicago?" Peter asked gingerly.

"I'm an Oklahoma girl," she said. "Don't get me wrong. I love seein' the world. That's why I do what I do. I get to see just about anything you'd ever want to see in my rig. I mean, I met your dad in Pensacola, Florida. We had what you'd call a whirlwind romance. Three sweaty nights at the Hilton."

She laughed at the memory.

"After he got a little taste, he followed me around like a puppy-dog. He even followed me back here to Oklahoma. And he came along with me on the road just about everywhere, but I could always tell that he liked the road better than he liked it here. That's not how I felt. This is my place. My home. I loved comin' home. I'm not sure that Henry ever did, bless his heart."

She hopped off the couch and walked toward the kitchen.

"That coffee should be done by now."

Peter followed her into the kitchen.

"Nancy," he said, "I really want to find that videotape."

She pulled two cups out of the cupboard, poured a cup of coffee, and pushed it along the counter toward Peter. He picked it up and blew on it. She poured herself a cup too.

"Well," she said. "Let's think about this. If Henry doesn't have it, and you don't have it, where could it be?"

"Do you think it's broken or something?" Peter asked.

"Nah," she said. "If it broke, he would have gotten it fixed or transferred it to DVD or somethin'. He must have given it to someone for safekeeping because he was worried he wasn't gonna make it. Does Sarah have it?"

Peter winced. "We don't know where Sarah is."

"Oh," Nancy said. She knew better than to go there. She took a sip of coffee as she thought about it some more.

"I talked to a few of his buddies from Vietnam..." Peter began.

"What about Hick?" she interrupted. "Did you ask him about it?"

"No," Peter admitted. "Do you have an address or phone number for him?"

"I think so..."

She had a little address book right under the phone a few steps away. She walked over, flipped through the pages, looked up Gary Hickman's name, and showed the address to Peter. Hick's phone number was crossed out for some reason.

"Is this an old address?" Peter asked.

"S'pose so," she said. "I'm pretty sure he's still in Milwaukee, though."

At least it's not too far away from Chicago.

"Do you know anything about Gary?" she asked.

"Not much," Peter said.

"He's a drunk," Nancy explained. "I never knew what your dad saw in that guy. He almost got thrown out of Stuffy's place once, and nobody gets thrown out of Stuffy's. He was threatenin' to tear out somebody's eye with his hook."

"Hook?"

"He lost his hand in the war," Nancy replied. "He has this metal hook now where his hand used to be. Swung that thing around when he got really drunk. It was scary. Henry was the only one in the world that could calm him down. If it wasn't for Henry, Hick would be dead in a gutter somewhere. For all I know, that's exactly where he is."

Peter was crestfallen. "Great."

"I shouldn't have said that, sugar," she said tenderly. "Those two were closer than brothers. Hick saved Henry when he took him to the doctor, and Henry saved Hick all the time. They both had this faith in each other that—I don't know how to explain it—to tell you the truth it made me a little jealous sometimes. Henry would drop whatever he was doin' and help Hick if he was in trouble, and Hick would do the same thing for Henry. It's the only reason I couldn't hate the guy. Henry's a good man, and if he says that Gary is a good man... then he's a good man."

They each took a sip of coffee. Nancy leaned back against the counter, and Peter smiled at her. Henry certainly had his faults, but he had great taste in women.

26

HOW TO SUCCEED IN BUSINESS

Dick Nicholson didn't see the newest member of his project team, Valerie Gordon, standing in his office doorway.

"Excuse me Mr. Nicholson," she asked. "Would you like a piece of pizza?"

He looked up from the desktop computer to see her pixie cut blond hair circling her angelic, youthful face. *What is she so happy about all the time?*

"Pizza?" mumbled Nicholson.

"Yes sir. They're serving in the lunch room, from Lou Malnati's, deep dish. Great pizza."

"What's the occasion?"

"I'm not sure, sir."

"No, I don't want any. And I suggest you bring yours back to your desk to eat. I need those depreciation figures this afternoon."

"Right."

"Hey, Val," Dick caught her as she was leaving. "Can you tell Kyle Petersen to step in for a moment?"

"Yes, Mr. Nicholson."

A few minutes later came a rap on Nicholson's open office door.

"You wanted to see me?" Kyle Petersen was about 45, with a permanently disheveled appearance, a mass of Larry Fine-inspired hair and a shirt that simply could not stay tucked into his crumpled khakis. He always looked as if he'd just woken up.

"Yeah, Petersen. Come in. How are the purchasing figures coming along for the new deep fryers?"

"Fine, sir. I've requested the bids. I'm collecting the numbers. I should have all the information from the possible suppliers by the end of the week."

"Great. I'm going to want to see all of those numbers. Make sure they come to me and only me. And I'll add them to the project numbers and deliver them myself."

"Sure," said Petersen. "Anything else?"

"Now that you ask," said Nicholson, leaning back in his chair and looking up at the still-standing Petersen. "How are you handling the distractions?"

"Distractions?"

"Well, O'Hern has turned the office into a club house, hasn't he? With pizza parties and personal pictures on the cubical walls and isn't there a baby shower next week?"

"Yes, Kim Coffman is expecting in a few weeks."

"And that's not distracting?"

"I hadn't thought of it that way, sir. But maybe you're right."

"Of course I am. Thanks. Just get me those deep fryer numbers as soon as you have them."

"Yes sir." And Petersen left.

A roar of laughter rose up in the distance, no doubt from the lunchroom.

"What is so damn funny?" said Nicholson, talking to himself under his breath.

And so he put his nose once again to the grindstone, staring into the spreadsheet analyses on his computer screen, attempting to draw associations and conclusions from the mass of calculations, charts and raw data. He knew that in the end his hard work would help him to prevail.

* * *

Reed sat in the lunch room enjoying the mix of seasoned Italian sausage, tangy tomato sauce and crisp, flavorful crust. It melted in his mouth.

When most of the department was hovering near the source of the marvelous aromas, Reed wiped the sauce from the edges of his mouth, took a gulp of soda and stood so that everyone could hear him.

"Can I have your attention for just a moment?"

The room quickly quieted down.

"Thanks. I just wanted to let you know that the pizza isn't just here because it's Wednesday, or because the 'new boss' wants to score some points. We are celebrating our first collaborative innovation award."

Everyone looked around the room to see if they could find a clue in one of their co-workers facial expressions.

"Joe Pantera, Carla Halberg and Tony Cooper have set the bar. They work on different project teams. They chose to discuss their separate projects together and found that they were duplicating work, bidding out similar projects for different regions. They agreed to experiment with combining the bids across regions. We believe that this idea will show us a significant savings. We don't know an exact number yet, but it should save us thousands of dollars in this year alone. Nice job."

Polite applause and smiles all around.

"So enjoy the pizza. Please take a moment to thank Joe, Carla and Tony for a delicious lunch. And let's do this more often."

* * *

"He what?!!!!!"

"He worked with the other regions on a cost savings idea," said Valerie, her perky blondness stopping in mid-smile. Nicholson got out from behind his desk. Young Valerie was uncomfortable.

"What exactly did he do?" asked Nicholson, trying to calm down.

"Tony figured out how to save money by bidding larger regions, working with East and South Central. Management is going to see if it works."

"Management," murmured Nicholson. "I'm management. I'm his boss. Why didn't he bring it to me?"

"Well, I don't think it was just his idea. I think he needed Carla and Joe's input to make it work," said Valerie. "And it still could fail," she added, attempting to soothe Nicholson.

"Val, honey, can you do me one favor? Can you go tell Tony I'd like to have a few minutes of his time?"

"Yes sir. And I'll have those depreciation numbers for you this afternoon."

Valerie left Nicholson's office feeling as if she'd ratted out Tony. She hadn't meant to. She arrived at Tony's cubicle. Tony was still accepting kudos from a few teammates leaning over the five foot high plastic and fabric walls.

"Tony," interrupted Valerie, "I'm really sorry but Nicholson wants to see you."

The other co-workers excused themselves.

"And I think it might be my fault," said Valerie. "I told him about the innovation thing, about the pizza and the idea that you, Carla and Joe had. He wasn't too happy about it."

Tony had been working on Dick's team for three miserable years now. He knew exactly what Valerie meant.

"Not your fault at all," Tony assured Valerie. "I totally understand. I'll talk to him."

Tony took a deep breath, gave Valerie a weak smile and shook his head. Only Nicholson could turn such a positive career moment on its head, making lemons out of lemonade. It was a long twenty foot walk to Nicholson's office door.

"You wanted to see me."

"Yes, Tony," said Nicholson, indicating without looking up from his paperwork that Tony should come in and have a seat.

Tony sat in silence and waited for Nicholson to finish whatever he was working on among the printed spreadsheets. Nicholson looked up finally. He was still not comfortable with Reed's new 'tie-optional' dress code. Ties were invented for a reason. And Tony just looked too relaxed in his bright blue polo shirt.

"How are those numbers coming on the expansion plans for Rochester?"

"They're going well," answered Tony. "I'm scheduled to meet with the contractors on the site of the new location in two weeks, to go over the final numbers. It shouldn't be too bad. These are the same contractors we used in Syracuse."

"Well," sighed Nicholson, "we had to move up the meeting to next Wednesday. Corporate wants the whole thing in place by the end of the month, so we have to get the details in sooner."

"But I'm on vacation next week," said Tony.

"That's what I wanted to talk to you about."

"What are you saying?"

"I'm saying that things change. Business moves fast, and some conflicts cannot be avoided. I'm sorry but I need you to be in Syracuse next Wednesday."

"But can't someone else go? I could ramp them up to speed."

"You know these contractors," insisted Nicholson. "You said it yourself. I want to make sure this thing gets done right."

"But my family…they're expecting me to take them fishing. We rented a cottage in Michigan."

"You can fly out on Tuesday, meet with the team in Rochester on Wednesday, file your report and be in Michigan by Thursday night."

"What about sending Kyle? He's walked through these kinds of processes before. He's done them in Buffalo and in Erie."

"Sorry, Tony. I need you for this."

Tony thought for a moment and had an idea.

"I could fly out tomorrow. I could get it done by the end of this week."

"Tony, I've already talked to Rochester. The earliest they can do it is next Wednesday, which is the latest we can do it. Now please let me get back to work."

Tony stood up without saying another word and walked out of Nicholson's office. He'd been planning the week in Michigan for months now. How would he break the news to his ten-year-old that Daddy was going to miss half of the week? But he also had a job to do. The family would have to do without him for a few days.

* * *

A young female voice answered the phone. "Monahan Construction. How may I direct your call?"

"It's Dick Nicholson at HKY in Chicago. Can I talk with Marty Coleman?"

"One moment."

Nicholson tapped his pen impatiently on his desk.

"This is Marty."

"Marty, it's Dick Nicholson. Listen, we need to move that cost evaluation meeting up to Wednesday of next week."

"That's no problem, Dick. We've actually got all the information together now. We could even do it sooner, later this week if you like, get it out of the way. Tony did such a great job last time that I know exactly what he needs."

"Well, Tony is busy this week. He won't be able to get there until next week."

"OK, then it's next Wednesday. We'll expect to see Tony that morning."

"Alright," smiled Dick, "I'll let Tony know it's all set."

Click.

Dick leaned back in his chair, very satisfied with himself.

"Nobody craps in my pool."

27

UNINVITED GUEST

I smelled it, dammit. There's no mistaking that gutshot smell... that bleedout smell. Dammit. That was no animal. How could I be so stupid? Never again.

Sergeant Retter?

Whaddya mean? Cover you?

You're not going out there?

Dammit. Dammit.

Holy shit. What was that whistle?

I can't lift my arm.

"Wait! Don't go out there! I can't lift my arm!"

Dammit.

"Hick. Tell him to stop. HOT ROD! Stay right there! Don't move."

What the hell is wrong with my arm? This thing isn't that heavy. Dammit, Henry. Get your act together.

Fuck! I knew that smell.

That gook smell. That Nuc Mam. Shit.

"Hick, I smelled it. I smelled them. Hick, talk to me. I let us down, man. I didn't say anything. I let us down."

I can't look.

"Sergeant Retter! Don't do it. I can't lift my arm. This rifle won't move."

"NOO!"

My God. My God. Dear God.

Please forgive me for what I've done.

Please forgive me for what I've got to do.

"HOT ROD!"

"RETTER!"

Say something. Say something. Let me know you're OK.

"SAY SOMETHING, DAMMIT!"

Why can't I lift my arm? Move you limp piece of shit. Move! If I can just get this damn thing to move. Move!

Fuck it! Blow that whistle right in my helmet. I've got to see.

Oh no. Oh no.

"RETTER!"

"NOOOOOOOOOOOOO!"

The blood curdling noise that jostled Katherine out of bed was the same one she heard last week, but that didn't make it any less disturbing.

"Henry," she said, pushing him in the back, "wake up. It's just a dream."

His big meaty midsection was thrashing, and her gentle shove seemed to have no effect. Henry's whole side of the bed was wet with his sweat. He wasn't screaming anymore. He was moaning. Dear God, it was awful moaning.

"Wake up, Henry!" she said. "It's just a dream. It's me, it's Katherine. It's me. You're OK. You're in bed in Chicago. You're OK."

She manhandled him with the second shove, desperate to wake him from his torture. He jerked forward, and landed hard onto the floor.

"Oh my God," she said, scrambling over to his crumpled body. "I'm sorry, Henry."

It was dark when Henry's eyes opened, but he could see her there; her disheveled silver hair tossing about, her white night gown clinging to her body. He couldn't see the features of her face in the dark, but the vision of that white night gown was like seeing an angel; an angel that was coming to take him home.

"Henry?" she asked. "Are you OK?"

Her voice brought him back.

"Katherine?"

"Yes, honey," she said. "It's me. I'm so sorry. I didn't mean to push you so hard. You were having another one of those dreams and I couldn't wake you up."

Henry groaned. The throbbing pain in his side was there all the time, and the dark pain in his brain had suddenly started showing up again when he closed his eyes, but now those more familiar pains were accompanied by more immediate pain--excruciating stabbing sensations in his back thanks to his tumble onto the floor.

"It's OK," he grimaced. "It's not your fault."

When Henry finally got back to his feet, he felt light headed.

"Don't go right back to sleep," she said. "Try to get your bearings."

His eyes adjusted to the darkness, and registered his location — a time and place far away from that appalling place in his mind — the place that had once again arrived unannounced and uninvited. The old wooden bedposts came into focus. The sheets and blankets strewn across the bed showed the strain of his struggle.

"Was I screaming again?" Henry asked.

"Come here, Henry," she said, opening her arms to him.

Henry staggered back onto the bed, and into her embrace. When she squeezed her arms around his back, the stabbing pain made him moan again.

"I'm sorry," Katherine whispered softly into his ear.

"I am too," he whispered back. "You didn't sign up for this."

"I signed up for you, Henry Stankiewicz. For better or for worse."

She didn't say the rest aloud, but they both knew the words.

In sickness and in health.

Until death do us part.

28

CLUB PARADISE LOST

Delmar was only a few blocks from Gina's apartment when he realized there might be a problem. It was a sensation he could not recall ever experiencing before. His legs were sweating.

Leather pants. The sales clerk at The Alley had insisted that leather pants made a statement. Delmar now knew what that statement was: Lose twenty pounds.

Delmar sat at the wheel waiting for the light to change, tightly wedged into this pair of black trousers. The pants complimented his new Doc Martens and the slick, black dress shirt that mercifully hung loosely over his waistline. Delmar wasn't sure if he'd be able to stand up without hurting himself.

But he looked damn good, he thought.

Delmar pulled up a few houses shy of Gina's apartment, just in case someone might be watching from a window and see him as he pried himself out of the driver's seat. He crossed the street. Circulation returned to his toes.

The street was dark at 9:30 on a Friday night. Usually Delmar's evening was slowing down about now. But he was playing in a different league tonight. And when you're 25 on a Friday night in Chicago, nothing happens until at least ten o'clock.

He entered Gina's building and climbed the stairs to her apartment. The squeak of the old wooden steps along with the slap of leather on leather between his thighs made quite a racket as he climbed the single flight to the second floor.

Delmar took a deep breath, straightened out his shirt and knocked on Gina's door. The door of the apartment across the hall opened and a young girl of about eight or nine peered out curiously. Delmar turned and smiled at the girl, waving to her. The girl smiled back and closed the door quickly.

Inside her apartment, Gina took one last quick look around to make sure all evidence of Emily was hidden from view. She opened the door and did a double take. The man in black standing at her door was shifting from foot to foot. It took her a moment to adjust to the 'new' Delmar. And had he forgotten to shave for a few days?

"Hi," Gina said, "Come on in. I'm just about ready."

Delmar stepped inside. Gina peeked out into the hallway. Emily was looking out again from Libby's apartment and gave her mom the OK sign, signifying that Emily thought Delmar was cute. Gina shushed Emily and closed the door.

"Give me just a minute. Sorry the place is such a mess. Make yourself at home."

Delmar considered sitting on the couch but worried that he might never be able to stand up again in these pants. "Thanks, I think I'll just stand. I've been sitting all day."

Gina left Delmar in the living room and went back to the bedroom for a few last minute adjustments. Off came the flower print top, replaced by a black pullover with the word "Cain" emblazoned across the front. Boots replaced her sandals and she was ready.

"Who's the artist?" asked Delmar as Gina re-entered the living room.

"The artist?"

"The drawing," said Delmar, indicating the construction paper masterpiece stuck to the refrigerator.

Damn, thought Gina. She'd missed one.

"Oh, that's Emily, the landlady's daughter."

"Do they live across the hall? I think I saw her at the door."

"Yes, that would be her. She's always watching who comes and goes."

"I think her painting is great. She's very talented."

"Well, we should be going," said Gina. "You said something about dancing. Have you got a club in mind?"

"I was thinking we'd check out The Iron Crystal. Sound alright?"

"Sure. I wouldn't have guessed the Crystal to be your scene."

"I'm a man of mystery," shrugged Delmar. "There's lots of stuff you don't know about me."

They flagged a cab on Addison and headed down to the club on west Diversey, better than driving and paying a valet twenty bucks. Delmar had done a little homework on the dance club after Oscar had suggested it. This was going to be an expensive evening, but it was worth it to impress Gina.

"Have you been here before?" asked Gina, as the cab pulled up in front of the club. Delmar paid the cabbie and was happy to be standing again.

"Not enough to say I'm a regular," answered Delmar. "How about you?"

"No, never been here. Too rich for my blood. But since you're buying," she said with a wink, "I thought I'd join you for the adventure."

The Iron Crystal prided itself on the fact that it looked like a warehouse. The marquee was a giant piece of sheet metal with the club's name in raised letters. The Crystal worked very hard at looking so unhip that it was very hip. It was a fine distinction.

Gina and Delmar got lucky. There was no line. Later tonight there would be a queue around the block. The immense body builder at the door asked for a $10 cover charge for each of them. Delmar handed him a twenty.

"And I'll need to see an ID for the young lady."

Gina obliged. When Delmar offered his own driver's license for examination, the bouncer nodded knowingly. "No need sir. Enjoy your evening." Delmar inhaled and squeezed the wallet back into his back pocket.

They entered the club and were immediately hit by a wall of sound. The hairs on the sides of Delmar's head stood on end. The room was crowded with attitude. These people had spent a lot of time working on their 'look', which appeared to be a studied carelessness, 'look at me' meets 'what are you looking at?'.

Delmar and Gina wormed their way through the crowd. All of the couches, overstuffed chairs and booths were taken, as were all of the tall stools at the long, chrome and steel bar. The DJ was hard at work destroying his patrons' hearing in a slightly raised booth in the opposite corner of the large main room. Delmar noticed that someone was screaming at him.

"Can I get you anything?" shouted the girl with bright green hair, no eyebrows and a bar tray of empty glasses in her hand. Delmar glanced at Gina, who seemed to be busy scoping out the room. The bass blaring from the sound system was beginning to make Delmar queasy.

"What would you like to drink?" he yelled at Gina.

Gina shrugged her shoulders.

Delmar was lost. *How can anybody communicate in a place like this? And is this the type of music she likes?* How could he bust his moves to this blare with no melody? He was in over his head. Delmar felt the entire evening slipping away. The girl with no eyebrows was still standing there.

"A double shot of Jameson, two Coronas and a club soda with a lime."

The dance floor was beginning to fill with people letting the innocuous semi-rap beat move them randomly around the dance floor. None of them seemed very happy about it.

"I'm digging the beat," he hollered at Gina. Delmar immediately prayed that she hadn't heard him. *'Digging the beat'? Oh my God, please tell me I didn't say that.*

The drinks arrived. Delmar handed the waitress a twenty. She signaled to him that he was still two dollars short. He handed her another five and she left without even asking if he needed change. Delmar held the beers in one hand and the drinks in the other.

"I didn't know what you wanted so I got a little of everything."

Gina grabbed the club soda. Delmar began to drink heavily. With nowhere to sit and no way to talk, the two were buffeted by the crowd like buoys in a hurricane.

The minutes passed like hours. They didn't say a word to one another. Delmar seemed to be nodding his head to the beat as he surveyed the room.

Gina finally excused herself to find the ladies room. "I'll be right back," she shouted.

Delmar was strangely relieved. He had finished the whiskey and was pounding down the second Corona just as the waitress was passing. He set the empties on her tray and ordered a second round.

Meanwhile, in the gaudy ladies' room Gina sat on an upholstered chair and closed her eyes for a moment. The techno volume was just a little lower in here and she could hear herself think. Why was she feeling so uncomfortable with him? Was this the same guy she'd felt so at ease with at Ponderosa? Was this really his scene?

Ten minutes passed.

Gina had not come up with any answers for the discomfort she felt, and so headed back. When she returned, there was another club soda waiting for her, and Delmar was holding a large, empty shot glass and two more empty beer bottles. He'd finished his second round. His eyes were a little glassy.

"Hey, there you are, Gina my queena." Delmar let out a belch just as he was leaning over to speak in Gina's ear. "Wanna dance?"

"Sure. Why not?"

They squeezed onto the dance floor and assumed the nonchalant aura of the crowd around them. Delmar wanted to kill Oscar now. All women love dancing? What a load of crap. They bobbed along with the incessant bass line. Delmar couldn't make any of his patented moves, like his killer robot dance. This wasn't even the type of music that would give him an excuse to touch Gina, to hold her. They just rocked back and forth, separately. Delmar felt the room beginning to spin.

Gina was seeing another side of Delmar, and it wasn't very flattering. He was way too old for this place, and he was trying too hard. It made Gina sad. Standing there attempting to be someone else, Delmar was pathetic. And now he was drunk and pathetic.

The beat moved them across the floor. Were they dancing or just being bumped around by strangers in the world's largest crowded elevator? When did this song end? Was it a song? Delmar was used to dancing three minutes at a time to catchy tunes with clever lyrics. He kept glancing to Gina for a signal that she'd had enough.

Gina closed her eyes and let the music carry her somewhere else. *Look at that. Maybe she's actually enjoying this.*

Eventually, Delmar noticed a couple leaving their seats at the bar. He and Gina made their way to the barstools. Delmar ordered another round. He couldn't think of a darned thing to shout at Gina to begin a conversation. He downed another shot.

Delmar caught Gina opening her cell phone and checking the time.

"I really should be going," she wailed into Delmar's ear. "But you can stay if you like. I just have to be up very early tomorrow."

Delmar looked at his watch. It was eleven thirty.

"I'll take you home," said Delmar. And they snaked their way out the front door. Delmar's head was pounding from the combination of too much alcohol, the deafening music and knowing that he'd somehow screwed up royally. The vibe with Gina was bad.

Outside, their ears still rang. Gina hailed a cab as Delmar held onto a light pole. Delmar turned away from Gina and puked onto the curb, splashing a little onto someone's red Ferrari, and a little onto his new shoes. His pants would not allow him to bend over and wipe off his shoes. The puke remained.

He felt better.

Gina pretended not to notice and held the cab door open for Delmar. Delmar squeezed himself into the cab, holding his breath. When the cab got them back to the street outside Gina's apartment, the romantic moment that both Gina and Delmar had secretly anticipated over the last few days faded away unrealized. Barf has a way of lingering.

Gina was even more gorgeous to Delmar as she stood on her stoop in the moonlight like an unattainable goddess, her brown eyes reflecting the street lamp, her statuesque frame taunting him like a car he could never hope to afford.

Gina saw a little of Delmar's charm return as he fumbled through his words trying to find something to salvage from this disaster.

"So, I guess the goodnight kiss is out of the question."

No reaction from Gina as far as Delmar could tell.

"OK, then. Are you fine going inside alone? I imagine you are. Alrighty then. I am going to go home now and hose myself down and try to figure out what the heck happened here." Delmar was struggling to balance himself on the sidewalk. He couldn't fit his hands into the pockets of his leather pants. "First, I'm gonna walk down to the Dunkin' Donuts and get a couple cups of coffee and a sandwich of some kind, and clear my head up a bit, but I'll be fine. Don't you worry about me."

Delmar started walking away, backwards, as if to fade into the evening. He continued. "In the immortal words of Gloria Gaynor, who by the way, they did not play at all tonight, 'I will survive'."

Delmar continued talking, now to himself, as he wandered down the street. Gina smiled as she opened the front door of the building, but Delmar didn't see it.

29

TWO SECONDS

Reed pulled out a Marlboro cigarette and lit it. Sitting on the cement landing outside the parking garage exit on lower Wacker was somehow calming on a normal day, but on a rainy day it was even better. The dirty water dripping off the street above was landing in a puddle no more than fifteen away from Reed. He watched it drip, drip, drip, as he took drag after drag after drag on his cigarette. Within a few minutes whatever stress had been bothering him had begun to dissipate into the ether.

"How's the boss?" Henry asked, making Reed jump.

"Oh geez, Henry, you scared me. I didn't hear you coming."

"How are things going?" Henry asked.

"Could be better," Reed admitted.

"Resistance to the new leadership?" Henry asked.

Reed nodded. "Nicholson."

"Ah," Henry said. "Sorry to hear it."

"Can I ask you a question?" Reed asked.

"Shoot," Henry said. He took a seat on the concrete landing.

"You're in charge of this shift at the parking garage, right?"

"Yup," Henry admitted.

"Do the rest of the employees buy into your management style?"

"Well, the only other employee down here is Ramon," Henry answered, looking around for Ramon. When he didn't see him, he continued in hushed tones. "And he's got to be nice to me because I'm the star of our bowling team. You know, you should really come out and join us some time."

"Thanks, I may do that someday," Reed responded.

Henry was about to launch into his bowling "fish stories", but was interrupted before he could complete a syllable.

"You know," Reed said, "This whole boss thing hasn't quite gone down like I imagined it would. A lot of people in the office have bought into my new approach, but obviously, not everyone is on board. I have a feeling some will never be on board."

"Nicholson's not playing, huh?" Henry said.

"He's taking his ball and going home," Reed replied. "I'm seriously thinking that he's going to destroy the whole atmosphere if I don't do something about it."

"Thinking of firing him?" Henry asked.

Reed shook his head.

"I just can't do that to him," he said. "He's a miserable jerk, but he's only two years away from his retirement."

"Can *you* last two more years with Nicholson?" Henry asked.

"I don't know," Reed replied. "A lot can happen in two years."

"A lot can happen in two seconds," said Henry.

Neither Reed nor Henry said anything for a few moments as that odd statement hung in the air. The street above was still dripping into the puddle below, but it was no longer calming to Reed. He needed to figure out what Henry was talking about.

"Are you saying that I should fire him?" Reed asked.

"No," Henry said. "I was just talking about how things can change in the blink of eye. Life is short. Who's got two years? Sometimes your whole life can change in two seconds."

Reed could tell that something was troubling Henry. "Two seconds?" he asked.

"Yeah." Henry paused. Did he really want to go there? No, he didn't, but he couldn't stop himself. "Mine did."

"What happened?" Reed asked.

Henry didn't respond at first. His mind was already there, the images had been burned there permanently, but they had never been transformed into actual words before. To make them come out of his mouth he would have to translate it into a foreign language; English. It never seemed possible before, but somehow he knew that if he opened his mouth right now, something inside him was going to force the painful words out of his brain for the very first time. He took a deep breath and tapped a vein.

"Back in Vietnam," he began tentatively. He hated that last word. It didn't come out naturally. But it did come out. And since it did, he knew what was coming next. Henry knew he wasn't going to stop. Not this time. He shouldn't. He couldn't. He cleared the lump out of his throat and continued.

"We were out on patrol. It was one of those unbelievably hot summer days. The humidity was unbearable, and we were wearing a ton of gear."

His words started gaining confidence, and then it happened. His mind was in the jungle. There was no turning back now.

"There are six of us: Sergeant Retter, Hendrix, Hick, Sonny, Hot Rod and me. Retter is the biggest horse's ass I've ever met. Total prick. He spits nails at us, and his favorite target for those nails is Hot Rod. Hendrix thinks it's a race thing 'cause Hot Rod is black and Retter is a redneck from Arkansas, but I just figure the Sergeant doesn't much care for Hot Rod for the same reason the rest of us don't like him. He's a junkie."

Henry continued, the lump in his throat now gone.

"That's the last thing you need out there, you know? You've got too much to worry about already. These patrols are always tense. I mean we're out there in the open, but they're hiding in the jungle. And there are booby traps everywhere. Every time a leaf moves, we're spooked. Every time we step on a branch, we're spooked."

Reed didn't even notice that his ashes were in danger of falling off the end of the cigarette.

"So anyway," Henry continued, "just as I think I smell something—a stinking gutrot, some dying animal, something in my mind saying beware, we hear a loud rustling coming at us from the brush, and Hot Rod lifts his rifle, and his finger is twitchin, ready to blast away. Then we see what's making the noise: one of those potbellied pigs. That really cuts the tension. We start laughing our asses off. Hot Rod is laughing too."

Henry smiled at the memory for a few seconds, before it began to fade. He almost whispered the next sentence.

"I was looking right at the smile on his face when the first bullet shattered his kneecap."

The ashes from the end of Reed's cigarette fell, luckily missing his pants, wilting harmlessly in the air as they slowly fluttered to the ground. Reed's attention remained rapt.

"Hot Rod takes at least a few more bullets before he goes down," Henry continued, "but I don't see any of them hit because the rest of us are just firing. I mean we have no idea where the bullets are coming from, so we're firing all over that damn jungle, hoping against hope to take 'em out." He rubbed the back of his neck. "We manage to crawl our way to safety in this ditch, but Hot Rod is still out there in the open. He's groaning, his blood is just dripping into a pool around his body, and he's completely helpless. Retter looks at us, and remember now, he hates Hot Rod… he had called him every name in the book, including—when he really wanted to get him crazy—a no-account nigger, and he says to us, 'Cover me'."

"And before any of us can even figure out what is going on, he's out there, trying to drag Hot Rod into the ditch with us. It's like the rest of us are paralyzed or something." Henry shook his head. "You know, it's funny how the sound of a bullet going right by your head will make you change your focus. That whistling sound doesn't sound scary at all—just whistling air—but your brain knows what it is, and your brain starts thinking about it. That's what the rest of us are doing in that ditch. Not Retter, though. Those gook bastards shot his whole body to pieces before we even fired a single shot to cover him. I mean it was two seconds. Just two seconds." Henry snapped his fingers. "Just like that."

Reed could see the anguish in Henry's eyes.

"Did either of them make it?" Reed asked tentatively.

Reed's question seemed to bring Henry back to the parking garage for a moment, but he didn't answer at first. It took him a little while to return completely, to regain his bearings.

"Not Sarge," Henry finally said.

"And Hot Rod?"

"He lost his legs, but he survived. Turns out Hot Rod wasn't such a bad guy after all. I got to know him a little better when we were both in the hospital. I mean, he was still a no-account junkie, but he was *our* no-account junkie. Know what I mean?"

"Yeah," said Reed, "I think I do."

"When we were recovering," Henry continued, "Hot Rod said that he and Retter had had a sit down a few days before Sarge died. Retter told him that the reason he was always on Hot Rod's ass was because he didn't think that Hot Rod was buying into the team. Here we were in a foreign country, with gooks behind every friggin' tree, and we were losing sight of the big picture, creating enemies amongst ourselves. Hell, we had real enemies trying to kill us. We didn't need any more. And you know what? Hot Rod *wasn't* buying what Retter was selling until this guy he was positive hated him, tried to save him. That's when he got it. That's when we *all* got it."

"In two seconds," Henry said, holding up two fingers. "Two seconds. After those two seconds, we knew that no matter what happened to any of us, no matter when or where it happened, we had to be there for each other. No matter what. No matter why. No matter how. Retter didn't think about it for a second. He just did it. The rest of us... hell... we thought about it for two seconds. Two seconds too long."

Henry trembled as he said it, and when he did, he felt the pressure release. Whatever force pulled those words deep out of him was through with Henry now. It was almost as if he could see the words floating away, fighting the raindrops in the air between Wacker and Lower Wacker, drifting away for good. Those words would never be spoken again. Henry looked at Reed to see if Reed could see it too, but his friend was deep in his own thoughts.

They didn't say another word. Two seconds turned into two minutes. Two minutes turned into twenty. The two men sat in silence together, staring at the dirty water dripping.

Drip, drip, drip.

30

THE TRUTH WILL SET YOU FREE

Gina, Kathy and Jose were busy cleaning up. The morning rush usually ended around 10, and they knew they had a good hour and a half before the coffee shop got busy again. If they cleaned up the mess quickly enough, they might even get a few moments to put their feet up and rest. It was a goal not often realized, but a goal they strived for daily nonetheless.

Gina was feverishly washing out one of the milk containers and didn't hear the Al Cappacino's front doorbell ring over the sound of the running water. Jose, on the other hand, got a good look at the man walking verrrry tentatively up to the register. He thought about warning Gina, but decided against it. This was one of those moments he could pretend not to understand English. He had been merely nodding at her vitriol over the last week anyway — keeping his head low, trying not to take any shrapnel. There was no way he was going to get in the line of fire now. Gina could probably throw his little 5'6" frame across the room if push came to shove. Considering who just walked into the shop, a push could be coming to shove any second. He skedaddled to the back of the store before she noticed.

Delmar cleared his throat. Gina didn't hear him. He jiggled his keys a little bit. Gina didn't hear him.

Kathy noticed there was a customer and was about to walk over and take his order when she saw who it was. She did an about face that would have made General Patton proud, and marched in Jose's footsteps toward the back of the store.

"I'll have the usual," Delmar finally said, his voice cracking slightly.

Gina's back stiffened when she heard his voice. She slowly turned off the water and wiped her hands on the towel next to the sink before turning around. Her face was expressionless.

"Black, right?" she asked.

"Like my heart," he replied reflexively.

Damn. Wrong time for that joke.

Gina poured his cup of coffee, being very careful not to make any eye contact. Delmar was staring at her, looking for signs of warmth. He wasn't getting any. He knew this was going to be uncomfortable, but he had no choice. He had thought of nothing else since he deposited his dinner on the sidewalk. He knew he had blown it, in more ways than one, but even that kind of humiliating embarrassment couldn't keep him away. There was something about this girl.

Gina slid the cup of coffee across the counter and waited for his money.

"How much is it again?" he asked.

"You know how much it is," she snipped.

Delmar cleared his throat again. "I was making sure the prices haven't gone up."

"Nope."

"Not even for morons that are still nursing a hangover from seven nights ago?"

"Nope," she said.

"Not even for people afraid to show their faces because of their embarrassing idiocy?"

"Nope," she said. "Same price."

There was definitely a chill in the air.

"Where have you been getting your coffee this past week?" she asked.

"I uh, uh... I've been afraid to come in here," Delmar admitted, as he dug into his pocket for the money.

Gina had promised herself that she wouldn't do it. She promised herself that she wouldn't say anything if she ever saw him again. But now that he was actually here in the flesh, she had to say it. She hated herself before the words even came out.

"Is your phone broken?" she asked.

"What?"

"Is your phone broken?" she asked again.

"Um..."

"It's customary to call after a date," she said. God, she hated the way she sounded. She sounded like her mother, but this had been bubbling up inside all week.

"I didn't think you'd..."

"Look," she said. "I kind of like you, Delmar, but life is too short to sit by the phone waiting for someone to call."

Delmar was stunned.

"Are you mad about the date or mad because I didn't call?"

Gina sighed. "Does it really matter? The point is I've been a raving bitch all week, and for what? I've got enough drama in my life. I don't need any more."

"I'm really sorry," he said. "I was too embarrassed to call. I puked on the sidewalk, for God's sake. I figured you never wanted to hear from me again."

"Never mind," she snipped. "Don't worry about it." She held out her hand. "That'll be two dollars, please."

Delmar handed the money to her and tried to establish eye contact. She was staring at the cash register as she slipped the two single dollar bills into the one dollar drawer.

"I don't know what to say," he said. "I came in here today because I've been thinking about you, and..."

"It's OK," she interrupted. She took a deep breath. "This doesn't have to be weird. You can still come here every day and order your coffee and we can be friendly. I'm just obviously not ready to date.

I promised myself I'd never be an idiot like that again, and after two dates, I'm getting all pissed because a guy didn't call me for a week."

Gina slammed the cash register drawer closed. Delmar couldn't take his eyes off her.

"Can I ask you something?" he said.

"Sure."

"You can tell me the truth," he said. "I'm a big boy. Was that the worst date you've ever been on in your life?"

Gina couldn't help herself. A smile struggled to her lips.

"That's what I thought," he said.

When Delmar saw her smile, he melted. How could he blow this?

"Maybe we can try again?" he asked.

"It's probably not a good idea," she said.

His disappointment was obvious. "I understand."

"Can I ask *you* something?" she asked.

"Sure."

"Have you ever worn leather pants before?"

Delmar could feel the color coming to his cheeks. He had to be blushing. "Was it that obvious?"

She nodded. "Have you ever been to that club before?"

He shook his head.

"Then why did you take me there?" she asked.

"The truth?" he asked.

She nodded.

"Before I answer, I need to know. Have I ruined my chances with you forever no matter what?"

She nodded again, this time with a hint of sadness on her face.

"Alright, what the hell," he said. He threw his hands up in the air, and gave his body the 'Price is Right Showcase' model wave. "Look at me. I'm pushing 40. I'm balding. I'm divorced. I'm boring. And look at you—you're young and beautiful and funny and absolutely perfect. I don't have the slightest idea what to do on a date with someone like you. I haven't dated anyone since 1991, and even then, trust me, I wasn't dating anyone of your caliber."

"Oh please," Gina said.

"Look at me," he said again. "I rent Port-A-Potties by day, and at night I go home, cook for one, and watch 'American Idol'. All of my friends are married and have kids. They don't want Uncle Delmar hanging around all the time, even though Uncle Delmar has nothing but time on his hands. Hell, my big night out is Thursday when I go bowling with my boss and his friends. And you want to hear something pathetic? I look *forward* to that all week long. It's the highlight of my week."

Gina didn't know what to say.

"Anyway, thanks for the coffee," he said. He raised the cup toward her as a goodbye and started walking toward the door.

"Delmar," she said.

He turned around. "Yeah?"

"Are you bowling this Thursday night?"

"Yeah, Waveland Bowl. 7:00."

"Do they have a place for spectators?"

"Spectators?" he asked.

She pointed to herself. Delmar would have been the worst poker player of all-time. He could barely contain the glee on his face, and Gina was thrilled to see it.

"I'd like to observe the real you in your natural habitat," she said. "You know like that Crocodile Hunter guy."

"It's pretty dangerous in there," he said, his smile overtaking his face.

"I'll bring a tranquilizer gun," she replied.

"You may need it," he said. "My teammates get a little wild sometimes."

"And Delmar..."

"Yes?"

"If I see you doing your Vin Diesel impersonation when I walk in that door, I'm walking right back out."

31

MOMENTS OF CLARITY

Reed stood at the bottom of the stairs dressed for work. He silently peered into the kitchen and watched Lucy as she mechanically moved about in her robe and slippers, making ham and eggs for him.

Reed snuck up behind his wife. "I love you," he whispered into her ear.

"I love you too," said Lucy, mostly as an involuntary reaction.

"I believe that ham frying in a pan is about the most wonderful smell I know. Right up there with its close neighbor, sizzling bacon, burning leaves in the fall, fresh flowers and whatever it is that you wash your hair with."

"Thanks, honey," said Lucy, still expressionless. "Can you please dance over to the refrigerator and grab the orange juice."

"Certainly." And he did.

Reed sat down to enjoy his breakfast, running his toast through the gooey yoke to sop up each last drop on his plate. Lucy watched him suspiciously from across the table.

"You know," Reed said, "I was thinking about that bus again."

"And what bus would that be?"

"That school bus. Senior year? The Art Institute field trip?"

"Ah, *that* school bus. Best five dollars you ever spent, as I recall."

"I had to think fast," said Reed.

"You know, to this day, when I see Amy Leahy, she still brings that up. She tells me that if she'd held out for ten, my whole life would be different now. I'm never sure whether she's taking credit or blame. But to get the record straight," said Lucy, smiling now, "I'm glad she traded seats with you."

"Did I ever tell you that I almost didn't get on that bus at all?"

"What are you talking about?"

"We were lined up to board four buses. We were all in one line. You were about ten people ahead of me. The bus monitor stopped the line just ahead of me, and told me I had to wait for the next bus. He turned away for a moment and I slipped onto your bus just as the doors were closing."

Reed picked up his orange juice glass. "Two seconds," he said.

"Two seconds what?" asked Lucy.

"That's how much time I had to make that decision, get on that bus and change my life. If I'd hesitated, I'd have missed my shot. I wasn't a rule breaker. The monitor could have pulled me off the bus."

"You're very resourceful," said Lucy with a wink. "You would have found another way to get my attention."

"I don't know," said Reed. "The prom was coming up. If I didn't move quickly, someone else would have asked you. I'd have lost my window of opportunity. And you just never know."

"You're amazing," said Lucy, picking up Reed's empty plate and bringing it to the sink.

"Really?" grinned Reed.

"That happened over thirty years ago. And this is the first time you ever told me that you snuck onto that bus."

"Like I said, I haven't really thought much about it until now."

"Reed O'Hern, you are downright diabolical."

"It worked, didn't it? The bus door was closing. The monitor was turned away. Two seconds changed everything."

"What made you bring this up now?"

"I was just thinking."

"I notice you've been doing a lot of that lately."

"Some of the most important things in our lives happen in two seconds, things that will affect us forever. You can prepare for them, you can consider what you might do in that situation. But you never know until it happens."

"Well, I'm glad you got on the bus," said Lucy.

Reed looked at his watch. He had to leave now to catch the train, but he felt compelled to say one more thing.

"Bad stuff can happen like that too." Reed looked into Lucy's eyes. "That drunk driver had about two seconds to choose between colliding head-on with that semi it was about to hit, and swerving into Will's car instead. It changed everything."

"It always comes back to that, doesn't it?" said Lucy with quiet frustration.

"It was only two seconds. But you know what else took only two seconds? That time he came home two hours late and I was ready to ground him, but instead I chose to hug him and tell him I loved him. Two seconds. The huge smile he gave us both as he looked into the stands after hitting his first home run. Two seconds. The morning when he was six and he gave me a big bear hug because he saw that I was sad when my mother died. Two seconds. We had thousands of great two second moments. We have been blessed. That's what I will remember. I refuse to have my life destroyed by two bad seconds. We need to appreciate more good moments. Life is short. And I know that's what he'd want us to do."

The last few words eked out of Reed's mouth. Lucy walked over to Reed, wrapped her arms around him and whispered in his ear. "I love you."

"I think this is one of those moments," said Reed.

"Yes, I think it is," said Lucy. "Now you'd better get to work."

On the way out the door, Reed glanced at Will's high school graduation picture hanging in the hall. Will was smiling back at him. Reed had never noticed that before.

* * *

By the time Reed arrived at the HKY building, he was completely composed. He rode the elevator in silence up to the Cap'n Slappy office suite. The pleasant buzz of conversation filled the air as Reed made his way to his back corner office.

"Good morning, Annie. How are you this morning?"

"Just fine, Reed. May I get you anything?"

"As a matter of fact, when Dick Nicholson comes in, can you please tell him I'd like to see him this morning. See if 9:30 works for him. Thanks."

"Yes sir."

Reed sat at his desk and began poring over reports. Charlie Turner stuck his head into Reed's office.

"Hey, does this still work now that you're the big cheese?"

"Come on in, Charlie. Have a seat. How's it going?"

"Good. Hey, it just dawned on me that this the first time I've ever been in this office when I wasn't getting my ass chewed out for something." Charlie sat down.

"I'll find something you've done wrong, if it will make you feel more at home," said Reed. "How's everything going out there?"

"Fine, fine."

"That doesn't sound fine."

"You can't turn around an aircraft carrier on a dime, or whatever that saying is."

"I think I know what you mean."

"Well," said Charlie, "Everyone knows that you mean well. The open door policy, the positive atmosphere; all great stuff, but I think they're afraid that you're being naïve, and that the sharks upstairs will catch wind of your human management style and put an end to it before it goes too far."

"What do you think?"

"I'm with you, boss. To quote the Elephant Man, 'I am not an animal. I am a human being'."

"Nice," said Reed. "I think to get the full effect you need to put a sack over your head."

"I'll remember that next time," said Charlie. "But it really doesn't matter what I think. What does Karen Barnett have to say?"

"I haven't met with her again since the appointment. I've just been analyzing the department reports, making some changes and recommendations and sending along my findings. So far she's been a rubber stamp, but it's still the honeymoon. I've got a meeting with her in a few days. Then we'll see."

"Did you see my report on the build outs in Columbus?"

"Yeah, thanks. It looks great. I think I'm going to recommend we go with the second option, using a smaller crew and doing one unit at a time. The loss in revenue for closing three stores at once for remodeling seems short sighted. Nice job."

"Thanks," said Charlie, getting up to leave.

"One more thing, Charlie. I'm not sure who else to ask about this. How has it been to work with Dick and his team?"

"Well," said Charlie looking out the office door to make sure no one else was within earshot. "To tell you the truth, he's keeping his team on a pretty tight leash, not allowing anyone to officially give data to other project teams without clearing it through him. And he hasn't offered any information for those cross-team efficiency papers you wanted. He wasn't very happy that Tony Cooper was in on that team award."

"OK, thanks. Stop by anytime, and I probably won't chew you out, but you never know."

"I'll keep it in mind, bossman." And he left Reed's office.

* * *

Nicholson was at the door.

"You wanted to see me?"

"Yes, Dick. Come in and have a seat."

"I hope this won't take long. I've got a lot on my plate as you know."

"Of course. Please have a seat."

Nicholson sat gingerly in the chair Charlie had occupied a few minutes earlier. He didn't move as fast as he used to.

"I'm trying to get some feedback on the new initiatives," Reed continued. "You're certainly senior on the staff. How do you think it's working?"

"I haven't had much time to devote to those initiatives. I've got a lot on my plate."

"I see," said Reed.

"Look, Reed, I just do my job. I keep my head down and follow my job description. It's been working that way for a very long time. And I will continue to deliver the information management needs to make financial decisions. I'm very good at what I do, and my team's numbers are always complete."

"I see. How about the cross-team efficiency programs?"

"I am responsible for my team. And we're doing our job," shrugged Nicholson. "I'll do what I can to help anyone else when I have the time. It's a matter of priorities with limited resources. I'm certainly not trying to be difficult. I wish you all the luck in the world. It'll be interesting to see how management responds to the 'new' purchasing department policies. In the meantime, I am at your service."

"Yes, well the current policies include sharing information for the cross-team efficiency programs."

"Got it," said Dick. "In two years, I'll be out of here anyway. Is there anything else?"

"No," said Reed. "That's all for now."

Nicholson got up without another word and left.

"Well, that went well," Reed muttered to himself.

32

CLIMBING MOUNT PAPER

Peter couldn't believe the amount of work he had. If he tried to pick up the stack of files that Buckingham had delivered to his office yesterday, he would get a hernia. But if he didn't plow through each and every file, he would never get to Milwaukee to continue his quest.

Kelly knocked on his open office door. "Is that you behind the mountain?"

He didn't respond. He just grunted. She closed the door behind her, just in case.

"Who is your favorite girl?" she asked.

He peered around the stack of files to see her smile. She walked around to his side of the mountain and gave him a peck on the cheek, before sitting on the only part of his desk that wasn't entirely consumed by paperwork.

"Why are you in such a good mood?"

"I was just in the bathroom with Lindsay McMahon," Kelly said coyly, "and she said something really exciting..."

"Ooh," Peter said, raising his eyebrows, "I think I like where this is going."

She punched him in the arm.

"Pervert."

"What?" he asked, lamely pleading ignorance.

"She said something exciting about *you*."

"Ooh," Peter said, evil grin added to the raising eyebrows. "Now I *really* like where this is going."

She punched him in the arm again. "Never mind, sicko. You don't deserve it."

Kelly walked toward the office door in a fake huff.

"Wait!" Peter said. His tone of voice was apologetic. "Wait. Don't go. What did she say?"

"I hate to disappoint you," Kelly said, turning back toward him with a pouty expression on her face, "but it wasn't anything sexual."

She was so sexy when she pouted like that. Peter pounced out of his seat, walked right up to his girlfriend, turned her around before she could reach the door knob, and gave her a long soft kiss on the lips. After a few seconds, Kelly came up for air.

"Do that again and I won't even remember what she said."

"Sorry," Peter said, still holding her by the shoulders, his face inches from hers. "Sometimes I just get carried away. So, what did she say?"

"She told me that SVE is looking to acquire Fetch!"

Peter waited for the big news.

He waited some more.

"So?" he finally replied.

"So?" Kelly said, disappointed. "What do you mean 'so'? I thought you would be beyond excited."

"I must be missing something," Peter said.

"She wants to get out of the Fetch! research," Kelly explained, still looking for the light bulb over Peter's head. "She has family coming in from out of town next week for her sister's wedding and will do just about anything to clear her schedule. And with an unexpected acquisition like this it could take weeks to do the research."

Peter was still confused. "I'd want to get out of it too," he finally said.

"Well that's too bad," Kelly said. "I just volunteered you for the job."

"You what?"

Peter walked away from her, and motioned toward his desk. "I can't start on a brand new acquisition right now. That's completely out of the question."

"She's willing to trade you," Kelly offered.

"Of course she is," Peter countered. Now he was miffed. "I'd take that trade if I were her too. Six days of work for several weeks of work. What are you doing to me?"

"Buckingham has already signed off on it," Kelly said.

That got Peter's attention. Buckingham had been treating him like a pariah since Peter returned from his "sickness".

"He has?"

"I talked to him," she said, proud of herself. "I know SVE is breathing down our necks on this, so I reminded him that you've probably done twice as much work on the SVE account as Lindsay, and that you could do the research in much less time than she could."

"And what did he say?"

"He said 'Good point'."

Peter didn't need Buckingham's kudos, but that didn't prevent him from feeling good on the unbelievably rare occasions he got them. For Buckingham that was high praise.

"He really said that?" Peter asked.

She nodded.

"Aw geez, Kel," he said.

Peter realized that Kelly was just trying to get him back into Buckingham's good graces, but dammit, under the circumstances, volunteering again was just out of the question.

"Ordinarily I would happily do this, but I just can't," he said. He was trying to sound grateful, but knew he wasn't pulling it off. "Sometimes you just have to put your foot down and say no."

"So you won't do it?"

The foot was coming down.

"No," he said. A no that was so emphatic it made Kelly wince.

"OK," she said, shaking it off. "I'll tell Buckingham and Lindsay. Don't worry, I'll come up with something."

She opened the door, and began to walk out while Peter settled back into his seat behind the mountain of work. When the door closed, Peter shook his head. He was feeling a little guilty about missing a chance to return to Buckingham's good graces, and more guilty about leaving Lindsay in a lurch, but he probably felt most guilty about hurting Kelly's feelings. He saw that wince. He hated that he had just done that to her.

"Dammit," he muttered aloud.

"I heard that," she said.

He peered around the stack of files, and she was still there. Despite his rejection of her idea, she still had a smile on her face.

"What is going on here?" he asked.

"You know that Fetch! research will require quite of bit of time spent at Fetch! headquarters, right?"

"Yeah. So?"

"You never asked me where they were located," Kelly said.

"OK, I'll bite. Where?

"Where did you say Henry's Army buddy lived?"

Her dazzling smile was extra dazzling as soon as the dense fog started to clear from Peter's overworked mind. He pounced out of his seat again, and this time the kiss was one for the record books. He actually pinned her to his closed office door as he hungrily devoured her. Kelly received it in the spirit it was intended, and though her soft moaning probably could have been a little softer, she couldn't help herself.

"Mmmm," she said when he finally disengaged the kiss.

"You really are something, you know that?" Peter said.

"You too," she said. "I've always been a sucker for a man that gets horny after hearing he's going to be shipped to Milwaukee."

33

HOPE

It had been nine years since the argument. Evelyn still blamed herself. She was the adult after all, and she should have known how fragile Sarah was. Evelyn had gone over and over it through the years.

If only….

Every night Evelyn left the front porch light on just in case. As she climbed the stairs tonight, she knew only another vigil awaited her. What else could she do? She opened the door to her apartment and flipped on the lights. The many photos of Peter made her smile. She hadn't screwed up completely.

Evelyn made her way, as she did every night, over to the small end table draped in lace and devoted to the memories of Sarah. She would be a young woman now, not the girl in these photos, with her wavy, light brown hair and her green eyes twinkling. Sarah's easy smile was frozen in time.

What would Evelyn say to her now? Just "I love you" and "please come home". She wondered if she'd even recognize Sarah's voice if she chose to call. Evelyn had made sure not to change her phone number through the years. She could afford a nicer place now, but she didn't dare move in case Sarah came looking.

She walked into the kitchen and picked the phone off its charger, walked back to the living room and sat once again in the armchair facing Sarah's photos. She had the number she wanted on speed dial.

"Detective Dunnington," a man's voice said.

"Hello, Vince. It's Evelyn Stankiewicz."

"Hi, Mrs. Stankiewicz. And how are you doing?"

"The same. I just thought I'd see if there's anything new. I hope I'm not bothering you."

"It is never a bother. How's Peter?"

"He's doing well. He's getting married, you know."

"You said you had a hunch. That's great. Pass on my congratulations to the groom. You know, our ten year high school reunion is coming up in a few weeks. Maybe I'll see him there."

"Ten years already?" said Evelyn.

"Yeah, time flies," said Vince. "So, how's everything else?"

"I guess that's why I'm calling," said Evelyn. "I checked online again. There's nothing new on the missing person sites."

"Unfortunately, the more time that passes, the less likely we'll find something."

"I just don't know what else to do. I Googled 'Sarah Stankiewicz' again and got nothing. And I haven't gotten any responses to my letter. I left it anonymous like you suggested. Maybe I should sign it."

"I don't think that's a good idea."

"What else can we do?"

"Well, as I've said before, when Sarah left, she was a minor and considered a runaway. Now that she's an adult, the law doesn't put much priority on finding her. She may just not want to be found. She wasn't kidnapped. She's not a fugitive."

Evelyn closed her eyes. She'd heard this before.

"I'll keep an eye out down here at the station. I'm a police detective and my jurisdiction ends at the city limits. But we get bulletins and there's always a chance."

"Do you need more copies of that photo?"

"I've still got it right here on my desk. We also have copies on file and online. There's not much more we can do, I'm afraid."

"How about another private detective?"

"Ron Draeger is the best I know. He spent two years and a lot of your cash and Peter's cash looking, but he came up with nothing. Frankly, I think you'd be wasting your money to hire someone else. I'm sorry."

Evelyn sat silently. She knew Vince was right.

34

BLINDSIDED AT THE ALLEY

"We're not used to playing with an audience," said Ramon.

"Excuses already?" said Oscar. "We haven't even bowled a freakin' frame."

Ramon took his ball from his bag and put it on the rail. "I'm just saying it could have an affect on my game."

"And how would we be able to tell?" asked Henry, tying his bowling shoes.

"Look," said Oscar, putting in his two cents, "I think we should try not to scare off Lolita. Who knows when Humbert Humbert here is gonna have another shot at teenage romance?"

Delmar tried to be serious for a moment. "Hey, guys, I'm begging you not to screw this up for me. I'm on thin ice already. Her name's Gina. And it would be nice if you were not complete asses in her presence."

"What would you like us to say?" asked Ramon.

"Ordinarily I would say to just be yourselves. But that's exactly what I'm afraid of," sighed Delmar.

"Why exactly did you invite her here anyway?" asked Henry. "Weren't you supposed to take her dancing?"

"Ixnay on the ancingday," whispered Oscar. "Sore subject."

"Oh, you didn't hear, Henry?" said Delmar. "Tell him, Oscar. Every woman loves to dance. Isn't that what you said? Tell Henry here how your worldly female wooing advice worked for me."

"Not good, apparently," said Oscar, shrugging his shoulders. "Although I still think it's a great date idea. Maybe Fred Astaire here just didn't have the moves. I can't be responsible for his lack of execution."

"Or maybe what worked back in the twelfth century when you were dating doesn't work here in the computer age," said Delmar.

"It couldn't have been that bad, Del," said Henry, "I mean she's coming tonight, right? So that's a good thing."

The Pin and Tonics, the top team in the league, were setting up on the next lane in preparation for their showdown with the Living Wills. With a single silent nod to Marge at the bar, Henry ordered the first round.

The teams shook hands and settled in. Delmar had been keeping one eye on the glass doors at the other end of the 40 lane building. Part of him still wasn't sure she would show up. That last encounter at the coffee shop seemed like a dream.

Then he saw her. His heart skipped a beat. Tall, dark and statuesque, by the rental shoe desk.

"OK, fellas. This is it. The eagle has landed. I'll be back in a minute."

Delmar moved quickly, nearly knocking over Marge as she delivered the beer. Gina spotted Delmar and they met halfway.

"Hi."

"Hi."

"I'm glad you made it."

"Me too."

Delmar looked into her deep brown eyes. Still too soon for that delayed first kiss.

"Well, uh, we're on 27, down this way. We're about to start the first game. I'll introduce you to the team."

The sounds of balls crashing into pins filled the air. The league occupied the entire bowling alley. Forty groups of four men each, in sets of matching shirts with names like the Gutter Snipes and the Lucky Strikes laughing, drinking and bowling.

"Ah, Delmar," Oscar called out. "There you are. I hate to interrupt you, you're up. Fire when ready."

Delmar and Gina walked down to the lane. Delmar's head was sweating again.

"Fellas, this is Gina Santelli. Gina, these are the guys. This is Oscar."

Oscar smiled and nodded politely, making sure to say nothing, the only way he could be certain that he would say nothing to embarrass Delmar.

"That's Ramon, the Hispanic guy wiping his hand on the towel."

"Hey, Delmar. I'm right here. I can hear you."

"I'm sorry. Is 'Hispanic' offensive now?"

"It's a pleasure to meet you, Gina," said Ramon. "Delmar, uh, you know the white guy right here, he's told us a lot about you."

"What has he told you?" asked Gina, smiling at the good natured banter.

Ramon went blank. He didn't expect her to actually ask. He couldn't think of a damn thing that Delmar had said.

"He said you were tall. And he was right."

Delmar interrupted. "And the guy hunched over the scorecard there is Henry."

Henry sat at the tiny table on the lane, his back to Gina, keeping score. He waved without turning to greet her.

"Have a seat wherever you like," said Delmar. "The bar maid will be around if you'd like a drink. We're running a tab. I have to go knock down some pins."

Gina sat at the farthest end of the long plastic bench and silently took in all of the energy in the room. Delmar lined up his shot. Henry got up from the table and walked over to Gina. He held out a hand to shake Gina's.

"Sorry about that. I'm Henry Stankiewicz. It's a pleasure to meet you."

Gina looked up and froze. She slowly shook Henry's hand and was glad she was sitting down. Her heart skipped a beat. Her mouth hung open for what must have been a long time. She said nothing.

"Are you OK?" asked Henry, looking down at Gina. "Can I get you something?"

Finally Gina could speak but weakly. "No thanks. I'm fine. Just a head cold coming on, I think. I get a little dizzy sometimes."

But inside, Gina was a mess. Her stomach was turning. All the blood was rushing to her head. If she had been standing, her knees would have buckled.

"All right," said Henry, "if you need something just holler."

Delmar picked up the seven pin for a spare. Henry stopped him on his way back to the bench.

"She seems like a real nice girl," whispered Henry, "but you'd better get her some water or something. I don't think she's feeling well."

Gina took a few deep breaths and tried to collect herself. Delmar sat down next to her. "I thought I had the strike there. Ah, well. Are you hungry? They have a decent grill in the back. It ain't the Ponderosa, but it's OK. I can get you a burger or something. And a drink."

"No thanks," said Gina. "But I'm gonna walk around a little bit. I just think I need a little air. Nothing to worry about. And I'll get some water at the bar."

"You want me to go with you?"

"No really. I'm fine. The team needs you, and I'm just gonna go grab a cigarette outside. I'll be back in a few minutes."

Delmar returned to the game. Ramon picked up a beautiful 5-10 split. Oscar ordered a second round.

"She seems like a sweet girl," said Oscar, looking back to where Gina had been sitting. "Hey, did she leave you again? I swear I didn't say a word to her. If she dumped you, it's not my fault."

Gina went to the ladies room and dabbed the sweat from her forehead with a paper towel. She had not been expecting this. And yet this was exactly the possibility she had been preparing for since she came back to Chicago.

Gina looked into her eyes in the mirror. It had worked, hadn't it? The years of hair straightening, the black hair dye, the tinted contact lenses. She had recognized him but he had not recognized her. She was sure of it.

Gina took a deep breath, ran her fingers through her hair, and drank a handful of water from the sink. Then she went outside for that cigarette. Leaning against a wall in the parking lot, Gina struggled to figure out how she was going to handle this? She really wanted it to work with Delmar. She couldn't just run. It would be too hard to explain.

He looked old, she thought. A lot older than he did in the pictures her mother had pressed into photo albums. In fact, if he hadn't said his name, Gina might not have made the connection at all. But it was him. Henry Stankiewicz.

Her father had returned to Chicago too.

35

PUSHING THE ENVELOPE

Lucy placed the marinating chicken on the bottom shelf of the refrigerator and returned to chopping the vegetables. She couldn't help but smile, anticipating Reed's reaction.

Friday had been Tuna Casserole Night for the last ten years. Will and Reed both loved it, it was an easy dish to prepare, and it didn't require a change to the schedule during Lent. She wouldn't make it every Friday night; there was an occasional Friday night fish fry back in the days that Artie and Laura still used to prod them to go out, and Lucy would occasionally order a pizza on nights she had to work a little late at the library, but when she'd pulled out the tuna fish can earlier today, something had clicked.

She cut the button mushrooms into thin strips and placed them in a bowl. She pulled the can opener out of the drawer and opened the bamboo shoots, rinsed them to get rid of the tinny taste, and tossed them in the bowl. The chicken was going to be a complete shock to Reed. The Moo Goo Gai Pan might require a defibrillator.

"Where did I put that ginger?"

She didn't find it immediately but she did locate the garlic. Breaking a clove off, she peeled it and began to mince it, all the while trying to remember where in the world she had left the ginger.

"Let's see here," she said. "I got home from the grocery store, brought the groceries into the kitchen, and... No, wait a second. I couldn't carry all of the bags. Did I leave one in the car?"

Lucy set aside the garlic, wiped her hands on her apron and walked toward the front door. The car was still in the driveway. She hoped there wasn't anything frozen or something that might spoil in that bag. The sun had been beating down on the car for over an hour now.

"There it is," she said, spotting it on the back seat. "I swear I'm losing my mind."

She looked inside the bag. Everything should be fine. There were a only few boxes of Triscuits, a jar of spaghetti sauce, a box of Rotini noodles, a jar of Spanish olives, and the ginger. Lucy held the ginger in her hand. It was still firm. Not a problem.

On her way back into the house she noticed that she hadn't yet brought in the mail. She brought it into the house and threw it on the little table by the door.

"I can't believe I didn't even check the mail," Lucy said, shaking her head as she returned to the kitchen with the grocery bag.

It was usually one of the highlights of her day. She normally would have already organized the mail hours ago into three piles—bills, correspondence, and junk/recycling. By this time of early evening she probably would have already filed the bills in the folders by the desk. Today was different. Everything else had to go on the back burner.

With the vegetables all ready to go, she retrieved the marinating chicken from the refrigerator, and the extra virgin olive oil from the pantry. She didn't have a wok, but Lucy knew that her big frying pan would work just fine. She turned on the front burner, and poured the olive oil in the center of the pan, shifting it from left to right to help the olive oil cover the base of the pan. After it warmed a little bit, she began throwing in the thinly sliced strips of chicken.

The sizzling was loud enough that Lucy didn't hear the door opening. Reed immediately smelled the Asian aroma drifting from the kitchen. He walked back out the front door and looked up at the address. Yep, he had the right house.

"I'm home," he screamed from the front door, "I think."

He couldn't believe the mail was in a disorganized pile on the table by the door.

"You're early," she yelled back.

"I took the earlier train," he said.

He walked into the kitchen with a huge smile on his face. "What on earth is going on in here? Have you been drinking?"

"Not yet, but I got a nice bottle of wine."

He kissed the back of her neck as she tossed the vegetables and a little more sauce into the stir fry.

"What are you making?"

"Moo Goo Gai Pan," she said.

Reed turned his wife toward him and looked in her eyes. There she was. The real Lucy.

"I *love* Moo Goo Gai Pan," he reminded her.

"I know," she said. "Remember that restaurant?"

"Of course. How could I forget?"

"Make yourself comfortable," Lucy said, "this will be done before you know it."

Reed kissed her on the lips, before leaving the room to change. Ever since he instituted the new dress code at work, it didn't take nearly as long to get ready for dinner. While he was upstairs hanging up his sport coat, throwing his shoes into the back of the closet, and putting on his slippers, Lucy was finishing up the dish and setting the table.

On his way back into the kitchen, Reed picked up the pile of mail and brought it to the table with him. It had been ages since he'd gotten first crack at the mail.

"You know what I remember most about that restaurant?" Lucy said, her back to Reed.

"The waiter with the Dracula haircut?" Reed guessed.

Lucy laughed. "No, actually I forgot all about him. I was thinking about that night we got caught in the rainstorm after the play. Remember that?"

"How could I forget?"

"Do you remember what you said to me that night?" Lucy asked. She turned around and looked at her husband.

He smiled and nodded. "I remember. It was the first time I had gotten up the nerve to say it. I also remember that after I told you that I loved you, you didn't say a word."

"I thought I was going to pass out or cry or say something stupid, so I said nothing."

"It seemed like forever."

"It was only two seconds," she said.

Reed smiled at his wife and she smiled back. *Yes, it was. Two seconds.*

Lucy handed Reed the bottle opener. "Can you open the wine?"

"Sure thing," Reed said. He jammed the corkscrew into the wine bottle and started to twist.

"I went to the grocery store today," Lucy said while stirring, "and I picked you up some San Pellegrino. It's in the fridge. It will go nicely with dinner if you want some."

"Thanks," Reed said. "Sounds good."

He pulled out the cork with a slight pop, and poured a little bit of chardonnay into Lucy's glass. While Lucy was putting the rice and the Moo Goo Gai Pan into serving bowls, Reed went through the mail. A bank statement, the cable bill, a flier for tuck pointing, an envelope of coupons from Super Savers, and... what the heck? It looked like a wedding invitation of some kind, but Reed didn't recognize the return address or the name. He opened it up and read the calligraphy.

Oh no.

Lucy arrived at the table with a bowl in each hand. She knew something was wrong immediately.

"You look like you just got punched in the stomach," she said.

Reed couldn't even look at her.

"What is it?" she said. Now she was getting worried.

Reed knew he wouldn't be able to hide it, but he also knew that he might not be able to say the words out loud. He had to be strong, he had to be strong, he had to be strong. He forced a smile on his face. "It's a wedding invitation," he finally said.

"Who's getting married?" she asked. She was still holding the bowls in her hands but the smile that had been on her face just minutes ago was long gone.

"I didn't recognize the name at first," Reed said. "It's from the bride's family."

"And the groom is?"

He looked in her eyes. He wished to God he didn't have to say it. "Johnny Flannery." Reed had said the name of Will's best friend thousands of times, but not in eight years.

"Johnny's getting married?" Lucy's eyes were already welling up, just like Reed's. "Isn't he a little young?"

"He's 26 now," Reed reminded her. He could barely get the words out.

Lucy put the bowls down on the table, and ran upstairs. Reed didn't call after her.

There was nothing to say.

36

YOU CAN'T GO HOME AGAIN

"How'd you choose this spot?"

"I don't know," said Henry. "It's a beautiful day. Seems like a shame to have lunch in some dark restaurant. Here, I got you a chicken breast sandwich, dry. And a Diet Coke."

Peter sat down on the ledge. Henry was right. It was a gorgeous spring day. Peter couldn't remember the last time he'd eaten lunch in Grant Park, even though it was just a few blocks from MacArthur Harrison Hyde.

"Thanks for buying," said Peter, biting into his sandwich.

"Consider it your legal fee. I signed those papers and I've brought copies for you. Thanks for doing that."

Peter looked closely at Henry. He couldn't decide if Henry looked weaker, or if it was just the sun at this angle.

"I'm glad you got these back to me," said Peter. "I'll be up in Milwaukee working with a client for a week or two, so I won't be around. I leave tomorrow."

Henry pulled out a greasy Reuben and a large Coke from the same bag and set them beside him, using the flattened paper bag as a place mat. He took in a deep breath of fresh air and admired the city skyline to the west.

"Nice town, Milwaukee. I used to have a friend up there. Don't know whatever happened to him," mused Henry.

"You've got my cell number if you need anything while I'm gone."

Henry nodded. "Yeah, I've got your number."

Office workers were scattered among the benches and cement landings along the park's walkways. Some even ventured out into the grass, to read or to nap. Henry was busy taking it all in.

"So, Henry, is there anything else I should know?"

"About what?" asked Henry, between bites. He had a dollop of thousand island dressing dripping down his chin.

"Oh, I don't know. Anything. You've got the living will now. How about a regular will? I feel strange asking you, but have you decided what to do with your stuff?"

"I don't have any stuff."

"Are you sure?"

"Nothing of any value. Just some clothes, tools, the truck. That's about it. I've got about enough in the bank to put me in the ground. I'm sorry. I really wish that I had something to leave you and your sister."

Henry watched a stunning blonde walk toward them in a short skirt and a very tight top, her hips swaying in the mild breeze off the lake. And then he watched her walk away. And then he noticed Peter deliberately looking away.

"She wants you to look," said Henry. "She worked very hard at the gym and the hair salon and the dress shop to achieve that look. The least you can do is appreciate her discipline and commitment."

"There are women out there who would find such gawking to be sexist."

"Yeah, well she ain't one of 'em. I can tell you that. And you know, just because I'm on a diet doesn't mean I can't look at the menu. I'm married, I'm not dead."

"No, not yet," said Peter. "Nice segue though. Where were we? Oh yeah. So you don't have anything of sentimental value, pictures, keepsakes, that you're keeping hidden away somewhere?"

"I did have some stuff I was holding onto. Some memories from when you and your sister were small. But I lost it somewhere along the way, like most everything else I ever had. Some people spend their whole lives collecting stuff. I could never hang on to anything."

A young couple walked by hand in hand. A skateboarder maneuvered down the sidewalk, weaving between the various pedestrians.

"Well, you should probably create a simple will anyway, something that just says that there isn't much, and how you want those assets distributed. It's easy and it will take care of some hassles after you're gone. No one wants three wives showing up with claims against your estate."

"OK, write me up one of those and I'll fill in the blanks. I imagine I'll owe you another sandwich. Hey, you've already doubled your fee. Well done."

"Henry, I've been meaning to ask you something else." Peter paused. "Do you have any idea how you got this cancer?"

"What kind of a question is that? How does anybody get cancer? It just happens."

"I mean, uh," and Peter was walking a fine line here. He didn't want to tip his hand. "Well, do you have any other health problems that could have made you more susceptible, anything that weakened your system?"

Henry looked into Peter's eyes to see if Peter knew. But Peter was a good poker player and gave away nothing.

"See, I was just thinking that sometimes these things are genetic and I want to know if there's anything that I should be concerned about for myself."

"Nothing that I know of. It just happened." It was clear Henry didn't want to go any further down that road.

"One more thing. I know you wanted me to keep this all to myself. Are you sure that there's no one I should tell about your situation?"

"Hey, I really don't want anybody to make a fuss. That's what would happen if your mother found out. I know there are some army buddies who would probably want to know, but they've been to too many funerals already. So how about we just keep this between us. OK?"

The sandwiches were finished. Henry slurped down the last of his Coke. Peter got up from the ledge and brushed a few crumbs off of his suit. Henry stayed seated.

"I do wish your sister was here."

"Yeah," said Peter. "Me too."

"What exactly happened there? I've only heard your mother's side of the story."

"Are you sure you wanna go there?"

"I'm dying. Just tell me what you know."

Peter looked at his watch and sat back down. He had the time. Did he have the guts? He closed his eyes for a moment as he began.

"It always goes back to that last night. I can't even remember what I did to make you so mad." Peter caught himself. He needed to stay strong and get this out.

"You didn't do anything, son," muttered Henry, his head down.

"I'm beginning to understand that now. But I was eleven. And every day since, I've had this reminder of that night," said Peter, pointing to the long scar on his chin. "It was my fault you left, my fault that the family split apart." Peter's voice was strained and hurt. "This was the last thing you gave me, and then you were gone by morning."

Henry reached out an arm to put on Peter's shoulder and Peter pushed it away.

Henry cleared his throat. "Leaving that house, that home, was the hardest thing I ever did. You gotta believe me."

"You could have gotten help," pleaded Peter. "They have resources and programs and therapy for the psychological hell you went through. But you just left. You were too proud to admit you had a problem you couldn't handle."

"I didn't understand it. I still don't," said Henry, shaking a little bit remembering his episode the other night. "But you're absolutely right. Leaving was the coward's way out. I was afraid they might put me away, or medicate me or do some head shrink mumbo jumbo on me. But I was also afraid that if I stayed, I might hurt you again, or your sister or your mother. I couldn't live with that. So I left."

Peter hopped from the ledge and slowly paced in front of his father. Peter had dreamed of this day, how he'd finally get up the nerve and tear Henry a new one, make him know every bit of pain he'd put the family through, and leave him a blithering, pathetic wreck. But now, instead, he saw a damaged, dying man. Peter stopped pacing, looked Henry straight in the eye and measured his words.

"You took the lazy way out, the easy way. Look what you've done. You left me thinking it was my fault. Mom tried to tell me different, but this scar was my constant reminder. You left Mom to raise us herself. And she couldn't handle it." Peter kept going. "And Sarah, well, I hold you responsible for that too."

Henry bowed his head, knowing he deserved every bit of it.

"Little Sarah," he whispered.

"Yeah," said Peter, "So back to Sarah. Those first years without you were pretty intense. Mom had to get a job. She was on edge a lot more often."

Henry dared to interrupt quietly. "Your mother seems to have done OK."

"It took a long time. She went back to school. She fought hard for everything she has. She's a different woman now, a lot stronger because she had to be. It doesn't justify walking out on us."

Peter looked around to make sure he wasn't speaking too loudly. "I did OK," he continued. "It was tough to see the other fathers watching their sons at our baseball games and encouraging them. I usually came to the games by myself. Mom would be there when she could, but she didn't understand the game. And anyway it's different to have your dad there, it just is. I looked up to you. I was eleven. You could do no wrong. You were my hero, and then you were gone. If you had died, that would have been one thing, but you just left. You just walked away."

"Son," Henry struggled for the words. "I am so sorry, but…"

"Don't interrupt me, Henry. I'm on a roll and I may never have the chance to explain this again."

Henry's eyes were tearing up. He nodded his head and continued to listen.

"I made it through. I focused on my schoolwork. I became more determined than ever to prove myself, to show that I could do everything for myself and that I didn't need anyone. My motivation was anger, but it worked."

Peter paused and his voice softened.

"It didn't work so well for Sarah. Mom always seemed to be harder on her, maybe because she was a girl. The rules were always tougher for Sarah. As she became a teenager, she started to rebel. First it was little things, like smoking, and not doing her homework. Then she was cutting classes. She started hanging around with a bad crowd at school and staying out 'til all hours. Her grades were awful. Mom didn't know what to do. Mom even set me up as an example, saying 'Peter never did that. Peter always gets good grades'. That made Sarah isolate herself from me too. I became the enemy.

"The final straw was when Sarah started seeing an older guy. She was about fifteen or sixteen because I was starting college. So it was just Mom and Sarah at home. Mom of course didn't like this guy, who was probably about 20. Mom said she'd throw Sarah out of the house if she continued to see him. Well, that was exactly what Sarah wanted to hear. When I came home from school one weekend, she was gone. Mom blamed herself. But I knew better. It was your fault, Henry. I've had a lot of time to think about it. Sarah must have seen that older guy as a substitute for you, even if she never realized it. You left a path of destruction in your wake. Some of us survived and some of us didn't. And you can't get it back."

Henry waited a moment to be sure that Peter was finished.

"Do you have any idea where she is now?" asked Henry quietly.

"No. A few of her friends said she had left town, that she and this 'Steve' had headed out to California. We let the police know. But they never found her. That's the reason Mom still lives in that old apartment. She could afford to buy a nicer place, but she keeps thinking that Sarah will come back. And she wants to be there when she does. It hurts Mom to even talk about it. She loves Sarah, but they left on such bad terms. It's been nine years since Sarah left and the pain is just as sharp today."

They were silent for a long time.

"I know that wasn't easy to say."

Peter took a moment to collect himself. "It had to be said."

Henry stared straight ahead, avoiding eye contact with his son. He didn't say a word.

Peter looked at his watch. "I gotta get back."

"Yeah."

Peter stood up and his face was still flush. He brushed the crumbs from his pants. Henry stood and faced him.

"I'll get the will stuff to you. I can mail it from Milwaukee."

"OK, yeah."

Now Peter saw how weak Henry looked, or maybe it was the effect of the conversation.

"Peter…" Henry began.

"I know," Peter interrupted. "You're sorry. I know."

"Yeah."

No hug. No embrace.

Just a quiet nod from Peter.

37

ANTICIPATION

Gina was feeling clunky and big and plain as she got ready for her date. She couldn't stand what was looking back at her in the mirror. She was taller than Delmar, might have even outweighed him by a pound or two, and that scowl on her face had been her constant companion for nearly five years. It made her look bitchy. Luckily Emily got rid of it with one comment before she left for her date.

"You look smokin' hot, Mom," she said.

* * *

As Gina walked from the bus stop to Delmar's apartment in Lincoln Square, she admired her reflection in the storefront windows. Her lacy brown top showed just the right amount of skin in her ample cleavage area, and matched the color of her eyes. Well, at least the color of her contacts. Her pants even managed to accentuate her curves without making her self conscious of her hips. Emily was right. When she took the time to fix herself up a bit, she *was* smokin' hot.

She pressed the button next to Delmar's name in the vestibule.

"Hello," came the voice through the tiny little speaker.

"It's me," she said.

The buzzer sounded, opening the door to the stairway. Gina made her way up the two flights of stairs to Delmar's third floor apartment. The stairway was well-lit, and carpeted with a luxurious Persian-style rug. Gina was officially jealous. Libby should have to see what a real stairwell looked like.

Gina's insecurities bubbled up to the surface again before she knocked on the door. She shook them off. She heard Emily say it again: "You look smokin' hot, Mom."

She knocked.

Delmar swung the door open immediately.

"Wow," he said, scanning her from head to toe.

"Oh, this old thing," Gina said, mimicking Violet from 'It's a Wonderful Life'. "I only wear it when I don't care how I look."

"Wow," Delmar said again.

"You already said that," Gina said. Delmar's reaction gave her another jolt of confidence. "Are you going to let me in, or do I have to stand in the hallway?"

"Oh, sorry," Delmar said. He motioned her in with his hand.

She smelled something wonderful as soon she entered the apartment. "What is that incredible smell?"

"That's dinner," he said. "It will be ready in about ten minutes. Can I get you a glass of wine or something while I finish up in the kitchen?"

"That would be lovely," she said.

Delmar scurried down the long narrow hall toward the kitchen, leaving Gina in the living room. She snickered to herself as she looked around. This place was obviously a guy's apartment. There wasn't even a hint of a female presence. The centerpiece of the room was the black leather couch. It was bookended by matching black leather La-Z-Boys. All of them faced the entertainment center on the opposing wall.

The entertainment center looked like it occupied the bulk of Delmar's time at home. The wide screen television must have been a 48 incher. On the shelf beneath the TV stood a 1990s component stereo system; receiver, cassette deck, VCR/DVD player, and a six-disc CD player. The speakers on either side of the entertainment center were three feet tall, and each speaker was flanked by a five foot tall CD rack. Delmar had a heck of a music collection.

"Mind if I put on some music?" she called toward the kitchen. Delmar cringed a little as he pulled the cork out of the bottle. Any hope he had of pretending he was cool was about to die for good. There was nothing even remotely contemporary in those CD racks.

"Sure," he screamed from the kitchen. "But you may not be crazy about my taste in music."

She smiled as she checked out his collection. Was there anyone else in the world that had the entire Barry White catalog? She pulled out a CD called "I've Got So Much to Give." It only had five songs, and the shortest one was almost six minutes long. She was still looking at it when Delmar returned holding two glasses of shimmering red wine.

"This is make out music, isn't it?" she asked.

Delmar blushed.

"Sadly, I listen to it for the keyboard work," he said.

Gina laughed, and took the glass of wine from her gracious host. She took a sip.

"Mmm, this is good. Is it Merlot?"

"Shiraz," he said.

Now Gina blushed.

"I don't know anything about wine," she admitted.

"I don't either," Delmar said.

They each drank another sip. Gina could tell that Delmar was afraid of making eye contact with her, and that was absolutely adorable.

"Need any help in the kitchen?" she asked.

"You can help with the salad if you want," Delmar said.

"I think I can handle that," she said.

On the way to the kitchen, Gina noticed the framed photograph of The Living Wills team wearing their bowling shirts—Delmar, Oscar, Ramon and Henry. She paused to take a look at it. Henry looked a little heavier in the picture than he had looked the other night.

"When was this picture of your bowling team taken?" Gina asked.

"Last year," Delmar yelled from the kitchen.

"Henry's lost weight," Gina said.

"I guess," Delmar said.

Gina was still in shock after seeing her father at the bowling alley, but she could tell right away that Henry didn't think he was talking to his daughter during their brief conversation. No, Sarah wasn't even there. He was talking to Gina. And Gina had a million questions.

"So how did you meet those guys?" she asked Delmar when she entered the kitchen.

"Oscar is my boss," Delmar said, his back still to Gina. He was busy stirring. "Henry is his best friend from high school. They reconnected after Henry moved back to Chicago a few years ago. And Ramon works with Henry."

"Where do those guys work?" she asked.

"A parking garage."

"They seem like real nice guys. That Henry is real character."

Delmar turned around a little to look at Gina. "Easy now. He's married."

Gina wondered if her mom knew that Henry had remarried. Who knows? Maybe she was remarried too. It was possible. It had been nine years. Apparently the world hadn't stop moving just because Gina had decided to get off.

"Don't worry, I'm not interested," Gina assured him. "He's old enough to be..."

She stopped herself. Better change the subject.

"What is that wonderful smell?" she asked.

"Turkey gumbo," he answered. "I usually only cook for one, so I hope you don't mind if I take advantage of a dinner guest to make a whole pot of gumbo. This way I can freeze the leftovers in individual portions for dinner next week. You can take some home with you if you like it."

"I'm sure I will."

Delmar stirred the gumbo some more. Gina giggled to herself when she realized she was actually checking out Delmar's caboose while he was stirring. She resisted the temptation to pinch it. Instead she stood next to him and looked at his creation. It had a beautiful light brown color, and the turkey, sausage, onions, and okra swirled up and down and around with each stir of the wooden spoon.

"Where did you learn how to make gumbo?" Gina asked.

"My mom," Delmar said. "She grew up in Louisiana." He blew on the spoon and tasted the gumbo to make sure it tasted right. "Yeah, that's good. Not as good as Mom's, but I think you'll like it."

"Does your mom live nearby?" Gina asked.

Delmar shook his head. "Lost Mom about five years ago."

Gina stopped chopping the cucumbers for a moment, put down the knife, and put her hand on Delmar's arm. She did it with tenderness, but she felt a little spark of electricity when she touched his skin.

"I'm sorry," she said.

"Dad's been gone for twenty years," he said, extending his arm for her touch again. Gina smiled at his approach. This guy was a dorky charmer. She touched him just the way she did a few moments earlier, but this time she looked deep into his eyes. Delmar flinched, but didn't avert his gaze. He put his wooden spoon on the counter, cupped her cheeks, leaned toward her, and paused for just a moment.

"I've been dreaming about doing this since the first time I saw you."

His kiss was soft and sensuous. Gina closed her eyes and lost herself in the moment. When Delmar finally disengaged, and pulled back to look at her again, he couldn't help himself. He kissed her forehead too. She giggled that he had go on his tiptoes to do it, but there was no doubt this man's tenderness was genuine.

"Whatever you were dreaming," she said, fanning her face with her hands, "keep dreaming it, because that was a hell of a kiss."

Delmar smiled.

She licked her lips. "And the gumbo really *is* delicious," she joked.

Delmar blushed. "Well good, let me put some in a bowl for you, because dinner is ready."

"May I use your restroom first?" she asked.

"Sure, it's the second door on the right."

"Thanks."

Gina touched his arm again and smiled at him on her way out of the kitchen. She was still smiling when she saw her reflection in the bathroom mirror a few moments later. That was the goofiest smile she had ever seen on her face. There was no doubt about it; the dorky charmer was sweeping her off her feet.

Once she regained her bearings, Gina looked around the bathroom. She had been in a man's apartment before, but the bathroom test was the one test that no man had ever passed. Men had a whole different definition of clean when it came to bathrooms. Delmar's bathroom, on the other hand, had shiny chrome faucets, a spotless toilet, an uncluttered vanity with only one jar of liquid soap on the counter, and a floor that looked like it had been mopped. Mopped! She peeked inside the shower curtain.

"I'll be damned," she said. There wasn't even hair in the bathtub. Of course, Delmar wasn't exactly blessed in the hair department, but still, what man didn't have hair in his bathtub?

As long as she was in the bathroom, Gina figured she might as well check out the medicine cabinet. She tried not to laugh when she opened it; Rogaine, Propecia, a spray can named Good Looking Hair, a Hair Growing Laser Comb, Dead Sea Mud, Hair Thickening Shampoo, and a jar of Emu Oil that claimed if it's "topically applied, it can stimulate melanogenesis in the skin and hair growth".

"That's gonna have to go, my friend," she said. But heck, if that was the worst she could find in his bathroom, this guy was a keeper. Gina flushed the toilet, and exited the bathroom.

"I'm in the living room," Delmar called.

As she walked in his direction she noticed that there were two bedrooms in this apartment. Gina had never lived in an apartment with an extra bedroom, but it seemed like an extravagance she could get used to very easily. Imagine if Emily had her own room?

Stop it, stop it, stop it! It's way too early to start thinking about things like that.

Delmar had set up dinner on the coffee table in front of the couch.

"Sorry about having to sit on the floor," he said. "I don't have a dining room table. My ex-wife took my old one to Vermont with her. I've been meaning to get another one, but I just haven't got around to it."

"That's fine," she said. She sat cross-legged across the table from him. The coffee table was actually quite beautiful. It looked like it was made out of black granite.

"Before we eat," he said, holding the stereo remote in his hand, "Do you mind if I play some music?"

"Barry White?" she asked.

"Even better."

He pressed the start button on the remote and the song began. It was a country and western song. She hoped that her disappointment didn't show. Gina absolutely hated country music. But when the lyrics began, she recognized the singer's deep baritone voice. He wasn't really singing. He was talking over the music. His words were clear as day; perfectly enunciated.

"He lay face down on the desert sand, clutching a six gun in his hand, shot from behind I thought he was dead, for under his heart was an ounce of lead, but a spark still burned so I used my knife, and late that night I saved the life, of Ringo."

"What in the world is this?" she asked. "Is that...

Delmar nodded. "Lorne Greene."

"He recorded a song?"

"This was a number one hit in 1964."

"Shhhh," she said. "I want to hear the words."

"I nursed him 'til the danger passed, the days went by he mended fast, and then from dawn 'til setting sun, he practiced with that deadly gun, and hour after hour I watched in awe, no human being could match the draw, of Ringo."

"Ha!" Gina squealed. "This is great. Emily would absolutely love this."

"Emily?" Delmar asked.

It was the moment of truth. If Delmar could be himself, she could too, right? Maybe it was time to spill it--although, she'd thought Sean wouldn't mind either. And look what happened with that jerk. Emily was probably right. It's too soon. Next date. Next date she'll definitely tell him. Especially if it goes this well.

"The landlady's daughter," she answered. "The one that watches 'Bonanza'."

Delmar nodded. "That's what I thought. The one I saw when I came to pick you up that night."

"She's the best," Gina said.

"She seems like a sweetheart," Delmar said. He looked like he really meant it too. Yup, next time she would definitely tell him.

38

A DICK MOVE

Dick Nicholson pretended to check the e-mail on his Blackberry for the fifteenth time. His cafeteria tray was littered with remnants of a corned beef sandwich he had eaten thirty minutes earlier, an empty bag of chips, and a barely touched fountain-Coke in a white Styrofoam cup. He had stopped drinking the Coke after two sips—the syrup to water ratio was completely off—and it made him sick.

On a normal day Nicholson would have gone back to the cashier and demanded his eighty nine cents back, but today he had bigger fish to fry. Today he was stalking corporate VP Karen Barnett again, just as he had done the day before, and the day before that. It seemed like Barnett was Ms. Popularity; always surrounded by co-workers and friends in the building's cafeteria. That's OK; Nicholson knew that patience was a virtue. He only needed a minute or two alone with her. In order for this plan to work, it had to be totally casual.

Barnett and her tablemates took their trays to the conveyer belt together. Once again it looked like Nicholson had endured the horrible cafeteria food for no reason at all. There was no way he was going to get near her with the boss's friends and colleagues hogging her time like that. But then he heard a sound that was music to his ears.

Barnett's cell phone rang. The VP pulled it out of her suit jacket pocket to see who was calling.

"I've got to take this one," she said to the tablemates. "Go ahead without me. I don't want to lose this call in the elevator."

When Nicholson saw what was happening, he knew it was go-time. He slowly meandered over to the conveyer belt, and casually placed his tray on the belt just steps away from Barnett. Barnett had her phone on one ear, and a finger in the other ear to drown out the sounds of the cafeteria. She was concentrating mightily on the conversation.

"Venezuela?" she said into the phone. "That's ridiculous. The beef at Custer's Last Burger is as American as Miley Cyrus. Yes, you can quote me on that. I'll double check with our purchasing director at Custer's Last Burger, but if he made a move like that it would have gone directly against our corporate orders. HKY is an all-American corporation."

When Nicholson saw that the conversation was going to last a little while longer, he slowly made his way to the elevator banks. Every ten or fifteen steps he casually looked back toward Barnett to see if she was still on the phone.

The elevator arrived and a dozen people walked into the open car. One of the women held the door for Nicholson, who was lamely pretending to tie his shoes.

"I'll get the next one," he said.

The doors closed. Another crowd formed, another elevator arrived, and Nicholson suddenly had another shoe-tying emergency.

"I'll get the next one," he said.

The doors closed again.

Finally Karen Barnett came strolling up to elevator banks. The phone was back in her pocket, but she looked a little distracted. Nicholson had to make a judgment on the spot. What was more potentially difficult? Waiting for an even more perfect casual moment alone like this, when the Purchasing VP of HKY might be in a better frame of mind, or cutting through the distraction first, and then unloading? Each approach seemed less than ideal. It had already taken three days for this opportunity. Another one might never happen. But if he was too obvious cutting through the distraction, it might tip off Barnett to his premeditation.

Nicholson looked toward the cafeteria. Nobody else was approaching. This was going to have to be the moment. Imperfect or not, it was time to leap.

"Karen?" Nicholson said.

Her head jerked as if being snapped out of a trance.

"Yes?"

Nicholson extended his hand. "Dick Nicholson. Purchasing at Cap'n Slappy's."

"Oh," she said, forced smile emerging. "Yes, right. Sorry about that. How are you, Dick?"

"Not bad, thanks for asking," he said.

Nicholson held his breath waiting for the next question. It was the key question to this entire plan. If it didn't come, he was prepared to abort.

"How are things going at Cap'n Slappy's these days?" Barnett asked.

There it was; the most natural small talk question of all time. Nicholson had to fight a smile.

"As well as can be expected," he said. "Reed is really trying hard. His wheels are moving all the time. It's only a matter of time before that translates into some sort of success. I'm sure corporate understands."

That statement hung in the air for a few moments. Not the type of reaction Nicholson anticipated, but at least he fired a first shot. If he was willing to bide his time and create another elevator meeting within a week or two, the next time the question may not be small talk. It might even lead to a requested meeting—which Nicholson could in all good conscience claim was not his idea, and then—

"Understand what?" she finally asked.

"Oh," Nicholson said casually. "I just mean that if the numbers aren't quite what they were under Anderson, you'll understand that it might take a new guy like Reed a little while to get his sea legs. Right?"

"Well I don't know about that," Barnett said.

Nicholson was ready for this. He looked horrified.

"Oh please don't take that as criticism of Reed," he said. "I didn't mean that at all. I probably would have kept things the way they were because I've always been one of those 'if it ain't broke, don't fix it,' kind of guys, but I have a lot of respect for some of the changes he's making in the office. You know what I mean? You've got to break it down, before you can build it up again. That's why Reed was such a good choice for the top purchasing job at Cap'n Slappy's. He's totally changing the way we do things, and I'll tell you what—if these new ideas work, within a year or two we could be sending you reports that will knock your socks off."

The elevator arrived, and Nicholson walked right into the empty car. Barnett followed him in, a perplexed expression on her face. Nicholson pressed 17. Barnett pressed 19. The doors closed.

"When you say a year or two..."

"Tops," Nicholson said.

"What about this year?" Barnett asked.

"Well, I can only speak for my team," Nicholson said. "He's been pulling some of my guys off their usual assignments to help with other teams, so my numbers would have been off a bit, but I put in quite a bit of overtime to make sure that didn't happen. I'm sure the other managers were doing the same thing."

Nicholson looked at the climbing numbers on the elevator wall. He had no more than a few seconds left before the elevator stopped at 17.

"Except..." he said, and let it hang there.

"Except what?" Barnett demanded.

"Oh it's nothing," Nicholson said. Slow down, elevator, slow down. Just a few more seconds were needed.

"Except what?" Barnett repeated.

Nicholson lowered his voice. He did his absolute best to squeeze imaginary empathy out of his mouth.

"I was just going to say, except most of those guys have little kids at home," he said. "And one of Reed's first announcements was that family comes first. Most of those other guys can't stay late like I can because they've got Cub Scout meetings and parent-teacher conferences and things like that. But I'm sure they've also figured out ways to get their numbers back to where they were. If not, they'll be darn close. If not this year, then next year for sure."

The elevator dinged. The door opened.

"Have a great day," he said. Nicholson exited without turning back to see the expression on Barnett's face. He didn't need to see it.

The door closed behind him.

Nicholson finally allowed himself to smile. He could see Reed across the room, standing next to Annie's desk, probably chatting the day away. Nicholson felt a surge of adrenaline.

"Don't crap in my pool, pal."

39

THE GIRL FROM IPANEMA

Delmar had a bounce in his step. He couldn't believe that Gina was falling for him, but there was no doubt about it. When she had come up for air after that first kiss and had that look in her eyes, he thought it might have just been the surprise of the moment. But when she had the same look after the second kiss. And the third. And the fourth...

Hell, this wasn't a bounce in his step. It was a leap.

Delmar didn't like to compare Gina to his ex-wife, but it was inevitable. Gina was the first woman he had been with since the divorce. It was only natural. As he bounced from sales call to sales call this morning, he thought about where it had all gone wrong with Lydia. What could he do to make sure he didn't make the same mistakes with Gina?

Lydia had always complained he didn't let her know the real Delmar, but there was a good reason for that. Lydia was always so serious, and she got more and more serious after they got married. She was always examining her inner self, looking for the answers to the big questions. Not only did Delmar have to fake an interest in the big questions, he wasn't allowed to bring up the little questions. Anytime Delmar began pontificating about the relative merits of Lenny versus Squiggy, she told him to stop joking around. He wasn't joking around. That's who he was.

And unlike Lydia, Gina actually seemed to get that.

Gina didn't expect him to read Deepak Chopra. She let him talk about "Bonanza". She didn't expect him to listen to Bjork. She let him spin his K-Tel's Super Hits of the 1970s.

Gina even told him to stop worrying about going bald. That wasn't something he ever expected to hear from a woman. Delmar had seen those glances to his balding scalp when he spoke to other women over the years, including Lydia. Weren't all women repulsed by that? How was it that Gina didn't seem to mind?

All those thoughts were swirling in his head as he sat in his car outside the coffee shop. There were a few more customers than he'd anticipated when he'd pictured this moment, but that wasn't going to stop him. The real Delmar was in the house, and the real Delmar was not going to be restrained or contained. *Buckle up, sister, it's show time.*

He opened the top of the boom box, made sure the correct karaoke CD was in there, and shut it again. Delmar grabbed the boom box by the handle, and exited the car. There was no turning back now.

When he entered the store, Gina was sporting her sarcastic coffee shop game face. She grinned ever so slightly when she saw him, and waved almost imperceptibly as he walked toward the back of the line. That grin and wave gave him the last bit of courage he needed. Delmar placed the boom box on the ground, and cleared his throat.

"Ladies and gentlemen," he said. "May I have your attention?"

Everyone turned to look at him.

"Would you all mind lining up to the left there? I need a little room here to form a dance floor."

Nobody moved.

"I need exactly three minutes and two seconds. If you move over there, I'll pay for all of your coffee."

That got their attention. The five customers formed a line away from the action, opening up a section of the floor for Delmar.

"I'll also need a dance partner," he said. He looked toward Gina who was now smiling broadly. "Miss, would you mind?"

"Delmar what are you doing?" she asked.

"Please," he said, gesturing toward the open space. "The dance floor awaits you."

"I'm working here," she said. "I'll get in trouble."

Kathy was standing behind the counter next to Gina. She elbowed Gina in the ribs. "It's OK by me," Kathy said. "I'm the manager on duty."

"Thanks a lot," said Gina sarcastically. The crimson was beginning to form in her cheeks. All eyes were on her. She wasn't accustomed to that kind of attention.

"Do you know how to Bossa Nova?" Delmar asked as she reluctantly joined him to a smattering of applause from the customers. She shook her head.

"Follow my lead," he said. "Back straight, knees bent, hips swaying, and eyes locked on mine."

He walked over to the boom box and pressed play. "The Girl from Ipanema" began. Over the opening notes of the song, Delmar extended his hand, and Gina grudgingly clasped it. When it came time for the words to begin, it was Delmar who sang them as he danced with her. His booming voice was on-key, delivered in the style, if not with the talent, of Robert Goulet.

"Tall and tan and young and lovely, the girl whose name is Gina goes walking, and when she passes, this guy she passes, says Aaaaah."

Gina was giggling now. "Oh my God."

"When she dances, she's like her coffee, robust and sassy, so I say softly, the only word that describes this Goddess is Oooh."

Gina was smiling despite herself. "You are such a dork."

Delmar didn't respond. The song wouldn't allow it.

"Oh, how I want her so badly, How can I tell her I love her, Yes, I would give my heart gladly, Sometimes you must take a chance, just show up and ask her to dance."

Delmar dipped her, pulled her back up, and stared into her eyes. Gina was flushed. He swayed softly as he sang the last verse before the bridge.

"Tall and tan and young and lovely, the girl whose name is Gina goes walking, and when she passes, this guy she passes, says Aaaah."

As the Stan Getz saxophone bridge kicked in, Delmar did too, dancing ever more intensely across the tiled floor. Gina was laughing so hard she struggled to keep up with him, but she did as she had been told. Back straight, knees bent, hips swaying, and eyes locked deeply on his. If she had looked at the customers, she would have noticed they were forming a circle around them to get a better look. All of them were smiling as much as she was. So was Kathy behind the counter. Even Jose stopped cleaning the tables to witness the spectacle.

Delmar spun her around, and pulled her back to him. Now they were dancing cheek to cheek.

"Oh how I want her so badly, How can I tell her I love her, Yes, I would give me heart gladly, Sometimes you must take a chance, just show up and ask her to dance."

One more spin and back to Bossa Nova positions for the last verse of the song.

"Tall and tan and young and lovely, the girl whose name is Gina goes walking, and when she walks by, I knows that this one's for me. Yes, this one's for me. Yes, Gina's for me."

The song ended, and Delmar pulled Gina in for a kiss. She lifted her back leg up as he kissed her, and the crowd erupted into applause.

Delmar and Gina acknowledged the applause with a wave. Delmar released his dance partner, and walked up to Kathy. He slapped a twenty dollar bill on the table.

"Whatever these people want," he said.

Delmar smiled at Gina as he picked up his boom box. She was still laughing as he started walking toward the door.

"Delmar," she called after him.

He turned around. "Yes?"

She had a huge smile on her face.

"You are such a dork."

He smiled back.

"I know."

40

Barkin' Up the Wrong Tree

The Hilton in downtown Milwaukee was a beautiful old hotel with a spacious lobby and all of the substantial architectural details you would expect of a major upscale urban hotel built in the early 20th century. It had long, winding staircases in the lobby and impossibly high ceilings, intricate detail and lush burgundy carpeting.

Somewhere along the line it had also been retrofitted with an indoor water park. So the seasoned business travelers now mingled with mobs of children wearing swimsuits and floatation devices. Peter enjoyed the dichotomy.

The late evening trip to Milwaukee had been an easy drive, a straight shot 90 minutes north of Chicago on 94. The whole way up, Peter hadn't thought much about SVE and their acquisition of Fetch!. There would be plenty of time for that in the coming weeks. His mind was elsewhere.

The next morning, Peter had breakfast at the hotel. He noticed the family at the next table, a father, mother, son and daughter about six and seven years old. The girl was telling a joke and they all laughed. The little boy glanced Peter's way and smiled.

Peter smiled back. He wanted to cry out to the boy to hold on to this moment, to be thankful for his family, to breathe it in and remember.

* * *

Fetch! headquarters was located in a new office building with a Starbuck's and a Potbelly Sandwich Works on the street level. Peter took the elevator to the 12th floor, told the young receptionist his name and took a seat on the edge of a black, vinyl chair in the waiting area. Magazines were scattered across the glass-topped coffee table: Dog World, Modern Dog, Dog Dish and others.

The walls of the lobby bragged about the company's illustrious innovations in the doggie chew toy industry. According to the timeline and photographs in the display, there had been a time when dogs had to resort to playing with bones and sticks. Rubber toys became popular in the early 1900s. It stayed that way until the big plastic breakthrough in the 1960s. The 'Doggie News' was the big Fetch! product of the 1970s, a molded, plastic, squeezable toy the shape of a rolled up newspaper. That was followed by the plastic steak and the plastic cat. The latest trend apparently was away from plastic toward 'greener', more biodegradable products. The most recent new product in the display was a piece of wood shaped like a stick.

"Mr. Stankiewicz?"

Peter turned his attention back to the present and the middle aged woman indicated with a wave that he should follow her.

"I'm Carol. It's nice to meet you, Mr. Stankiewicz."

"Thanks. Nice to meet you as well," said Peter.

Peter followed his hostess through a maze of twists and turns, past cramped offices and rows of cubicles, past small conference rooms and a lunch area. Boy, Peter thought, all office space looks the same. Same white walls, beige cubicles, drinking fountains. They arrived at a tiny, windowless office filled with boxes and boxes of documents. The metal desk in the center of the office was cleared except for a phone and an inbox. The white walls were bare.

"This will be your office. If you need anything, I'm at extension 153. I'll let Mr. Ruscheinski know you're here." And she left.

Peter sat in the standard issue, high backed chair and admired his new home. There would be no easy way to go through all of these documents. The boxes were at least labeled: supplier contracts, sales division, employee benefits, etc. And they were dated going back at least 20 years. Yee hah, let the fun begin.

Peter spent the morning getting his bearings, sorting the documents into categories. He arranged the stacks of boxes accordingly around the office and began developing his game plan. There was only one way to knock out a project like this, and that was one small step at a time. He would start with the employment contracts.

At noon, Peter took a break, grabbed a sandwich at the Potbelly's and then went for a walk. He found himself back at the Hilton. He reached inside his pants pocket. There was the old address that Nancy had given him and the page he'd printed off of MapQuest. Peter looked at his watch. Only nine minutes away, according to the sheet.

Twenty-five minutes later, Peter pulled up to the address. No one had mentioned to Peter that Gary had been living at the YMCA. Peter walked up to the front desk. The clerk looked up from his Sudoku.

"Can I help you?" he mumbled in a smoky voice.

"I hope so," said Peter. "I'm looking for someone who used to live here."

"Well, I think you just answered your own question. He ain't here." And the man picked up a pencil with his nicotine stained hand and went back to his puzzle.

"I'm a relative. I've lost touch with my uncle."

"You don't look like nobody's relative. You look like a cop."

Peter understood. They probably didn't get a lot of guys in suits and ties here.

"I'm not a cop."

"OK, I'll tell you what then. Mr. Dowling will be back from lunch at one o'clock. You just sit over there and read you a magazine."

Peter looked at his watch. A quarter to one. He sat down. They had a more diverse reading selection here than at Fetch!. Peter picked up a Highlights from May 1996 and thumbed through an article on molecules.

At about 1:15 a tall, thin man in his mid-30s walked out of a back office. He wore a polyester sport coat and a well worn pair of grey dress slacks. He crossed the large, open room and walked directly over to Peter.

"Good afternoon. Are you being helped?"

Peter stood. "I'm waiting for Mr. Dowling."

"I'm Joe Dowling. How long have you been waiting?"

"The man at the desk said you'd be back from lunch at one." Peter gestured over to the desk, which was now unoccupied.

"Ah, that would be Benny. Please come on back."

Dowling led Peter to a dark office that had been paneled about 40 years ago.

"Please have a seat. I have to apologize for Benny. I'm afraid he took too many bennies back when they were called bennies. I never went to lunch. I've been back here the whole time. What can I do for you?"

"My name is Peter Stankiewicz. I'm looking for a man who used to live here. He's a friend of my father's." Peter paused a moment realizing that was the first time he'd actually referred to Henry out loud as his father since he was eleven.

"I see," said Dowling, "And what led you here?"

"This is the last address he gave us. It was several years ago."

"Well, there are a lot of men who pass through here. They have some of the hardest luck stories you'd ever want to hear. And they don't usually stay in touch once they've left. A lot of them just survive on the street."

"I know it's a long shot." And now Peter pulled his trump card. "My father is dying and I was hoping to let his friend know."

"I see. Well, I've been here about five years. We have 20 rooms. So we've probably had over 100 men stay here in that time." Dowling turned to a file cabinet. "I can't give you personal information, but if they left any forwarding address, that might help. What is the man's name?"

"Gary Hickman."

Dowling pulled a file out and sat back at his desk.

"I remember Gary," said Dowling, thumbing through the file. "It's hard to forget Gary. He's such a little guy with that mop of gray hair and the hook for a hand. He left, well let me see, here it is, he left about two years ago. They tend to just leave without much explanation."

"So you have no idea where he might be now?"

"No. I'm sorry."

"What if he left something behind? Some belongings? Would you have a record of that?"

"Each man has a locker when they're here. But when they leave we clean out anything left behind. We would have a record of it here, just in case there was anything of value. But there's nothing in Gary's file, except this P.O. Box number. Would that help?"

"It's better than nothing I suppose," Peter said as he wrote down the number. "Thanks for your time."

Dowling followed Peter out to the lobby.

"Mr. Stankiewicz," said Dowling, scratching his head. "Did you ever get the feeling that you've had a conversation before?"

"I guess so," said Peter. "Why?"

"Well, there's a lot of things to keep track of around here, and I'm not the most organized man. But I seem to remember that someone else came looking for Gary about a year ago or so." Dowling closed his eyes to jog his memory. "He also asked if Gary left anything behind. A large man, older, maybe about Gary's age. Does that make any sense?"

"Yeah," smiled Peter. "It makes a lot of sense." Henry had been here too, no doubt looking for the tape. Peter was on the right track.

The men shook hands.

"Thanks for your time, Mr. Dowling."

"I hope you find Gary. If you do, tell him he's welcome to come back if he likes."

"I'll tell him if I see him."

Out at his car again, Peter checked the time. 2:00.

By the time I get back to Fetch! it will be almost three.

He turned his cell phone back on. One missed call, from Buckingham. It could wait.

41

PINS, PAIN AND PIZZA

Waveland Bowl wasn't far from Gina's apartment. On a nice evening she might even walk. However, the late spring weather had turned unseasonably warm. And Gina remembered her mother's old saying that "horses sweat, men perspire and women glow." Gina knew better. Walking two miles in eighty degree heat, she'd have glowed right through her blouse. She took the Addison bus instead.

Walking through the glass doors, Gina was met by the familiar cacophony of bowling balls rolling down hardwood floors, hitting pins and echoing through the building along with pinball dings and pings, cash register rings, beer bottles clinking and the laughter and chatter of camaraderie amid the crowded lanes. She was beginning to understand Delmar's attraction to the sport.

Gina made her way to lane 27 and sat again at the end of the plastic bench.

The boys were deep in conversation.

"Selling like hotcakes. I've heard that before. What the hell does it mean?" asked Ramon.

"What are you talking about?" asked Oscar.

"You said your new port-a-crapper, the Turdinator, or whatever you called it, was 'selling like hotcakes'. And I just wanna know what the hell that means."

"It's just a figure of speech."

Delmar had not noticed Gina yet. He grabbed his 16-pounder and stood at the line. He tried to focus on the pins and shut out the chatter of his teammates.

"Because I'm not even sure what a hotcake is, to tell you the truth," continued Ramon. "Is that a pancake? Or is it a cake that was just yanked out of the oven? That wouldn't sell very well at all, I wouldn't think. I like cold cake."

Henry was the first to spot Gina.

"Good evening," he said, walking over to her. "Back for another evening of stimulating intellectual conversation?"

Delmar landed a strike.

"I'm just here for moral support," Gina smiled.

Gina tried to remain cool. Nothing in Henry's manner suggested that he had any idea who he was actually talking to.

"Well, between you and me," said Henry, "I don't know what you've been doing, but I can't remember ever seeing Delmar so upbeat before. It's gotta be you."

Delmar came over to greet Gina with a long kiss.

Ramon and Oscar noticed and exchanged a knowing glance.

"Henry, you're up," yelled Oscar from the scorer's table.

Oblivious to the chaos around him, Delmar saw only Gina. "I'm glad you made it. The Gutter Snipes are a good team, but the pins are falling our way tonight. Do you need anything?"

Gina grinned. She didn't need anything at the moment. This was perfect.

* * *

The Living Wills went on to an impressive victory. Delmar was in the zone all night, scoring a 207 in the final game. He was on fire. They shook hands with the Snipes and packed up their equipment.

"Who wants to go to Luigi's? I'm buying," Delmar announced.

"As rare as that occasion is," said Oscar, "I better get home. I've got a client presentation in the morning. The huge Oktoberfest in

Lincoln Square is rethinking their outdoor bladder relief needs. Beer equals urine, and that's a lot of urine."

"Hey, Oscar. Remember there's a lady present," said Ramon.

"Yeah, well it's a natural bodily function. And it happens to be how Delmar here pays the rent, so there's gonna be a lot of excrement in her future."

"How about you, Ramon?" asked Delmar. "Join us for a pizza?"

"I better not. I have to watch my girlish figure."

"Henry?"

"Sure. Why not? You bowled a great game tonight, Del. You should have to buy someone a meal. It may as well be me."

A lump formed in Gina's throat.

* * *

Luigi's was right across the street from the bowling alley, a neighborhood joint that was still open at 10pm, but the rush was over and a table was easy to find. Gina, Henry and Delmar found a booth, and Delmar excused himself to find the men's room. Gina and Henry sat across from one another.

"He's a good man."

Gina smiled. "Yeah, I know."

"I really don't like to stick my nose into other people's business, but Delmar is a class act. He's had a few tough breaks, but he's older and wiser now. I can see, for example, that his taste in women has improved tremendously."

Gina blushed.

Just then a sharp pain tore through Henry's lower abdomen and he leaned over. He sat back up and closed his eyes. Although he was doing his best to hide the pain, his face lost all of its color. Gina quickly poured Henry a glass of water from the pitcher on the table. Henry took a large gulp and a deep breath. The blush returned to his cheeks quickly. He wiped the cold sweat from his forehead with a napkin.

"Are you all right?"

"Yeah, it's nothing," winced Henry. "It happens once in a while. I've talked to the doctor about it. He says it's just part of getting old. It always passes pretty quickly. Let's not make a big deal out of it. No need to concern Delmar."

"OK," said Gina.

Delmar returned and remained standing, looking around the restaurant. "Looks like we're on our own. I don't see a waitress. Who needs a drink?"

"Just seltzer and a lime for me," said Henry.

"Make it two," said Gina.

"You guys are a cheap date. I guess I'll be drinking alone." Delmar journeyed off to the long, oak bar at the far side of the room.

Henry changed the subject. "So tell me about yourself."

"I live near Wrigley. I work at a coffee shop. Not much more to it."

"There's always more to it," said Henry. "How about your family?"

Was he messing with her? Did he know?

"I'm kind of estranged from my family, I guess you'd say."

"Ah, well, that makes two of us."

"Is that right?"

"Yeah. I've got a son and a daughter. I see my son once in a while now. He's a hotshot attorney downtown. My daughter," Henry slowly shook his head, "I haven't seen her since she was a little girl. I really screwed that one up."

"Oh," said Gina, taken aback, trying to stay collected. She fumbled with the plastic table cloth. "Where is she?"

"That's the thing. I don't know. My son doesn't know. Their mother doesn't know. When I left, she was about eight."

"Uh huh."

"Yeah, well, I've made a lot of mistakes. But not being there for my kids. I can't even....My son, Peter, he seemed to turn out OK I guess. But Sarah," Henry's thoughts were taking him back to a better time, "she was my little sugar plum. You know she used to beg me to throw her in the air..."

Gina couldn't help herself now. She was about to say, "Then why did you leave?"

"All right, party animals," Delmar interrupted, "two seltzers with lime. I also took the liberty of ordering a large sausage pizza. It should be out in fifteen minutes."

Delmar took his seat next to Gina and raised his glass.

"To friends," said Delmar. "I had a great game tonight. But it was so much better because you were there."

"To friends," repeated Gina and Henry as the three clinked their glasses.

42

THE GIFT THAT KEEPS ON GIVING

Delmar drove around the block twice looking for a parking space on the street. It was one of those dreaded mid-week street cleaning days in Chicago. Every single space on the west side of the street was open because it was illegal to park there on street cleaning days. Of course, that meant that every single space on the east side of the street, the legal side, was taken.

"Screw it," he said.

He pulled right in front of Gina's building and parked in a street-cleaning space. He didn't really have much time to stay anyway. This would be the classic 'zip-in and zip-out' surprise visit, stoking both of their imaginations for a fun-filled night tonight. He wouldn't be here long enough to get a parking ticket.

Delmar walked up the creaky wooden stairs to Gina's apartment. He knocked on her door, barely able to contain the smile on his face. She was going to love this little present Delmar had brought for her at Zach's Tracks.

Nobody answered.

He looked at his watch.

"Hmmm. I know she's not working. I wonder where she is."

Delmar thought about staying and waiting for her on the landing, but his internal city of Chicago parking clock was ticking. One or two more minutes could cost him fifty dollars.

That was when he got a great idea. This present wasn't really for Gina anyway; it was a gift for Gina to give to the landlady's daughter. *Why not just eliminate the middle man?* Emily had to be home from school by now. It was already four o'clock.

Delmar knocked on the door across the hall.

He could hear rustling. Someone was fiddling with the lock. Two deadbolts and one chain later, the door opened. A large woman with disheveled orange hair was staring at Delmar. She had a confused look on her face as if she had just woken up from a nap.

"Good afternoon," Delmar said.

"Who are you?" Libby asked.

"My name is Delmar Dunwoody," he said.

At first it didn't register. Libby just stared at him blankly until she connected the dots.

"OH!" she said, suddenly very excited. "You're Gina's new boyfriend!"

"Yeah," he said. He sure liked the sound of that.

"Why don't you come in?" she implored. "Can I offer you some tea or something?"

"No thanks," Delmar said. "That's very kind of you, but I can't. I've got to get back to work."

"Don't be silly," Libby said. "There's always time for a little tea."

"No really, that's really nice, but I'm parked illegally outside."

"Well, OK..." Libby said.

He held up a Lorne Greene CD. "I have a little gift for Emily. Is she home?"

"Why don't you give it to her mom?" Libby asked.

Delmar stared at her for a moment trying to figure out if she was joking or not. She didn't appear to be.

"Her mom?" he asked.

"Yes," Libby said. "I think she went to pick Emily up at school today. There was some sort of after-school function. A science fair or something like that."

"I see."

But Delmar did not see at all. Now that he was looking at her, it did seem a bit unlikely that this woman was Emily's mother. Grandmother, maybe. But mother? How did he get that so wrong? He began the questioning tentatively.

"I'm sorry, but I'm a little confused here," Delmar said. "You *are* Gina's landlady, right?"

Libby slapped her forehead.

"Oh, how rude of me," Libby said, extending her hand. "I haven't properly introduced myself. Yes, I'm Libby."

"Nice to officially meet you," Delmar said as he shook her hand. "I've heard a lot about you." He didn't quite know what to say next. "Um... I don't want to pry, but how are you related to Emily?"

"Related?" Libby said. "I wish I was related to that little angel. I'm just her neighbor and babysitter." Libby pointed past Delmar. "They should be back soon enough. Why don't you just slide the CD under her door?"

Delmar was dense sometimes, but he wasn't that dense.

When he turned around to see which door she was pointing to, all he could do was silently hand the CD to Libby, and walk away.

43

I'll Make Him an Offer He Can't Refuse

The thoughts were flying through Reed's brain as he made his way from his office, through the sea of cubicles, out the glass doors, to the elevator and up to the corporate suite two floors above. If anyone along the way had acknowledged Reed or tried to get his attention, he hadn't noticed.

"Ding," rang the elevator, announcing his arrival on 19. Too late to back out now. What's the worst that could happen? They could fire him. That might not be so bad. Or they could give him back his old job and bring in someone new, or someone old. Reed had done his best. He'd tried some new things. But it didn't seem fair for management to make judgments so soon. Reed needed more time.

"Good afternoon, Mary. I'm here to see Karen."

Reed tried to conceal his angst and stood motionless.

"Of course, Reed," said Mary. "Please take a seat and I'll let Karen know that you're here."

"Thank you."

Reed sat with his file folder full of numbers uncomfortably perched on his lap. He continued to tell himself he had nothing to worry about. And each time he thought that, it just made him more nervous. He wiped a bead of sweat from his brow.

Mary returned to her desk.

"Karen will see you now."

"Thank you again."

Reed stood and walked to Karen's door, entered and closed the door behind him. Karen was sitting at her desk reading some sort of report. She looked surprised to see Reed there when she looked up.

"Ah, Reed, come in, come in. Have a seat. Let me just finish this."

Reed sat silently and again observed how amazingly spotless this woman's desk was.

"Alright," she said finally. "Sorry to keep you waiting. How's everything going down at CS Purchasing?"

"Fine," said Reed, not sure of where this was going.

"Good, good," said Karen, appearing to measure Reed with her eyes. "Now I have been going over your numbers, and comparing them with the historical data from your department."

Karen pulled a file from seemingly nowhere. Reed recognized his own handwriting on the manila tab. It was last week's departmental report.

"I know it's not fair to make long-term decisions based on such a small body of data," she said, "but we have no choice but to draw some preliminary conclusions. We have to extrapolate this information into the future. We can change horses in midstream if we have to. I had put my money on you, but I always knew that I could go to Plan B if I needed to."

Reed shifted in his seat.

"But it looks like I won't need to," smiled Karen.

Reed couldn't hide his confusion. "Excuse me?"

"The numbers look good as far as I can tell. You've got some new ideas for cost savings that look promising. Your team is still generating the information we need. It looks like a smooth transition from Anderson to you. Nice job."

"Thank you ma'am," grinned Reed. "Frankly I'm relieved. I didn't know what to expect when you called me up here."

"I apologize if I left you in the dark. I didn't mean to. I try not to play mind games. But my husband tells me I'd make a good poker player."

"I imagine that you would."

Reed began to stand. "Is there anything else?"

"Just one thing, Reed."

Reed sat back down. "What's that?"

"How are things going with Dick Nicholson?"

"As well I can expect, I guess. Why do you ask?"

"Well, of course this is completely off the record," said Karen, pausing and becoming very serious. "I never liked Dick. I inherited Conrad Anderson when I got here, and he always protected Dick. I tried to stay out of their way, and Dick seemed to be getting his work done, so I let it go. I thought it was just a personality thing and I'll be the first to admit that you don't need to like everyone you work with, as long as you get the work done."

Reed nodded, feeling a little more at ease. "Off the record, I feel the same way. Dick comes with the job. So I am learning to manage it. I'm even reading a book called *How to Deal with Difficult People*. I am considering Dick Nicholson a leadership development challenge."

"I appreciate your positive outlook. And I'm glad to see that you are doing some homework. Those are both signs of a good leader."

"It's still early," sighed Reed.

"Well, I admire your patience. Personally, I'm still working on that trait," she said. "I had a passing conversation with Nicholson in the elevator the other day."

Reed braced himself.

"I'm sure he thought he was being subtle. Between the lines he implied that you were a risky choice for Anderson's spot and that the changes you were making would take a long time, if ever, to yield any positive results."

"Dick is old school," said Reed. "He doesn't like change. But he does his job."

"If it were just a matter of personality, I might just let it go. But I spoke to a few others in your department. I hope you don't mind." She paused. "I found out some interesting things. Dick Nicholson has point-blank told his budget team not to participate in your cross-regional, cost savings analyses. That is clearly insubordination.

One employee told me that Dick deliberately scheduled an out-of-town meeting for him when he knew that this employee would be on vacation, forcing this employee to unnecessarily cancel his vacation plans. This was apparently in retaliation for sharing information with other teams. We don't want that kind of poison spreading through the department. Good people may leave. Good projects may be compromised. And it would have an adverse affect on the bottom line."

Reed leaned forward before speaking. "Look, I'm new at this. I've worked with Dick for a long time. Until now, we had completely separate responsibilities, and that's the way Anderson liked it. I enjoyed not having to work directly with Dick. But now I have to, and I'm struggling with how to deal with him. He only has a couple of years left until retirement. Believe me, he tells that to everyone every chance he gets. I can't fire the guy."

"I'll take care of it," said Karen leaning back in her chair.

Reed felt like he was sitting across from Don Corleone. "You'll take care of it?"

"I'll ask Dick to bring me everything that he's working on, and I'll break the news to him. It wasn't your idea, it was mine. And I'll make sure that Dick can stay around until his retirement. I've spoken to HR and found a place for him. Based on his years of service, he will be incredibly well paid for his new responsibilities. His last day in CS Purchasing will be Friday. Unless you don't agree. It's your department."

"No, no," said Reed. "Thanks for helping out the new guy. Now don't take this the wrong way but next time I'd like to handle it myself."

Karen smiled. "I was hoping you'd say that."

44

DECONSTRUCTING DESTRUCTION

Emily's tongue was hanging out of her mouth like Michael Jordan as she concentrated on cutting the heavy pink construction paper. This was the kind of homework assignment she absolutely dreaded. She was doing very well in school academically, but her fine motor skills were coming along a little slowly. Cutting was the worst; especially heavy paper like this. Every few seconds she had to stop because it was hurting her hand. She tried her pouty face one more time.

"Please help me with this, Mom," she said.

Gina didn't seem to be paying attention. Emily said it again.

"Mom, can you please help me cut this?"

"Oh," Gina replied. She absentmindedly grabbed the scissors from Emily and helped her finish cutting out what appeared to be a pig. The curly tail looked more like a French fry, and the head was almost triangular now, but thanks to Gina at least the legs looked like actual pig legs. She handed it back to Emily, and drifted back into her own thoughts.

What on earth had she done wrong? For the past four days she had been beating herself up, reliving every moment of her brief relationship with Delmar, looking for the clues she must have missed. Was it the time she made fun of his leather pants? Did she pick the wrong "Bonanza" cast member? Did she go too fast or too slow in the romance department? It must have been the joke about the Rogaine. Guys are so sensitive about their hair loss.

"Mom, do you think this looks like a pig?" Emily asked.

"Uh huh."

"I think it looks like a pink horse," Emily said.

"Uh huh."

Even in Gina's young and stupid pre-Emily life, when she had dated a bad boy or two, she had never been stood up for a date. If those animals had done it to her, she would have been ready for it. That was part of their attraction—they lived life on the edge, they were unpredictable. But Delmar? It was like a punch in the gut coming from him. That song and dance at the coffee shop was the most romantic thing anyone had ever done for her. And now this? It just didn't add up.

"Oh no," Emily said.

"What is it honey?"

"I think I left my glue stick at school," she said. Her lip started to quiver. "How am I going to glue this into the barnyard?"

"I think I have another glue stick in our room," Gina said. "I'll get it."

She walked into her bedroom, sat on her bed, and opened the top drawer of her nightstand. She saw something out of the corner of her eye. It was her reflection in the mirror on the opposite wall. Gina turned her head and stared at herself. Sitting sideways like this, dressed in her sweatpants and pajama top, she shuddered.

Ugh.

She thought her hips looked enormous, and boy, what an unflattering way to display her tummy. Maybe Delmar got the same view one night. Gina also thought her face, with all the makeup washed off, looked as plain as can be. She could see how someone could lose interest in that face.

Ugh.

"Mom, did you find the glue stick?"

Emily was standing at the door, looking at her mother.

"Right," Gina said. She resumed the search through the nightstand drawer, hastily rearranging things, trying to uncover the pink and blue glue stick.

Emily came and sat down next to her mother.

"Are you OK, mom?"

"Yes," Gina said. "I'm just upset that I can't find this darn thing."

Emily wrapped her arms around Gina's waist. "I'm sorry, mom," she said as he she looked up at her mother's face. "I'm sorry you're so sad. I'm sorry about Delmar."

Gina hugged her back. Emily was such a great hugger.

"I'll get over it," Gina said.

"But you really liked him, didn't you?"

Gina had to turn away.

"Maybe something happened to him," Emily surmised. "Maybe he was in a car accident and is sitting in the hospital somewhere trying to tell the nurses that he has to call you to apologize for missing the date. Maybe he can't communicate because his voicebox was knocked out in the crash, and his hands are broken so he can't write it down either."

Gina smiled at Emily.

"I called his office every day this week," Gina said. "He's been there; the receptionist told me she saw him. He won't return my calls. He won't return my e-mails. Nope, sorry, honey. He just decided he doesn't want to see me anymore."

"Did he break up with you?"

"I guess that's what he's doing."

"But why?"

"That's the part I don't understand," Gina said. She was fighting hard to hold back the tears.

"Boys are really weird, aren't they, mom?"

Gina sniffed and smiled. "Yes, they are."

There was a knock on the door. Gina looked at the clock. It was 9:30 at night. *Who could be knocking on the door at 9:30?* Emily pounced out of bed and started heading for the door.

"Wait honey," Gina said. "I don't want you answering that. Let me get the door."

She grabbed her big fluffy white terrycloth robe to cover up her pajamas, and put it on as she strolled back into the living room toward the front door. Whoever was there knocked again. Gina looked through the peephole and saw the big orange hair. The door swung open and Libby had a big grin on her face.

"I didn't wake you up, did I?" she asked. "It looked like the lights were still on."

"No, we're just finishing up Emily's homework," Gina said. "What's up Libby?"

"Oh, I was just cleaning up the table in the corner," Libby said. "You know the one that has all of those old magazines?"

"Yeah..."

"I thought, what if I ever need to have a dinner party or something? Where are we going to eat dinner? I just had to clean off the table or else we wouldn't have room to eat. Did you know that I have some good china from my mother? She had eight place settings of everything, and it's really beautiful china. The plates have gold trim, and the design is blue flowers. I think it's Wedgewood or something like that. I mean, it's really nice, and I thought, what if we actually used it sometime? It hasn't been used in twenty years, probably not since my father died. Mother didn't bother to entertain much after that. She just put the china in the closet in the back bedroom, and covered it with towels so it wouldn't break. I really don't even go back in that room too much to tell you the truth because it just reminds me of her. Anyway, after I clean off the table, I'll go check on the china—I'm sure it's still beautiful, and then we can have a dinner party if you want."

Gina just stared at her strange landlady.

"Um, OK," Gina finally said. "Is that what you wanted to tell me?"

"Uh huh," Libby said. "What do you think?"

"Just the three of us?"

"And your boyfriend," Libby said.

"Oh," Gina replied.

"He's wonderful," Libby said. "Funny and friendly, just like you said."

"You met him?" Gina asked.

"Didn't I tell you? He came over here a few days ago. I invited him in for tea, but it's a good thing he didn't come in, because like I said, that table was a mess. It's still pretty bad, but I'm making progress."

"Why was he here?"

"Oh dear," Libby said, slapping her own thigh. "I completely forgot to give it to you. Hold on for a second."

She retreated into her apartment across the hall. Gina could hear the ruckus of items being tossed about. While Gina waited in the doorway, Emily came and stood by her side.

"What's going on?" Emily asked.

"I'm not sure," Gina said.

Libby bounded back to the door with a CD in her hand. "Here it is!" She handed it to Emily.

"'This is a present for you," Libby explained. "It's from Delmar. Want to hear something funny?" Emily was staring at the CD cover, which featured a picture of Lorne Greene. "He thought I was your mother or something. I told him that I wished I was related to you, because you're such an angel. I tried to get him to slide the CD under your door, but I guess he was afraid you'd step on it or something, so he just gave it to me."

Emily and Gina looked at each other, mouths agape. Emily dropped the CD on the floor and ran to the bedroom. Gina ran after her.

Libby stepped into the apartment and called after them: "It's not that bad, really! He's actually a wonderful singer!"

45

THE ACCIDENTAL DETECTIVE

Peter's cell phone rang. He made note of the caller's name and answered.

"Heartbreak Hotel, how may I direct your call?"

"Where are you?!!" said Kelly in a very loud, strained whisper.

Peter imagined her covering the phone with her hand, and peeking out of her office to be sure they weren't being heard.

"I'm enjoying a latte at a place called Java the Hut, reading today's Milwaukee Journal-Sentinel and looking out on a lovely Wisconsin spring storm. How are you?"

"Buckingham wants your ass on a plate," Kelly whispered angrily. "He's going ballistic. The client is ranting about your vanishing act. You're not answering Buckingham's calls, and now he's on my case because I was the one that recommended you for this assignment. Other than that, everything is just peachy."

"I'm sorry," said Peter. "I'm sorry that you're catching heat for this. As far as Buckingham goes, I'm doing the work. I stay late, I get there early. I actually get a lot done when no one is there. They'll get their report."

"Then why don't you just answer his calls?" Kelly was exasperated.

"To tell you the truth, I kind of enjoy imagining him flipping out," said Peter, sipping his coffee. "He's such a control freak and I'm just out of his grubby reach. It's gotta be killing him. He's been getting under my skin for three years now. It's a little bit of payback I guess."

"So you're sitting in a coffee shop just to bug Buckingham?"

"No. I'm actually following up a lead on Gary Hickman."

There was a long silence on the line.

"Peter," she said, "I understand that finding this video is important to you. But is it worth losing your job? You don't even know if this video exists. And if it does, what are the odds that some vagrant wandering the streets of Milwaukee is holding it? I think you've gone around the bend. I love you, but this is nuts."

"I've considered that possibility. But I found out something the other day that makes me think I'm close."

"Really?" asked Kelly, "What's that?"

"Henry was up here. About a year ago. And he was looking for the tape. He must not have found it, and I don't think he found Hick. But I'm so close. Even if Gary doesn't have the tape, I have to find him now. I still have to tell him about Henry. It's like investigative police work, hunting down a missing witness. I've actually been mistaken for a cop. It's kind of fun."

"Well I'm glad someone is having fun. What kind of lead are you following, Columbo?"

"I found out Hick's got a P.O. Box," Peter said. He had an air of mystery in his voice. "I stopped by the post office yesterday and asked the clerk. He told me that the guy with a hook for a hand picks up his mail twice a month. Another of my sources thinks it's linked to his disability checks, on the first and the fifteenth. Today's the fifteenth. So I'm on a stake-out across the street from the post office. It's the only way I could find him. If I just left a note for him he might not respond. I need to be here when he shows up, and hope I can talk to him. It's the only shot I've got right now. If I miss him today, I've got to wait two more weeks. And I'll be finished with this Fetch! research long before that."

"Sounds like a great plan, Sherlock," answered Kelly. "What if you miss him? It gets delivered on the 15th, but what if he doesn't show up until the 20th? Are you gonna sit there and sip coffee for a week? Explain that to Buckingham."

"Crap," said Peter dejectedly. "It all sounded so logical in my head."

"Believe me, no one wants you to find that tape more than I do," said Kelly. "And fast. I just want you to wrap this whole thing up so we can restore a little order around the office here. Besides, I miss you. You may be a nut, but you're my nut."

Just then Peter spotted a short man in old jeans and beat up boots moving slowly across the street and toward the post office. He had a grey hood covering his head to protect him from the rain. His hands were in his pockets. Peter watched closely as the man approached the front door of the post office. The man pulled his hands out of his pockets to open the heavy glass door.

There it is!

"Gotta go," said Peter absently into the phone. "Love you." Click.

"Can you please at least call Buckingham and...."

But Peter was gone, out of the coffee shop and dodging traffic and puddles as he crossed the street.

Peter entered the post office, wiped his feet on the mat and looked around. Peter's prey was standing at the large, long table in the center of the lobby filling out a form of some kind. Peter approached quietly. He didn't want to frighten him off. The man pulled his hood back and revealed a head of sparse, dark hair. Peter moved toward the table and noticed something else that was odd; the man had two hands.

Peter looked around, confused. They were the only two people in the room aside from the clerk behind the partition. Peter looked again at the man in the hood. He held a gleaming silver cell phone in his hand. One mystery solved, yet a larger mystery remained. Where was Hick? Peter headed for the door, his head down.

"You missed him." The voice came from behind the partition.

"What was that?" asked Peter, approaching the clerk.

The clerk set down the paperback crime novel he'd been poring over and took off his glasses to see Peter better. It was the same clerk Peter had spoken with yesterday.

"The guy with the hook. He came in earlier than usual."

"Damn," mumbled Peter to himself. "Well, thanks anyway."

Deflated, Peter began to leave. Then a light bulb went off. Peter turned back to the clerk. "Where's the nearest bar?"

"That'd be Cal's. Just around the corner."

Peter turned to leave again.

"Only one problem," added the clerk.

"What's that?" asked Peter.

"He's got a four hour head start on you."

* * *

Cal's Lounge was conveniently located next to a currency exchange. It was a drinking man's bar, dimly lit and quiet, cheap and undiscriminating. Even on this rainy day, Peter's eyes had to adjust to the darkness of the tavern. Several men sat separately at the old, oak bar. None looked up from their drink to acknowledge Peter. A small television high on a shelf in the corner blared a local news report that no one was watching. Peter stood at the end of the bar nearest the door. The bartender, a large man in a smaller-than-necessary white t-shirt, and an unlit cigarette dangling from his lips, met Peter at the end of the bar.

"What'll it be?"

Peter looked at his watch. It was only two o'clock. *Ah, well, when in Rome…*

"I'll have a Miller Lite."

The bartender returned quickly with a bottle of beer and a small glass.

Peter could now clearly see his quarry at the far end of the bar. His graying head bobbed slightly and his eyes were closed. He scratched his head with his hook. Several empty shot glasses sat on the bar before him.

Peter walked the length of the bar and stood next to the man, who was singing some sort of tune to himself as if he'd been transported in his mind to a better place.

"Hick?"

No response.

"Hick?" asked Peter, louder this time.

The bartender looked on. He knew that Hick had been overserved but he didn't want to see the poor little guy get hassled.

Hick lifted his head slowly and looked toward Peter with two red, glassy eyes. His body swayed in the bar stool and his voice was a slur. "Who the hell are you?"

"I just want to talk to you," said Peter.

"Go away," grunted Hick. "I don't know you. Leave me alone."

"It will just take a minute," insisted Peter.

Hick mumbled something unintelligible and appeared to be falling asleep.

"My name's Stankiewicz. Peter Stankiewicz."

Hick swiveled in the chair, opened his eyes and attempted to stand.

"Stankiewicz?" Hick managed to say, and then collapsed onto the sticky bar floor.

46

OH, WHAT A TANGLED WEB WE WEAVE

"I'm just asking. Why do they call it a pair of panties, but it's only one bra? It seems like it should be the other way around."

"Ramon," sighed Oscar as he tied his bowling shoes. "What do you do all day that you've got time to consider such crap? Are the exhaust fumes in that parking garage getting to you?"

"*What?*" asked Ramon, placing his ball on the return. "You never wondered about that? I mean there's two up here, and there's only one …"

"I understand the question," interrupted Oscar. "I'm just amazed that you expend any energy on finding an answer."

Henry walked up to the lane. "Evening, boys. Where's Delmar?"

"I haven't seen him yet," said Oscar. "But he was at the office today. And he said he'd be here."

Henry sat down with a groan and tried to catch his breath without the others noticing. He needed a minute before he'd be able to bend down and change his shoes.

"Here's Romeo now," said Ramon as Delmar joined them at lane 26.

Delmar was moving at half speed. He slowly pulled his ball from its bag and placed it in the ball return, sat without saying a word and stared at his shoes.

"So where's the ball and chain, Doctor Love?" asked Oscar.

"Not here," mumbled Delmar. "Can we just bowl?"

"We gotta wait for the opponent," said Oscar. "The Pin Pricks always run a few minutes late. We've got time. What's eating you anyway?"

"She dumped you," surmised Ramon. "Oh, man. I'm sorry."

"I did not say that she dumped me!"

"So she didn't dump you," said Henry. "That's good. Right?"

"I dumped her."

Henry, Ramon and Oscar silently watched Delmar for a moment in surprise.

"I hadn't even considered that possibility," said Oscar.

"I'd really rather not talk about it," said Delmar.

"OK," said Oscar and Ramon simultaneously.

"Delmar," said Henry calmly, "I'm sorry. We're all sorry. Gina seemed like a very nice girl. But things don't always work out. So whadd'ya say we have a few beers, have a few laughs and bowl? There's nothing better to help you forget about a failed romance."

"You oughta know," said Oscar.

* * *

The Pin Pricks were formidable. And Delmar's game just wasn't there. The beer didn't seem to help like Henry had thought. Delmar was in a deep funk.

Oscar was at the line, trying to pick up a spare.

"You sure you don't want to talk about it?" Henry asked his depressed friend. Delmar just shook his head.

Oscar picked up the spare but it wasn't nearly enough and the second game ended with another decisive victory by the 'Pricks'. Henry excused himself and went to the men's room. He wasn't sure what was going on inside him but the pain was sharp and he needed a little privacy. A bathroom stall would give him a few minutes and maybe the pain would pass. He closed the stall door, sat down and closed his eyes.

* * *

"OK," said Oscar to Ramon and Delmar back at the lane. "Let's just play this last game for pride. We'll have some fun. And we'll live to fight another day."

"You're a regular Knute Rockne," said Ramon.

Then she walked in.

Oscar saw her first. "Oh, Romeo. I believe Juliet is at the balcony. And she brought company."

Delmar turned. Gina stood behind the row of plastic chairs, her eyes ablaze, holding Emily's hand. She had the Lorne Greene CD in her other hand and whipped it at Delmar's head, but he ducked and it landed on the ground. Emily shook nervously at her mother's side, and it was clear she had been crying.

"What do you have to say for yourself, chicken shit?" yelled Gina.

Oscar and Ramon sat back and folded their arms. This was going to be good. Even the Pin Pricks stopped their chatter to watch.

"What are you talking about?" said Delmar from fifteen feet away.

"You're just like the others!" yelled Gina. "You find out I have a daughter and you run. You didn't even return my calls to talk about it. A good man doesn't do that."

"Oooh," said Oscar under his breath.

"What are you talking about?" said Delmar. He was calm but intense. "I'm not mad that you have a daughter. I think it's great. I'm upset because *you* lied to *me*! You told me Emily was your neighbor's daughter. You hid her from me. I thought I knew you better, and I thought you knew me. I trusted you. And you lied to me about the most important thing in your life. How can I believe you now? What else have you been lying to me about?"

Gina stood in silence. There were a few other things. Tears were rolling down Emily's cheeks again.

"Emily," said Delmar, walking closer. He softened his voice. "I am so sorry that you were put in the middle of this. It's not your fault, OK?"

Emily nodded silently, sniffling.

Delmar was now standing directly in front of Gina and looked her in the eye. "I put my heart on the line and you stepped on it. I made a fool of myself pronouncing my feelings in front of a bunch of strangers at that coffee shop. I thought we had something here. But if you think you have to lie to me, I was wrong. Now if you don't mind, the guys and I would like to bowl."

Gina stormed her way toward the doors dragging Emily behind her. Henry exited the men's room holding his side. He was moving slowly back to the lane, and didn't see Gina and Emily until they nearly ran him over.

"Gina," said Henry, caught off guard.

Henry looked down at the eight-year-old girl at Gina's side, at her soft brown curls and her sparkling, green eyes. Before he could say anything, Gina ran for the exit with her daughter.

"Holy crap," said Henry to himself.

The likeness was unmistakable.

47

THE PRESCRIPTION

Reed took a deep drag on his cigarette and kicked his feet back and forth against the concrete landing. Lower Wacker was dark and dingy as ever, but the temperature was nearly perfect. Reed really enjoyed his cigarettes on days like today.

"There he is!" Henry said.

Reed turned around to see the familiar sight approaching, but was a little surprised by what he saw. The normally robust Henry was moving kind of slow. His face was abnormally pale and his eyes had big black bags below them.

"You feeling OK?"

"Not really," Henry admitted, grunting as he took a seat next to Reed. "Don't worry—I'm not contagious."

Reed didn't smile. "Maybe you should go see a doctor."

"Naaah," Henry said. "What's he gonna say? 'Henry, you're getting old.' Oh really? Gee thanks, Doc. I had no idea."

Reed still looked concerned, but he could see that Henry wasn't receptive to further overtures. "Well, I hope you feel better."

"Thanks," Henry said. He took a deep breath, and seemed to settle in to his concrete seat. "So, what about you? Everything OK up on 17?"

"Surprisingly, yeah" Reed admitted. "Nicholson was transferred."

"So everyone is in line now?"

"Not exactly," Reed admitted, "but it's heading in the right direction. I'm optimistic."

"That's the spirit," Henry said.

"I wish things were going that well at home," Reed said.

"Uh oh. Problems with the missus?"

"You could say that," Reed said.

"Now you're in my wheelhouse," Henry said, rubbing his hands together. He held up three fingers. "I'm on wife #3. If there's one thing I understand, it's problems with the missus."

Reed chuckled.

"Well, this one is a little complicated."

"They're all complicated," Henry replied.

Reed took another drag from his cigarette. When he blew the smoke out, it hung in the air in front of him. There wasn't a hint of wind on Lower Wacker this morning, so Reed had to create it himself. He waved his hand to move the smoke along and out of Henry's personal space.

"Sorry about that."

Henry closed his eyes while the smoke dissipated. "Not a problem."

Ramon saw Henry and Reed talking and waved.

"What's up, Reed?" he yelled.

"Just getting some marriage advice from Henry here," Reed explained.

"HA!" Ramon laughed.

Henry chortled a little too.

Nobody said anything for a few seconds as they listened to the sounds of the bustling city streets above them. The noise was constant and continuous, but because it never abated it was almost like it wasn't there at all. It was just part of the setting. Part of what made Chicago Chicago.

"So," Henry said. "Your wife isn't happy with you these days?"

"It's not me," Reed said. "It's..."

"The usual?" Henry asked.

"Yeah," Reed admitted. "What bums me out about it now is that she was really coming along. I was starting to see that sparkle in her eyes again. Starting to see that smile more often. Starting to remember what it was about her that made me fall in love with her all those years ago. Then that stupid wedding invitation showed up, and I lost her again."

"Wedding invitation?" Henry asked.

"Yeah," Reed explained. "My son's best friend is getting married. It just reminded Lucy that we're never going to see our boy get married. We'll never be grandparents..."

Reed had to stop.

"I see what you mean."

"Yeah," he replied. "There's nothing I can say or do now to bring her back. It's just going to take some time."

"How about you?" Henry asked. "How are you doing? That must have hit you like a ton of bricks too."

"I'm OK," Reed said. "I don't know why that is. It stung for a day or two, but honestly, I'm ready to start living again. That's probably why it's so hard to come home to that."

"You know what you need?" Henry proposed, raising his voice. "You need a night out with the guys."

Reed laughed out loud. "Yeah I do."

"Then do it."

"I don't have any guys," Reed said.

"C'mon," Henry protested. "You must have some old buddies you haven't seen in awhile. Guys you used to hang out with."

"Not really," Reed admitted. "Lucy and I went out with another couple for awhile, but they stopped calling us. I guess we haven't felt that social."

Henry didn't need an explanation.

"And before that," Reed continued, "our lives were consumed doing the usual stuff... PTA, Cub Scouts, baseball, basketball, piano lessons, you know, family stuff. For 18 years we were busy all the time. I haven't 'gone out with the guys' since the first year or two of my marriage."

"Well then it's settled," Henry said. "You're coming out with us."

Reed looked at Henry to see if he was serious.

"I don't know."

"What do you mean, you don't know?" Henry asked, slapping Reed on the shoulder lightly. "You know. You know. You need to get out of the house. Come bowling with us on Thursday night."

"I suck at bowling."

"We all suck," Henry said.

"Speak for yourself!" Ramon screamed, obviously listening in on the conversation.

"Hey Ramon," Henry called. "Tell this guy that we'd love to have him."

"He's right," Ramon screamed. "Come on out. We almost never win, but we have a blast."

Reed started to smile. "I don't know."

Henry pointed to Reed's smiling face. "See. There it is. You know you want to do this. C'mon, Reed. I've been trying to get you to come out and play for the last couple of years. If you don't want to bowl, that's fine. Just come and hang out with us." Henry raised his voice in an obviously overstated fashion to complete his thought. "Ramon buys drinks for everyone all night."

"I DO NOT!" Ramon screamed.

Henry winked at Reed. "OK, he doesn't. But I'll buy you a beer."

"I don't drink," Reed pointed out.

"I don't either," Henry said. "Ever try an O'Doul's? It's really pretty good for a non-alcoholic beer."

Reed smiled again. "You really don't drink?"

"Haven't touched a drop in years," he said. He raised his voice intentionally again. "BUT RAMON DRINKS LIKE A FISH. They have to restock that place every Friday morning."

Ramon started walking toward the conversation, and flipped the bird at his old friend on the way. Henry returned Ramon's one-finger wave with an exaggerated "queen at the parade" wave, exposing all of his teeth in the process. Reed couldn't help but laugh at the exchange.

"You know," Reed said, "Maybe I will come out. Where do you bowl?"

"Do you know Waveland Bowl?"

Reed nodded.

"That's our joint," Henry said. "The house that Stankiewicz built."

"HA!" Ramon said.

"What time?"

"7:00," Henry said.

Reed turned to Ramon, who was now just a few feet away. "You sure you don't mind if I freeload for a night? Not to bowl, just to watch."

Ramon smiled. "Love to have ya. As a matter of fact, why don't you stay home Henry, and let Reed here take your place?"

Henry rattled his fist like Ralph Kramden, mockingly ready to send someone to the moon.

"Looking forward to it, gentlemen," Reed said.

"Great!" Henry said.

"We'll have fun," Ramon added.

Reed got up and walked back toward the elevator, while Ramon helped Henry back up to his feet. Henry called out to Reed just before he was out of sight.

"Hey Reed, by the way, I forgot to ask you. Where did they end up transferring Nicholson?"

"Let's just call it customer service," Reed called back. He was grinning from ear to ear.

48

THE HAIR OF THE DOG

"I'm glad to see you've made yourself at home," said Peter. The hotel room was littered with several trays from room service. Hick was wrapped in a thick, white hotel bathrobe. He lounged leisurely in one of the queen-size beds, three pillows propping him up, and a can of peanuts and the TV remote control in his lap.

"Thanks," said Hick in a gravelly baritone. He lowered the volume on ESPN's 'Poker Tour 2005.' "I hope you don't mind I called room service. Three times. I also got some toiletries and whatnot sent up. I didn't want to use yours."

"I appreciate that," said Peter. "You clean up pretty good." Hick had obviously shaved and showered. The hook was still there though. Nothing would fix that.

"I also sent my clothes out to be washed, seeing as I only got the one set," added Hick. "I found this fancy robe in the john. It's a pretty nice setup you got here, Peter. Looks like you done real well for yourself."

"Not as well as you might think," said Peter, looking out the window to see the view of Milwaukee at sunset. "Have the barber, the masseuse or the manicurist stopped by yet?"

Hick popped a handful of peanuts into his mouth. Peter loosened his tie and hung his suit jacket in the closet.

"That was a joke, right?" asked Hick.

"Right," said Peter.

"I also raided your mini-bar. I hope you don't mind. You understand you shouldn't leave an alcoholic alone in a room with a mini-bar."

"I hadn't considered that," said Peter. "You look pretty sober to me."

"Compared to what?" belched Hick, pulling an empty beer can from the pocket of his robe. "I gotta say I'm a whole lot cleaner than when you found me. But you wouldn't like me sober. I don't like me sober."

"Well, you seemed sober enough when I left for work this morning."

"A temporary condition. I don't even remember how I got here. You didn't drop one of them roofies in my drink, did you? I heard about guys that try that crap."

"No, Hick. But we did enter through the parking garage last night so that I didn't have to drag you through the lobby." Peter noticed his own bed had been made. "I see housekeeping came by. Did they ask you any questions?"

"Nope," said Hick. "They didn't speak no English. I just sat in the chair over there and lifted my feet when they vacuumed. They brought fresh towels and made the beds real nice."

There was a knock at the door.

"Hey, that's probably Carlos with my clothes," said Hick.

Peter answered the door, slipped Carlos a five and returned with Hick's well-worn flannel shirt, jeans and underclothes.

"Put these on," said Peter. "I'm starving and I'll take you to the sports bar on the corner. They make a great burger. Of course, you're probably not hungry."

"No, no, no. I could eat. Just give me a minute to get dressed."

Hick hopped out of the bed and another empty beer can dropped onto the floor.

* * *

Murphy's Sports Bar had a menu that was much more imaginative than its name. Peter enjoyed his Piggly Wrigley, a burger wrapped in bacon and topped with a slice of goat cheese. Hick ordered the Ground Drool Double, two 1/3 pound patties drenched in barbecue sauce and served with a lobster bib and a dozen moist towelettes.

Hick held his pint of ale in his good hand. "To Henry."

"To Henry," agreed Peter as he raised his own pint.

"Thanks for letting me drink. I appreciate the fact that you ain't trying to save me. I heard so many damn lectures over the years and it's just a waste of breath."

"I'm not here to rescue you, Hick."

"I only been drinking beer today, Peter," said Hick proudly. "I want you to know that's like going cold turkey to a hard drinker like myself."

"I'm flattered," answered Peter.

"So how is Henry? Last I heard he was still in Chicago. I ain't much for staying in touch, but I knew *that* much. I know he musta sent you here. God bless that man. I don't know what I done to deserve a friend like Henry."

"Henry's not doing well," said Peter. "That's why I wanted to find you. The doctors aren't sure how much time he has left."

Peter sat quietly while Hick absorbed the news.

"Sorry to hear that. What's he got? Did liver number two give out?"

"He's got cancer. I guess when you've got a transplanted organ and you're on these anti-rejection drugs to suppress your immune system, you're susceptible to some pretty nasty stuff."

"Ah, crap, that's terrible," said Hick.

"I guess you're lucky. Henry destroyed his liver. But yours seems to be OK."

"What are you talking about?" asked Hick seriously.

"I mean all those years of hard drinking. I'll bet the two of you really tore it up in the old days. Henry's liver just couldn't take it."

Hick set his glass down and looked Peter squarely in the eye. "Your father was never a drinker. Oh, sure he might hoist a beer once in a while on a hot day, or if there ain't nothing else around. But I never once saw him drunk. He likes hanging out in bars because of the atmosphere, that's where his friends are. He loves to be social, but that's as far as it goes."

"But he had a liver transplant."

Hick shrugged. "I ain't a doctor. I just know what I know. By all rights, I should be the one with the bad liver. Your father's a stronger man than me." Hick took another bite of his burger and sauce rolled down his chin and dripped onto his lap.

Hick caught Peter staring at the hook.

"You noticed this, huh? I thought your dad maybe told you. I lost it in the same firefight that sent Henry home. Henry took a bullet to his left shoulder and another to his right arm. I got hit by a piece of shrapnel, it slashed through the hand and tore it to shreds."

"I'm sorry," said Peter.

"Hey, what are ya gonna do, huh?" shrugged Hick. "This was my ticket home. Lots of guys, like Retter and lots of others never even made it off the damn battlefield." Hick took another drink and continued. "Some guys like Hendrix and Sonny made it through without a scratch, except for the stuff they can't get outta their heads. Some wounds, they're harder to see. Now take your father. I guess his fate was sealed when he went after Hot Rod."

"What do you mean?"

"Your dad never told you this?" asked Hick.

"No," said Peter, hoping Hick would continue.

"Well, we were crossing this open field through the jungle, which was probably a mistake, but it seemed quiet enough. Then before we can react, bullets are flying and Hot Rod's hit. We all hit the ground. We're in the weeds and we crawl over to this ditch, the only place to hide out there so it's pretty damn obvious where we are. Hot Rod's wailing out there, and without a thought Retter runs out to drag Hot Rod back. I'm looking out, trying to provide some cover for

Retter, firing into the trees. And right there in front of my eyes Retter is mowed down by a barrage of sniper fire, the most violent thing I ever seen. The rest of us are in the ditch, and Sonny is on a walkie-talkie trying to call in some air support."

Hick took another drink of beer and Peter leaned further forward. "Well," Hick continued, "Hot Rod is still out there, bleeding. He's in the weeds about ten yards away, in the direction of the trees where the Viet Cong are waiting. We can hear him moaning. Henry runs out to Hot Rod. He gets hit in the shoulder on the way out. He makes it to Hot Rod, whose freakin' legs are tore up. Henry lifts Hot Rod and carries him back to the ditch, and gets hit again in the arm on the way back. I get hit by shrapnel from a grenade launched from the trees. Then we get lucky. The next ten minutes feel like hours but then this Huey appears like a vision, swoops in and torches the jungle. We get Medi-Vac'd out. Me, Henry and Hot Rod go to the field hospital. And Retter goes to heaven I guess."

Peter sat stunned.

"Your father didn't have to do that, you know. We all had a gut check lying in that freakin' ditch. Hot Rod coulda bled to death out there and nobody woulda asked any questions. But Henry, dammit, he brought Hot Rod back. I'll never forget that moment back in the ditch with Henry holding Hot Rod in his arms, both of 'em covered in blood. Henry musta been running on pure adrenalin. We didn't even know he was shot 'til we were in the damn helicopter. I know Henry would never say it but he's a friggin' hero. And more than that, he's a good man, the best man I ever knew."

Peter took a long drink of his beer and said nothing.

"War is hell, Peter. We all handled it different. Me, I found the bottle. It numbs everything. You don't just shrug off something like war. It becomes a part of you."

"What about Hot Rod? What happened to him?"

"Some guys had to escape, even while it was going on. Hot Rod shot heroin. It happened to some guys over there. The constant threat of your own violent death when you're twenty years old does some strange shit to you. Watching your friends get blown up in front of your face. Anyways, they sent Hot Rod home to Atlanta. His legs were gone, he was in a chair. He did alright for a while. We'd see him at reunions. Sometime in the mid-80's he got real bad. He couldn't get a job. Turns out he had hepatitis, probably from sharing needles with another junkie in Nam. Henry went down to Atlanta to help Hot Rod, just like he done back in the war. Matter of fact, Henry was with Hot Rod when he died. It hit him really hard. I don't think I can explain it to you. War does crazy shit to a man's head, even if he gets out alive."

Peter hadn't even touched his burger. But he wasn't very hungry.

"Look," said Hick, noticing that Peter was lost in thought. "I hope it was OK for me to tell you all this. Somehow I thought Henry woulda."

"Yeah," mumbled Peter, taking another drink of his beer.

"Anyway, now you know."

"Yeah," said Peter again, returning from his thoughts. "I'm learning all sorts of stuff. Hey, you know I found out that Henry was up here about a year ago, looking for you. But I guess he didn't find you."

"Nope. Woulda been nice to see the old guy," smiled Hick.

"I think he might have also been looking for a video. You know anything about a video? One of my family, my sister and me?"

Hick smiled. "I might."

Hick reached under his collar and showed Peter the long silver chain that was around his neck. A key was dangling from the end of it.

"I got a safe deposit box. It's down at First National. That tape is the only thing in it. You know there been times when I wanted to end it all, but I knew that Henry needed me to hold onto that tape. I tell you it kept me going. I'd do anything for Henry, you know."

Peter ordered another round and his appetite returned. Hick just winked.

49

THAR SHE BLOWS!

When Delmar was running late like he was this morning, he had a few rather extreme shortcuts that saved him about ten minutes. All of them involved slightly illegal maneuvers, like driving about twenty five feet the wrong way on a one-way street, cutting through a medical supply company's parking lot to avoid a stoplight, and coming in the back "Trucks Only" entrance of the BM&P parking lot.

But he had no choice. He came in through the back entrance again this morning, drove past a sea of port-a-potties that stretched out as far as the eye could see, and around the warehouse-shaped brown brick building into his parking spot in the opposite corner of the front parking lot.

He looked at his watch: 8:07 a.m.

"Crap," he said as pulled the key out of his ignition. He grabbed his cup of coffee and his briefcase and sprinted toward the front door.

The receptionist Bridget tried to talk to him as he ran past her. He didn't respond. He just opened the door to the conference room.

Oscar Case looked up from the end of the table. He looked at his watch; not amused.

"Three days in a row, Delmar," he said.

"I know, boss," Delmar apologized. "I've been getting coffee at a new place and their line just moves so damn slow."

"We have coffee here, you know," Oscar pointed out.

"I'm not sure that brown liquid in the coffee-maker meets the legal definition of coffee," Delmar said, eliciting giggles around the table. The other salesmen were all in their seats, and each of them had some sort of purchased coffee in front of them.

Oscar didn't join in their frivolity. "I'm serious Dunwoody. Get your ass in here on time."

"I know. I'm sorry."

Delmar took the last empty seat, placing his briefcase on the table in front of him.

"We were just discussing the latest complaints from Carpentersville Rib Fest," Oscar said. "Before we were so rudely interrupted, Keith had the floor. He was telling us that they were balking about using us this year. What seems to be the problem?"

"You know how that lady is, boss," Keith said. "She is absolutely positive that we have Japanese toilets that will explode on her."

"Didn't you tell her that our models are from Taiwan?" Oscar asked. "And that the whole exploding toilet thing is an urban legend?"

"Yes I did," Keith continued, "but she said she saw it on the Internet. Something about the combination of methane gas, hot temperatures, and what happens when the fans aren't working properly..."

"The shit hits the fan," Brian the new guy said.

Everyone turned toward him and glared.

"Sorry," he said.

"Tell her that Snopes.com has debunked the whole exploding toilet thing," Oscar said. "Send her the link. That usually ends it."

"But there was one suspicious incident in Japan with Ishikawa's EasyFlow 360," Keith pointed out. "You heard what happened there, right?"

"Dung Pao," joked Brian.

Everyone glared again. This time Brian slouched in his seat.

"That hasn't been debunked yet," Keith continued. "They just added it to the bottom of the exploding toilet page, and its final assessment says 'Insufficient Evidence'."

"It's on the same page?" Oscar asked.

"Yup."

"Crap," Oscar said.

"I got the same routine from Stuart at Page Construction last week," Delmar piped in. "I just told him we don't use the EasyFlow 360s because those things are way too high-tech for us."

"But why are they exploding?" Keith asked. "Shouldn't we be worried about that?"

"If we were in Japan, then yes," Oscar said. "But I'm not worried about toilets exploding thousands of miles away from us. You know what I'm worried about?"

The four salesmen all looked down and muttered it at the same time.

"Leads."

"Right!"

"What have we got?"

Keith, Brian, and Stephen each had a half dozen or so to pursue. Oscar talked them through the possible objections, how to counter them, and of course, the nearest bakery to visit before the sales call.

"Frosted cookies," he reminded them again.

Each man nodded at the sage advice.

"OK, Delmar," Oscar said. "What have you got?"

"Um..." He couldn't make eye contact with Oscar. "I've got a few possibilities, but I didn't bring them with me. I have them written down at my desk. I'll drop by your office in a little while and let you know."

Oscar was staring at his star salesman and protégé, just waiting to meet eyes with him. When Delmar sheepishly looked at his boss, Oscar bared his gritted teeth.

"Gentlemen," he said, never averting his stare from Delmar's face, "would you mind giving us a moment?"

The other salesmen nearly sprinted out of the room.

"Close the door behind you," he reminded them.

When the door clicked shut, Oscar pounced.

"You have to get over this broad," Oscar said. "Dammit-- I need the real you out there, Delmar, the best damn salesman I ever trained, not this guy, this guy... this guy impersonating you. Do you know how quickly this office will sink if we have to count on nimrods like Keith and Brian? For God's sake—snap out of it!"

"It's not quite that easy," Delmar said.

Oscar exhaled. After looking at the droopy expression on his friend's face, his tone of voice changed. He spoke as softly as he could manage. "Look, I know you really liked her..."

"I thought she was the one," Delmar said.

"I know, but c'mon, here. You weren't even like this when you got divorced. That had to be worse than this."

Delmar didn't say anything.

"I'm not trying to be a dick, and I know we go way back, Delmar," Oscar said, "but I really do have an office to run here. I can't have my best salesman—the example for my entire staff— moping around the office. And poor Bridget at the front desk. Think about her! She's the one who has to explain to everyone that your voicemail isn't working. We both know it would be working just fine if you'd just erase that twenty minute voicemail Gina left you."

"I know," Delmar said. "I know. I'll get Bridget some frosted cookies."

"Don't get her cookies," Oscar said. "Erase the damn voicemail so that you have room on that thing for real clients needing real toilets."

"OK, OK," Delmar said. "I'll take care of it. I promise. I'm just not quite ready yet..."

"When will you be ready?"

Delmar took a sip of coffee rather than answer the unanswerable question. Blech. This new coffee place wasn't cutting it.

There was a knock on the door. "We're still in a meeting," Oscar yelled.

"OK," Bridget said from the other side of the door. "I'll take a message. Delmar's voicemail is still full."

"Is it a client?" Oscar asked.

"No, it's personal," Bridget replied.

"Wait a second," Oscar said. He ran over to the door and pulled it open with a swoosh. "If it's Gina, put her through. He'll talk to her *right now*."

Delmar was horrified. He waved his hand back and forth. "No, no, no..."

"It's not Gina," Bridget said. "It's a little girl."

50

GUESS WHO'S COMING TO DINNER?

Emily was perplexed. "Mom, is it fork on the left side, and spoon and knife on the right, or is it the other way around?" She was busy setting the dining room table with Libby's newly unearthed china and silverware, while Gina was stirring the spaghetti sauce in their little kitchen.

"Nobody really cares, honey," Gina called toward her daughter.

"Maybe not for a regular dinner," Emily said, as she switched them back and forth trying to see which one looked correct. "But for a dinner party it should look like a restaurant."

Gina smiled.

"I don't think Libby will even notice," she said. "Just pick one and do it the same way on all three place settings."

After Emily settled on putting the forks on the left, she joined her mother in the kitchen.

"It smells good, Mom," she said half-heartedly. She didn't say another word, but the way that sentence was left hanging in the air, Gina knew there was more. She stopped stirring and looked at her daughter.

"But what?"

"I didn't say but."

"Emily..."

Emily tried to say it gingerly.

"But... do you think spaghetti is fancy enough for a dinner party?"

Gina put her hand on her hip. "I'd hardly call dinner with Libby a dinner party."

"But we're using the china!" Emily pointed out.

"So? You can eat spaghetti off china too. Trust me. This will be like gourmet dining for Libby. I've seen her eating cold SpaghettiOs right out of the can. A night without SpaghettiOs or macaroni and cheese is like a night at the opera for her."

"If you say so."

Emily hugged her mom.

"What is that for?" Gina asked.

"Nothing."

Emily released the hug and looked up at her mom's face.

"I like your hair that color," she said.

"It's my natural color," Gina said. "I had almost forgotten what it was."

"It looks just like mine now."

Gina smiled. "It looks better on you."

"And your eyes are the same color as me now too," Emily added. "I like it when you don't wear those color contacts. Do you think we'll look like sisters when I get a little older?"

"I wish," Gina said.

She put a small spoonful of sauce on the wooden spoon and brought it up to her lips. It was a little hot, but after blowing on it a bit, she managed to taste it. Not bad. Maybe a tad heavy on the basil, but much better than the generic spaghetti sauce that was in the jar fifteen minutes ago.

"Mom," Emily said, still by her mother's side. "Want me to stir that while you get dressed?"

Gina looked at her daughter again. The hand went right back to her hip. "What's wrong with what I'm wearing?"

"Oh nothing," Emily said. "It's one of my favorite tops."

Gina kissed her daughter on the forehead. "I'm not changing."

There was a knock on the door.

"I'll get it," Emily yelped and ran around the corner toward the front door. Gina giggled at her daughter's excitement. It reminded her of her own mother's excitement on dinner party nights. Maybe the girly-girl thing skips a generation.

Gina heard the door open, but instead of Libby's voice, she heard a man's voice. She couldn't see who it was because a partitioned wall stood between them, but she certainly knew the voice as soon as he said...

"Hello Emily."

Gina dropped the wooden spoon into the sauce. "Oh my God." She looked at her outfit again. "Oh my God." She fiddled with her hair, straightened her blouse, and started to walk out from around the corner, but then stopped. Started again, and stopped again. There was no way to escape from inside the kitchen. If she left the room, he would see her. Even though she wanted to do nothing more than run away, her body was frozen in place. But her ears perked up to listen to the conversation.

"Thanks for inviting me," Delmar said.

"You're welcome," Emily replied.

"I found another copy of the CD for you," Delmar said. "The other one was a little trashed."

"Sorry about that," Emily said. "Thank you for the CD."

"You're welcome. The bottle of wine is for your mom. She liked it when we had some at my apartment a few weeks ago. I hope it goes with dinner."

"She's making spaghetti," Emily said.

"I love spaghetti," Delmar said.

"If she knew it was you she might have made something fancier, and might have worn something a little nicer, but..."

Gina shook her head in the kitchen, and muttered under her breath. "Oh great, just great."

"Um, where is she?" Delmar asked. His voice sounded nervous.

"She's in the kitchen," Emily explained. "It's right around the corner."

"Where?" Delmar asked, pointing. "Over here?"

"Yeah."

Gina could hear their footsteps approaching. Her heart leapt into her throat, and she staggered back and forth wondering what to do. The footsteps stopped just around the corner, out of her view. She was holding her breath and didn't even realize it.

"Are you going in there?" Emily asked.

"Yes," Delmar said, but his legs had stopped moving. He was awaiting Gina's emergence. His stomach was all tied up in knots.

"She might yell," Emily whispered. "She's kinda mad you haven't returned her call."

"I know," Delmar whispered back. "I'm sorry about that. That wasn't very nice, was it?"

"It wasn't nice of her to lie either," Emily whispered. It was more of a stage whisper, easily overheard by her mother just around the corner. "But like I told you on the phone, that was all my fault. I was just worried that if you knew that she had a kid you wouldn't want to date her anymore, and she really really likes you. I mean she *really* likes you. I've never seen her like this before. You know what she told me that first night you went on a date?"

Gina had heard enough. This had to be stopped and stopped fast. She whirled around the corner before Emily could say another word.

"OK, Emily," Gina said. She was glaring at her daughter. "Thanks for all your *help*. Don't you have some homework to finish up in the bedroom or something?"

"Not really."

Gina simply pointed toward the bedroom. Emily sheepishly but obediently disappeared from view within a few seconds. The door closed behind her, leaving Delmar and Gina face to face for the first time since the blow up in the bowling alley.

They stared at each other. Neither one could formulate a cogent thought.

"Um, I'm so, you know, we have good china," Gina said, averting her eyes and pointing to the table. "It belongs to the landlady. That's who I thought was coming over for dinner tonight. Emily didn't tell me that—"

"I like your hair," Delmar interrupted.

Gina turned back toward him and looked in his eyes.

"It's my real color."

"It looks nice. And your eyes?"

"Real color."

"Lovely."

"Still need contacts," Gina said. "I'm blind as a bat."

"Me too."

"Wait a minute," Gina said, light bulb going on over her head. "It's Thursday night, why aren't you bowling tonight?"

Delmar gulped. He was afraid of speaking because he was sure he wouldn't be able to spit it out. "Some things are more important than bowling."

Gina instantly softened, and Delmar noticed.

"Is this the part where you start screaming at me?" he joked. "Emily told me you were mad at me."

"Of course I am, you big jerk," she said. "I apologized a thousand times on that voicemail. I'm not a big apologizer, but I felt terrible for creating a scene. For telling you... well, for everything. But after you didn't call back, I just started getting pissed. Every day you didn't call, I got more and more pissed."

"I'm so sorry," he said. "I guess I have some explaining to do, don't I?"

"Yes you do," Gina said. "But I do too..."

"Emily told me," Delmar said. "She called me at the office today."

"I didn't tell her to do that," Gina said. "I would never do that."

"I know," Delmar said. "She really is something, isn't she?"

Gina smiled. Emily, ear glued to the bedroom door, smiled too.

"Look," Delmar explained. "I practiced what I was going to say to you on my way over here, so let me just say it, OK?"

Gina nodded, but the anxiety returned to the pit of her stomach.

"I was talking to Oscar today just before Emily called and he said something that really made me think. He reminded me that I wasn't even this hurt when I got divorced. That's something that really hit home. I was thinking about it all day."

He cleared his throat. Gina didn't dare say a word to interrupt his train of thought. She waited for him to continue.

"I finally figured out why that is. Even though we were married, I never really felt like I could be myself around Lydia. I knew what she wanted me to be, and I tried to be that—and wow did I suck at it."

Gina laughed. Delmar did too. It helped him continue.

"And at first I tried to do the same thing with you. That's why I took you to that stupid night club. And you were going to get rid of me then too."

"Do you blame me?" she asked. The memory brought a smile to her face.

"No," he said. "I don't. I don't at all. But then you did something she didn't do. You gave me a second chance. And I decided, the hell with it. No more being what people think I should be. I wanted you to love me for me, and if you didn't, it wasn't meant to be. So I put it all out there for you. I let you see how pathetic my personal life was. I told you that bowling was my favorite thing to do. I let you rifle through my embarrassing record collection. I even threw out my emu oil for you. I was balding right before your eyes, in the open, for all to see."

That made Gina laugh again.

"But that day I came to your coffee shop and professed my love in front of everyone—that was the real me. That's how happy you made me. For once in my life, I let it all hang out. In the open. In public. And after I did that, after I really let it all hang out, I found out that you hadn't been doing the same for me..." he said, his voice trailing off. "You were pretending that—

" —I'm so sorry," she said.

"Let me finish," he said. "I kept thinking about my ex-wife—and how that ended. I didn't feel any of this then—not any of it. It didn't hurt as much when she left me, because she didn't leave me. She left the person I was pretending to be."

Delmar looked into Gina's real green eyes.

"But I'm happy I didn't show her the real me," Delmar said, his voice gaining strength, "because if I had, I wouldn't have met you."

Gina didn't say anything at first. She just stared at Delmar.

"Aw shit," Gina finally muttered, and stomped on the ground. "This is going to sound real bad after that beautiful speech."

"What?"

"OK," she said. She hesitated to continue. This whole honesty thing was much harder than it looked. "OK, there's one more thing. But this is the last thing I haven't been completely honest about, I promise."

"What is?"

"It's going to sound really bad, but I have a good reason, OK?"

"What?"

"Promise me you won't get mad."

"I won't get mad," Delmar said. "Not if it's the truth."

"OK," she said, and exhaled. She dug deep to conjure the words that hadn't been said out loud in eight years. "Here it is. My name isn't really Gina."

"What?" Delmar said.

"What?" Emily said, her ear still glued to the bedroom door. She said it loud enough that both Delmar and Gina looked in the direction of her voice.

Gina answered both of them. "I mean, it is Gina now, but I wasn't born Gina. I had to legally change it because my creepy ex-boyfriend, Emily's father, was a stalker, and I didn't want him to find us."

"So what is your real name?" Delmar asked.

"It's Sarah."

"Really?"

"Yeah. Sarah. Sarah *Stankiewicz*."

Delmar was taken aback. "You mean like Henry?"

"Yes, like Henry."

"Well what kind of a coincidence is that?"

"The kind of coincidence that happens when your father is Henry Stankiewicz."

51

SPEECHLESS

Maybe Henry was right, thought Reed. Maybe he needed a little break. The office was becoming less stressful now. But it was still work. On the other hand, going straight home to Lucy was becoming more stressful. Maybe he needed an outlet. Maybe going bowling would be fun. Reed couldn't remember the last time he'd had fun.

Reed had driven to work this morning. The trip reminded him why he normally took the train. The Dan Ryan had been backed up with a gaper's delay, which drove him nuts. The train was faster and he could actually get something done.

Now, after a full day of meetings and cost analyses, Reed relaxed in his Camry, heading north on Lake Shore Drive. He'd stayed a little late in order to miss the worst of the evening rush hour. As he drove, he admired the breathtakingly expansive lake to the east; man and nature right up against one another.

Reed exited at Belmont, wound his way west and north past Wrigley Field. Being from the Beverly neighborhood on the South Side, Reed was a dyed-in-the-wool White Sox fan. But he still appreciated the charm of the 'Friendly Confines'. Luckily there wasn't a game tonight. He headed west on Addison Street to Western Avenue.

Reed spotted the huge neon sign and pulled into the parking lot behind Waveland Bowl, unsure of what to expect. He knew Henry would be there, and Ramon from the parking garage. Reed would be the outsider, but something told him that accepting Henry's invitation was the right choice. Maybe it was Will. Camping and now bowling. "What's next, son?" he said to himself as he opened the building's glass doors.

Henry was sitting just inside. He got up slowly when he spotted Reed. Henry gritted his teeth to mask the sharp pain in his gut. "There he is. Glad you could make it, Reed."

"Thanks, Henry. I'm glad I'm here too."

"Great, great," said Henry, leading the way to their lane, 22 tonight. Half way there, Henry stopped at the shoe counter. "What size do you wear?"

"Huh?" said Reed. "No, that's OK. I'm just gonna watch, like we said."

"Yeah, well about that," chuckled Henry. "We just found out that our fourth won't make it tonight. Girl trouble. So it turns out you're here on the perfect night."

Reed watched Henry warily. Had he been hoodwinked?

"Look, Henry, I haven't bowled for decades."

"Well it's still the same game, roll the ball, hit the pins. C'mon. We really need you. Otherwise we'd have to forfeit. We truly don't mind if you suck."

"Alright," said Reed after a moment. "Ten-and-a-half should do it."

"A pair of your finest ten-and-a-halfs for my friend," said Henry to the clerk.

Reed carried the shoes to the lane.

"Fellas," announced Henry, "This is Reed. He's got a 210 average and he's going to clean house tonight. Reed, these are the fellas. You know Ramon, and this is Oscar."

Henry sat down to rest. He was breathing heavily.

"Nice to meet you, Oscar. Good to see you, Ramon," said Reed, nodding and shaking hands. "I'm afraid that the 210 would actually be closer to my total score for three games."

"Perfect," said Oscar. "Then we're right where we'd be with Delmar. You'll fit right in."

"Hey, Reed," said Ramon. "Do you drink?"

"Actually no, not anymore," shrugged Reed.

"Well, do you buy?" asked Ramon.

"Sure," smiled Reed.

"Even better," said Ramon. "You're officially one of us. Congratulations. But I recommend you lose the sport coat."

* * *

Dick Weber's Illegitimate Children had considered protesting Reed playing as a sub. There were teams that brought in ringers. But after watching Reed take a few warm-up throws, the 'Webers' relaxed. Reed was just as bad as he'd said he was. And the evening progressed as expected. The Living Wills kept it close, but lost.

"Hey, Reed," said Oscar. "That wasn't bad at all. I'm glad you joined us. I hope we can call you if we ever need a sub again."

Reed laughed. "You can't be serious."

"Sure he's serious," added Ramon. "The good bowlers we know won't bowl with us. They are all on much better teams. We're just happy not to have to forfeit."

"Well," said Reed, "with a vote of confidence like that, how could I say no? If you guys ever need a fourth and you don't care that I suck, I'd love to join you."

Marge came around to clean up the bar debris, glasses, bottles and wrappers that the team had accumulated through the evening. "Last call. You guys want another round?"

"Actually," said Henry, "Why don't you bring out that bottle now. Thanks."

And Marge left.

"A bottle?" asked Reed.

"Is it that time of year again already?" asked Oscar. "Time really flies."

"Yes, it does," said Henry, wiping cold sweat from his brow with his bowling towel.

Marge returned with a tray carrying the chilled bottle of champagne Henry had brought and four tumblers. "Sorry about the hardware, honey," said Marge. "We don't even keep champagne in the building. So we ain't got those fancy tall glasses neither."

"This will be perfect, Marge. Thank you." And Henry uncorked the bottle. Reed was completely in the dark. Henry, Oscar and Ramon seemed to know the drill.

Henry filled the glasses and passed them around.

"Reed, I know you don't drink but this is a special occasion, an important anniversary. We do this every year. You can just hold the glass, or smell it, or whatever. But I would really like you to join us."

Reed nodded his head and took a glass in hand.

The lanes were emptying out. The team was now among just a few stragglers left in the building.

Henry cleared his throat and stood facing his three friends who sat quietly in the plastic chairs. "Now, this is a special night. We are all blessed by the people in our lives, and it is important to recognize those people, whether they are here or far away, whether they are with us or they have passed on. Tonight, like every year, we recognize such a person. Eight years ago tonight, I was on my way out. My liver was shutting down and they gave me twenty-four hours to live. My only hope was a liver transplant."

The glass shook in Henry's hand. But he continued.

"On that same fateful day, a family that I didn't even know was going through heartache that I can only imagine," said Henry, his voice quivering. "Their young son had been in a terrible car accident. His broken body was in a hospital bed, being kept alive by machines. This family, at the same time as being crushed by this tragedy, made a selfless decision. After saying goodbye to their precious boy, they decided to abide by their son's wishes and donate his organs. In the depths of their incredible pain, they gave life and they saved my life. Eight years of sunrises and sunsets, to enjoy my friends and my new wife, to reconnect with my son. I haven't taken a single one of those days for granted. All of these amazing things were made possible by the kindness of strangers. To this family I owe everything. We drink to their beautiful generosity, and we hope that they may find comfort that some good came from this tragedy."

Oscar and Ramon raised the glasses to their lips. They'd heard it before. But this time Henry stopped them. "Not yet, fellas. For tonight is even more special than that. Tonight we have the unbelievable opportunity to actually thank these wonderful people in person. Or at least one of them."

And then Henry turned to Reed, tears pouring down his face. And now the shock on Reed's face was turning to recognition ."To young Will O'Hern, and to his father Reed. There is no way I can ever repay you and Lucy for your selfless act of kindness. And nothing I can do will bring back your beautiful boy. But I hope there is some comfort in knowing that your son's death has brought life. God bless you."

Reed rose unsteadily to his feet. How could this be? Henry moved forward and gave Reed an awkward bear hug. Reed stood frozen, utterly without words.

52

Two More Seconds

Lucy was asleep on the couch when Reed walked in the door. She was covered with the burgundy blanket they kept in the front closet for cold winter nights of television viewing.

The lamp next to the couch illuminated more than just his sleeping wife. The Yellow Pages were on the coffee table, open to the listing of hospitals. The cordless phone sat on top of the phone book, and there was a box of Kleenex right next to it. Several crumpled tissues were strewn about the table.

Reed's heart sank as soon as he saw the scene before him. He knew immediately how big of a mistake he just made. How could he have been so stupid? He sat by her side on the couch, and gently touched her shoulder.

"I'm home," he said. He kissed her on the forehead.

"Where in the world were you?" she asked groggily.

"I'm sorry that took longer than I thought it would," Reed said. "Henry and I started talking and the time just flew away. I didn't realize it was this late."

"You should have called," Lucy said.

"I did call," Reed said. "From the bowling alley."

"You said you'd be home in a few hours," she said. "Not five hours. You should have called again."

"My phone is sitting right over there on the table," Reed pointed out.

"I know," she said. "I heard it ring when I called looking for you. You should have borrowed someone else's phone."

"I know," he said.

"I was worried sick. You know where my mind goes, especially today of all days."

"I know," Reed replied. He glanced over at the Yellow Pages, and shook his head. His mind probably would have gone there too. "I'm sorry, honey."

"So what is this big news you told me we needed to talk about?" she asked. Lucy's eyes were still blinking, trying to get adjusted to the light. When she finally focused enough to see him, Reed's concerned facial expression made her nervous all over again. "Did something happen?"

"Yes," he said. "I have something really important to tell you, but I'm not exactly sure how you're going to react."

The color drained from Lucy's face, and her shoulders tensed. "What happened?"

"Actually something amazing happened," he began. "But I'm worried how you're going to take it. Henry told me something about Will."

Lucy suddenly couldn't even look at her husband. She got up and tried to get away, but Reed grabbed her hand and urged her to sit back down.

"You need to hear this."

"I don't need to hear anything," she protested. She struggled to get away from his grip. "I just spent the last three hours reliving the night he died, sure that my husband was dead now too, and that's enough for one night. I'm going to bed."

"Please, honey," Reed said, hanging on for dear life. "Let me finish. Henry and I talked all night because he had something important to tell me."

"No more," she said. "I can't handle anything else right now." She tugged, but Reed wouldn't let go.

"Do you know where Henry lived before he came to Chicago?" he said. He held on for dear life, and just spit it out. "Oklahoma. Oklahoma, Lucy. He lived there exactly eight years ago."

When she heard the name of the state her son took his last breath in, she stopped struggling for a moment, and looked at Reed. He was fighting back tears.

"Please Lucy," he said. His voice cracked a little as he said her name. "Please sit down. I need to tell you this."

Against her better judgment, Lucy quietly sat back down next to Reed. She couldn't look in his eyes anymore, but she did manage to eke out a question.

"Did Henry know Will?"

"Not exactly," Reed explained. "But he lived near the school — just an hour or so away from downtown Norman. Henry was very sick back in those days. The doctors had told him that he was going to die in a day or two if he didn't get a new liver, so they moved him to the top of the liver transplant list. And that morning at the VA in Oklahoma City, while he was making his final peace with God, he got the call. Henry got his call the same night we got our call. Do you remember that night?"

"Do... I... remember?"

"I know you remember," Reed cringed. Bad choice of words; *real* bad choice of words. He was trying to be as soothing as possible. He needed to start over.

"That night on the phone," he said. "I had to answer all those questions about him — before we flew down there to bring him back home..."

Lucy's eyes were closed, and her entire body was tensed.

"He was an organ donor," Reed said. "Remember? They asked me if I had any objections, and..."

Now Reed couldn't continue for a moment. He took a deep breath.

"I didn't even think about it, honey," he finally said, gasping between breaths. "I just said it was fine. I didn't even think about it.

Two seconds. That's all it was. Two seconds. They asked... and I said yes, and... I never... thought... about it again. When we got down there I signed all the paperwork, but I didn't even read it. I couldn't think about anything but Will, and how empty my life would be without him..."

Reed broke down and could barely sputter the words.

"God, Lucy, you know how much I loved that boy. I loved that boy more than I loved life itself. I have begged God to take me too, and cursed that bastard because He wouldn't. I cursed Him every night. It's not right for the son to go before the father. It's not right. But He just left me here to ache in my heart every single day... I miss our boy so damn much..."

Reed couldn't regain his composure for several seconds. Lucy tried to comfort him by putting her arm around him. "Me too," she muttered. "Me too."

She handed him one of her wet Kleenex, and he wiped away as much as he could. There was so much more to tell, but no way to get the words from his heart to his brain to his mouth. It took him several seconds to recover. He took a deep breath, and forged ahead.

"But until tonight," Reed said, "I only thought about what was gone, not what was still..."

Lucy's mind started racing. "Wait a minute."

Reed looked at her. Was that a trace of recognition in her eyes?

"Did Henry..." she asked.

Reed nodded.

"Henry got Will's liver?" she asked.

Reed nodded again.

"But how in the world did Henry... and you..."

"That's what I wanted to know," Reed said. "That's why I'm so late tonight. I had a million questions too."

Reed placed the wet Kleenex on the coffee table.

"After the procedure," he explained, slowly regaining his voice, "he asked the hospital for his donor's information. Apparently I had told the hospital that I didn't want to share any personal information with the recipient. It must have been one of the questions I had to answer, or something I signed when I got down there. I don't even remember them asking me about it... but I was... so... so..."

"I know," she said.

"And so," he continued, after another long sniff. "So Henry wasn't given our name. He was only told that the liver came from an 18-year-old male who died in a car accident. That immediately touched a nerve with him, because Henry had a son about the same age. After he got out of the hospital he scoured the papers looking for stories from that day. As you can imagine, not many 18-year-olds died in Oklahoma around that time, so when he saw the story about the accident, he knew. And when Henry read that Will's hometown was Chicago — same town Henry's son lived — and that he was going to be buried here, he saw it as a sign. A sign that he had to come home too."

"But the parking garage..." she said.

"Henry said he was looking for a job when he came to town, and he couldn't explain why, but he saw the ad in the paper for the opening at the garage, and he was just drawn to it. Looking back now, all he remembers is that he was drawn to that ad. He had never worked in a parking garage in his life."

"He didn't know you worked there?" she asked.

"He had no idea. He didn't even realize who I was the first couple of years we talked to each other. He said that there was just something about me that he connected with. His gut just told him we would be friends. And you know what, Lucy," Reed said, turning to face his wife, "I felt the same way the very first time we talked. You know me. I'm not that comfortable talking to strangers, but I felt comfortable with Henry right away. I felt like I had known him for years."

Lucy's mind was reeling, thinking back.

"Henry told me that the day I confided in him about Will was the first time he asked me my last name, and it almost took his breath away."

"Why didn't he say something?" she asked.

"Because we signed the forms saying that we didn't want the recipient to know, and he didn't want me to think he was some weirdo stalker. When he realized who I was, he wanted to do something to pay us back but he could never think of anything; nothing that could pay us back for what we had given him. We had given him eight years of his life -- how do you pay somebody back for that? He had no money. He had no possessions."

"I always thought it was so weird that you listened to him..." she said.

Reed nodded. He wiped away the tears with the back of his hand. Lucy put her arm around her husband.

"You know what's funny though?" Reed said. "He felt like he didn't give me anything, and kept apologizing for that, but he gave me something that nobody else could have given me. Before I knew any of this, he had already saved me."

Lucy got a lump in her throat, and the tears rolled down her cheeks too.

"You've seen it," Reed said. "I was just going through the motions, just biding my time, just waiting to die. I wasn't alive at all. Nothing should have been able to reach me—I was a dead man walking."

Lucy nodded. She knew that feeling all too well.

"But something inside him reached inside of me."

"What made him tell you this tonight?" she asked.

"Because Henry is dying," Reed said. "He has cancer, and he wanted me to know before he was gone. He wanted both of us to know. Will gave Henry his life back, but Henry gave that life right back to me. Didn't I tell you that I felt like Will was somehow behind all this? Didn't I tell you our boy is looking out for us..."

Reed couldn't continue. He looked at Lucy, and she was struggling as badly as he was, but through the tears, and the pain, he saw something else.

He saw her smiling.

53

THE LONG WAY HOME

"I am still mad at you," said Emily, crossing her arms and gritting her teeth.

"I know," said Gina. "And I'm sorry. It was just a lie that got out of hand. You know how I always tell you not to lie? Well, this is why. Things become a big mess."

Gina and Emily sat on the bench at the bus stop, waiting for the westbound Addison 152. At six o'clock the buses come fairly regularly with people spilling off of the El and heading home.

"Look," Gina said. "I am so sorry. But believe it or not, I started all of this because I loved you. Even before you were born, I made choices I thought were the best for you. I guess you're old enough to hear this now."

"Hear what?" Emily was intrigued, but still kept her arms folded.

"When your biological father found out that I was going to have a baby, he freaked out. He wanted me to, well, not have you. He threatened to hurt me. So I left."

"What's 'bijocolical' mean?"

"Biological. It means he helped make you. But it's not like being a 'dad.' A dad is someone who loves you and helps you grow. A dad doesn't hurt you."

Emily looked east. No bus in sight. Gina continued.

"Well, I didn't want him finding me. I was afraid of what he might do. I figured it was easier to hide in big cities with a lot of people. I moved to Seattle and he found me there. One day he showed up at the store I was working at, and said he was going to hurt me if I didn't do what he said. So I left again. I left Seattle. I changed my name, and I changed how I look. I moved to Denver and that's where you were born. My name was now Gina Santelli, so when you were born you were Emily Santelli. Those are actually still our legal names. Now I've been living that lie for so long that it seems like the truth. But that's all changing now."

"Is he still looking for you?"

"I don't know. When we were in Denver, I typed my real name into the computer to see if I could learn anything. Someone had put my name and description on the Internet with a letter asking for information. But they didn't give their name. I think it was him. I was afraid if I stayed somewhere too long he'd find me. So we moved to Kansas City and then here to Chicago."

"Aren't you scared he'll find us now?"

"I saw what all the lies were doing. To you. To Delmar and me. And then when my own father didn't recognize me. I don't know, something said I should stop hiding. I can't let some shadow run my life anymore."

"What would he do to us?" asked Emily. "You said he didn't want me."

"It doesn't matter. I wanted you. And you will always be the most important thing in my life. I would never do anything to hurt you. I thought I was doing the right thing by not telling you this stuff. But now I want you to know the truth. I can't lie about it anymore. I hope you're old enough to understand."

The bus pulled to a stop at the corner and mother and daughter climbed aboard. It wouldn't be a long ride. They found two seats together near the rear of the bus.

"Why did you pick Chicago?"

"I grew up here. I thought it would be better to come back to a city I knew. After awhile I realized that coming back here made it even more important to keep up the disguise. He might think to look here for that same reason."

Emily looked around the bus now, thinking that any one of these men might be her father.

"Emily," said Gina. "My mother had warned me about this man. But I didn't listen. Think about how mad you've been at me the last few days. When I moved away from home I was 16, and I was at least ten times madder at my mother than you have ever been at me. I thought I knew everything, and I thought my mother was ruining my life. I know now that I was wrong. And I hope you're never that mad at me. Everything I do, even the mean stuff, I do because I love you. My mother never told me that. Or if she did, I wasn't listening. My mother, your grandmother, still lives in Chicago. I don't know if she's still mad at me, but I'm not mad at her."

"But she doesn't know that," said Emily. "You should tell her."

"One step at a time, baby. One step at a time."

Gina stood up and Emily followed her mother to the rear door of the bus. They got off at Leavitt, stood on the corner waiting for the light to change and walked south.

"So where are we going?" asked Emily.

"Something happened the other day completely by accident. My father, your grandfather, found me. Or I found him. I'm not sure."

"So we're going to my grandparents' house?" said Emily excitedly. She was walking quickly to keep up with Gina's pace.

"Close. My father ran off when I was about your age."

"Why?"

"I don't know. Maybe we'll find out tonight. But now that I've seen him again, I actually think that your grandfather is a lot like me. We even look alike."

About one block down Leavitt, Gina pulled a scrap of paper from her pocket and glanced at the address she'd written down. Delmar had given it to her. They stood on the sidewalk and looked up at the nicely maintained bungalow.

"If your father ran away, he didn't go very far," said Emily.

"He took the long way." Gina turned and bent down to look Emily directly in her eye. "Are you ready for this?"

"Are you?" asked Emily, holding her mother's hand.

They climbed the front stairs together and rang the doorbell.

Henry answered the door, still in his work shirt and gray khakis. His face went ashen when he saw the two of them standing there, with their soft brown hair and green eyes.

"Hi," nodded Gina. "I'm not sure if this is proper etiquette, but I thought we should stop by. Is this OK?"

"Absolutely," said Henry. "Absolutely. Please, please come in."

Henry ran his fingers through his thinning hair, and moved jerkily about the entranceway, ushering the two girls into the living room. Katherine entered from the kitchen.

"Well, who do we have here?"

"Katherine," said Henry, clearing his throat. "This, uh, this is my daughter Sarah. Or is it Gina?"

"I'm still working on that."

Henry continued. "And this, uh, this one over here, the smaller one, uh…."

Gina saved him. "This is Henry's granddaughter, Emily."

"I have to sit down," said Henry under his breath. He found an armchair.

"Hello Emily. I'm Katherine. And how old are you?"

"I'm eight," answered Emily politely.

Katherine glanced to Gina, then to Henry. An awkward silence filled the room, finally broken by Katherine.

"Eight, my goodness. Well then maybe you can help me in the kitchen. I'm baking some chocolate chip cookies and I need a tester."

"Sure!" said Emily. She took one more long look at the man who was her grandfather. She had so many questions.

"Come on, sweetheart," said Katherine. And Emily followed.

Gina and Henry were left alone in the living room. Henry sat uneasily in his armchair. Gina stood with her arms folded, leaning on her left foot.

"I'm not sure how this is supposed to go," said Gina sharply.

"I, uh, I thought about this day," said Henry. "I thought about what I'd say. But now that you're here, I don't know. Can I get you anything? A glass of milk?"

"No thanks," said Gina.

Silence.

Gina began again. "I'm not sure why I came. I guess it's for Emily. She's been asking lately about family and stuff."

"Yeah," said Henry hesitantly, "Family is good."

"Yeah. And then you appeared out of nowhere. That is the weirdest thing, that you know Delmar."

"Maybe that was what they call fate. I don't know. Life is like that sometimes."

"Yeah, maybe. When you introduced yourself to me I about had a heart attack. I didn't know what to say. I guess I still don't. When did you know it was me?"

"I still can't believe it's you. But now with the hair and the eyes…"

"When did you know?"

"I didn't have a clue until you brought Emily to the bowling alley. She's the spitting image of you at that age. That I remember." Henry shifted in his chair to ease some discomfort. "Then I asked Delmar a few questions. About your family, and what he knew, and your age and where you grew up and it all started to make some sense. But to tell you the truth, until you just walked in this house, I wasn't sure I wasn't just dreaming."

"I was mad at you for a long time," said Gina, now pacing the floor in front of Henry. "I think I still am. I'm still a little confused about how I feel. But that conversation at the pizza place, when you didn't know it was me….Are you sure you didn't know?"

"I swear," said Henry, raising his hand.

"Well, you said some things. Some nice things. And I've been thinking that it would be good for Emily to know her grandfather. Delmar also seems to think you're a good guy. I know a little about running away now myself. It gets tiring."

"I'm sorry," said Henry leaning forward. "I have done some stupid things in my life but leaving you and Peter was the worst. If I could go back, I'd do things so much different. I am so sorry."

"You're not off the hook yet. I'm gonna need a little time."

Gina finally sat, uncomfortably, on the edge of the couch and faced her father.

"So you said you see Peter once in a while?"

"Yeah, he's a fancy lawyer downtown. He and your mother are very close. When I came back to Chicago, I called Evelyn and I talk to Peter every now and then. He's doing well. He may or may not be getting married, depending who you talk to."

"Does he know about me and Emily?"

"The only person I mentioned it to is Katherine. Like I said, I wasn't even sure myself until just now. You want me to tell Peter?"

"Yeah, I guess that would be good. Emily should meet him too."

"Emily. She seems like a sweetheart." Henry paused looking for the right words. "You don't have to tell me anything, OK? About where you've been, what you've done, your hair and eyes or Emily or anything you don't want to. There's a lot of water under the bridge. I screwed up, and I can't get those years back but if I could, I would."

"So then I'll ask," said Sarah. "Where have you been?"

"Well, it's been almost twenty years. I've been all over. Atlanta, Florida, Oklahoma. I got married a couple more times. I worked. I kicked around. I know I didn't make much of my life. Seems like I missed the best parts."

"You make it sound like it's over," said Gina.

"Yeah, well," shrugged Henry.

Gina stood again and paced. Henry watched her. She stopped and sat again.

"I gotta say this. It's been, well, I just gotta say it." Sarah took a deep breath. "You hurt me. You hurt me and I can't just let it go. I was your little princess, your sugar plum, and…."

Gina was breaking down. Henry got up slowly but then sat back down, unsure of what he was supposed to do.

"....and then you were gone. You were my daddy. I was eight. Eight. And you just left. I just, I don't know. It's a lot, OK, it's a lot."

Gina pulled a tissue from her pocket and wiped her nose. "God, I didn't want to cry. Dammit."

"What do you want me to do? Anything," said Henry in a hoarse whisper.

Gina sat back on the couch. "I know one thing you could do for me."

"Anything at all," said Henry.

"There's a little girl in that kitchen who's never had a grandpa before."

"I'm not sure I know how to be a grandpa."

"It's easy. Just treat her like she's your world. Spoil her. Ask her questions. Talk to her about anything. And listen. Just listen."

"OK. Anything for you," Henry said softly.

Emily burst out of the kitchen, carrying a large silver plate of fresh baked cookies She set them on the coffee table. Katherine followed with a pitcher of milk and some glasses. Henry and Gina both quickly dried their eyes.

"I'm sorry. I tried to stop her," said Katherine. "She was so excited."

"It's OK," said Gina.

"Who wants chocolate chips?!" announced Emily.

Henry stood up slowly, seeming even larger than usual next to Emily. "I don't think we've been properly introduced, young lady. I'm Henry, Henry Stankiewicz. But if you'd like to call me Grandpa, that would be OK too."

He held out his large, calloused hand for Emily to shake. Instead she wrapped her arms around his waist. Henry hesitatingly returned the hug.

"Now, Emily," said Henry sitting back in his chair. "Tell me all about you."

54

SWEET HOME CHICAGO

Traffic coming in on the Edens was awful. Peter's trip home from Milwaukee had been a breeze until he hit the northern suburbs of Chicago. You'd think people would be leaving the city in the afternoon rush instead of crawling toward it. But Peter tried not to let it bother him. He was done. The Fetch! analysis was complete, and he'd done a damn good job of it if he did say so himself. Now he was heading home to see his baby. What could be better?

Peter had plenty of time now to think about what he would say tonight, moving at about five miles per hour staring into the back of the white panel truck directly ahead of him in the center lane. He'd bought a bottle of good champagne, some ice, and a cheap Styrofoam cooler at a liquor store near the hotel. It was chilling in the trunk. He didn't have a ring. That would be presumptuous. If she said yes, they would pick one out together.

His phone rang on the seat next to him. It was her.

"Hello, my love," said Peter.

"Hi, where are you?" asked Kelly.

"Well, first of all I've put you on speaker phone so I don't kill myself before I see you. But I'm not sure that what I'm doing actually counts as 'driving'. At this rate I should be home by September."

"Do you have company with you?"

"Company?"

"Hick."

"I offered," said Peter. "But he didn't take me up on it. I gave him some cash, including enough for a train ticket. He said he'd come visit Henry when he was up to it. Of course, he could be drinking that money right now. What can you do?"

"You can get your cute, young attorney body over here pronto. That's what you can do," answered Kelly. "I'm at your condo."

"I'm doing my best. Good things come to those who wait I guess."

"Well," whispered Kelly in her sexiest voice, "I'll be waiting."

"And I'll be idling," said Peter.

Forty minutes later, Peter was finally exiting at Ohio Street. Traffic had lightened up a bit. He pulled into the condo building's parking garage and quickly found his spot. He bounded out of the car, grabbed the few essentials, his phone and the videotape, popped the trunk, took the champagne from its icy cocoon, leaving his luggage and briefcase for later, and sprinted for the elevator.

What would she be wearing? Peter rode the elevator alone up to the fifth floor and tried to remember her smell, the scent that he'd missed so much. Should he knock on his own door or use his key? Knocking would be more romantic. He held the champagne in his left hand and knocked with his right hand, which held the video. He then stood back from the door and waited, his heart beating quickly.

Peter heard the chain on the door being slid open, than the deadbolt. He held his breath. Kelly opened the door. The serious look on her face threw Peter off.

"Katherine just called. Your father's in the hospital."

"What?" asked Peter. "What happened?"

"Put your things down. I think we should go now."

Peter hustled into the apartment, set down the champagne and his things, and went right back to the door where Kelly was waiting.

"I'm sorry this isn't the homecoming you were expecting," said Kelly.

Peter's head was spinning as he locked the door and they headed for the elevator. "Did Katherine say what happened?"

"She said the ambulance took him last night. He collapsed at home."

"Last night? Why didn't she call earlier?"

"She knew you were coming home this evening."

"Yeah, Henry called yesterday morning. I told him I'd see him when I got home. He sounded fine. Dammit."

"Anyway, she said she didn't want you to get you anxious about something you had no control over. She thought it was better to wait, since you'd be home tonight anyway."

"She's probably right. I would have been a basket case." Peter paced the elevator all the way down to the garage level.

"I think I should drive," said Kelly.

55

THE FOURTH

Reed strolled through the doors of Waveland Bowl and started scanning the lanes, looking for a familiar face. He didn't see any of the guys after his first scan, but he heard Ramon's voice.

"I'm telling you," Ramon said. "It makes zero sense. Zero."

Oscar's voice was next.

"Fine, I won't call it a restroom anymore."

Reed followed their voices, and finally spotted them. Another person was there with Ramon and Oscar—a slightly younger guy—but no Henry. All three men were busy putting on their bowling shoes.

"Think about it," Ramon continued. "Do you ever really rest there? No."

"When you sit on the john, you're resting," Oscar countered.

"You *sit* on these johns here?" Ramon asked. He had a grimace on his face. "You're a braver man than I am."

"You know what they need around here?" Oscar said. "Those paper rings to put on the seats."

"An Ass-Gasket?" Ramon said.

"It would help," Oscar said.

"Call it a washroom," the younger man said.

"That's true, you do wash in there," Oscar pointed out.

"But it's not the primary reason you go," Ramon said, slamming his shoe down on the bench next to him to provide the exclamation point. "You go in there to piss. That's it. You only wash after you've taken care of business."

"So are you saying we should call it the piss room?" Oscar asked.

"It's more descriptive than restroom or washroom, isn't it?"

"I always call it the bathroom at my house," the younger man said.

"Fine," Ramon countered. He was getting exasperated. "At your house, you can take a bath, but they don't have a bath in the bowling alley, do they?"

"Actually, I never take baths," the younger man said. "I'm a shower man."

"My point exactly!" Ramon said.

Reed cleared his throat to announce his presence. Ramon saw him first.

"REED!"

"Hey guys," Reed said, a big smile on his face.

Ramon jumped over to the back of the plastic chairs and led Reed over to the "player side" of the lane.

"Have you met Delmar?" Ramon asked, pointing to the younger man.

"Don't think I have," he said.

The two men shook hands.

"Nice to meet you," Delmar said.

"Delmar is Henry's son-in-law," Oscar teased.

"I am *not*," Delmar said. He grinned at his boss, then back at Reed. "I'm dating his daughter. It's a long story."

"Talk about an understatement," Ramon said.

"Where is Henry?" Reed asked. "I went down for a smoke today and he wasn't there. Ramon, I didn't see you down there either. I wanted to let you know I would be coming tonight. Hope you don't mind if I just showed up."

The three men looked at each other, and the smiles quickly drained from their faces. None of them was quite sure how to proceed.

"Henry's in the hospital," Oscar finally offered.

"WHAT?" Reed said. "I just saw him yesterday."

"He went in last night."

"Oh no."

"It's pretty bad," Oscar said. "We all went over there to visit him this afternoon."

"That's why I wasn't in the garage when you came down this afternoon," Ramon added.

"He couldn't talk much, but he was the same old Henry," Oscar said. "He told us he would kill us if we didn't show up here tonight and have a good time."

"The Banana 7-10 Splits offered to forfeit when we told 'em," Ramon said, "because they love Henry too, but that wouldn't be right. Henry wouldn't approve."

Ramon nodded toward the other team, also putting on their bowling shoes. In another circumstance Reed probably would have been amused by the logo on the other team's bowling shirts — the old characters from the late-1960s kid show, "The Banana Splits". Each team member had embroidered the name of one of the characters, Fleegle, Bingo, Drooper, or Snork, above the picture of that character. The concept somehow didn't fit the men wearing the shirts, each of them easily in their mid-50s.

"We're going to do what Henry said," Oscar added. "It won't be easy, but we're determined to have a good time. In Henry's honor."

"What hospital is he in?" Reed asked.

"Illinois Masonic," Delmar said. "But visiting hours ended at seven."

Reed was deep in thought, standing among the men, wondering if he could escape from the office tomorrow to visit Henry, or if he should do it after work. His mind was spinning. Henry hadn't looked good recently. Hopefully it wasn't because he stayed up so late last Thursday. That did seem to take a lot out of him. But he was so happy that night when he finally spilled the beans. He was joyous. Just thinking about the expression on Henry's face was enough to make Reed smile. He could almost feel him here, in the bowling alley, willing his buddies on. Reed's train of thought was interrupted by Ramon.

"Go get your shoes," he said.

"Huh?"

"Your shoes," Oscar said, pointing to his feet.

"Oh," Reed said. "Don't you have a fourth?"

"Yes, we do," Delmar said. "You."

"Henry told us not to get a sub," Ramon explained, "because he said a fourth would show up."

"And here you are," Oscar said. "Hurry up. You have to hear this story about Delmar and Henry's daughter. It's a doozy."

"Yeah, hurry up," Ramon said. "Fleegle's already taking his practice shots."

Reed scurried over to the front desk. He pulled his cell-phone out of his pocket and dialed it. Lucy answered on the third ring.

"Hello?" she said. She sounded a little winded.

"Honey, it's me," Reed said. "Everything OK?"

"Sorry," Lucy said. "I just ran up from the basement. The tape measure was in your toolbox."

"The tape measure?"

"I'm measuring the room right now," she said. "I think the queen size bed from Mom's house will fit, but I just want to make sure."

"So you're really going to do it?" Reed asked.

"I already have," she said. "You should see the room. It's completely empty, except for the desk and the bookshelf."

"You're keeping the personal stuff, right?"

"Of course I am," Lucy answered. Reed could hear the smile in her voice. "I'm keeping his varsity baseball picture on the bookshelf, and I moved a few of his trophies down to your workbench. I still have to find a spot for two boxes of keepsakes, but the rest of it is going. I already called Goodwill about the clothes."

"I'm proud of you," he said.

"So what are you calling about?" She asked. "I thought you were going over to say hi to the bowling team."

"I'm here," Reed said. "But Henry's in the hospital, I'm afraid."

"Oh no! Is he OK?"

"He's pretty sick," Reed said. "But he issued orders from his hospital bed that the team has to have a good time tonight. They're bowling in his honor. Mind if I join them?"

"Not at all," she said.

"I obviously remembered my phone," he joked. "I should be home before midnight."

"Have a good time," she said. "I'm not waiting up for you this time."

"Please don't," he said. It was almost his turn in line. "See you later, honey. I love you."

"I love you too," she replied.

Reed closed the phone, and turned his attention to the burly woman behind the counter, semi-patiently awaiting his request.

"Can I help you?" she asked.

"Your finest pair of 10 ½'s please," he said.

Just like Henry would have done it.

56

BUCKINGHAM FORTRESS

Peter picked up the phone, and dialed her extension.

"Lindsay McMahon."

"Hi Lindsay, it's Peter," he said.

"Great work in Milwaukee," she said. "Thanks again for volunteering to do that. If there's ever anything I can do for you..."

"Actually," Peter said, "that's why I'm calling. There is something, if you don't mind."

"Oh," she said. "Um, OK. What is it?"

"I'm going to be spending a lot of time in the hospital. I don't know how long. My dad is really sick, and..."

"I'm so sorry to hear that," she said. "I know this is going to sound bad after you helped me out and everything, but..."

"You're too busy," Peter said.

"Swamped."

Peter held the phone up in the air and stared at it for a few seconds. He just knew she was going to say that.

"I understand," he answered.

"Have you asked Kelly?"

"Buckingham won't let her leave the Bramel/Placko merger right now," Peter said.

"What about Bill Schumacher or Dan Erazmus?"

"They're already on Lundberg/Goonan with me," Peter explained. "They're the ones I need to find help for..."

"What about..."

"I've asked everyone else, Lindsay. You're my last hope. I'm desperate here."

There was a long uncomfortable silence before she answered. Peter could hear her sighing.

"OK," she finally said. "As long as it's OK with Buckingham."

"Thanks Lindsay."

* * *

Buckingham's executive assistant Klaus Roberts was his gatekeeper, but he was much more than that. He was feared nearly as much as Buckingham himself. Klaus was always businesslike and curt in his responses, and never ever wasted a moment of time. If anyone called him they had to get to the point right away. If they e-mailed him, everything had to be perfect.

Peter casually strolled up to his desk. Klaus was busy, as he always was, so Peter simply stood next to him until he had a moment to look up.

"He's in a meeting," Klaus said.

Peter could see into Buckingham's office behind Klaus. He was sitting at his desk, engrossed in a report of some kind.

"He's not in a meeting," Peter said. "The door is open. I can see he's not in a meeting."

Klaus stopped typing for a moment, turned around, and looked into the office.

"Fine," he said. "He's not in a meeting. But he's busy. I'll tell him you stopped by."

"I need to talk to him *now*," Peter said.

Klaus looked at Peter. He wasn't accustomed to that kind of impertinence from anyone, let alone Peter. Peter didn't even come down this hallway more than a few times a month. Klaus picked up the phone.

"May I tell him what this is regarding?" he asked.

"Just tell him it's important."

Klaus resisted the temptation to hang up the phone and shoo Peter away. He dialed Buckingham's extension. Peter could hear the phone ringing in Buckingham's office, but the boss ignored the telephone. It rang three times with no movement from Buckingham at all.

"What do you want, Stankiewicz?" Buckingham hollered from his desk.

"I need to talk to you about something important," Peter hollered back, staring at the sighing partner.

"Can't this wait until later? I'm up to my ears here."

"It's important."

"You've got thirty seconds," Buckingham said.

Peter scurried in the door before the boss changed his mind. He didn't bother taking a seat in one of the leather chairs opposite Buckingham's desk. He remained standing, awaiting his attention.

"Speak," the boss barked.

"I need some time off," Peter said. "Lindsay said she could cover for me for a little while."

That got Buckingham's attention. He put down the file in front of him and looked up at his young associate.

"First you ignore my calls, and then you have the balls to..."

"I couldn't get reception in the..."

"Bullshit."

"Mr. Buckingham," Peter said, attempting to be respectful. "You admitted yourself that the Milwaukee research was good work. And I was..."

"Forget it, Stankiewicz," his boss interrupted. "Not this time. I was talking to Cal Averill yesterday, and we agreed it might be a good idea if you switched over to his team for awhile. He's a little shorthanded right now. I was going to tell you this afternoon, but I might as well tell you now. You need to report to him on Monday."

Peter knew what that meant. There was a very good reason Averill was shorthanded. He was the biggest prick in the firm and nobody wanted to work with him. Any attorney assigned to work with that partner was being given a gigantic hint.

"Just because I didn't return your calls?" Peter asked.

"Of course not," Buckingham lied.

The two men stared at each other. Buckingham had eyes of steel. Peter knew it was probably fruitless, but he gave it one last try.

"I'd like to urge you to reconsider," Peter said. "You know I'm not a slacker. My father is in the hospital. He's dying and I don't know how much time he has left. I want to be there for him. I need to be there."

"I'm sorry to hear that," a surprised Buckingham responded. He rubbed his temples, and softened his voice. "Look, I'm not trying to be an ogre here, but the Averill thing is a done deal. He really does need someone. I'll talk to him, and see if he'll agree to let you leave a little early every day if you want to spend a little more time with your dad..."

"I think we both know what he will say," Peter said.

Buckingham shrugged his shoulders. "You never know."

"I guess this is it, then," Peter said. He extended his hand for a handshake. Buckingham stood up and shook it. "Thanks so much for the opportunity, Mr. Buckingham. Who knows, we may run into each other again someday in the future."

"It's not like you're moving to Timbuktu," Buckingham said. He had a sympathetic smile on his face. "You're only moving to a different floor."

"Actually," Peter said, "I'm moving a lot further than that. Please tell Mr. Averill that I won't be reporting for duty."

Buckingham's smile faded immediately. "What?"

"Today is my last day at MacArthur Harrison Hyde."

57

SAY UNCLE

"Good afternoon. You must be Mr. Stankiewicz's son."

"Yes," Peter said, and stood to greet the doctor as he entered the room. "Peter. Peter Stankiewicz."

Henry's room faced east and therefore got very little sun in the afternoon. The overhead lights were dimmed. Peter had come here immediately after clearing out his office. He'd been working on the New York Times crossword puzzle in the room's only comfortable chair, using a small table lamp for light. Henry was sleeping. The drugs they'd been giving him were wearing him out. A tube was helping him to breathe. He looked very uncomfortable, unshaven and very pale.

The doctor read Henry's chart and turned his attention to Peter.

"I'm Dr. Rudoren. I'm treating your father's cancer. Do you have any questions for me?" said the doctor in a thick New York dialect. Dr. Rudoren was a very tall, thin man with a very long face. He stood on one side of Henry's bed, Peter on the other.

"Are you sure it's OK to talk right here?" asked Peter, indicating his sleeping father.

"We won't wake him up, if that's what you mean. And I won't tell you anything that your father hasn't already heard."

"Well, when they brought Henry, er, I mean my father in the other night, there wasn't much explanation of what was going on. I thought cancer came gradually. Why would he need to be rushed to the hospital?"

"Your father has been in a lot of pain for some time now. The other night he just couldn't stand up anymore and he collapsed at home. The type of cancer your father has is especially nasty. It's rare, it's very aggressive and unfortunately people in Henry's condition are much more susceptible."

"Because of the anti-rejection drugs for his liver?"

"You sound like you've done your homework."

"I've been reading up."

"Well, unfortunately you're right," said the doctor. "And now I'm afraid that the cancer fighting drugs will just hurt him more. These are very powerful drugs. His organs, not only his liver, may not be able to take it."

"I do have one other question, Dr. Rudoren. I know that you're not the liver specialist, but is there anything in those charts that explains how my father got in this shape to begin with, why his liver failed eight years ago?"

"Have you not had this discussion with your father?"

"My father has not exactly been Ward Cleaver, if you know what I mean. We don't have many heart to heart talks."

"Well, I can only tell you what I know. Your father has type C Hepatitis. Hepatitis C is contracted through blood to blood contact with an infected person. It's not something you just randomly or casually get. Years ago people might have become infected by donated blood during surgery, before we knew enough to test for it. There have also been cases of people contracting it in hospitals. And it's been known to be spread by people who share needles, like heroin users."

"I can't imagine my father ever shooting drugs. He barely drinks alcohol."

"Well, hepatitis can remain dormant for many, many years. Your father could have contracted the disease thirty years ago. It showed itself fifteen years ago and led to the transplant eight years ago. That's very possible."

"Thirty years ago?" said Peter under his breath. And then a light bulb went off. "Holy Crap, that's it! Hot Rod!"

"Excuse me?" asked the doctor.

Peter sat back down, and looked at his father still sleeping. The only sounds were from the monitors on the doctor's side of the bed.

"My father was in Vietnam," explained Peter. "A man in his unit was a heroin addict. My father carried his bleeding body off of the battlefield and was shot twice in the process. They bled all over each other. Years later that man died of hepatitis."

"If that's true, there's a possibility that they are cause and effect."

Peter looked down at his father, still asleep. Did Henry know? Of course he knew. And of course, Henry wouldn't have told anyone.

* * *

"I found a couple of people in the hallway who wanted to say hello," said Katherine entering the room with a bag of sandwiches.

Peter and Henry looked up from the game of rummy they'd been playing on Henry's serving table and saw the two female figures standing in the doorway. Peter stood in stunned silence.

"Peter," Henry said in a dry, scratchy whisper, "I think you remember your sister, Sarah. And this is her daughter, your niece, my granddaughter. Her name is Emily."

"But, how did...?" started Peter.

"Peter," said Gina. "It's good to see you."

"Yeah, but..." said Peter.

Katherine chimed in. "I brought enough sandwiches for all of you. I think I'm going to leave you all to talk." She leaned over the bed and kissed Henry on the forehead, brushing his hair with her hand. "I love you," she whispered. Henry gave her a wink.

"Thanks, Katherine," said Peter. And Katherine left the Stankiewiczes to catch up. They all exchanged long looks.

"So," said Peter, not quite knowing what to say. "I have a niece. Hello, Emily. I'm your uncle. Whoa, I've never said that before. I have to get used to that. Uncle Peter."

"Ladies," said Henry softly, "I am thrilled to see you both. I'm sorry I must look awful with these tubes and things. But it's good to see you anyway."

"Emily," said Peter, "Has anyone ever told you that you look like your mother?"

"Not until the last week or so," said Emily.

Peter looked confused. Henry noticed and jumped in. "I think we all have a lot of catching up to do. Why don't you all grab a sandwich and find a seat? I'll be having an I.V. for lunch, but you all go right ahead. And if you don't mind, I'm going to rest and let the three of you do all the talking."

Henry leaned back on his raft of pillows. At this moment he felt no pain. Peter still obviously had no idea what to say. Gina saw the discomfort in his eyes.

"You probably have a million questions," she said.

"I'm just thankful you're OK," he said. "I've had nightmares about what could have happened to you."

"I'm sorry," Gina said. Her lip began to tremble. "I'm fine." She inhaled and tried to be strong. "Same pain in the butt little sister as always."

Peter walked over and gave his sister a long hug.

"Sarah," he said warmly as he let her go. "God, it's so good to see you, you little..."

"Careful," Gina said, with a laugh. "Little ears."

"Right," Peter said. He winked at Emily.

"Her name is Gina now," Emily said with a smile.

Peter looked at Emily. "Really?"

Gina laughed. "Long story."

"I've got nothing but time," Peter said.

"And her last name is Santelli," Emily offered.

Peter looked at his sister. "Are you married?"

"Nope," she said. "Never married."

"Sooo..." Peter said.

"Bottom line is that I'm back now," she said. "And Emily's right. My name is Gina Santelli."

"There has to be a story there," Peter said.

"Well," Gina said, "the Cliff Notes version is that I was trying to get away from someone. Emily's father."

Peter glanced Emily's way.

"Emily knows," said Gina. "It was hard. But she's a big girl now, and I had to tell her the truth. Right, honey?"

"Right," said Emily proudly.

"I got scared when I saw this unsigned letter on the Internet looking for me," Gina continued. "That's when I knew he wasn't going to give up, and I had to do something drastic. So, I legally changed my name. Emily was born Emily Santelli."

"Where did you get the name Santelli?" Peter asked.

"Remember my teddy bear?" Gina asked.

That made Peter smile. "Ellie? You wouldn't go anywhere without that thing."

Gina nodded. "And who gave me Ellie?"

Peter looked at Henry. Gina furrowed her brow at her brother, and gestured toward Emily. It took him a second, but he finally figured it out.

"Oh," Peter said. "Santa, right?"

"Yup," Gina said. "And because I was about to get the only gift that I would love more than that teddy bear, I wanted her to have a very special name. Santa + Ellie – Santelli."

Gina stroked Emily's hair. Emily smiled at her mom.

"Corny, isn't it?" she asked.

"Very," he said. "But I think it's nice."

"Me too," said Emily, and hugged Gina.

"So why did you call yourself Gina?" Peter asked.

"I just thought it sounded Italian," she said with a chuckle. "I even dyed my hair and got colored contact lenses to look more like a Santelli."

"And he never found you?"

She shook her head. "But I kept seeing these anonymous letters on the Internet looking for me."

"Wait a second," Peter said. "Anonymous letters?"

"Uh huh."

"That wasn't him. I know who posted those."

"Who?"

"Those were from Mom," Peter said.

* * *

"Hi, Uncle Peter!" said Emily, running into the room.

Peter looked up from his novel. He stood and stretched, and Emily gave him a big hug around his waist. By now Emily had gotten used to the sight of her grandfather sleeping, surrounded by monitors and tubes running in and out of him. The electronic beeping didn't bother her anymore. Peter held his finger to his lips to remind his niece to talk more quietly.

"Hello, sweetheart," said Katherine sitting on the edge of a chair in the corner. "Where's your mommy?"

"Hello, Katherine. Mommy's at the end of the hall, talking to the doctor about something. Did you bring it, Uncle Peter? Did you bring it?"

Peter held up the video tape. Gina joined them in the room and went straight to her father's side, looking at all the machines.

"I wish I knew what all this stuff meant," said Gina. "I want to do something."

"I know," said Peter. "And he's not getting any better. He'd never say it, but you can tell that the pain is getting to him. They've upped his pain medication this morning, and he comes in and out of it. He's been sleeping nearly all day."

"Hi, Katherine," said Gina, stooping to give her a hug. "I'm sorry I wasn't here earlier today. Emily had choir practice right after school and she's missed the last three."

"You made the right decision. You didn't miss anything here."

"So, what's with all this?" asked Gina, indicating the TV/VCR that was sitting on a rolling cart at the foot of Henry's bed. "Did Dad finally say it was OK?"

"Yeah, luckily the hospital still has a VHS player. Dad had a nurse haul it in last night. He told me to bring the tape with me today. I'm not sure what he's been waiting for. I know he wanted to wait until the time was right, whatever that means."

"Can we watch it? Can we watch it now?" asked Emily.

"I think that would be a good idea." The voice came in a raspy whisper from Henry, who was now trying to sit himself higher in his bed. Peter and Gina knew the drill. They each took a side and gently lifted their father by holding him under his arms and putting more pillows behind him to prop him up.

"Are you ready for this?" Peter asked his father.

"I know every frame of this thing by heart. I thought it was lost forever." And now Henry was looking directly at Gina.

Peter plugged the TV into a wall socket. The chairs were arranged as best they could without disrupting the monitors. Gina sat to Henry's right, holding his fragile hand. Emily sat on her mother's lap. Katherine sat to Henry's left. Peter popped in the tape, pressed play, and then stood behind Katherine with his arm on Henry's shoulder.

The tape began with a pan of the old house, the one they'd had to sell soon after Henry had left. There was Evelyn modeling the latest in gardening clothes, the backyard, the chain link fence. A little girl ran into the frame in a sun dress and barefoot.

"Mommy, is that you?" said an amazed Emily.

"Yes, sweetheart."

"It looks like me."

"I know."

The picture jumped to a birthday party. Peter sat anxiously at head of the table wearing a cone-shaped hat that announced that he was eight. The family sang. Peter blew out the candles.

The Stankiewiczes sat, mesmerized by the distant memories flashing across the very small screen. A thirtyish Evelyn being surprised in the kitchen by Henry wielding the camera and begging him to turn it off; Peter swinging a whiffle bat in the backyard; Peter and Henry playing catch; Peter and Sarah wading in a small, inflatable pool; Sarah in a tutu practicing for a recital in the living room; a large, strong, young Henry standing in a t-shirt and shorts in front of the house. He easily held Sarah and Peter simultaneously in his arms, and then spun them around, all three of them giggling. There were a few minutes at Christmas, opening gifts under the tree. Peter gave a big "Yeah!" when he opened a Tonka dump truck. Then Sarah, in her princess pajamas, her long soft hair still mussed from sleep, walked straight to the camera until her dimpled face filled the entire frame and whispered "I love you, Daddy."

That was the last image on the tape.

58

PATIENCE REWARDED

G ina looked at the house.
"*Where have you been all day?*"
Silence.

"*Don't just walk away from me. I want to know where you've been. You certainly weren't at school. I got another call from the attendance office.*"

"*I don't care,*" she mumbled.

"*What?! Look at me when I'm talking to you.*"

"*I gotta get out of here.*"

"*You're not going anywhere until we finish this conversation.*"

"*Watch me. See? I'm stuffing my stuff into this box, see? All my stuff. Are you watching me? Cuz I'm leaving. I've had enough.*"

"*You're sixteen. Sixteen. You can't just go. How will you get along?*"

"*I'll figure it out. Now step out of my way, please.*"

"*You're leaving with him, aren't you?*"

"*What does it matter? I'm leaving.*"

"*He's too old. You're too young. He can't take care of you. He'll leave you. And then where will you be?*"

"*I guess I'll be right where you are. Ain't that right?*"

Slap.

"*I gotta go.*"

"*I didn't mean it. I'm sorry. Please, let's talk…*"

Quick steps echoing down a long stairway to the front door.

Slam!

Canned music from an ice cream truck rolling slowly down the street snapped her out of it. The little boy nearly ran Gina down as she stood in the parkway.

"I'm so sorry," said his mother, running to Gina's side. "He's been waiting all day for the ice cream man. I hope he didn't hurt you."

"No, no. I'm fine," smiled Gina. "I used to do that same thing."

The boy and his mother flagged down the truck while Gina went back to staring at the old two-flat which held so many memories. How long had she been standing there? Her hands shook as she considered her next move.

It was 7:15. She'd be home by now. Had she seen Gina standing out here on the lawn? Gina slowly walked up the front sidewalk and checked out the yellowing label taped under the doorbell. Stankiewicz. Yep, this was still the place.

Henry had said it briefly at the hospital yesterday, and then he let it drop. "You know, I'm sure your mother would like to see you." And that was all.

Gina closed her eyes, rang the bell and braced herself for the unknown.

"Yes?" a tinny voice said from the speaker next to the doorbell.

Gina pressed the button down. "Yes, uh, Mom?"

The speaker clicked off.

"Mom? Hello? Hello?"

Gina could hear the interior door at the top of the stairs open, and then the echo of each step down. Gina paced the porch and was at the farthest corner when Evelyn stuck her head out the door.

"Sarah?" she asked softly.

Gina turned to face her mother. "Hi, Mom."

"I can't believe it," said Evelyn, walking onto the porch. "I, I just can't believe it. I mean Peter told me the other day that he'd seen you but…"

"Yeah, well, here I am," shrugged Gina, still keeping her distance.

"Yes, yes. Well, would you like to come in? I could make some tea or something."

"OK," said Gina.

Gina followed her mother into the building and up the stairs that she hadn't climbed in over nine years. Someone had painted, but the stairwell still smelled the same, warm with the faint scent of flowers and pine. The two didn't say a word until they entered the apartment.

"Can I get you anything? A soda, or tea or something?"

"Water would be fine. Thanks." Evelyn went to the kitchen, and left Gina standing in the living room and looking around. She noticed all of the photos of Peter. Who could miss them? Of course he was the 'good' child. Then she noticed the smaller shrine, and the pictures that looked so much like Emily now.

"Here you are," said Evelyn, handing Gina a glass of ice water and motioning Gina to sit on the couch with her. "I've been thinking what I might say if you stopped by. I mean I've been thinking about that for nine years now. But even more since Peter said he saw you. And I still don't know what to say. Except one thing I've been practicing for a long time." Evelyn looked Gina in the eye. "I'm sorry."

"Look, Mom, you don't have to..."

"No, I do, I do. I am so sorry. I prayed that I'd be able to say that to you one day. It feels so..." Evelyn struggled with her words and began to cry. "I don't know why I'm crying. I'm so happy. It doesn't make any sense. But, I just never thought this day would come. Look at me, I'm a mess."

Evelyn grabbed a tissue from the box on the coffee table and tried to dry the tears.

"Mom," said Gina. "I'm sorry too. You were right. Wow, I bet you never thought you'd hear me say that. But you were." Gina smiled. "I know you only wanted the best for me. I see that now. Maybe it took having my own daughter to understand what you were going through. Oh, my God -- did Peter tell you that? Did you know? I have a daughter."

"Yes," said Evelyn with a warm smile. "Peter told me."

"And Steve was an absolute jerk. I left him before he hurt me. So you were right."

"Well, I don't take any comfort in being right about that. I'm just so glad to see that you're alright."

"Peter told me about your anonymous letter on the Internet. I had seen it. I thought it was Steve looking for me. I'm so relieved it was you."

"I never gave up hope."

"I know."

"And I'm a grandmother. When will I get to meet Emily?"

"Emily is very excited about having a grandmother. I didn't bring her tonight because, well, one thing at a time. I thought we should talk first."

"Yes, yes. Of course. I'm just so happy that you're alright."

"Look, Mom. I said a lot of things that stupid teenagers say…"

"Please," interrupted Evelyn, "That was so long ago now. I understand."

Gina nodded. Evelyn smiled. They sat silently on the couch for a long moment. Gina tried to imagine her mother sitting here among these pictures every night, alone, waiting. Evelyn considered her next words carefully. She didn't want to push too fast.

Gina leaned toward her mother and gave her a hug. Evelyn awkwardly returned the hug at first, and then held onto her daughter tightly. Another long moment passed.

"Now," said Evelyn as she stood, taking a breath and wiping her eyes. "Would you like a piece of apple pie? It's store bought."

"Sounds great."

59

PEACE

"I'm just walking in now," said Peter into his cell phone as he entered the lobby.

"Give your dad a hug for me," said Kelly. "He looked awfully uncomfortable when I was up there the other night."

"Yeah, but he was happy to see you. Hey, by the way, Henry's friend Reed stopped by last night to see him. Man, have I got a story for you! I'll tell you when I see you. You won't believe it."

"OK. I'd better get going. I still earn a paycheck, you know," said Kelly.

"I don't miss the firm for a second," said Peter. "I got everything I needed from that place. I got you."

"Go see your father. I love you."

"I love you too," said Peter, hanging up as he approached the guard desk.

He signed in.

"How are you today, Phil?" Peter asked the security guard.

"Just fine, Mr. Stankiewicz. Have a good day."

Peter clipped the security pass to his shirt and headed for the elevator. He entered the fourth floor hallway and walked to Henry's room as always. He knocked on the heavy wooden door and opened it without waiting for a response. He stopped in his tracks. The room was empty. No Henry, no machines, no personal items, just the sterile smell of new sheets.

Peter spun around and nearly ran into the nurse entering the room.

"Where is he?"

"Mr. Stankiewicz has been taken down to the ICU. They took him down this morning."

"How bad is it?"

"I'm not the right person to ask. The ICU staff can answer your questions. The ICU is on the second floor. Your pass will let you onto the floor, then ask the attendant at the desk."

Peter left immediately. When he found Henry's room, Katherine was already there.

"Peter," said Katherine, "I'm sorry I didn't get a chance to call you. It all happened so fast. When I got here, they were already working on him frantically."

Henry had even more tubes and pumps and drains in him than he'd had before. He was unconscious and nearly unrecognizable behind the breathing tubes and tape.

"What happened?"

"His kidneys have begun to shut down. The doctors knew something like this would happen. They wanted to talk to me about our options but I told them to wait until you got here. You're his son, after all. And his lawyer."

Dr. Rudoren knocked on the open door, making Peter jump a bit.

"Peter, Katherine. Let's find a room down the hall where we can sit. I can let you know what's going on."

Dr. Rudoren led them to a small, windowless room with an oval table in the center, surrounded by plastic chairs. On the table sat a large box of tissues. How many times had this same conversation taken place in this room? Peter and Katherine sat together, facing the doctor.

"This is the most difficult part of my job," began Dr. Rudoren. "But I understand that it is even more difficult for you. So I will lay it all out and then answer any questions you may have."

Peter clenched his hands on the table in front of him. Katherine reached over and put her hand over his.

"Henry is dying," said the doctor. "We can continue to fight his cancer, but the drugs are very powerful and they have already begun to shut down his kidneys. We could put him on dialysis, but it would be permanent. He would never leave that room. If we stop treating the cancer, the cancer will kill him. Either way, he's heavily sedated and may never regain consciousness. We've given him morphine for the pain. His lungs are filling with fluid and he's not breathing on his own anymore."

Peter cleared his throat. "So there's no chance that he can live without the machines?"

"I'm afraid that's correct," said the doctor.

Peter leaned forward on his elbows and closed his eyes for a long moment.

"Henry made the decision for us. He has a living will. He would not want to live like this. I know what he wants us to do."

Peter looked to Katherine for confirmation. She nodded slowly through a veil of tears. She squeezed Peter's hands even more tightly.

"Doctor, I do have a question," Peter said softly. "Can we call my sister and wait until she's here? In a cab, it would be thirty minutes or so."

"Of course," he replied. "I'll leave you alone to make that call, and I'll meet you back in Henry's room. You have the condolences of my entire team."

* * *

Gina arrived twenty-five minutes later, still in her barista outfit. She hugged Peter. Katherine wiped the mascara running down Gina's cheeks. A short time later, nurses quietly came into the room, followed by Dr. Rudoren. One by one, they disconnected the machines that were keeping Henry alive, until the only remaining monitor measured his pulse. His heart rate was beginning to slow.

Gina walked toward the bed. Her hands shook as she placed them on either side of Henry's head. She leaned forward, kissed him on the cheek and whispered in his ear, "I love you, Daddy."

Peter was next. Gina stepped back. Peter came forward, and kissed his father's clammy, cold forehead. "You are a good man," he said, "a good man."

Peter took a deep breath to compose himself.

Katherine came to her husband's side one last time and gazed into his peaceful face, his eyes closed, the pain gone, the fight over, and she said with a brave smile and tears rolling down her cheeks, "Goodnight, sweetheart. I enjoyed every minute of it. Now it's time to rest."

The pulse monitor flat lined.

60

SHOULD OLD ACQUAINTANCE BE FORGOT

The Millgard-Roth Funeral Home had been a Jefferson Park institution for half a century; a favorite final stop for the neighborhood's working class Polish and German families. When the Stankiewicz clan walked in the front door, a man with a polyester suit and a noticeably bad hairpiece greeted them. He asked them to follow him into his office for final instructions. He spoke with a calm soothing voice to all seven of them; Katherine and her son Kevin, Peter and Kelly, and Gina, Emily and Delmar.

"People will begin arriving in thirty minutes," he said. "Visitation is from 3 until 9, and that's a long time to be standing in the receiving line, so we always advise families to allow some time to sit, to make sure you retain your strength. That couch in the front of the room is reserved for the family. Also, you must allow yourself a little break to eat some food. Henry's office sent some sandwiches, which we'll keep in the refrigerator in the basement."

Peter smiled at the mention of Henry's "office".

The funeral director looked at Emily.

"And for you, young lady, there are a few tables downstairs in our break room. We have some paper and markers down there."

Emily smiled.

"I'll take you down there in an hour or so," Delmar said to Emily. "We can draw pictures together. You know, I was a pretty good artist in my day. My Aunt Cynthia still has one of my drawings on the wall in her basement."

"What did you draw?" Emily asked.

"Her dog; it was a Schnauzer named Heidi."

"How old were you when you drew her?"

"Twelve."

"Where is Heidi now?"

That brought a round of laughter.

"She's been dead for twenty five years," Delmar said.

"Is the paper you drew her on all yellow and crumply now?" Emily asked.

Delmar went down on one knee and whispered to Emily. "No," he said, "But my Aunt Cynthia is."

* * *

Gina and Peter agreed that Henry didn't really look like himself in the open coffin. For one thing, he was wearing a suit. Katherine had handled that detail. His hair was also perfectly parted. Henry almost never bothered with a comb. That didn't look right.

They stopped staring at him when they heard the commotion of people beginning to arrive. The old woman Peter and Gina always called Aunt Martha was the very first mourner through the doors. Nobody seemed to remember how she was related, but they all knew she would be there. Aunt Martha treated the obituaries like her very own social calendar.

The first thing Aunt Martha did was point at Kelly.

"Is this her?" she asked Peter loudly.

"No, *that's* her," Peter corrected, pointing to Gina.

Aunt Martha gave Gina a dismissive wave. "I know Sarah. I mean your fiancé. Is this your fiancé? Your mother told me you were getting married."

Gina laughed out loud.

Peter looked at Kelly, shrugged his shoulders, and decided to stop fighting it. "Yes, this is her."

Aunt Martha patted Kelly on the hand a few times. "There's no ring," she observed.

Kelly looked at Peter to explain.

"We're going to go pick it out together," he said.

"That's a good idea," Aunt Martha said. "Men don't know anything about jewelry."

Aunt Martha nodded toward Katherine. "So, this one's the new wife?"

Gina laughed out loud again. She had forgotten how blunt the Stankiewicz clan could be. Katherine was unfazed.

"That's me," Katherine said. "Wife Number 3."

"Henry was a good man," Aunt Martha said. "After my Richard died, he bought me a whole case of Vermouth."

If there was an explanation, Aunt Martha wasn't providing it. She simply smiled at everyone one more time, and made her way toward the guest of honor. As soon as the old woman knelt in front of Henry's open coffin and closed her eyes in prayer, the Stankiewiczes met eyes, and were on the verge of a highly inappropriate funeral giggling fit. They walked a few paces away from each other, regained their composures, and returned to the receiving line.

* * *

The whole meet and greet process was a little overwhelming, but as tough as it was for Peter and Gina, it was even more difficult for Katherine. She only knew a few of these people, and though she had managed to sneak several breaks to sit with her own children for awhile, she always dutifully returned to take her place in line when Peter and Gina needed a break. For the time being, she was the lone Stankiewicz on duty.

"I'm so sorry for your loss," a blonde woman said to her.

"Thank you for coming," Katherine said. "How did you know Henry?"

"I knew him in Oklahoma," the little blonde explained. "Came up as soon as I heard."

The two women looked at each other.

"Are you Nancy?" Katherine asked.

"That's me," Nancy confirmed.

Katherine smiled. "Henry would be so happy that you're here."

* * *

Henry's army buddies were sitting in the last row of seats.

"When are you heading back?" James asked.

"Tomorrow."

"Where are you staying tonight?"

"I figured I'd head out toward the airport after the wake," Sonny said. "There are a lot of hotels out that way."

"Why don't you stay with Susan and me," James said. "I can give you a ride to the airport tomorrow."

Sonny laughed, and nudged his buddy in the side. "I've been married a long time, Jimi. That's not the sort of offer you can make without checking with your wife."

James puffed out his chest. "What are you talking about? I'm the king of the castle, and what I say, goes!"

Both men laughed.

"Yeah, sure," Sonny said.

They sat in silence for a few moments, as the long line of mourners seemed to come to a standstill. They couldn't see who was taking more than the customary few seconds to comfort the family, but whoever it was didn't seem fazed about the traffic jam he or she was causing.

"Good turnout," Sonny said.

"Not bad," James agreed. "Just missing Hick."

Sonny nodded his head.

"Did you hear that Peter talked to him?" James asked.

"No!" Sonny replied and turned toward his friend. "So he knows about Henry?"

"Uh huh."

"How did he take it?"

"Peter told me—'Nothing like telling an old alcoholic that his best friend just died.'"

"Yeah," Sonny sighed.

"Think we'll ever see him again?" James asked.

"Maybe someday," Sonny answered, his voice cracking. "Hopefully before Henry, Retter and Hot Rod do."

The two men didn't want to look at each other anymore, so they allowed their eyes to wander. Sonny looked at the seats filling up around them, and James looked at the line of mourners, now suddenly moving again.

That's when he saw her.

At first James thought he must have been seeing things. He wanted to be absolutely sure it was her before mentioning anything, so he looked at her again. There was no doubt about it. He would have recognized that face anywhere. James nudged Sonny in the side.

"Is that who I think it is?" he asked. "She looks about the right age."

Sonny followed the subtle head nod toward the receiving line. About ten paces away from them, a striking young woman was awkwardly looking ahead, trying to get a glimpse of Henry in the coffin.

"Wow," Sonny said. "I think it is."

* * *

The funeral director with the bad hairpiece tapped Peter on the shoulder.

"Mr. Stankiewicz," he said. "It's almost time for your remarks. I'm going to make an announcement for everyone to take their seats in just a few moments."

"OK, thanks," Peter said. He turned to his sister. "Gina, you better run downstairs and get Delmar and Emily. I'll handle the line."

As Gina worked her way through the crowd, the next person in line extended her hand to Peter.

"Sorry for your loss," said the young woman. She looked to be in her early twenties. Her skin was a stunning coffee brown, and her big beautiful eyes were hard not to notice. "I don't remember your dad very well, but my mom told me he was a good man."

"Who is your mom?" Peter asked.

"Her name is Diana Wilson," the girl said.

"Have I met her?"

"I don't think so," she said. "She lives in Atlanta. I live only twenty minutes away from here, so I told her I'd represent the family, and pay our respects."

"Did she know my dad?"

"Yes," the girl said. "Your father and my father served together in Vietnam. Mom says he spent a lot of time with us when I was very little."

Peter looked at her closely.

"Are you Hot Rod's daughter?" he asked.

She nodded.

"Well then you must know these guys," Peter said, nodding to the two gentlemen making their way up to say hello. She smiled, but it was obvious she had no idea who they were.

"Henrietta?" James asked.

"Yes," she replied.

"Nice to finally meet you. I'm James. Your dad called me Hendrix. This is Sonny. We served with your dad."

"You look just like him," Sonny said.

While Sonny talked to Henrietta and Peter, James subtly pulled the camera-phone out of his pocket and took a surreptitious photo. That was something he never thought he would see in his lifetime. Henry's son and Hot Rod's daughter—together in the same picture.

*　*　*

By the time Gina got Emily's stuff cleaned up in the basement, the announcement had already been made for everyone to take their seats. Gina, Emily and Delmar made it to the parlor entrance, only to discover that there were more people than chairs. The doorway was blocked by the overflow crowd.

Gina, leading the way, tapped on shoulders to make a pathway to their seats.

"Excuse me," she said to the big burly man. He got out of the way.

"Excuse me," she said to the elderly couple. They got out of the way.

"Excuse me," she said to the little woman.

When the woman turned around, Gina was a little taken aback.

"Mom," she said. It still sounded odd.

The two women stared at each other for a moment, until Gina grabbed her mother's hand, and dragged her along with her. "C'mon," Gina said. "We've got to get to our seats."

"It's not my place," Evelyn protested.

"Baloney," Gina said.

"But Sarah," she protested.

Just as she was going to firmly put her foot down, Evelyn met eyes with Emily. She was standing next to her mother, gazing in wonder at her grandmother. Evelyn couldn't help herself when she saw that miniature Sarah. She broke into a big smile. "C'mon Grandma," Emily said, returning the smile.

Evelyn was powerless to resist them from leading her to the front row. Katherine and Nancy smiled warmly at Evelyn, and immediately scooted over to allow room for everyone. They all managed to squeeze in, but only because Emily sat on Evelyn's lap. Grandmother and granddaughter both looked thrilled with that arrangement.

At the podium, Peter saw the scene on the couch and smiled, before returning his attention to his prepared remarks. He tapped the microphone.

"Excuse me, everyone."

When the crowd saw Peter at the podium, they quickly hushed and moved to their seats. He waited until all eyes were on him.

"I want to thank everyone for coming out tonight," he said. "I know I speak on behalf of the whole family, when I say..."

Peter paused for a moment. He cleared his throat like he was going to continue, but then he picked up the piece of paper from the podium, calmly folded it a few times, and held it in the air.

"You know, I had a speech written about Henry... about Dad," Peter continued, "but..." He shoved it in his pocket. "I don't feel right telling you about him, because you've been telling me about him all night. All of you know him. In fact, all of you heled *me* get to know him. I hope you don't mind, but I'd just like to thank you for that. There are a few people in particular."

Peter looked at his mother.

"First of all, Mom. When you sent me out to tell Henry's army buddies about his illness, I really thought you were doing that for Henry. But that wasn't it at all, was it? You sent me out to learn more about Dad—to understand the reasons you could forgive him. Isn't that right?"

Evelyn smiled.

Peter smiled back. "That's what I thought."

Peter looked over toward Sonny and James, still standing near Hot Rod's daughter. "It worked, you know. When I met those impressive guys, the obvious respect and admiration they had for Dad really did make me look at him differently. You know what, guys?" Peter said, addressing them directly. "I even talked to Dad about it. I told him that you guys considered him a hero. You know what he said?"

They shook their heads.

"He said that you guys were full of crap."

Everyone laughed, including James and Sonny. Those words most certainly came directly from Henry.

"Nancy," Peter said, looking at the petite blonde sitting between wife #1 and wife #3. "After that one conversation with you, I never looked at Dad the same way again. You filled in the blanks about those years away from home. Without that, I don't know if I ever could have forgiven him. You showed me how to do it."

Nancy brushed the tears away.

"And Katherine," Peter said. "You taught me something about Dad too. When I first met you I thought, 'What's this classy lady doing with my dad?'."

Another round of sniggers.

Katherine's son Kevin reached over from the second row and squeezed his mother's shoulder on the couch. She reached back and held onto his hand.

"But then after getting to know you, and watching you with him, I realized something. The things that you loved about him—his love of life, his enthusiasm, his spirit, his big loving heart—that's what I loved about him too. I wanted to be just like him when I was boy, and thanks to you, I remembered why."

Through her tears, Katherine smiled.

"And then tonight, I heard so many more great stories about Dad from everybody that came out to say goodbye to him. I want you to know that my sister and I truly appreciated hearing each and every one. I know I speak for Sarah when I say that it fills our hearts to see the impact Dad obviously had in this world. You certainly don't need to hear a speech about Henry Stankiewicz to realize what a special man he was. You just need to look around this room."

Peter looked back toward the coffin. "Take a look, Dad. It's standing room only."

Peter had to compose himself for a moment before returning his sights on the mourners packing the room.

"So," he said. "I hope you don't mind that I didn't deliver the speech. I know for a fact that Dad will forgive me, because, well, he told me; 'Nobody wants to hear a speech'."

The mourners laughed.

"But there is one thing that I promised him we *would* do," Peter said. He gestured to Delmar in the front row, who nodded toward Oscar and Ramon. They stood up, and made their way to the podium. "I'd like to bring Henry's bowling team up here. These guys were there in the hospital room with me when Henry brought this up, and they promised to carry out Henry's final wish."

Peter stepped to the side, as the three men arrived at the podium. They were holding their bowling jackets in their hands. All three of them took off their sport coats, and put on the bowling jackets, just steps away from Henry's coffin. Oscar held an extra jacket in his hand. Delmar and Ramon deferred to Oscar who stepped up to the microphone.

"Henry was my friend for fifty years," Oscar said, choking up a little. "I already miss the heck out of him." He paused, digging deep for his composure. He took a deep breath, exhaled, and then continued while he held the jacket in the air. "This is Henry's bowling jacket. I jokingly said to him that we should bury him in this jacket, but he said no, he wanted us to give it to someone."

Oscar left the podium, and waved for Ramon and Delmar to follow. They went to the third row and stood next to Reed.

"Reed, this is Henry's final wish," Oscar said. He held the jacket out to him.

Reed looked stunned.

"It's going to be a little big on you," Oscar continued, "but we would be honored if you would take Henry's jacket, and his spot on the team, to become an official member of the Living Wills."

Reed looked at Lucy. She was holding her hand over her mouth. He stood up, removed his suit coat, and put on his new bowling jacket. Everyone applauded as Reed turned around a few times to show the jacket to every part of the room. His eyes were filled with tears, but he was also beaming with pride.

While Oscar, Ramon and Delmar returned to their seats, and Peter thanked everyone one last time, Reed sat back down next to his wife.

Lucy rubbed the name of the team written in script on the breast of Reed's jacket.

"You never told me what the team was called," she said.

When Reed looked down at the jacket, and read the name again, he saw what it meant for the very first time.

"The Living *Wills*," he said. He looked back at Lucy.

"The *Living* Wills," she replied.

61

JUSTICE

"You won't have to wash a single dish,
Just get your kids some deep fried fish,
Hot and juicy, everybody's happy,
When you make the trip to Cap'n Slappy."

"OK, OK. We'll stop at Cap'n Slappy's only if you promise to stop singing the darned commercial," said Mom.

A roar went up from the back seats of the mini-van as Dad maneuvered into the crowded parking lot. "Yay!!!" cried the five children in unison.

Dad found a spot and everyone piled out of the van.

"No running. This is a parking lot," shouted Mom. "There are cars that might not see you. Bobby, hold your sister's hand. Ryan and Joe, turn off the Game Boys and pay attention to where you're walking. Meg? Where's Meg?" She turned back to the car where Meg was still locked in the car seat. "Why didn't someone unlock your sister? You guys go inside and find a table. I'll go to the counter and order. I'll take Meg with me."

Dad and the older four kids walked in and were nearly hit by a flying stuffed toy, coming from the direction of the pirate ship jungle gym. The place was packed with small children eating greasy fish products and slurping down soda at cramped tables. Those who weren't sitting were running somewhere or another.

"Dad," yelled Bobby over the noise of perhaps forty screaming children, "We're going on the ship."

The four siblings took off their shoes and climbed aboard.

Dad crossed the sticky floor to a large table which was unoccupied except for the various litter left behind by the last customers. Dad threw down a jacket on a chair to mark his territory, piled the debris on a plastic serving tray and set it in a nearby waste can. He used several Cap'n Slappy nappies to wipe the liquid mess from the table.

"Ryan, let go of your brother's foot," Dad shouted as the two boys climbed the ropes to the crow's nest, but he could not be heard above the din.

Dad tried to relax at the table. All of the other parents here had the same look on their faces. Surrender. Yeah, there was healthier fare. Yeah, the place was absolutely insanely loud. Yeah, someone was probably going to kill themselves climbing all over that indoor death trap pirate ship. But it was cheap, simple and filled their bellies for a while. Tomorrow we can feed them some carrots.

Mom arrived with a tray stacked with assorted fried delicacies. Meg waddled behind her mother and climbed onto her daddy's lap.

"Where are the hush guppies?" asked Dad.

"They're in there," said Mom exasperated, "Under the Slappy Sauce. I bought the whale sized box. It's in the treasure chest. Honey, can you round up the troops?"

"Sure" said Dad. He got up and made his way to the ship. He stepped onto the foamy, ocean blue padding and started searching for recognizable traits among the sea of mini-pirates. Many wore pirate hats and eye patches, making identification more difficult.

"You gotta take your shoes off."

Dad heard the shout and turned to see a teenager in a Slappy's Crew outfit and chewing gum. The boy folded his arms in front of him, his eyes were half-closed.

"What?" asked Dad.

"You gotta take your shoes off," repeated the boy, now rolling his eyes back in his head. "We run a tight ship."

"I'm just collecting my kids," explained Dad.

"Whatever," said the boy, shrugging his shoulders and walking away.

"Dad! Dad!"

Dad recognized the voice. He looked up and saw Bobby hanging over the side and yelling from the upper reaches of the ship.

"Dad! Joey dared Ryan. The sign said 'poop deck'. And so Ryan did!"

Other children heard Bobby, or perhaps saw the mess, or smelled it and went running.

"Abandon ship! Abandon ship!" It was the teenager in the Crew outfit. "Everybody climb out. We have to swab the decks!"

Children climbed out of portholes and trap doors and jumped from the ropes covering the ship. Dad counted twenty-seven kids, but where was Ryan?

Bobby finally appeared, carrying Ryan down the gang plank to his father. Ryan's pants were still around his ankles and he was crying. Joey followed, his head down.

"I didn't think he'd do it, Dad. I'm sorry."

Noticing an even greater than normal level of chaos, a gray-haired man in his early sixties, clearly the restaurant manager, moved slowly from behind the counter to check out the situation. His navy blue polyester Cap'n Slappy jacket had epaulets on the shoulders and grease stains across the wide belly area.

"What's going on, Timmy?" he asked the teenager gruffly.

Before Timmy could answer, Dad chimed in. "My boy had a little accident on the poop deck. I'm very sorry."

"Timmy," said the manager, "Take care of it, will you. We really need to change the name of that deck. I knew it was just a matter of time."

"Look, I'm really sorry," said Dad. And then Dad remembered an old sales trick that people like to be called by name. He read the manager's name which was embroidered onto the jacket. "I'm sorry, Dick."

"It happens," said Dick. And then he mumbled to himself as he walked away. "Why do they always have to crap in my pool?"

THE LIVING WILLS

Acknowledgements

The Living Wills was improvised, conceived, improved, and fine-tuned at The Catalyst Ranch in Chicago, Illinois. The atmosphere at the ranch was outstanding for creativity, and we are eternally grateful to Eva and the rest of the staff for letting us set up shop there. We highly recommend the ranch to anyone looking for a space to generate creative ideas together, no matter the size of your group or the scope of your endeavor.

We'd also like to thank everyone that helped us improve the book by reading various different drafts of the manuscript and offering their honest opinions. Among those helpful souls were Bridget Kaempfer, Susan Sullivan, Brent Petersen, Jim Coffman, Rick Kogan, Mary Kopale, Gil Herman, Ralph Leonard, Bob O'Connor, Kim Strickland, and William Petersen.

We would also like to recognize Don Sanetra, Doug Stevenson, John Robinson, the Oak Park men's group and all of our other friends who encouraged us along the way. A special nod to Gary Bailey.

Others provided their expertise in certain specific fields, and we tip our caps to them as well; including attorney Peter Tomczak who schooled us on the life of a young attorney in a big law firm, and the American Liver Foundation and Kevin Gianotto, as well as Dr. David Bosch and Gift of Hope who gave us those all important medical details. (Please take a moment and sign up to be a potential organ donor. You can save a life and change the world with a stroke of your pen.) We also greatly appreciate our editor Lisa Mottola Hudon. She provided us with the kind of line-by-line input that was invaluable. You have no idea how much you helped us, Lisa.

Our former radio bosses Jonathon Brandmeier and Steve Dahl & Garry Meier deserve our gratitude as well. We were working for them when we met each other about twenty years ago in the hallways of WLUP-Radio Chicago. That was a special place in those days; a place where the spirit of creative collaboration thrived. Our common experience at the Loop was immensely helpful in our collaboration process.

We also came at this from slightly different perspectives too, Brendan from a world of improvisation and Rick from a world of writing, and for that we are also thankful. Specifically, Brendan, would like to thank the improvisational theater community in Chicago. He still feels a strong influence from his years with the iO, Del Close, Blue Velveeta, Prefontaine, the Second City Conservatory and the Players Workshop. Many improv techniques were liberally used in the writing of this novel. Rick would additionally like to thank four people who have supported him in his writing endeavors, specifically Pat Colander, John Landecker, and the late Sandy Stahl, who believed in his writing when no one else did, and Olga Gardner Galvin who really taught him how to write.

Jon Langford is an awesomely talented visual artist, and we are thrilled that he was available to create the cover art for this novel. Please buy Jon's art. And see him play amazing punk-rock-country music with his bands, the Mekons, the Waco Brothers, and others when they come to your town. Siena Esposito is a great friend and a very talented graphic artist whose skills were invaluable in the design and overall 'look' of the book's cover. If she had a band, we would also suggest that you go see her play.

We're also very excited to be the first book published by Eckhartz Press. David Stern did more than just publish this book for us. He inspired some of the more entertaining personality traits of one of the Living Wills characters. If you were ever one of David's clients during his previous life as a salesman, you know the power of his frosted cookies. Eckhartz Press staffer Kelly Hyde was an unsung hero of this project as well.

To our veterans; America's heroes. We hope that the pages of this book fully express to you how much we appreciate your incredible service and sacrifice.

We dedicated this book to our deceased parents, Brendan's mother, and Rick's father, but it goes without saying that we have just as much appreciation for our living parents. Brendan M. Sullivan, always encouraged Brendan's creative endeavors and supported this project, and Hildegard Kaempfer has always been there for Rick, in good times and bad.

Above all, we'd like to thank our families. Between the two of us we have seven children (that's right, *seven*). Thanks to Charlie, Mac, Harry, Rose, Tommy, Johnny, and Sean for not complaining when we needed some time to write. Our wives Bridget and Susan had a lot to do with that. This process required them to put in a lot of extra time and effort to cover for our absence, and/or cut through our creative fog. We're very lucky guys to have such understanding and supportive wives and kids.

Unbelievably lucky.

About the Authors

Rick Kaempfer has written for magazines, newspapers, radio, television, advertising agencies, websites, and/or blogs for the past twenty five years. In 2007 his satirical novel "$everance" was published by ENC Press. The Chicago Sun Times called it "whiplash fast, choke on your coffee funny." He also co-wrote "The Radio Producers Handbook" with John Swanson in 2004 (Allworth Press), and contributed to the book "Cubbie Blues: 100 Years of Waiting til Next Year" (Can't Miss Press, 2008). Rick currently writes two weekly parenting columns ("Father Knows Nothing" and "Suburban Dad"), a humor column for Shore Magazine ("A Fine Mess"), and is editor-in-chief of the Cubs history website Justonebadcentury.com. When he's not writing, Rick is a full-time chauffeur for his three boys Tommy, Johnny and Sean.

Brendan Sullivan is a creativity coach, helping organizational teams, leaders and individuals to realize their potential to be creative, innovative and collaborative. His clients include Kellogg's, PepsiCo, Harley-Davidson and many others. He is a renowned keynote speaker on the topic of collaborative creativity. He'd be happy to talk to your company, association, school, writer's conference, organization, etc. (www.creativitycoach.net). This novel is a living, tangible example of the power of collaborative creativity. Don't tell them, show them. Brendan's also been a professional improvisational actor, a radio producer, a commercial/film actor, a comedy writer and lots of other stuff. Mainly he's Susan's husband and the father of Charlie, Mac, Harry and Rose.

Author's Note

This novel was conceived, developed and written in what we've come to learn is a fairly unusual way. "The Living Wills" was written through improvisation, brainstorming mind mapping and other ideation techniques, as an experiment in pure collaborative creativity. Rick and I had no pre-conceived ideas about the content of this novel, absolutely none. All we had was our own creativity, Rick's wisdom and experience as a writer and a set of mutually agreed-upon rules, based upon my years as a professional improvisational actor and my extensive experience in applying these rules with corporate clients to improve their ideation, problem solving, team development and leadership skills.

These rules include true mutual respect, trust in yourself and your team, active listening, playfulness, being 'in the moment,' taking risks, supporting someone else taking a risk, accepting one another's ideas, finding the positive and building on that, saying 'yes…and' first and creating a safe and healthy environment for all of this to take place.

These concepts can be applied to any collaborative endeavor when you are creating something new or improving something (a novel, a new product, a better mousetrap, an office layout, a team, a marketing campaign, etc).

I happen to have an awesome partner in creating this novel. Rick's talent, experience and wisdom made this work. And there's no replacement for that. The rules stated above are not a substitute for education, knowledge, experience and talent. But the rules tremendously increase the odds that the collaboration will be successful.

These rules are really based in common sense. But as a good friend of mine says: "Yeah, it's common sense, but is it common practice?" Our own hang-ups, fears, judgments, prejudices, egos, need for control, politics, lack of confidence, overconfidence, analysis and other weird stuff can get in the way of healthy collaborative creativity.

Rick and I agree that neither of us could have written this novel alone. We held fast to these rules of improvisation when things got rough, and they pulled us through. When we trusted our system, the results surprised us. And we had a blast! It reminded me of being on stage and creating something with my improv teams, Blue Velveeta or Prefontaine. If you've seen or performed true improv on stage, you know what those moments are. Even if you haven't, I know you've had moments in conversation where ideas flow because you're 'playing nice together.' All we did was ritualize these steps to improve the likelihood of those moments happening.

We realize that movies, television shows and songs are often written in this way. We aren't even saying that other novels have not been written this way. We just haven't seen them. The co-authored novels we've seen appear to be written by a team with separate roles (perhaps the crime novel written by a writer and a real detective), or they're ghost-written. But we're not taking credit for something new. These are simple ideas that have always been around.

If you're interested in learning more about our collaborative creative process and how to apply it to your world, we're available to discuss our process with your group. I'm also available as a keynote speaker, workshop designer and facilitator. I'd love to help you to achieve your collaborative creative potential. It's a lot of fun and it works.

Brendan Sullivan
www.creativitycoach.net

The Living Wills is available at:

www.eckhartzpress.com

**ECKHARTZ
PRESS**